Nobody but Walker

Sweet McKenna Book Three

Christine Young

Published by Rogue Phoenix Press, LLP
Copyright © 2021

ISBN: 978-1-62420-644-3

Credits
Cover Artist: Designs by Ms G
Editor: Sherry Derr-Wille

Published in the United States of America

Chapter One

Scottish Highlands 1748

Walker Endicott, tenth Earl of Briarwood, sat atop his stallion staring across the meadow at the McKenna keep. Sun glinted off the battlements. A soft breeze flew the McKenna standard. The scent of summer wildflowers coupled with the ever-present heather assailed his senses. Above it, the flag of Scotland flew. Bittersweet memories assaulted him, tormented him as he stared at the peaceful scene. For a moment in his life, he thought he had found love here, a forbidden love. Crissie could never be his. Too much stood between them. Though he could see her one last time.

He'd been gone now for a year. His travels took him to Paris then the Bordeaux region of France, family business of a necessity he couldn't ignore even while his musings were of Crissie McKenna and this small part of the highlands where his heart belonged. When he closed his eyes, he could always see her lying in the dark green moss, her dark hair spread out around her, silver-blue eyes shimmering with passion. When he thought of her, he would always remember the sweet fragrant scent of orange blossoms along with the musk of a warm willing woman. His return was in question. While he'd written to her, he received no response in return.

He didn't like himself very well, the way he treated the lass the day he left the country and Crissie behind. What he'd willingly as well as eagerly taken from her a year ago had been hers to give. So many times he told himself it wasn't his fault. She practically begged him. Still, he should have been a gentleman and told her no. She had a way of bewitching him, her piquant face, slightly turned up nose coupled with the simmer of those sensual eyes always enthralled every sense he possessed. Whenever he imagined her arms around him, her legs cradling him between them, he was reminded of her, wrapped in the sweet memories she evoked.

He didn't, could not have told her no to save his soul.

No, he wanted her with an explosive need within himself he'd never felt before. His body succumbed to the months of denial he inflicted on himself. Never before in his life had he been celibate for so long. The truth of the matter was that he felt that way every time he saw her, stood close to her, caught the elusive scent of oranges and lemons. The silken length of her hair never failed to draw him, provoking him to touch. The soft curve of her breasts always left his fingers itching to possess. That day she was a fire in his soul he couldn't battle. He could not tell her no when all he wanted for the last month or so was to possess her, claim her as his. She could never be his.

She ran after him.

Begged.

So, he did.

Still, he wouldn't be staring at the keep situated high on the hilltop if he had not been forced into another mission involving the unveiling of the McKennas. He would never have returned. Because she never answered his letter, he assumed she didn't want to see him again. Perhaps she couldn't forgive him for taking what she offered, her innocence. It was his now. Maybe he couldn't forgive himself for the rutting bastard he was that day.

Refusal of the assignment had been first and foremost on his lips until he realized if someone else was given the task, they might well ferret out the truth about the McKenna clan, a story best left untold. If the truth were to be discovered, he feared for Crissie. He had to get her out of the highlands even if she protested. He would find a way. The list of reasons in his mind to say nay to the assignment was short, but he felt if he'd given in to his superiors, they would have listened.

Ah, but he thought that perhaps he should take a room in the village beyond instead of assuming he might be welcome in the keep. He wasn't at all sure of the greeting he would receive from the McKenna lass or her brothers. Despite his resolve, he yearned for her, thought of little else when he was at rest than the feel of her lush curves pushed softly against his length. God's fish, when he closed his eyes, he vividly recalled her naked, sunlight shimmering over the gentle slope of her hips and the ripe swell of her breasts. He remembered the lush fall of her dark black hair as he wound the silken length through his fingers.

Walker let out a long slow breath of air before hitching in another deep gulp. Prudence dictated he should avoid her. Should do everything in his power not to see Crissie McKenna. He couldn't do that. She stirred a fever in his blood he couldn't douse. Even now when he tried desperately to put thoughts of her to the back of his mind, the image of her with moistly parted lips, her long hair curling down her back and through his fingers sent heat straight to his loins. He recalled the way her lush breasts with the rose tips pushed against his chest, the way her sweetly rounded buttocks felt beneath his hands.

"You're an utter ass and a foolish idiot," he mumbled, starting his horse down the trail to the keep not to the village. His heart hammering beneath his ribs, he knew he had to see her; could not rest this night until he discovered the truth of their heated parting. He would find a way to keep her safe from the intrigue he was forced to take part in.

She never wrote him. He wondered at that after he sent a letter to her at least once a week until he realized she did not answer back. But then, perhaps she decided what happened between them the last day was for her a mistake. Well, if she thought that way, she was right. It was tantamount to the biggest mistake she'd probably made in her entire young life. To him, he would never forget the feel of her body next to his. For the rest of his life, he would remember. He couldn't have her though. Couldn't do right by his mistakes. The wrong he inflicted would never be righted.

If her brothers learned what passed between them that long ago day, he might very well be giving his life into their hands. She wouldn't

3

say anything. It was, after all, her virtue at stake. Still, he decided he needed to stay alert to any pending situation.

The short distance, now that he was almost at his destination, seemed to go on endlessly. Beneath his chest his heart pounded, thundering against his ribs. As to what he would say to Crissie McKenna when he saw her, he didn't know. In his mind, he thought of a thousand different things. None of which satisfied him. Possibly, she would speak first taking the initiative, setting the stage for the direction of his comments. Sweat trickled down the back of his neck. Unending nausea settled in his gut.

Why didn't you write? was one of the first thoughts rambling in his head. Somehow, after all this time, he didn't think it prudent for him to blurt something like that out before he actually had a chance to find out what she was feeling for him. The only women he had encounters with were widows when he was out of town, his mistress when he was home. He never bedded virgins. Well, what they did that day in the secluded glen could hardly be considered bedding.

Bloody eyes, but she might have married someone in the last year. He couldn't fault her for that since he gave her no indication that he might want her for a wife. Nor did he promise to return.

He did want her every way possible.

He couldn't have her though. Couldn't ask her to wed him. That fact gnawed at his gut, churned in his stomach until it soured. The taste of that fact so bitter he couldn't swallow. To ask Crissie McKenna to be his wife and have his children was a dream that would never come true. He would have to live with that fact, accept whatever she was willing to give. She wasn't the kind of woman to become a man's mistress. In any case, neither her brothers nor her father would ever allow anything such as that.

As he approached the gate, he was sure he heard a low murmur of voices rise around him. The sound so bitter and angry, he didn't understand. He wondered if it was because he was a captain in the English army. Now, for all practical purposes he was a civilian. Something hit him on the shoulder. Another missile hit him in the small of his back. He found himself pummeled from all sides. Curses were spewed at him.

What the devil?

He sat up straighter, looking around for the assailant or assailants, knowing the English were still not liked around these parts. He had not expected this type of welcome. After the battle of Culloden, he well understood the sentiments. This was far too brazen to be about that battle. It seemed personal to him. Hell, he wasn't even wearing the soldier's uniform. He was dressed in civilian clothing.

"Sassenach!" The jeer hit him hard. "Sassenach!" was called out over and over again. A tomato hit his face, juices sliding downward pooling beneath his collar. Taking out a handkerchief he wiped it away.

"Bloody Englishman, go home!"

"*Yer* not welcome here after what *ye* did."

What I did?

He ducked the next pebble hurled at him, dismounting before handing the reins to a young man who suddenly appeared from nowhere. By mere inches he avoided another small rock directed at him. Beneath his breath, he swore as he headed toward the main hall. Has everyone gone mad?

"What the devil is going on?" he asked the lad, hoping the boy knew something he could pass on to him as he followed the young man into the stable.

"People around here don't like the English. You in particular have stoked their rage. Best you don't let either of the McKenna brothers or the laird see you. Doubt if you're welcome. Might not live long enough to discover the truth. Secrets are never kept in small villages. Probably should mount on up and ride out of here if you value your life. Do *ye* want me to take care of your horse?"

Sometimes little boys had too much to say. Sometimes they didn't say enough. "Yes." He wasn't going anywhere until he got to the bottom of the hate. "Don't go too far away though. I might be leaving sooner than I planned."

A seething anger built inside as his long strides brought him closer to his destination. The building anger was directed at Crissie. She had to be the source of this debacle.

"They won't like you any better in the village," the lad went on to say. "Of all the McKennas, Crissie's one of their favorites. She holds a special place in everyone's heart."

Blessed hell, he would have never expected her to say anything about that day. He was more perplexed than ever. It was then he saw her. His heart caught in his throat, raw with emotion. Rushing after the few women who deigned to throw the pebbles at him, she was shooing them off with her hands. Unconfined, her long dark hair was waving in the breeze, curling softly around her shoulders as it fell from the pins she used to hold the mass in place. He wished he could see her eyes; sure, they were brimming with passion the burning hunger he so vividly remembered. The women seemed to get the idea, leaving as she bade them.

Walker turned his gaze to his savior, waving her arms, his protector. He stifled the chuckle welling up in his throat. When he caught her attention, she stopped, her hands falling to her sides. For several seconds she stared fixedly at him. She stepped back; her hands now clutched at her throat as if she just now realized who he was. A moment later her skirts were swirling around her ankles as she turned from him. Her pace quickened until she was running toward the hall.

Bloody hell.

His breath caught. She was more beautiful than before if that was possible. More than ever, he knew he had to talk to her, discover the truth about her strange reaction. By his estimation she should have been running to him not away. His strides were longer and faster than hers. He caught her arm, twirling her around. Her eyes were blazing pools of molten blue-silver. By God, she was glorious in her anger. Never before had he seen her like this. The need to enfold her in his arms surfaced with a vengeance.

Yet, the fury she exhibited burned a hole deep in his heart. By the way her eyes shimmered and her body tensed he could swear what she felt for him at this moment was a deep-seated rage. He didn't understand. She was going to tell him if he had to tear the words from her throat.

"Let me go, Sassenach," she gritted out between clenched teeth while trying to wrench her arm from his grasp. "You don't belong here. Go home to your precious Englishmen. To Ireland, to wherever it is you come from. Leave me alone. I don't want you here."

Suddenly, his calm was held onto by the slimmest of threads. "No, not until you explain to me what is wrong with you, with everyone." With one hand, he gestured to the yard. "Why are people throwing rocks and vegetables at me? What the hell have I done? I haven't even been in the highlands for a year. We need to go somewhere private."

Once more, he looked around the yard. It seemed they had an audience he didn't want. The people of the clan quietly fanned out around them, belligerence on their faces.

"Now you want to know? Now you care? Yes, it's been a year, a very long year for me at least." Her icy words were coated in sarcasm while she still tried to jerk her arm away. "Let me go." Her voice held steel.

"Yes, now I want to know. Yes, now I care. Would it be so hard to explain? I'll not let you go until I'm satisfied."

He watched her sway slightly. She was thinner than he remembered, her breasts larger. She was just as beautiful, maybe more so than in his memory, her hair as black, her eyes as silver. He struggled with a breath of air as his gaze traveled the length of her body. A slow realization coupled with a question formed.

"You've no rights here, Walker. Go back to England or Ireland or wherever it is you call home," she repeated as if he didn't hear her the first time. "I dinna want to see you ever again." She unexpectedly fell dead still, her eyes nearly crossing. Her voice lost the steel while she whispered, "Please..."

Suddenly, the top of her gown was damp, the wet stain growing larger as they stood in the hot noonday sun. A heated blush spread across her face. He watched with a fascination and wonder he didn't understand as he tried to piece together the reasons for this. The thought hit him full in the gut. Unreasonable anger simmered, escalated with a resounding force he couldn't put aside. His brain didn't work as quickly as the words tumbling from his mouth.

"By God, you little harlot. No wonder you don't want to see me. No wonder you never answered my letters."

Unable to help the seething fury, he pushed her away from him. She stumbled. Her eyes blazing, the rage she now felt at his words evident in the changing color of her eyes. Christ, he shouldn't have said that. He didn't mean it although there was a shadow of doubt in his mind.

"How dare you!"

She whirled, her dress rising above her ankles, running full out away from him. Her skirts were hiked nearly to her knees so she could take longer steps.

He wasn't sure what possessed him. All his instincts kicking in told him to mount up and ride in the opposite direction. He understood he should put miles between them. Instead, without batting an eyelid, Walker followed her into the hall, matching her stride for stride then up the steps to the rooms above, oblivious to the possible scandal.

He didn't care.

Just wanted to glean the truth.

When she thought to slam the heavy wooden door to her chamber in his face, he caught it with his boot. Pushing it open, he stepped inside fascinated by the scene enfolding in front of him. Slowly, he shut the door behind them. He leaned against the solid wood; his arms crossed in front of him as he surveyed the dimly lit room.

A baby was crying in a crib near her bed. He could barely see one tiny fist waving in the air. His gut churned over while his heart forgot to beat. Even though questions abounded, deep in his soul he knew the babe was his. She hovered over the crib, caressing the baby even while her shirt was slipping from her body then her sodden chemise.

Her milk-swollen breasts were naked to his gaze. Yes, she was indeed larger. He understood why. Now, she wore nothing from the waist up, her breasts swaying beautifully as she picked up the child. She didn't look at him. It seemed she pretended he wasn't there, in her room, watching her.

He neglected to breathe.

It appeared she was more concerned about the babe than she was about her partial nudity. While he watched spellbound, she picked up a small blanket then the baby who seemed to stop crying the moment Crissie held the child. He was so intrigued; he couldn't move nor could he remove his gaze from the captivating scene before him.

Without sparing him a glance, she sat down in a large wing chair near the fireplace. The babe's greedy little lips fastened onto a nipple. His breath caught what there was of it, captured in the back of his throat. She didn't look at him though she must have sensed him watching her. The small blanket she'd been holding covered her a few seconds later, the child's head as well as her breasts.

Walker didn't understand the sudden rise of fury to his chest, didn't comprehend the compelling need to watch her feed his child or the protectiveness that filled him so completely. Abruptly, he didn't have a doubt in the world that this child in front of him at Crissie's breast was his.

Purposeful long strides took him to a spot in front of the pair. He needed to know if the child was a boy or a girl. Supposed he would have to wait until they finished with the meal. Wasn't sure if he possessed the patience for such a thing. All he wanted was to hold the babe in his arms, uncover his arms and legs, count toes and fingers.

Outraged at her audacity, he pulled the covering from the child's head. "The babe needs to breathe."

She gasped. Brilliant red heat flooded her cheeks, her dismay clearly evident in the narrowing of her eyes. For a second, she looked down at herself before lifting her angry gaze to him. Still, she said nothing. He wanted to know what was going on behind those silver-blue eyes.

"Don't want my child to smother to death while eating. Is the babe a boy or a girl? Crissie? Don't you think I deserve to know?"

Even while he asked, he wasn't sure if she would tell him. Despite her reticence, he would discover everything. Now, she glared at him unspoken emotions glistening in her eyes. She had no reason to be angry with him.

"If I'm a harlot, you've no rights here. So, you *dinna ken* whose child this is, do you? Why should I tell you something you'll take exception to?"

She didn't make an effort to cover herself. Her resentment was so very evident. He deserved what she tossed out at him. Somehow, he would find a way to make amends.

In any case, she must know he wouldn't allow her to continue on that vein. True, he said something with no basis. He wasn't going to allow her to constantly throw it in his face just so she could continue the argument. She switched sides, her breasts lush and beautiful, swollen with the milk feeding his child. They swayed. He controlled his desperate need to reach out and caress the soft fullness revealed to him. An overwhelming rush of emotions nearly sent his knees buckling followed by an overwhelming fury that she never had the decency to tell him his child existed.

"Why didn't you tell me? You could have written. I would have been here for you. You didn't have to go through this by yourself." His voice was so very much calmer than his seething emotions.

"I did write. I wasn't by myself. I've my family. At least they don't burn hot then cold." She began to hum softly seemingly to the babe in her arms, ignoring him or perhaps ignoring the fact she was naked from the waist up.

"*Nay.*" One hand slashed through the air. "*Nay*, you did not. Don't lie to me. You wrote no letters. I received nothing in the mail."

How dare she lie to his face? If she wrote to him, he would have arrived in the highlands before she could even blink. Would have cancelled all the business that seemed so important at the time. He would have been here for her.

A little bubble of milk appeared on the child's lips as the infant pulled away to stare at him with large golden-brown eyes, his eyes. The lashes closed slowly then opened again when the babe seemed to notice him staring at him, noticed the caress of his finger along the soft cheek of the infant.

His.

"You can believe what you will. Roby, you know my brother, delivered them for me to Inverness. They should have been received."

She rose, walking toward her wardrobe, the babe on her shoulder. With great finesse she managed to cover herself with a dry chemise. She walked around the room until a tiny burp issued forth from the baby.

With all his heart, Walker wanted to believe her. Every instinct he possessed cried out to him she told the truth. There was no reason for her to lie. Still, the facts were in front of his face. He received no mail from anyone here, from any McKenna. If he had, he would have replied immediately.

While he wanted to jerk the babe from her arms, he did not. "What is the child's name?"

She whirled, still clutching the baby to her shoulder, one hand cupped around the baby's head. "Now you care? Now after over a year you want to know details?"

While she still sounded furious, her words were soft, hesitant as if she hoped for something more. Besides what he offered right now, his strength and support, all she could possibly hope for was for him to wed her.

He could not.

"If you had told me, I would have been here. Doubt it not," he reminded her, his voice soft. "I will take care of the two of you."

"If? If you say?" One of her finely sculpted dark eyebrows rose toward the heavens. "If is one pretty big word to be ignored for a year."

"Then the babe is three months old?" He was calculating backward from the day he left, the day he took her virginity. Blessed hell, but he wished she had bothered to tell him.

"Yes."

"The name?"

He wasn't sure what demons drove him; fury, curiosity, possessiveness. The list could certainly go on. If he so desired, the name would be changed. She would not saddle him with some Scottish name that would haunt his child forever. A good Irish name would be appropriate.

She stared at him, tears brimming in her eyes spiking her lashes. "He's been baptized. *Ye* cannot change his name."

"Him? I've a son."

His heart swelled with pride coupled with the fury he had not known before. He could never get back this time with his son. He felt robbed. Cheated. By God, he would not squander any more time with the babe.

"His name?" he queried again trying to keep the tenor of his voice in check. If he had to shake the words from her, he would. Damn his good intentions.

She blinked a few times. He wasn't sure if the gesture was to rid herself of the evident moisture in her eyes or to infuriate him further. He was sure he was going to misplace all sense of patience. His hands fisted at his sides, he glared at her and waited. Hoping she understood in this he would not be denied.

Slowly, Crissie looked at him, a soft expression suddenly in her eyes as she pulled in a long breath of air. "I'm sure you won't like it. You have no say since the child is not yours."

"The hell he isn't."

He never realized those long months he spent with her before their intimacy she could be so infuriating. Before, she'd always seemed so biddable, sweet natured.

This time her smile was soft and beguiling, tempting him with a promise. What that promise was he wasn't at all sure, retribution possibly. He had the uneasy feeling everything she told him before was a lie.

"Ian Walker McKenna." Her whisper reached his ears with a shudder and a sigh. "I'm sure you won't want another man's son with your name."

"Ian Walker Endicott," he told her, his voice countenancing no argument. He wished she would stop, remembering his earlier accusation. "The last name will be changed. You can count on that. You and I both know this boy is mine. He will be legitimatized. My heir."

"So, you say." She set the child in the crib.

Turning her back to him she slipped out of the wet gown before quickly putting another one on.

Desperate to set this untenable situation to rights, he stabbed his hands through his hair thinking of the right words. After a few more seconds of watching her back while wishing he could see all of her, "I'm sorry I called you a harlot. There was no call to do something like that. I would take back the words if I could. I cannot." Once more he thrust his hands through his hair. "It's just that..." He didn't know what to say. One time. One time and he sired a child. It wasn't unheard of. He knew it happened, just not to him.

In his ecstasy, he forgot about protection, forgot she was untried in the ways of love and contraception. He'd been so shocked when she rode after him, stunned when she wanted him to make love to her. Lord, but the heat of the coupling, the frenzy, the desperate need she generated in his loins, he didn't have the good sense to withdraw. Didn't know if he could have done such a thing even if he thought of it.

He hadn't.

"Is there anything else you would like to know?" Her voice was soft in the stilted silence of the chamber.

He didn't answer. He was pacing the room, distraught by this, frustrated by the lost year, afraid he would lose his son if he didn't immediately rectify this situation. The boy was going to live with him. If she wanted to be part of the lad's life, she would have to come with them. Hell, from the beginning, he meant to take her with him. They were leaving now, this afternoon. Staying where her people despised him wasn't tenable. He didn't care who would try to stop them. They were leaving within the hour.

"No?" she asked seeming bemused now that she thought he would go without a fight.

"I'll be back in a few minutes. Pack a small bag for you and Ian. Something you can hang from a saddle. We're going home."

Walker didn't wait for an answer or a comment. He left with every intention of speaking his mind to her father. He would return as soon as he set everything to rights. He heard her last comments just before the door banged shut behind him.

"Like hell I am. I'm already home."

Stepping back inside the room. "If you don't pack a bag, you'll be wearing that same gown from this moment until your things can be shipped to my home in Ireland. Your father won't, can't stop me from taking my son no matter how much he'd like to do just that. I'm sure you would like Ian to have a few things to change into from one day to the next." He stopped talking. His angry gaze bored into her. When he started again, "Of course, you don't have to come with us. It's your choice."

"You're talking to father?" Her fingers wove into the fabric of her gown, her eyes wide while drops of moisture clung to her lashes. "He won't let you take my son."

"I guarantee you, he won't say *nay* to this. A man should raise his son. Your father understands that."

"As should his mother."

He smiled at her. It was the first since he saw her in the courtyard. "So true. I'm glad we are in agreement. Of course, it is solely up to you if you accompany me. I won't force you. Your choice."

~ * ~

Crissie was so incensed all she wanted was to throw things at him; yearned to deny him his son. She wouldn't. At this moment, she truly didn't understand what he was about. Why he wanted her to pack a bag. He wasn't going to take Ian from here. The right wasn't his. Deep in the farthest reaches of her heart, she knew her father would not stop Walker. Ian was his son. Connal would expect them to work this out between them as adults. A wobbly breath of air slipped into her lungs.

She sat down next to the crib, stroking the babe's back, cooing soft words as she watched him sleep, his little bum high in the air. Ian was her life. Once she thought herself in love with Walker. That emotion was precisely why she threw herself at him that long ago day. Thoughts of Walker like this as an infant gave her reason to grin.

Nay, he was not so sweet now. There were no sweet bones, sinews or muscles in his body.

When she saw him in the courtyard less than thirty minutes ago, her heart had stopped beating. He was everything she remembered, tall and powerful. His legs so long, thighs so heavily muscled his buff britches fit as if they were a second skin. His brilliantly polished black knee-high boots shone in the sunlight. The shoulders she clung to so many times were broad. One strand of his tawny hair slipped to fall across his forehead, shielding his golden-brown eyes from view. In her estimation there was no one more handsome, more striking and commanding. Her pulse quickened at the sight. She ran from him, not because she was afraid of him but because she was terrified what he might think when he saw the child.

Her worst fears were confirmed when he called her a harlot. He thought she gave herself to another man. Heat stained her cheeks. One time. She got pregnant from one time with him. She never thought that would happen. Lilly, her brother Brady's wife, told her it was possible after the fact. Unfortunately, by the time she knew and confided in her, it was too late to take any precautions.

What was she to do now?

He said they were leaving, going to Ireland.

Nay.

Her heart lurched to her throat. He was asking her to give up the only life she knew.

For a few tenuous minutes she struggled to breathe. Fought for control of her emotions as they splintered into a million shards inside her chest. He wanted her to pack two bags small enough to be tied to the saddle. He was taking Ian, with or without her.

I have no choice.

Suddenly, she stood straight, racing around the room, desperate to complete what he asked before he returned. He wouldn't wait. Wouldn't give her two more seconds to finish putting their things together. So much was needed. She had to think. His determination coupled with the anger she saw in his eyes was terrifying. She didn't know he could be this way. He'd always been so gentle and sweet, given her anything she asked for. His kisses melted her heart. She turned to liquid in his arms.

She thought she loved him.

That was then.

This is now.

He was a dangerous formidable man. Not one to trifle with.

Tossing clothing from the armoire, she heaved a huge sigh as she stared silently at the items strewn on the floor. She didn't know what to take. She'd never been farther away than Inverness. Her father took her brothers to Edinburgh on occasion. She never went with them, content to stay in this tiny part of Scotland. The highlands were all she'd ever known. Tears ran down her cheeks.

He expected her to travel to Ireland.

She didn't think Ian was old enough to make such a journey.

An hour passed by then two. She sat in the wing chair watching the clock, her hands trembling, her breath shaky. The bags were set at the door. Still, he didn't come. It would be time to feed her son. He would have to wait to leave. If he objected, she would make him wait. After all a babe had to be fed. He might be cruel to her, never to the child.

She must have dozed. The sound of the door opening woke her. When she opened her eyes, Walker stood over her, hands on his narrow hips, his very presence commanding. She wanted to fight him, dispute his dictates. Taking Ian from this home was not something she wanted for her son. It didn't seem she had much of a choice though.

"Are you ready?"

She rose then nodded to the two bags resting by the door. "He will need to eat soon."

"When he does, we'll stop. Perhaps you can learn to feed him while we ride," he told her with no emotion whatsoever as he picked up the bags before holding the thick wooden door for her.

In her arms, Ian nestled against her breasts, his sleepy-eyed stare so endearing she felt the twinge of her milk as it started to let down for him. "He needs to eat now."

Halfway out, he stopped. "Is this some ploy to keep us here longer than necessary? It won't work."

"If I don't feed him this instant, I will have to change my clothing.

Lest you forget what happened last time. You understand I would not be able to go far without sickening if I was forced to ride in a wet gown."

"Very well."

She heard his impatient grunt before she turned her head to hide the smile. "It won't take long. Twenty minutes or so then we'll be on our way. You will not lose much of your precious time on this irrational quest of yours. Still, you will have to learn to deal with the needs of a babe. Your child. You will come to realize Ian comes first in everything. A new concept for you, I'm sure."

He sat down to watch. She understood all too well if she tried to hide from him, he wouldn't allow it. Resigned, she undid the front fastenings, smiling when Ian's tiny rosebud mouth latched on to her. She always felt such joy when he nuzzled into her, his lips sucking on her.

Some of her anger dissipated while Walker was gone. Now, it returned full force as she watched him, his gaze riveted on her breasts. He would allow her no privacy. She understood. Would have to accept. Those days before he left, she wanted him desperately. He sparked a desire in her no one else ever had. Still did. Even now, when he acted so very arrogant and condescending, she couldn't deny the inferno sweeping through her body when he looked at her. Somehow, she thought, if he would just kiss her, she could forgive him any and all indiscretions. She would willingly go with him anywhere without one objection.

Nay, that was not true. She would not go willingly as his whore.

By the tight line of his mouth coupled with the narrowing of his eyebrows, she didn't for one second believe a kiss might be forthcoming. He was angry, furiously so. Absently, she stroked Ian's cheek, cupped the downy top of his head with her palm. This little boy was so very precious. She didn't understand how Walker could even think to take a three-month-old baby overland to Glasgow then by ship to Ireland. In her estimation he wasn't thinking straight.

Ian seemed to sense her mood. He looked up, his golden-brown eyes staring at her while his little fist was clenched on her breast. She switched sides with him, giving her the other nipple. He would be finished soon. They would be on their way. To what end would this unsolicited journey lead them. She doubted if it would lead to anything good.

"I would have thought my father would put a stop to this sudden nonsense," she said as curiosity began to get the best of her. Her father had not been angry with her when he finally discovered she carried a child within her. Though she knew he was disappointed. He and her mother supported her through the long trying months before Ian was born. The delivery had not been easy. She swore at the absent father, cursed him as the pains became too much to bear. Then the sweet innocent babe she now held in her arms came screaming into her life. Without a doubt Ian Walker McKenna was the most priceless being on this earth. He was her sunshine.

"Connal understood a man's got to raise his child. I didn't force you." He stopped for a moment. "When we made love. Suppose I've got you to thank for that." His voice was a sultry soft murmur, showing none of the impatience she was sure he was feeling at the delay.

No, at the time I told father I loved you. Also told him you returned the love. I was a foolish child. No longer. I'm walking into this with my eyes wide open.

She lifted her shoulders, trying not to disturb the babe. "Everyone saw me race out of here to catch you. They also saw my slightly disheveled state when I returned more than an hour later. Never thought to hide it. Never thought there would be consequences."

"Guess you wouldn't." He sounded insincere to her ears.

Crissie remembered how in awe she felt, how strange to know the man she loved reciprocated her feelings. She was floating on air when she returned to the keep. Naivety led her to believe he loved her. He never said the words. Never would, she was sure. All he wanted of her now revolved around the child.

"One might say I had absolutely no idea what happened to me. My feelings..."

He did take advantage in ways though. She didn't understand at the time what she felt was lust not love. He alone spurred the fires in her body she didn't understand. He could do that to her. That day he stole her heart. Since then, she'd been trying to take it back. Now, when she looked into his eyes, she was sure the feat would be impossible.

Roby, her older brother knew sooner than anyone else. She didn't know how he *kenned* she was with child. Didn't ask. He stood by her. Went with her when she told their parents. Connal's disappointment in her was so very easy to read in his eyes. If she could, she would have melted into the walls. Roby placed reassuring hands on her shoulders. Even before she told them, she thought to make some excuse to go after Walker. She was mightily glad she did not. These extra months without him near gave her much needed time to think or to vanquish him from her heart.

What was it about men that they needed to control every situation?

"What were your feelings, Crissie?"

"What were yours?" she shot back unwilling to put her heart on the line.

She would never tell him how much she thought she was in love with him. Never tell him how broken she'd been when he never wrote. Or when he didn't care enough about her or her child when she told him of Ian.

"At the time, shocked. I'm not going to deny anything. I wanted you from the first moment I saw you. Made a promise to myself I would have you." For a few seconds he looked away. "No matter what."

Her laughter was bitter, strained to her limits. "It worked out for you then, didn't it? You got more than you bargained for."

"Yes, but not as I planned," he spoke slowly, his gaze resting on her lips, moving lower to linger on her breasts. "I gave up my plan because you were too much a lady for me to take advantage of you. I knew you would never lie with me without benefit of marriage." He lifted his broad shoulders, the fabric of his shirt straining against the muscles. His smile failed to reach his eye. "Then you did."

"When I threw myself at you, you didn't have any trouble doing just that. Did you?"

"No. It was all I'd wanted since I was assigned here. Everyone told me I didn't stand a chance in Hades with you. I did woo you tenderly still hoping I would taste a small part of you. When I was called back to Ireland, I thought a few kisses was all I would get from you. Then I got more."

"A hell of a lot more."

She thought she saw him wince. Probably because of her profanity not because of what she implied.

She so needed to end this conversation. Ian was staring at her, no longer nursing. "We should go now. If you want to get off before it gets dark, that is."

Crissie rose. After burping Ian then walking him to sleep, she wrapped another blanket around the sleeping child.

With her back stiff, unknowing what was before her, she followed Walker Endicott, the tenth Earl of Briarwood from her chamber, from the keep where she grew up. In favor of a new one, she left her old life behind. They rode for a few hours. Her arms grew sore and stiff from holding Ian. Her back ached. She bit down on her lip in a feeble attempt to keep the pain at bay. He completely disregarded her, overlooked the possibility that she might be struggling in his efforts to get as far away from McKenna land as soon as possible.

He let her catch up to him. "Can you make it another hour to the inn or would you like to make camp here?"

Her jaw dropped at the two impossible decisions he presented her with. She hoped he would offer to carry Ian for her. Warring with the option of telling him the truth she blurted. "I cannot possibly carry him any farther without dropping him. There is no way I want a three-month-old child to spend the night on the ground in the wilds. Do you think of no one except yourself?"

His once mild features changed to anger, his brows narrowing. "You should have said something. Do you expect me to read your mind?" His low harsh voice was a side to him she'd never seen. He reached for Ian, cradling him in his strong hold.

Tears pricked the back of her throat. Her arms tingled where the blood seemed to rush back into the numb limbs and fingers. She turned away from his probing glare trying to ignore him, fighting the overwhelming exhaustion. She didn't say anything simply because she didn't wish him to believe her helpless or weak. Before they started on this journey, she determined she would never complain or ask anything from him. There was coin in her pockets. She would pay her way. Owing him anything was unconscionable.

One of his tawny eyebrows rose in question. "Nothing to say?"

Well, she had a lot to say. In this case biting her tongue was the most prudent choice. "Thank you for carrying my son. It seems I've been alone and doing that very thing for what at this moment seems a veritable lifetime. The inn will be much nicer than the forest floor."

His laughter sent a shiver of anger through her. He corrected her. "All prim and proper are we now? Remember. My son. My heir." He settled Ian on his shoulder before kicking his black stallion into a canter.

She watched his back, the smooth play of his muscles as he so easily rode away from her. He carried the babe with little effort. He wouldn't slow his pace. She understood. Still...

Still what? She urged her horse to a gallop until she caught up to him.

"Thought for a moment you weren't coming. Perhaps second thoughts," he told her, his voice bland.

Third thoughts too.

She gritted her teeth to keep the reply on the tip of her tongue from bounding forth. Instead of words that would do neither any good, she smiled. It wasn't a sweet smile, probably bordered on mocking. Try as she might she just couldn't conjure anything pleasant.

Less than an hour later, they rode into the yard of an inn. Rustic Inn was the sign above the door. Dear God in heaven, she prayed it wasn't too rustic. All she wanted now was a bath as well as food for herself along with the privacy to nurse Ian. After that she wanted a nice warm bed. What she'd been through this day, she didn't think that was too much to ask for. She would pay for it if it was the only way to get what she needed.

Walker helped her down, held on to her waist for a few seconds while she struggled to get her legs back in working order. They had not been on the horses for more than a few hours. God in heaven what was she going to do tomorrow when he was sure he intended to ride all day? Walking with a slight limp while rubbing her thighs, she followed him inside.

He registered for a room before she had a chance to tell him she would stay in her own as well as pay for the separate lodging. When she moved toward the desk to do just that, he took her by the arm propelling her toward the stairs. For a second, she tugged on her arm. When he didn't release her, she let him have his way. He would anyway. She was too tired to argue over a room.

While he opened the door, she kept quiet choosing to keep her complaint private. When he handed her Ian, she smiled at him. "Where are you going to sleep?" Perhaps she shouldn't have said that. Maybe she should have waited a little longer to let him know her intentions.

His grin broadened to show his even white teeth behind the lips she so longed to touch, to kiss. "With you."

"We can't possibly share a bed, we're not..."

"Lovers?" he quirked, a tawny eyebrow lifting upward. "You're holding the proof that we are."

"No. One time does not make us lovers." Unable to look at him, she turned her back, doing the only thing she could think of to keep her emotions from escalating.

"We made a baby together, Crissie. We can obviously share a bed. Unless you forgot."

She didn't dare say what was on her mind as the door opened. She gasped in a sharp breath, knowing everyone would think they were married. Better than believing she was his whore.

The innkeeper along with his staff arrived with a cradle as well as a tub. Buckets of steaming hot water were carried in behind the man who smiled at her knowingly. Crissie couldn't help herself. She grimaced. Then she let out a long slow breath of air, feeling the momentary anger at this intolerable situation fade. She would make the best of this. Just the thought of all that hot water started to relieve her sore muscles. If she wasn't already halfway to hell, this was almost heaven. For the time being she decided she would ignore the sleeping situation. She could deal with it later.

Walker spoke to the man for a few minutes before he set Ian in his cradle. He turned to address her; his words tenderly spoken. "I believe the water is for you. If you don't take too long, we can use the same water." He busied himself with the fire, setting a few logs on it watching as they flamed to life.

She let out a long slow breath of air before straightening her shoulders. Understanding she needed to make her wishes clear, she said, "I suppose it's too much to ask for you to leave."

"Suppose it is. We've seen each other. I've kissed most every part of you, although there are a few places... Best you hurry. I've a feeling Junior is not going to have a lot of patience if his mama doesn't feed him right away."

He sounded so agreeable, so sincere, so very condescending and presumptive. Crissie struggled with the need to argue, to vent her feelings. She understood he wouldn't bend in this. She comprehended he wanted her with no commitments attached. She couldn't do that, not to her son, not to herself.

Walker would do just as he pleased. He sat down stretching his long legs out in front of him after he poured himself a glass of brandy, something else he must have ordered before they found their room. His lashes lowered, fanning out across his cheeks.

"Water's getting cold."

Quickly, her back to him, she disrobed, her breasts so full and now unconfined they hurt with every small movement. It was time for Ian's feeding. Walker was right, she needed to hurry with her bath. There was little to no time to soak and enjoy the marvelous heat. The water was everything she dreamed of. With a soft sigh she settled into the heat, allowing the warmth to soothe the soreness accrued today from the hours in the saddle. She permitted herself a few minutes with her eyes closed.

The tender touch to her cheek surprised her. Her lashes flew open. She stared into the honeyed eyes of the man she loved with all her heart. Months ago, she wished her feelings away. Thought for a few fleeting weeks she succeeded. Now that he appeared so suddenly into her life, she knew that love for him would never leave her.

I need to learn to deal with it, ignore the ache in my heart.

"*Dinna* touch me. You've no right," she whispered softly.

Even to herself she heard no conviction in the words. How could there be when she wanted more than anything to feel the tender strokes of his large hands on her flesh. He'd kissed her so many times, lovingly caressed and held her. No matter her intentions or his, she could not let him have his way. Despite her past actions, sex before marriage was not appropriate.

"You cannot mean that, lass." His soft, wet lips followed the path of his long, slender fingers while his words whispered across her cheek. "What difference can it make now? We both want each other in the most elemental ways."

She jerked away, her body melting into the heat he offered as well as the flames he so easily fanned inside her. She could not let him do this to her. She needed to be strong for the sake of her son. Could not fall into his arms again. It was sensations just like these that had her racing after him that day so long ago. *The day that changed her life forever.* She couldn't allow him to coax her from her decisions, from her principles. While in so many ways she didn't regret lying with him, it had been a bad decision. If for no other reasons, her son would be brought up a bastard.

"*Aye*, I do. As you said I need to hurry. Ian will be screaming soon. Already he's making those tiny demanding noises that tell me he's ready to have his dinner. See, he's kicked free of his blanket. His chubby little arms and legs are waving in protest."

She brushed his hand away then washed the rest of her. Tonight, she didn't have the luxury of washing her hair. It needed time to dry. They would leave early in the morning.

To her amazement, Walker backed away, resuming his seat near the fire, sipping the drink he poured earlier seeming to brood. She let out a long slow breath, understanding this was just the beginning. He would not give up. Wasn't a man to forego his pleasures. Staying strong where his tender coaxing was concerned would be difficult. God willing, she didn't intend to stray.

Not now.

Not ever.

She finished with the soap. When she was rinsed, he stood by the tub, a huge bath sheet extended for her use. As she stepped from the water, he wrapped it around her. While he watched his smile broadened.

"I will give you time to get used to me," he murmured as he began to strip his clothing from his tall, powerful frame. "Soon you will want me as much as I want you."

Time to get used to him. What did that mean?

For a few seconds she observed, fascinated by the play of muscles across his naked chest, the tawny hair curling provocatively there. She remembered the feeling of it pressed against her breasts. Remembered how she twined it through her fingers. Remembered his scent, a bit spicy and male. She swallowed hard, closing her eyes before turning abruptly away from the sight of him.

From her bag she pulled out a long white nightgown, one that buttoned to the neck. She picked Ian up from the cradle, cuddling him to her before she unfastened the nightdress far enough for him to suckle.

Just as she assumed, Walker viewed her. She kept her gaze on him wary of his every move. He seemed oblivious to her blatant perusal. Humming a tune, he washed then rose, the water sluicing down his long firm legs across his well-shaped buttocks. When they made love that day, she never really saw all of him. She touched and stroked him, held him in her arms but...

He was a perfect specimen of a man.

Walker pulled on the doeskin pants he wore that day. When the knock on the door came, he opened it making sure he took the tray from the servant before the person could see inside the room. The scent of the fresh baked bread and hearty meat stew sent her stomach into a tailspin.

"Are you hungry?" he asked smiling broadly, his eyes glistening. As he watched her nurse, he poured a goblet of wine for her, brought it to her. "This will help you relax."

"Famished," she murmured as she drank down a large portion. She did need to relax. Somehow, she knew that while he was part of this room and there was only one bed, relaxing was most likely not in her future.

"Did I ride you too hard today, Crissie? I was eager to get you away." He sat down beside her a bowl of stew for her in hand. She couldn't eat the stew until Ian was finished. The huge slice of bread he handed her that was smothered in butter and honey was perfect. She bit into it, closing her eyes, delighted with the warm yeasty taste.

"If you are asking me if I'm sore, I am." She bit off another large chunk of the bread, chewing contentedly as he dished up a plate for himself. "Not used to spending so long in the saddle."

"Yes, I am sorry for your pain. You have to tell me how you're feeling."

He picked up Ian, holding him to his shoulder as he rubbed the child's back. The large burp made him laugh. "He likes his meal. Can't say I wouldn't like some of what he's getting also."

"You won't. Get what he's getting." With an exasperated sigh, she set the spoon down that had been halfway to her mouth. "What do want from me, Walker? I won't be your whore or your mistress. I've heard no words about marriage or love. All I've heard is the demand that you would take Ian from me. I could come or go as I pleased. What the hell do you want from me?"

His brows drew together, his voice suddenly harsh. "I cannot wed you or anyone else. You best come to understand that. My son will grow up feeling his father's love. His mother's also if she chooses to stay with him."

She gasped at his words, swore softly beneath her breath. "Can't or won't?"

~ * ~

Connal found it incredibly difficult to keep from looking at Wynnie and seeing the disapproval so blatant in her eyes. Walker presented no choices when he came to talk to him. There was nothing he could do to keep Walker from taking Ian. Hell, he could have insisted Crissie stay here. Walker certainly didn't look as if he wanted the mother to come with him.

"Tell me what happened this afternoon." Roby sat down on the opposite side of Connal, a glass of ale in hand. He didn't appear at all pleased with the situation. "You say Walker took off with Ian and Crissie? I can go after them. Bring my sister as well as the babe home. They don't belong with that Sassenach bastard."

"*Aye*, that he did. No, you cannot interfere in their private relationship."

Connal didn't' want another argument. He had spent most of the afternoon defending his inaction to his wife. Didn't need to have the same conversation with his youngest son. Brady would come along and a repeat of today's events would have to be hashed out.

"I could bring Crissie and the babe back. Take Kit with me," Roby offered once again, grinning as if he already understood what was happening. "Never did like that particular Sassenach."

"You liked him well enough until you learned he was the father of Crissie's child, until you understood how he took advantage of her," Wynnie said in a soft voice seeming to need to tell her youngest son to go after the couple and bring her child and grandchild home.

Roby's unfettered hand was fisted, the knuckles on his ale glass white. "He did take advantage even though Crissie said she was willing. She was innocent, naïve in the ways of men and women. She would have had no idea of the consequences of the quick dalliance. Walker did."

"Well, they are gone. He did explain to me why he couldn't wed her. The entire story is unsettling at best. Maybe in time, things will change in Crissie's favor."

"Why is that?" Roby asked, his voice harsh.

"He is already wed to another," Wynnie spoke before Connal could say the damning words. "Damn his everlasting soul to hell!"

"And you want me to believe that Englishman didn't take advantage of my sister?"

"Not me," Connal said softly, hands in the air as he slanted his wife, a look that only the pair understood. "Crissie wants us to believe in her."

"That tale is hard to swallow at best. The Sassenach should be hung by his balls," Roby said watching the door as if he hoped Crissie and Ian would be walking inside as they spoke.

"*Aye*, it's hard to accept," Connal agreed. "In this case, Crissie made the only decision she could. Walker was hell bent on taking both of them away from here. Says we are all in danger, but he didn't explain why or how. Said to be very careful. I got an ominous feeling from his words."

"So, what is it he plans to do with her when they reach his home? Keep her as his mistress or his whore? Set her up in a home nearby when he can visit at leisure? Use her when it pleases him?" Roby asked, his anger blazing. "What is he planning on doing with the child? He still needs his mother. The bastard wouldn't dare hire a wet nurse with Crissie in such jeopardy."

Wynnie reached out touching her hands on both her husband's and her son's hands. "I believe that will be up to Crissie. I'm sure she is aware of his wishes by now. He's an honorable man. He will abide by what Crissie wants. I'm sure he won't take advantage of her again. Unless she's willing."

Roby let out an astounded chortle. "Honorable? You are far too naïve, mother. He will try to seduce her. Will do so until she gives in to his wishes. The way she feels about the man, he will achieve his desires with few difficulties."

"You've never bedded a woman?" Wynnie asked directing her attention to her son. "You've never coaxed and sweet-talked until you got your way?"

Connal watched his youngest son squirm. "I've never gotten one with child, never an innocent maid. Don't intend to do so anytime soon."

"That's good to hear," Connal said reflecting on his past as well as his actions until he met his wife, his mate.

He did protest, did ask to speak with Crissie before they left. Walker refused. Connal supposed he could have argued and won that particular battle. Walker had been right, however, in his conviction that what transpired was between the two of them and he didn't want interference to complicate things.

Walker didn't speak of love. Connal had a strong suspicion the Englishman did love Crissie. Wed to another. It was hard to believe.

Walker told him it was a betrothal made by fathers when the children were born. Walker had been married nearing ten years now. He said he was nineteen at the time. Had never consummated the marriage to his wife.

No, Walker's marriage was not one of love but of duty. It was easy for Connal to read the truth in Walker's eyes. Easy to see how much he regretted that marriage. He suspected they lived in separate bedrooms. Connal could well understand Walker's need for a warm willing woman in his bed.

He just wished it wasn't Crissie filling that position. For he had no doubts that she would end up in the earl's bed again.

Chapter Two

It took them two weeks to get to Glasgow then the port and the ship that would take them down the Firth of Clyde then into the North Channel and on to Belfast as planned. He spent every night in the same bed with Crissie barely touching her. This was the last night on the ship. He closed his eyes, wishing he dared reach out, stroke the gentle swell of her hips as she lay beside him, her back against his chest. He wanted to right all her problems. Instead, he made them worse. It wasn't what he intended. Hell, he didn't know what he wished for.

She sighed softly, nestling her gently rounded bottom against the cradle of his thighs. He couldn't help the groan of pleasure at her actions. It seemed his rod was ever ready for her, ready to test her tight velvet sheathe, to probe and explore. Prepared to take what she offered sweetly once so long ago. What little he had of Crissie was not enough of Crissie. Still, she would have no real part of his tender coaxing. Whenever she told him no, even when it sounded more like please, he let her go. Someday, she would change her mind.

Someday.

Someday seemed a hell of a long way away.

However, she was not immune to his advances. In his arms she shuddered with the pleasure of his kisses, of the dance of their tongues. Before she melted completely, she would always tell him to stop. Over the week, he wanted to believe he made a few strides toward coaxing her into his bed. If he was honest with himself, she was more stubborn now to deny the pleasure they could find in each other's arms than when they first left McKenna land behind. In reality his sexual ploys and temptations were losing ground.

Crissie was becoming ever more stubborn and determined to keep him at arm's length.

Mayhap, he should back off. Honestly, he didn't know how he could do that when every part of him screamed for sexual release that only Crissie could give him. No other woman would do.

Everything he could possibly think of to woo her, he'd done. Even gone as far as learning to change Ian's diaper. He spent time every evening playing with his son. A task he thoroughly enjoyed. Now, he made it a point if the wee lad woke up in the middle of the night for a feeding, he would get up before Crissie in order to change the babe's diaper. The simple gesture saved her time, let her sleep longer. Over the past week, she lost weight, her smile never evident. He knew she was sad and depressed. But then he would ask himself, what did she have to smile about? The journey was too much for her. Ah, but she worried about the trip where it concerned Ian not her. Ian was doing fine, more than fine.

When he implied that he went above and beyond what was expected of a father looking for a compliment or two, she simply told him it was the least he could do when he put her through nine months of torture coupled with the added agony of giving birth.

He wasn't in a position to argue the fact. He wasn't there for her. More often than naught he was worried about her. She was exhausted, sleeping almost as much as Ian. Still there were dark circles beneath her eyes. When he brought food to her, she seldom ate more than a few bites. He could see her bones protruding. He was thoroughly glad the trip had almost come to an end. Praying now she would begin to rest as well as eat.

She never complained even when he avidly watched her disrobe or nurse the little one. He sighed softly, rolling onto his back, one arm thrown over his eyes. If given the opportunity, she would leave him. More than anything he wanted to marry her, claim her as his.

Nothing had changed in his life.

Cursing his wayward thoughts, he rose striding naked to the tiny window overlooking the ocean. The captain's cabin was his this trip simply because he owned the merchant vessel. There was some trade between Belfast and Glasgow that he capitalized. Mostly this particular ship carried commuters from the two countries. The majority of passengers came to visit family members for various reasons; birthdays, holidays to name a few. This one ship was full because it was summer and a good time to travel.

When she turned over, he was greeted with the sight of one beautifully shaped breast sticking out from the bodice of her gown. She must have been so exhausted when she finished nursing Ian last night, she had forgotten to button her nightwear. His body tightened even more as his gaze cast hungrily over her. Inwardly, he groaned as he decided he would pay a visit to his current mistress as soon as he got Crissie settled in his townhouse in the city. He needed release from this constant torment. Was smart enough to understand that Crissie would not see to his pleasures or hers, at least not anytime soon.

He planned to change that.

He just wasn't sure how.

She would not be pleased to find herself installed in his home. He wasn't going to let her live anywhere else. When push came to shove, she would admit that she wouldn't leave Ian to live in a home where the boy would not see his father on a daily basis. He made it perfectly clear his son would live under his roof. The cradle would be kept in the master suite until Ian was old enough to have a room of his own. That fact didn't give Crissie very many choices.

His strides long he covered the distance between them quickly. Sitting on the bed he set his hand on her shoulder. Her long sooty lashes fluttered open. "Walker?"

"Time to get up, lazy bones," he said softly, grinning at her sleepy silver-blue eyes. Running a fingertip along her collarbone then down between her breasts, he watched the soft quiver of anticipation.

She tried to deny him but her body betrayed her at every gentle stroke of his fingers. Heated flush rose from her breasts to her cheeks.

She closed her eyes, sighing softly. "Don't want to," she murmured. Her hand rose to touch his, to stop his tender explorations.

"You should not be doing that."

He ignored her last words. "Would you like me to join you in bed? We still have time to make love, for me to send you to a place of ecstasy," he said softly, continuing the teasing assault on her senses.

He understood she must be still too sleepy to object over much, to say nay with conviction. A tiny mewling sound of pleasure slipped from her lips at the same time her small pink tongue painted a dewy line across them.

"*Nay*," she whispered, arching her back as his fingertip slowly dipped beneath the fabric. His palm brushed across a hard puckered tip then moved to the other one. "Walker..."

His name quivered on her lips.

He liked the way it sounded.

He wasn't about to withdraw until she implored him to do just that. The palm of his hand traveled between both breasts. Her pulse at the tender juncture between her neck and her shoulders pounded. She didn't seem to be quite awake. She hovered somewhere between dreams and reality.

Slowly he bent closer, captured her mouth with his, delicately nibbling along the length to the corner then to the other side, knowing the pleasure he induced. Once more she swept her tongue across her lips leaving a path of compelling moisture everywhere it touched. He met it with his, pulling it into his mouth. She tasted of everything good about the morning.

He knew the minute she woke fully as she stiffened, her hand held his against her breast, her eyes huge livid pools of molten steel, "*Ye ken* I *dinna* want you to touch me."

"What I *ken*, sweet darling, is that you melt under the stroke of my fingers, surrender to my lips when they attempt to possess yours. You want me. It's long past the moment to admit to the fact."

Quickly, she sat up pushing his hands aside. Deeper heat enflamed her cheeks, a tiny drop of milk hovered on the puckered nipple he just adored. "*Nay*. I *dinna* want you, Walker Endicott. You cannot seduce me. I won't let you. Nor will I be your mistress."

"I do believe you protest over much as well as too often."

What Walker understood was that if he so desired, if he wanted to push this tiny bit of lovemaking to its ultimate conclusion with her, he could. He wasn't going to do that, simply because next time he made love to Crissie McKenna he wanted her begging him not saying *nay*.

He stood, the proof of his desire more than evident to her gaze, "You will want me. I promise you that. There will come a time when you ask me to make love to you. Mayhap even beg." With that said he pulled on a pair of buff-colored pants and a white shirt then finished with his boots. Striding from the cabin, he stopped for a moment at the doorway. "Take your time with Ian. I'll bring breakfast. We should dock in a couple of hours."

"What next?" Her eyes were huge pools of silver surrounded by blue-ice, her breathing erratic as he watched her.

This was the first time during the entire journey she asked what would happen when they reached his home. She showed little to no curiosity about her fate or details about their destination. "We will settle in for a few weeks in my home in Belfast. You look quite done in, Crissie. You need to rest before you sicken. We cannot travel again until the sunken hollows beneath your eyes vanish."

"What next?"

"We will travel to my country estate southwest of here. That is where we will spend most of our time. Where Ian will grow up."

When he left, he understood she would have more questions. After this, he would have a difficult time keeping her in his bed. There would be no obvious reason. His homes had more than one bedroom. He would figure out some way for her to make the decision to share a bed. Dictating to her was abhorrent, even in this situation.

Perchance he could find a way. He would have to think on the possibilities, as he wasn't averse to a little blackmail. She would, after all, want to be close to her son. He grinned as he strode outside into the crisp sunshine of a perfect day. This morning there were few clouds anywhere in the sky. A slight breeze blew from the west. It was a beautiful summer day.

For a few minutes he stood at the bow of the ship watching as the landmass approached. He would find some way to bind her to him. He had to. Living without her in his life as well as his bed was not a tenable option for him. In time she would come to love him. In time she would understand why they couldn't be wed. His was a promise to his father that needed to be kept despite the horrible situation.

Striding to the small kitchen, he piled a tray high with food coupled with a pot of tea as well as cream and lemons. He didn't care if he gave her enough time to dress and feed Ian. Having seen her with nothing on every day during the trip, one more time should not bother her overmuch. Since Ian started on oatmeal, her breasts were a bit smaller, not so filled with the milk for his son. He wanted to watch them change, damned the time of her pregnancy, which he missed. From here on out he intended to enjoy every moment with the woman he loved along with the growth of his son.

When Walker stepped inside the cabin, she was on the bed asleep. Ian was crying, waving his arms and legs angrily. He didn't understand how she fell so soundly asleep in such a short time. Didn't understand why Ian's cries did not wake her.

He dropped the tray on a nearby table before rushing to her side. His hands on her shoulders, he shook her. "What is it, Crissie? Wake up?"

She moaned softly. It was then he realized she was warm, too warm. He didn't know what to do? Quickly, he picked up Ian, jiggling him trying to stop the crying. Lord, but he needed some help in here.

Keeping Ian on his shoulder with one hand, he dipped a cloth into the small basin of water. He ran the coolness along her forehead across her cheeks then down her neck. Prayed this was caused from exhaustion and nothing else. She mumbled something, batting his hand away in protest. It seemed she tried to sit up then fell back with a silent shudder. Suddenly, her eyes were open but they were glassy looking. She blinked a few times, brushing damp hair from her face.

"What happened?" She clutched her gown together before reaching up for her son. "I'm so tired."

"You tell me?" Walker watched her lips thin, watched as she once more bared a breast for the babe to suckle. He propped pillows behind her back as she nestled Ian to her. She was flushed but now seemed better. When he touched her again, she was only a little warmed, most likely from sleep. She was fatigued he realized. At the same time, he understood in his eagerness to get home he pushed her too hard.

"I don't know," she told him her eyes wide with what appeared to be genuine fear. "One minute I was watching you leave while wondering about what was going to happen in the next weeks and months then you were hovering over me. I guess I fell back to sleep."

"When we get settled in Belfast, I'll fetch a doctor for you. As for now, I'm not leaving your side."

He hoped this was nothing more than overwhelming fatigue he saw in her face linked with the weight loss. During the long weeks of their journey, she'd not been eating right, mostly moving her food around on the plate. He knew in his pressing need to reach Ireland he overtaxed her strength. Would not have done so if she even once told him she could not go any further.

She had not.

Bloody eyes. but he wasn't a mind reader. How could he know she was ill equipped to keep pace with him? She had always seemed so strong so self-reliant. While she was small, he never thought of her as fragile or delicate.

I should have known. Should have seen the tiredness in her eyes, the violet-blue smudges beneath.

"I don't suppose you'll give me the option of living in a separate home," she spoke softly, staring at her son, not deigning to look at him.

Her small hand caressed Ian's head. Her lashes were lowered, fluttering elegantly across the fragile bones of her cheek.

"Only if you want to live separate from your son. Ian will live with me. Your living quarters are up to you." He spoke evenly trying not to put any of the anger he felt about her request into the tone of his words.

Not only was he battling with her to remain in his bed, now it seemed she wanted to argue about staying in his home. In his arrogance he had not expected that.

"You do know what the good people of Belfast will call me if I stay in your home, unchaperoned, with a small babe."

"Enlighten me."

He did know what was coming. Frankly, he didn't care what anyone thought or said in private or in public. If he could help it, Crissie McKenna wasn't going anywhere.

Her eyes flashed, heat once again rose to her face, stained her breasts where Ian was suckling. It seemed she could not hold her irritation in check. "You damn well know."

"Does it matter that I don't think of you as a whore or as my mistress? You are a beautiful woman. A woman I care deeply for. A woman I long to shelter and protect. What is done in the privacy of my home should stay there." He spoke with a calm that didn't reach through to his core. "If you live in a separate house, even if you pay all the bills, when I am seen coming and going on a daily basis I might add, you will then be called my mistress. Is that better?"

Angrily, he slashed his hands through the air. His jaw was clenched so tight his teeth hurt. This conversation was one he understood was coming. Still the spoken words were repugnant to him. "Is that what you want?"

"You could send us back."

"Never!"

Finally, he lost the tiny bit of control he garnered during her questioning. His son and hopefully Crissie would stay with him forever. He would find some way to do so. In any case, sending her back into the dangers surrounding her family, the clan Chattan, was not going to happen.

For a moment she lowered her eyes, her lashes dark against the snowy whiteness of her cheeks. When she looked up, "Perhaps you could take Ian so I can dress and eat. Have you eaten?"

So, it was to be this way. She would end the discussion before it was finished, before she admitted she would remain with him. "No, I haven't."

He reached out for the babe then stepped back so she could dress, his gaze focused on the slender curve of her back, the flare of her hips when her nightdress slid to the floor.

Walker wasn't at all sure why he insisted on tormenting himself. Watching her naked, gazing at her when she bared a breast to nurse their child, staring while she bathed, sent his already engorged rod into a tempest of desire he couldn't douse. Because of it, he was constantly on edge saying words that shouldn't have been spoken.

They ate in silence. Their meager belongings were atop waiting departure. When they finished, he carried Ian while Crissie walked beside him, her chin held high, her shoulders stiff. When they began this trip, he was sure she would succumb to his every wish just as she'd surprisingly done in the highlands. She was proving a formidable woman, staunch in her most fervent beliefs. Hell, if he wasn't already wed, he'd marry her today.

Walker didn't just want her now. He wanted her forever.

"So, this is Ireland," she whispered as the land grew closer. "Seems much like Scotland."

"It is. Since we are neighbors, much will seem the same. Here in Northern Ireland, it is not as cold as the highlands though. We are a *wee* bit farther south."

"I see," she murmured, her fists clutching the rails, her expression rather bland. "Does it rain a lot?"

"We have our fair share of rain, sunshine as well."

He looked to the sky, which was still bright with the kiss of the sun although unlike an hour ago, dark clouds lined the horizon to the west. "It will probably be raining by tonight. After we land, we should make haste."

"If that is the case, I hope we'll be settled into our new lodgings by the first sprinkles. I don't care to get drenched." Her voice was flavorless yet her stance was still rigid, her shoulders stiff.

It seemed to Walker she appeared to be in battle with the world or at least his part of this world. His body shook with the need to share everything with this lady, the woman who bore his son, gave him his heir.

When he thought of the betrothal, leading to his wife, his child wife, despair threatened to swamp him. Charlotte was a meek woman, one who trembled if her shadow surprised her. They'd never lain together. Never consummated the marriage decreed at her birth. If he truly wanted, he could have the marriage annulled.

Deep in his heart he couldn't do that to Charlotte or his father. He'd sworn to wed Charlotte. She wouldn't understand, would be ostracized by her peers, her small circle of friends. Yet he yearned to think of himself, to see to his needs as well as Crissie's.

Before they wed, the lady in question wanted to hide herself in a nunnery, give herself to God. Now that Charlotte wed him even though the marriage was not fully completed, she would never be allowed such a privilege. The marriage was a horrible mistake, the passing years even worse. For the longest time he didn't care. Indeed, he used it to keep a few cloying women at bay. He kept one mistress.

But now...

Now, this lady beside him would never wish anything of that nature. She was wild and passionate. Even after a year the taste of her lips, the silken texture of her flesh was still easy to recall, the way he felt when he was deep inside her. He wished she would let loose with her temper. The fury at this situation she was in, he knew simmered just beneath her skin. He saw it every time she looked at him. Still, she refused to show her true feelings to vent her anger. If she would succumb to the tempest boiling inside, perhaps they could get past the blasé indifference and figure out what they both wanted.

The gangplank was lowered. Walker hailed a carriage just off the wharf, giving the directions to the townhouse. While they rode in silence through the streets, Crissie looked out the window as they passed through town. She was by nature curious. Her curiosity coupled with her intelligence always intrigued him. If they could get passed the tiny obstacle of his marriage to another, they would do well together.

He'd sent word ahead that he would be at the house. His two maids along with his cook met them at the door. Walker introduced them before handing the cradle to the upstairs maid, asking her to place it in his room.

The way Crissie stiffened didn't surprise him. One of the maids stared at her with disdain written clearly in the set of her mouth linked with the slant of her eyes as her gaze skimmed over her. Walker made a note to himself that he would have to talk to his staff. Right now, all he wanted was to get Crissie and Ian settled in to his suite of rooms upstairs. If she needed to take a nap before dinner, that was what he wanted for her.

"Would you bring us tea and a light snack just enough to tide us over until this evening. We've had little to eat this morning and afternoon."

The cook smiled at Ian, then, "I could bring more than a light snack. If you'd like, perhaps some bread and cheese. Have nice thick slices of ham also."

"Thank you." Walker extended his free arm to Crissie.

Ian was snuggled into his shoulder, his head bobbing, golden eyes wide and alert as if he was either looking for something to eat or trying to observe his new surroundings.

To his surprise, she accepted the proffered arm, climbing the steps to the second floor. He heard the long drawn in breath of air. Noted the wariness in her posture. "You will like Belfast."

His attempt at small talk was met with stilted silence. Down the long hall, he entered the master suite. Once again coming as no surprise to him, she stiffened. "This is our room. I hope you will share it with me. If you would like a bed of your own," he led her through an adjoining door, "you can sleep here."

"I see you put the cradle in your room."

"He's my son."

"I have to feed him, wake with him in the middle of the night. You wish for me to disturb you as well."

"All true. We both understand that he is sleeping now through to early morn. The choice of a bedroom is also your prerogative. I've merely laid out the ground rules. Ian, until he is old enough to reside in the nursery, will sleep in this bedroom with me. You may sleep anywhere you like. If this adjoining suite is not to your taste, feel free to pick any room in this house for yourself."

His attempt to be magnanimous fell on deaf ears as he watched her bristle more with each condescending word. In truth he was giving her more obstacles than choices. In reality there was only one obstacle, that was Ian.

Turning her head away, he assumed so he wouldn't hear her one whispered word. "*Bassa.*" He kept the chuckle behind his teeth. Perhaps he was a bastard.

"I'll have my things put in the adjoining room," she said softly as she removed the bonnet on her head.

At her directive to move into the other room, he stifled the sudden surge of annoyance. His ploy had not worked, at least not yet. Time would tell. *All I have to do is wait her out.*

"As you wish."

He could well-afford to appear magnanimous.

"I would like to freshen up before we eat. Do I have authority with your servants or do I have to wait until you request something?"

"I will make sure they understand that you will, if you like, assume the duties of the mistress of the house." Wrong word. He heard her suck in her breath, flashing her distaste.

"Thank you," she said without a hint of emotion. "Now, do I order the bath or do you want one also?"

"I will happily wait until you finish." He pulled the bell cord.

A few moments later a maid entered. "A bath please, for the lady."

She curtsied then left. True to form the hot water arrived and was then taken to his dressing area. Crissie watched wide-eyed, her hands trembling as she fought to keep her impatience in check. He was underhanded. He did only have one tub. Before the water was dumped, yes, he could have put the tub in the other room. He was sure he heard the word *bassa* again. Perhaps this time he deserved the label more than the last. No, both actions were underhanded. They might however begin to get him what he wanted most, her willingness to be held in his arms.

"Do enjoy." He nodded to the dressing room.

With her back still rigid, she retrieved a fresh gown from her bag. Head held high, she marched into the dressing room. He heard the soft thump of her slippers as they hit the ground along with the swish of her clothing, imagining the removal of each garment. Next the lap of water against the sides of the tub held him intrigued.

He laughed softly, wishing he dared go to her, wash her. *Nay,* he would not goad her further. Perhaps playing the gentleman would serve his purposes better.

He set Ian on the floor then lay down beside him, tickling his tummy. Ian gurgled and smiled as he waved his arms in the air, enjoying the attention. Walker called Ian's name. The little boy turned to look at him. Found himself perched precariously on his side.

"Come on, you can do it, little man." Walker laughed out right as Ian fell backward. A few seconds later, the little boy was on his side again. He blew tiny bubbles from his lips. This time he rocked. Once more he fell back.

The two played the game over and over again. Suddenly, Ian fell on to his tummy, his eyes wide with surprise. Walker laughed again so very amused as well as proud of his son.

"Crissie! My god, Crissie, you've got to see this."

When he rose to get her, she was standing between the two rooms, a puzzled look on her face. Her skin was pink from the heat of the bath, flushed more as she realized she wore only the towel.

"What is it? Is Ian alright?" She walked to him, bent down on the other side of the little boy.

"He rolled over. Ian rolled from his back to his tummy all by himself. You have to watch him," Walker said proudly, knowing he was grinning like a besotted fool.

On his stomach now, Ian was trying to push himself up with his hands and arms, rocking back and forth. "Place him on his back so I can see."

As Walker did her bidding, he said, "There are no guarantees, you know. It took several tries."

On his back now, Ian looked peeved to be there again when he already changed his position. "I don't think he wants to perform for us."

"Just watch." Walker tried again, calling Ian's name, presenting him with a toy to persuade him.

"He must be tired," Crissie said when the feat was not accomplished a third time. He looked at his mother, blowing more bubbles. "He only has one thing on his mind right now."

Walker, laughing at himself said, "As do I."

~ * ~

At Walker's words Crissie felt heat filling her from the tips of her toes to the top of her head, tumbling inside. She'd been around him as well as her brothers too many times not to understand the meaning of his words. Yet his antics on the floor with their son were endearing. She wanted to join him there even though she was completely naked beneath the towel.

"I'll be right back," she told both of them as she bent to place a quick kiss on her son's forehead.

Striding into her new room, she closed the door behind her then quickly dressed. During her bath, she decided he could dictate all he wanted. If he wanted to keep Ian in his room with him and wake up in the middle of the night when Ian needed his nightly feeding, so be it. He could do just that. In her mind Ian was swiftly approaching an age where he could sleep in a room nearby, a nursery for her son becoming more accomplished with each passing day. Most nights he slept until early morning.

Dressed now in a clean gown, still barefoot, she returned to find Walker holding her son high in the air above him while he lay on his back. Ian's little arms and legs were waving wildly. Pressing the back of her hand to her mouth, she stifled the gasp of fear threatening to ripple out.

"He likes flying," Walker said, nearly grinning from ear to ear as he dodged a drop of drool slipping from Ian's smiling little mouth.

"I see. Hand him over then why don't you see to our pre-dinner snack. I'm starving."

"I won't hurt him," he said with a bit of defensiveness coating his voice. "He shouldn't be coddled if he's to grow up to be a fine man." He cleared his throat, "The snack will probably arrive before I've finished with my bath. You will take care of it?"

She smiled at him, sitting in one of the chairs facing a window overlooking the bustling city, Ian at her breast. Walker's booted steps led to the dressing room. She heard the slosh of the water. Closing her eyes, she wondered just what she was supposed to do. He was incorrigible. She knew eventually she would give in and he would get his way. So, why spend the time fighting the feelings he so easily brought to the forefront, feelings he manipulated with finesse. *You're a devil, Walker Endicott. No doubt about the fact.* Crissie found herself in a quandary she had never before thought would be hers. It felt much the same as when she discovered her pregnancy.

Principles. Morals. Values instilled since she could remember was why she would struggle within herself. Why she would persevere resisting his ardent sweet-talking until she could no longer do so.

Truly, she didn't like the position he placed her in with no remorse on his part. To her this wasn't a game to be played. It was her life. She didn't know if he was her mate or if someone who wasn't a shifter could be another normal person's mate. Possibly that was only something shifters experienced.

She did love the man.

The knock on the door brought her attention away from her musing to the heavenly aroma of fresh cooked ham along with warm yeasty bread just from the oven. Her mouth watered while her belly grumbled. For the first time in a week, she was hungry.

She decided then and there she would make the best of this situation at the same time standing as long as she could by her values. She broke the code once. She prayed for strength now. Still, she wondered when faced with the prospect of a life with no physical love would it be so horrible for her to give into his vigorous pursuit of carnal pleasures. In time he might feel more for her than simple lust. She also wondered if love could grow from lust. More than anything she longed for him to love her.

"Set the tray on the table." Crissie looked up to see Walker with a towel around his waist, drying his hair with another his golden eyes alight with amusement. "Could you bring a bottle of wine too? I don't think we're going to go downstairs for dinner tonight. We'll eat here. This should be more than enough."

"Are you going to dress?" she asked then immediately regretted the question when his smile broadened and his eyes twinkled.

"If you ask nicely."

With a faintly languid gesture, she shrugged, "Do you care, Ian?" She kissed the boy on the forehead. "I don't. You can certainly do as you please. You will anyway," she added as an afterthought.

"An answer true to my heart. I'd much rather you didn't dress. It would be my utmost pleasure if we sat at the table stark naked with the sole purpose of feeding each other while easing the potent hunger in both of us."

At his blatant words she turned away to hide the tiny smile she tried to keep hidden. Felt a shimmer of passion. "What are we going to do the next days before we leave here? For that matter when are we leaving?" She sipped the wine he poured for her, feeling the sweet texture as the liquid slipped down her throat gently warming her insides.

He sat down close to her, the naked length of his muscular leg brushing against her skirt. "We could explore the city. Go to a pub or two where we can enjoy a meal along with the ambiance. There is also the farmer's market to appreciate. If you were to feel romantic, we could stroll hand-in-hand along the river."

"I'd like that. We left in such haste, I'm in need of a few things." She held up her free hand feeling strongly about her next statement. "I've coin. I will buy for myself what I need. Perhaps we could go shopping."

"Your things should be here in a day or two. However, I fully intend to purchase anything you think you might need in the interim. You will not spend your money on necessities. That is my role now."

The one breath she inhaled lay trapped inside her throat. She slanted him what she hoped was a fierce glare as she was at the same time shaking her head to deny him what he seemed to think was his responsibility. "*Nay*, you will not purchase my favors. I will not owe you my body because you buy things for me. If I am to stay with you, I will do it my way. There will be no compromise on this. You can buy things for Ian since he is your son. Not for me."

"You cannot stop me, Crissie. I don't expect anything from you that you are not willing to give. Makes no difference if I purchase a dress or a bonnet or the most expensive piece of jewelry money can buy."

He took Ian up in his arms accompanied by a quick cuddle before placing him in the cradle. He graced her with a broad smile effectively ending the bent of the last conversation. "I must have worn him out. He's asleep already."

She sipped in a shallow breath of air holding it in her lungs until her thoughts were in control. Just enough so she could once more speak her mind. "You are ignoring what is right in front of your face. I'm not going to argue with you. Do what you want. I'll do as I please."

By insisting on this course, he was making her plight worse. The servant who brought the tray of food looked at her as if she was lower than the dirt beneath her feet. Did he not see or did he choose to ignore what was obvious? With a long-held sigh and trying not to look backward, she decided she would have to ignore what others thought.

Walker seemed to be doing just that, discounting the situation. He was oblivious to everything around him.

"And what would that be?" he asked biting into a piece of ham.

For a few minutes she didn't answer as she concentrated on her food as well as filling her stomach. She didn't want to get sick. She acknowledged he was right about her health. Her eyes were sunken as was her belly. She wasn't eating enough to look out for herself or her son. Escalating and rolling emotions were the cause. All that would change now that she set her course.

"I wasn't going to mention it again. Promise this will be the last time. The servants here think of me as your paramour. I don't know if there is any term I can accept. They all sound so foul and degrading they make me cringe. Did you see the way that servant looked at me when she brought the tray into the room? It made my stomach roll. Truly, she believes I'm with you for what you can give me."

"I did tell you I would speak to them."

She waved her hand in the air, furious with his blasé nature. "Speaking to them will not still their thoughts or the truths they believe in their hearts." She wiped her hands on a napkin. "For better or worse that's all I'm going to say on the matter. I am done with it."

"Good, then I've some business to attend to. I'll be gone the rest of the afternoon perhaps into the evening. Make yourself at home. Explore if you would like. Before I leave, I will make sure all know this is your home as well as mine. You are not to be opposed in any request or deed." He laughed, "Short of burning the house down."

"Business?" she queried surprised that he would leave this evening when they just arrived. "What kind of business?

"Well," he said hesitating but a moment as if he diligently searched for the right words, "I did leave the highlands in a bit of a rush. Some explaining to my commanding officer is in order. He will want to know why and if I'm going to go back."

"Are you? Going back? Do you have a choice? You were dressed in civilian clothing when I first saw you. You told me you resigned your commission. Surely they cannot command you to go." Her heart caught in her throat at his words. "Why were you there?"

Suddenly his appearance at her home seemed suspect. She thought from the moment she first saw him, he'd not returned for her. Now, she was positive of that truth. Her nerves twisted inside. Her stomach turned sour. The food in front of her became unappetizing despite her best efforts.

"I'm not at liberty to say."

More clarification hit, her eyes widening with recognition. Her breath caught in the back of her throat. "You're a spy. Aren't you? You're spying on my family."

His silence coupled with the set of his jaw told her she hit on the truth. "Or you're still looking for stray Jacobites who fought in the battle of Culloden. You believe my brothers are involved. When will this ever end? Those people deserve to live in peace. They fought for a cause they believed in. Now it is over."

When he looked away for a moment, she learned more truths, thoughts she was sure he didn't want her to comprehend. "No, that was not your intention, was it? There is something more nefarious you are involved in. What then?"

Crissie was hit with an even stronger realization his presence might not have been because of her but because of her family.

"Tell me it's not true."

"What is not true?"

She could hardly blurt out her suspicions. If he didn't suspect or know about her father's and her brother's ability to shift into an animal form, she couldn't put the thought into his head. Throughout the generations her family spent much time putting down the rumors they were shifters. They always feared capture in their other form. Had always agreed that if any one of them were indeed found and restrained while in their cat form they would not be rescued. A rescue might put the entire clan at risk.

"Nothing," she murmured, downing her wine before pouring herself another liberal amount. For countless minutes she looked away, concentrated on the window, the rain sluicing to the ground. Wind whistled across the glass panes.

"There are no reprehensible purposes in the highlands set by the British government. My mission there is just to survey what has already been done. Nothing nefarious, I assure you."

She knew he was lying just as surely as she understood his meeting this evening was about her family. It seemed to her he tried to reassure. Well, it wasn't working despite the fact she wanted desperately to believe his words. Her heart lurched at the thought her family might find betrayal at the hands of this man, the father of her child.

"Just by you."

"No, it's not what you think, Crissie. At this moment I can't explain. You will need to have faith in me until, until there is some understanding as well as trust between us. As long as you fight me, fight our relationship, there can be no trust and no communication. Secrets cannot be shared. I cannot tell you things that might put your life at risk or mine. Sometimes ignorance is the best means to stay alive. When and if you are ever confronted, you can simply and truthfully say you don't know anything."

The words he said rang true. Indeed, there were too many secrets between them. She couldn't blurt out that she wasn't a shifter. He need not fear betraying her. If she were wrong about his intentions, he would think she was crazy. Instead, she held her breath until she gained some semblance of control. "When will you be home?"

"Don't wait up for me. You need your rest."

"Then I'll move Ian's cradle into the adjoining room." She thought her voice sounded calm.

"If you do, I'll simply move it back. My son sleeps in the master chamber as should his mother. I've no say where his mother sleeps though. Choose whatever you like." With a soft resigned sigh rattling from him lips, "I know you will."

He was then out the door. As much as she tried to school her temper, her annoyance coupled with irritation escalated to a point where she was throwing pillows at the wall wishing the pillows were something harder and directed at Walker's head.

After a while, she did calm herself. Allowed herself to breathe deeply taking in several long breaths until her heart no longer raced. She decided she needed more wine. If there wasn't any left in the bottle, she would ring for another bottle. Perhaps she would anyway.

The tiny sleep noises coming from Ian's cradle brought her back to reality. While she would have loved to drink enough wine so she would no longer feel, she didn't have that privilege.

His whore. His lover, his mistress. What the hell did he want from her? None of those titles sat well with her.

Her son.

She could take his dictates, put up with the untenable position he put her in or she could leave. He would not let her take his child.

Nor did she want to love the blasted man.

It was with considerable agony that Crissie finally resolved her feelings while plotting a course of action for at least the near future. She couldn't even imagine the distant future. As she thought time and again, as she knew every second he held her, she could not refuse him or hold out for long. His kisses generated irrefutable sparks coupled with undeniable longings within her.

While she thought about her heart and how he possessed it, she also tried to figure out the best way of holding her love apart from him. Idly and with no apparent destination, she wandered through the upstairs rooms. Finding a duster in a corner closet, she began to clean. While she did, she hummed to herself. His maids did need direction, a great deal of it. What must be year old dirt covered shelves and knick-knacks. His home had not been kept up while he was away.

After several hours, she was satisfied that the first layer of dirt and grime had been removed from the suite of rooms that composed the master chamber. Carrying the half empty bottle of wine with her she made her way to the third floor. Here she found all manner of different rooms. Some were meant for the hired help who also lived and worked in the townhouse. One large room was obviously a playroom. Old toys were stashed away in boxes.

Smiling happily at her discovery, Crissie sorted through one large box finding several suitable toys for Ian, among them several horses along with wooden soldiers. She stuffed them in one pocket of her dress deciding she would return on the next day to find some more things for him to play with. Holding the bottle of wine to her lips, she drank long and deep letting the sweet liquid settle in her stomach. She found she was hungry again but she ignored the rumble thoroughly enjoying the moment at hand.

In another room, she found trunks of old clothing. In another no longer wanted furniture was piled high on top of each other. The scent of old wood and dust filtered through her senses. She pushed away cobwebs, sneezed from the dust she raised with her cleaning. Suddenly exhausted, she sat down on one of the chairs that was perched atop another. It rocked precariously before finally settling to a standstill.

Crissie found herself in front of a window looking out on a velvet dark sky dotted with a few twinkling stars. The storm must have passed.

Between clouds she saw the hint of a slivered moon. A shaft of light filled the tiny room. The stars were not so bright as she remembered from the highlands. A wave of homesickness washed over her as she longed for the place of her birth.

Here she was in a townhouse in the outskirts of Belfast alone waiting for the father of her child to come home. It was not something she would have expected two short weeks ago. She drank from the wine, once more emptying the bottle. It dropped from her fingers finding purchase atop a table before rolling to land on a rolled-up carpet then the floor. She heard it spinning until finally it too stopped. Silence echoed in the small cramped room.

She realized she needed to get down, should go see how Ian was faring. Unexpectedly, she wasn't quite so sure how exactly she was going to go about this feat without hurting herself or toppling all the furniture. She was positive if she tried, she would land haphazardly on her rear, in the process embarrassing herself. Of course, at the moment there was no one to see her fall from grace.

"Well," she murmured, "there is nothing to do about this except do the best she could." She stood on the arms of the chair below her planting her hands on something she hoped was solid. She felt a bit wobbly. Closed her eyes. Froze. The entire stack rocked before shuddering then shifting beneath her weight. She held her breath trying to move as slowly as possible.

"What the hell do you think you are doing?"

Walker's harsh words startled her as she lost her balance, her arms whirling in the air. Strong hands encircled her waist, his fingers biting into her. Oh dear, he was angry with her. This time, she did suppose he had good reason. He lifted her from her perch on top of the chairs. While she thought she would land in his arms, it seemed the lower chair shifted causing her to move.

Instead of landing safe and secure in his arms, she landed on top of him on the floor. When she pushed off his shoulders, she stared into his laughing golden eyes that seemed to be sprinkled with dots of deep brown. Perhaps he wasn't angry.

"It's not funny," she murmured.

"You're drunk, Crissie. I've never seen you this way. It's rather endearing though. I'm sure there are lots of ways I've not seen you."

She punched his shoulder. "Am not. Let me up. Have to see to Ian."

"He's sleeping. What were you doing up there?" he asked again, his voice gentle. "You're covered in cobwebs. Hopefully, there are no spiders inhabiting your hair." He brushed a few sticky strands away and off her hair. "Along with the dust of years of neglect."

"If you must know I was doing the job your servants are supposed to do. If there are any spiders in my hair, I hope they crawl onto you."

Suddenly he rolled, pinning her to the floor. "You don't say." His lips captured hers, hard and demanding at first before gentling. The kiss turned slow, languorous.

Intoxicating.

Undeniable magic.

All the exquisite delights she always felt with his kisses bombarded her. Heat coupled with desire roared to a tempest inside all her most vulnerable parts. Never could she be immune to this enchantment he generated within her. His large hands slipped beneath her rear, pulling her against his hard arousal. Her fingers wove through his hair as he deepened the kiss taking outrageous advantage of her feelings for him along with her half-drunken state.

He told her he would do so.

And so, he did.

Finding sensitive erotic places to stroke and tease to his command, he continued to coax her surrender. *Nay, not this soon, please give me strength to withstand this onslaught for a few more days.*

Crissie didn't have the will to tell him *nay*. If they stopped it would have to be because Walker stopped. She desired his hands and his lips, all of his body more than she ever wanted to admit. His large hands found their way beneath her skirt, smoothing along her legs, to settle more intimately on her soft belly, teasing her with expectations of more erotic caresses.

Unable to help herself she moaned softly, the tiny ripple of noise telling her how thoroughly she was losing herself to this man.

She heard the soft masculine chuckle confirming his win. His hands continued their bold, teasing exploration down her legs, settling her skirt as he reached her ankles. He stood then, pulling her up with him. Her body stretched tight against his, his arousal pulsing against her now so very obvious.

"As much as I would like to continue this while you are more than willing, perhaps a cleaner space might be a bit more romantic."

Feeling chastised and still vulnerable to his sexual prowess she lowered her lashes. When she looked at him again, his smile was tender as he gently brushed his soft lips along the width of hers.

"I didn't start this." She tried to protest, but his finger on her lips silenced her.

"No, you did not. As I told you before, I want you begging me much as you did the day my son was conceived. Nothing else will do."

She was mortified that it was Walker who stopped the love play. If he chose to take her on the dirty attic floor, she would have allowed it. Brushing off her skirts, she strode out the door. Back in the master suite she checked on Ian.

He followed a little later with two pitchers of clean water. "You've several smudges of dirt on your face. Thought you might want to clean up before you crawl into your cold bed."

Those words surprised her drastically. Also caused a slight feeling of rejection she didn't want to admit to reeling inside her. It seemed she managed to convince him she didn't want to sleep with him. She peeked at Ian who was still sleeping soundly.

Using the water and a small mirror she cleaned her face. "Did you have a nice evening?"

He laughed, "Did you?"

"Why do you always throw questions back at me without answering mine? It's irritating."

"Why indeed?"

"You, Sir, are incorrigible. I will say goodnight."

Her legs trembling but keeping her head held high, Crissie walked what seemed an eternity to go into the adjoining chamber. Once inside she shut the door. The wood shut with a resounding bang she didn't intend. Sitting on a chair in front of a fireplace that had neither logs nor flames within, she let a tear slip down her cheek. She was beside herself with insecurities pounding in her head.

What was she to do?

The soft sound of her door opening had her lifting her head in surprise to see Walker framed by the muted light behind him.

"You must keep the door open between us. I won't have it any other way."

Crissie inhaled a long-ragged breath of air. *Keep the door open between us.* How prophetic. Just how could she do that when he opposed her at every turn, generated such confusion that reached into her very soul. She no longer knew how to cope with him. Wasn't sure she wanted to.

Nay, she had to be strong. Had to stand firm. In the end she would win out over him. At this moment she didn't know how.

She would win and, in the process, get everything she ever wanted.

Or would she lose her soul?

Stand firm.

~ * ~

Charlotte Endicott strode through the small home Walker settled her in after their marriage proved disastrous for both of them. She was afraid of the man she wed. Had begged and cried for her father to send her away until there were no tears left inside her to shed. Her father gave her to the earl with no concession to her feelings. She didn't want to be with a man. Other desires consumed her.

In Walker's defense, he tried to be gentle with her. She rebuked him at every turn. Finally, he gave up. She was glad of that for herself but not for him. She never wished Walker ill will. She just didn't want to wed him. She didn't want him to kiss her or put his rod inside her. *Nay,* she didn't want anything to do with marriage to anyone, not just the earl. When she met Anne, her feelings changed. She wanted to be with her, lie with her, understanding her feelings would not be accepted by anyone.

Her father insisted even when he was given a means to recover from the damage to his pride. Pride. That was all it was that drew her father to manage her life so thoroughly they were both miserable. She could never tell him her preferences.

Now, she heard Walker had a new mistress. Deep down she was happy for him. He deserved love in his life. She certainly couldn't give him the happiness he merited. Charlotte's only wish was that he would find a way to annul their defective marriage then wed this other woman. If he did annul it, she would be left with nothing. There had to be another way.

Perchance he didn't love this other lady.

In that case why bother.

They would be here at the estate in a few days. Walker wrote to the estate manager. He told her of the pending arrival of her husband, asking in the next breath if she wanted to move into the main house. He asked only because in the next breath he told her about the woman Walker was bringing with him. The manager thought Charlotte should be there to be his wife.

Aye, he was coming along with the son she never would be able to give him. That was the only thing she felt bitter about. She would have liked to have a child. As things stood now, she never would have that opportunity. Unbidden, a tiny flame of jealousy took hold, simmered, then leapt higher.

Charlotte wondered if this new woman understood exactly who Walker Endicott, the tenth earl of Briarwood, really was. He had secrets. Secrets he didn't even know she uncovered. She laughed softly. She had almost been willing to bed the man until she discovered the fact.

Walker still didn't comprehend the extent of her knowledge. It was information she held close to her heart. If he had not been such a gentleman, giving in to her fears and leaving the bedroom when she asked, she might have exposed him. At one time she thought to do just that so she could be well and truly rid of her husband.

Ah, but she supposed the telling of his secret should be between the unlikely pair. It was up to Walker to tell her. Supposed they also had a lot of discovery to do if they were to stay compatible. Most women didn't want to be second to a wife. Charlotte suspected this woman was much the same.

She didn't know why, but deep down she believed this lady would change her life as well as Walker's. A tiny ripple of apprehension ripped through her growing in size the more she considered the possible consequences.

"What has you so deep in thought, milady?" her maid, Laura asked, her voice soft. "You look as if you've seen the devil himself."

"Walker is bringing a woman here to live. It's not just any woman. Seems she bore him a son, his heir."

"He would have to denounce you. I doubt he would do such a thing. How long has it been since the two of you wed?"

"Ten years in August," Charlotte said, studying the trees outside her window, thinking hard about this new situation. Walker never brought women to the home. He'd always had more consideration for her.

"He has not done so yet."

"True, but he's never had a son to consider. To my knowledge, save this boy, he has no other illegitimate children." Charlotte turned then a strange feeling settling in the pit of her stomach.

"That you know of."

"None that he thought to bring here, along with the mother. That in and of itself tells us a wealth of things about the lady, now, doesn't it?" Maybe she should be looking for somewhere else to live. Her father, after the way she shamed him, would never allow her to move home.

She was solely at the mercy of her lord husband. Well, it seemed to her she always had been. Nothing here was new. She would have to think of some way to change that. By his grace he allowed her to live in comfort. She was able to purchase anything she ever wanted or needed. Feeling more need for privacy, it had been her choice to move from the main house to this smaller guest home.

What should she do now? All would be better off without her. *Nay*, all would be better off without the new lady.

"If you chose to leave the estate, I'm sure he would pay for a home. He's always been generous," the little maid who Charlotte adored spoke with a knowledge that belied her age.

"My leaving would solve none of his problems if he does indeed love this lady as I suspect he does. Possibly on the morrow I should seek out the minister to see how I could obtain an annulment of our marriage. It could be the wedding gift I've never given him," Charlotte mused as she tried to think of any other solution. She couldn't even think right now. Her mind was in such a jumble of confusing thoughts.

"I will go with you if you like."

"I'm sure that won't be necessary, but I do appreciate your offer. No, you need to remove yourself to the main house to make sure everything is in order for Walker as well as his son."

"*Aye*, milady but I do think you should not be left alone."

Charlotte laughed, a small brittle sound to her ears. Brittle, that was how she felt. As if she could be snapped into two pieces by the slightest pressure. For ten years she knew this time was coming. Understood eventually her husband would find a woman good enough and strong enough for him. He would want to be rid of her then.

Well, she would wait to meet this lady. If she was all that or even more, she would make her decision then.

Chapter Three

Walker was pleased with this evening's progress. Crissie didn't want him to stop kissing her when he picked her up off the floor. While her seduction would not be easy, he determined it was coming along just fine at the moment. He would take his time. When he watched her stride stiff shouldered into the adjoining room, he knew a moment of anger before he tempered that feeling with the confidence he felt in the ultimate outcome. When necessary and with the proper reward at the end, he could be a patient man.

She would come to him, hopefully tonight, if not tonight, then the next. He smiled tenderly at the way her eyes simmered with the desire he freely coaxed from her, at the soft silken texture of her flesh undulating across his fingertips. The tiny sounds of pleasure he heard from her, aroused him as no other woman. For the longest time, he watched the opening to her room, wishing he would see her walk through the door to him.

He stood, stretching. At Ian's cradle he tenderly stroked the little boy's back then the soft roundness of his cheek, marveling at the amazing creation in front of him. He would have to go back to the highlands soon to unfinished business but not until he spent a few days here in Belfast with Crissie and not until she was settled in the country manor of Briarwood.

Exhausted by the rapid trip to Belfast along with the emotional upheaval, Walker stripped, washed quickly then settled into the bed he wished he was sharing with the woman he was coming to care for more than he ever thought possible. Unable to sleep, he stared at the ceiling above, his hands clasped behind his head. Time ticked by slowly, subtle night sounds filtered in through the slightly open window. He closed his eyes but found sleep eluded him.

It seemed his eyes had only been closed a few seconds when he felt gentle warmth consume him, felt the outlines of a rounded bottom pushed against the cradle of his thighs, his body instantly fully aroused. The delicate scent of orange blossoms tugged at his senses. His hand settled on the soft curve of her hip. He didn't understand why she was in bed with him, but he wasn't going to complain.

This was exactly what he prayed for.

Sunlight was just peeking in through the window. The day, he hoped would be warm and delightful. A stroll through town might prove interesting. First thing after breakfast he meant to find a nanny for Ian so Crissie would have more time for him. Had the perfect woman in mind. Selfish, he supposed. He needed to bind her to him, before he left for the highlands. He would have to extricate a promise from her that she wouldn't leave while he was gone.

Ian would wake soon. Before that happened, he wanted to set Crissie on fire again, coax her body into craving his more than ever before. His hands explored sweet tender flesh beneath the nightdress she wore, deciding then and there that if she were to come to his bed from this point on, she would wear nothing at all. He would have it no other way. To be in his bed or not was her choice. What she wore was his.

The fabric inched slowly up. She moaned softly pushing her bottom against his heavy arousal. God help him but he was stimulated beyond endurance. His hand cupped one soft breast. His palm rubbing across the tight puckered bud that tipped it. He pushed aside her braided hair, nuzzling at the nape of her neck.

To his surprise she turned toward him. "Sit up and lift your arms for me."

To his astonishment she did. He quickly rid her of the fabric that separated their bodies before tossing the offending gown to the floor. She settled against him. Her breasts pushed against his chest. His hands on her buttocks pulled her closer. His lips molded over hers, taking her mouth with reverence. He slid his tongue along the seam until she willingly parted for him allowed him inside. Let him explore the dark sultry depth, which tasted of the sweetest mint.

Her eyes opened wide. As if finally understanding what she was asking from him or perhaps not, "What?" She pulled away from him, a tiny look of confusion on her beautiful face. Her silver-hued eyes studied him intently. For a few seconds she appeared puzzled. "What are you doing?"

"Enjoying you. You came to me or have you forgotten?" he asked watching for her reaction for any attempt to hide the truth.

There was none.

"I was cold," she murmured as strands of her silken hair slid across his arms. The tips of her breasts tantalized him with the steady movement across his chest. His open hands slid up and down her back.

"Is that all? The only reason? Tell me the truth now."

His fingertip rested beneath her chin, he lifted so he could look into the silver-blue depths of her eyes, more blue than silver at the moment. Perhaps read all her thoughts.

Her long, dark lashes fanned across her cheeks. Then she opened her eyes for him again. Her murmur softly spoken, "Nothing really, I missed you. You're warm."

Beneath his chest his heart lurched. "After so many nights you've become used to sleeping next to me?"

Not giving her a chance to answer knowing this time was rapidly coming to an end simply because Ian would wake soon, he captured her lips with his. He coaxed and teased her until tiny purring sounds emanated from deep within her. He squeezed and cupped her breasts, worked the tight buds with his fingers. Her fingers wound into his hair, pulling his face closer even while she explored within his mouth.

God, but he didn't want this to end so soon. Ian was crying now. He pulled away from her, smoothing damp strands of her hair from her face. When she looked at him, her eyes were slightly glazed from the passion they shared. Now, he was about to deny her the ecstasy he knew her body craved. He would have to wait.

Another time and it would be hers.

Confident that moment would be sooner than later, he gave her rump a tiny whack. "Best you get up before he screams his head off."

She was sitting up now, pushing her hair away from her face, her breasts swaying provocatively with the movement. He grumbled deep inside not feeling as if he actually made progress when indeed he had. Much to his surprise she appeared completely at ease with her nudity.

"Could you change his diaper while I put my nightdress back on?" she asked, her smile sweet.

He wasn't at all sure what to make of the impish grin he witnessed. "Yes, but I would prefer you remain as you are."

"Once again, I would be cold. Do you want your servants to see me when they bring in the morning tea?"

In this she was right. With a quick move, he tossed her the gown. He watched her as she slipped it over her head, preparing herself to feed his son.

Before she could completely get comfortable on the small chair where she fed Ian last eve, he had the boy diapered and clothed to meet the day. Still feeling the profound reverence of having a son, Walker placed Ian in Crissie's arms. Stepping back, he allowed his gaze to linger on them before turning to the dressing room to prepare himself for the day. Before he left, he walked back to her.

He kissed her as well as Ian on the forehead. "I'm going to make preparations for our exploration of the city. I've also made arrangements for you to hire a nanny to watch over Ian when we cannot. You will, of course, have time to interview her. If you wish we can hire the lady today."

Crissie's eyes seemed to cross as she thought on all he said. "I never thought..." She ran her tongue across her lips. "Never thought to have a nanny. At home there was always someone to take care of a child when the parents wanted a few moments alone."

"Then you are fine by this? A nanny for Ian?" He quirked a tawny colored eyebrow upward. "I hoped you would be. You need time to yourself. We need time together."

"I would like to learn a little about her first. If you don't mind?"

He sat down. "I'm to meet her in twenty minutes. She was my nanny."

"So, she is old." A smile twitched softly on her lips, ones he wanted to taste again.

"Not so much. She lost her husband a few years back. A child to take her mind off the loneliness will be good for her. I trust her implicitly."

Walker realized he did indeed trust her. She knew and kept secrets about him few others were privy to. In fact, he trusted her with the very essence of his life.

"Of course, go fetch her. We can sit down with a cup of tea and get to know each other. Perhaps your cook wouldn't mind making something else."

Walker left with a feeling of relief. Crissie needed time away from the child while he yearned for more time with her. Before he left for the highlands, he needed to extract a promise from her to stay at the manor at least until he returned. At that time, he might be able to give her proof of his intentions where she was concerned. After meeting with the possible nanny last night, she agreed to be at his home by eight o'clock. It was nearing that hour now.

When he stepped into the drawing room, she was waiting for him, a cup of tea in hand and a scone on a small plate beside her.

"Rose, you're early." He hugged the older lady before pouring himself a cup. "We can talk a few minutes. It will give Crissie a little more time to get ready for us."

"Shouldn't she come down here?" Rose asked looking to the steps for an answer. "I'd like to meet the lad too. Does he look like you?"

"Perhaps, but I didn't give her the directive. Possibly we should leave it up to her. As to who he looks like, you will have to see for yourself."

"Always the tease," Rose laughed.

"Never."

"Of course you are and proud of it."

"We can argue the point later," he said blandly.

"Now, I'm not being a busy body." She leaned forward patting him on the hand a smile crinkling the age lines around her eyes. "I didn't have to be in this house for more than a few seconds before I heard the gossip that your lady is not your wife but a mistress. You need to quell that nonsense quickly even if it is true. Gossip has no place in a respectable home as well you know."

He felt the snub from his employees not from Rose. She was merely interested so she would know how to proceed. "Crissie is not my wife. I'm still wed to Charlotte. You're right however, the gossip needs to stop."

"A terrible mistake, my dear boy, just terrible. This special lady of yours is your mistress? If I were to give you any advice, I would tell you now, end the fiasco that started ten years ago with either a divorce or an annulment. My dear boy, you deserve to be happy." After a lengthy pause, "Does she know you are wed?"

The lump in his throat seemed to stick and claw at him. He was about to say yes, she was his mistress but she couldn't disrespect Crissie that way. He loved her. Dear God, it was the truth. He did love the woman upstairs, the one who bore him a son. Until now, he had not realized the truth.

I love her.

"*Nay*, she is not a mistress to me but I've no idea what to call her since Crissie cannot be my wife. I cannot wed. Nor can I shame my father by setting aside my wedding to Charlotte."

What a conundrum. Until now the marriage made little difference in his life.

"Of course you can, dear boy. Charlotte doesn't want to be married to you any more than you do to her. She will agree to anything you suggest in order to gain her freedom. Talk to her. I assume we will go to the country manor in a day or two. You will have time then. However," a few seconds later after seeming to think a while, "will Charlotte accept your new woman?"

He could think of no argument to give Rose nor did he have an answer to her question so he reverted back to his original statement. "I would not shame her father or mine. The betrothal contract was legal and binding as was the wedding."

Rose pinched the bridge of her nose making a face at him. "This has a stink that needs to be washed away before you lose what is most important to you. Then there is the fact that you should not have to lose all that is good in your life over something put together by two doting fathers long before their children were born. Fathers who had no idea how their children would grow up or what they could possibly want in their lives."

As much as he knew Rose to be right on this score, he didn't know how he could ever go about doing such a thing to Charlotte. She would be devastated as well as embarrassed. If he ended the marriage, he would make sure she would continue to be taken care of financially. Still, he needed to consider his feelings along with Crissie's. What a mess he'd made of his life so far.

Rose was right. The problem simply stated, how was he going to set this to rights?

After taking another sip of her tea, Rose spoke again, "I know you and you're about to tell me you could never dishonor Charlotte. Do me a huge favor, yourself as well, think on this. Charlotte loathed you from the moment she learned of your secret. She loathes men in general. You're fortunate she has not given you away."

Having noticed a shift in the air, the scent of babe and orange blossoms of Crissie following, he looked up to see Crissie, with Ian in her arms strolling into the drawing room. At the sight, his heart caught in his throat. He didn't think he could bear it if anything happened to her.

Walker stood, extending his arms for Ian. He cleared his throat. It was still husky and raw with desire, "You came down. I wasn't sure..."

She held her hand out to Rose, "I'm Crissie McKenna, Walker's friend. He's been kind to help me out when I was in need of someone."

He blanched at the word friend thinking of the way she melted in his arms, the way her sweet kisses heated and aroused him to his very soul. Hell, sweet? No, wicked and hot. She was anything but a mere friend and she knew it, said the single word to absolve him of any interest in the boy.

Rose stood to greet her also extending her hand. "Nice to meet you, my dear. "I'm Rose Dahling. I've known this rascal since he didn't have an ounce of common sense," looking at him with a tilted head then a slight snort of derision. "Not sure he has any now. He got into more trouble than any of the other children. Sometime I'll have to tell you about some of his more daring exploits. My dear, you don't need to tell fibs about yourself. We both understand you're far more than a mere friend to Walker. You mean a lot to this young man, and in that case at least to me you are a treasure to know."

"Thank you," Crissie said as a small tear slipped down her cheek, a flush rising there. "He must have been caught more than once," Crissie laughed softly seeming to push away the earlier tear as well as the obvious embarrassment generated from Rose's assessment of their relationship, her smile lighting the entire room.

Lord, but he wanted her to look at him with that smile on her face. He craved the intimacies with her she still denied him. What would it be like to hold her in his arms again, to make love to her or even be able to claim her as his wife? A deep pit of despair closed over him at the thoughts swirling in his head. He could not, would not let her go even if she deserved better than what he could give her.

"*Aye*, that he did. He was an adorable little rascal. Seems now he's grown into an adorable man, handsome devil. Now tell me, what do you want to know about me?"

"Besides Walker's endorsement of all your sterling qualities, I suppose your qualifications. He would hire you this instant but I have to know more about the woman who will look after my son in my absence."

"Our son," he corrected her quickly.

"Our son," she conceded with a nod, knowing then that Walker must have told her everything. "Do you have children?"

"Three boys and a girl. They've all married and gone to live in cities other than Belfast. I've twelve grandchildren. Hardly ever see them. Sometimes they visit at Christmas or invite me to their homes for their birthdays."

Crissie looked at Walker who was tickling Ian until he was giggling delightedly then he was holding him over his head. "I pray you will not be tossing my son like that. It near kills me to see Walker doing such a thing. He plays far too rough for my taste. Don't you think he is a bit young for such roughhousing?"

"If you care to look closely, I'm not doing any tossing," Indignantly, Walker interrupted the conversation between the two ladies.

"*Nay*, I've the same gut reaction," Rose said. "Men are like that, though. He will *nay* harm the lad. Soon he will be tossing him in the air and you will lose whatever air you have left in your lungs at the time."

"You will not coddle my son. He has to learn how to be a man. A boy needs to be strong and sturdy," Walker said with a chortle as he stopped the game they were playing. Then with a sheepish grin, "He loves it. The higher I hold him the better."

"While I'm not a tutor, I will be happy to look after him and play with the little boy. He looks just like Walker at that age. Why he even has his father's amber-gold eyes." She looked to Walker sharing the secret silently that Rose spoke of earlier.

Walker nodded, his expression turning grim. He would have to find a way to deal with the secrets between them. First however, he meant for her to tell him the truth about herself.

"Ah, then he is more like his father than just his eyes and what seems to be the color of his hair."

It appeared Rose wanted to say more but stopped, her smile vanishing as if she held some secret close to her chest.

"Yes, he does have my eyes."

"You can ask me anything anytime. Walker tells me we will be moving to the country manor in a few days. I will travel with you. Stay in the main house if that is your wish," Rose said calmly.

Rose did understand everything. All the problems as well as the good things that would come about once Crissie reached her new home. He prayed she would be content if not altogether happy.

"To be honest, I'm overwhelmed by all this. I don't have a notion of what I would like."

"You don't have to make a decision today. Just soon enough so I can pack my belongings so to be ready when Walker decides to leave town. I do know he has unfinished business to attend to before he can leave. By the way, I understand the problems you young people are going through. An archaic betrothal that should have never been legalized then condoned with a marriage vow that hangs over his head. I won't' sit in judgment of you. Both their fathers should be ashamed of themselves for arranging this travesty. All they managed was to ruin two lives."

Crissie was shaking her head, looking to Walker before turning her attention back to Rose. "I don't understand."

"What you and Walker feel for each other is not my business. Even if he hasn't said the words, he loves you. I can tell just by the way he watches you. In time all will work out. I'm absolutely sure of it." Rose smiled then, before reaching out to pat her hand.

Walker felt heat rise to his cheeks at Rose's words. How the devil did she know what he felt? He just figured it out a few minutes ago himself. For too long he thought his emotions for Crissie revolved around the most intoxicating lust a man could feel for a woman.

It was more than sexual attraction however.

What he felt was love.

"For now, do you think Rose will work out?" Walker handed the child to Rose who clasped him to her ample bosom, stroking his back as she cooed nonsense words to the little man.

Ian clearly liked her. He gurgled and smiled at her while she grinned down at him.

Turning to Crissie he held out his hand, hoping she would accept the invitation. "I've had a coach brought around to the front. Are you ready to explore a bit of the city? I can show you the sites. We could also get a bite to eat and drink or both."

She nodded. Still, she held back looking uncertain as she watched Rose play with Ian. After seeming to inhale a large breath of air. "I'll get my cloak."

"If we're not back in a few hours, the cook knows what he can have to eat," Walker spoke to Rose as he watched Crissie's swaying skirts. He was looking forward to a few hours alone with her.

As they walked out the door then into the carriage, he felt her holding back. "Everything will be fine. You'll see. Do you like Rose?"

More than anything, he wanted Crissie to like his old nanny. She was outspoken. What she told her about his earlier days were true, every word.

"I've never left him for more than a few minutes. Never been out of the house and left him behind," she murmured softly while she let him help her with the cloak before offering her his arm.

"You will have to get used to the feeling. Ian will thrive with Rose as another friend as well as teacher. He doesn't need his mother every second of the day. You will see. This small change will be good for the boy as well as you, perhaps even for us."

He was hoping it would be good for them. While he wanted her to stay with him, he would have to find a way to bind her to him so thoroughly she would never choose to leave.

"Still..." She turned to look at the house as the carriage began to pull away. "He is so young."

Rose stood on the porch, Ian in her arms, waving.

"Come here."

"What?" She blinked at him, seemed to watch as he pulled her into his arms for a kiss.

He set her aside, grinning besottedly. "A kiss and more of that when I get the opportunity." He loved the soft flush of color rising from beneath the collar of her gown to settle on her cheeks. He craved to see if her breasts were that same shade of pink even while he remembered their one moment of sweet sexual intimacy.

"Where are we going?"

"Where would you like to go?" he asked her, grinning while he still marveled at the color painting her face.

"As you well know, I've never been in the city. So, I couldn't say." Her voice held a bit of mocking disdain.

"Close your eyes and don't open them until we reach our

destination. We'll stroll through the shops and pubs in the heart of the city. You can have anything you would like."

"Something to eat would be nice. We didn't get anything for breakfast before you drug me from the house. I did have a cup of tea, but I'm afraid that isn't enough."

"Drug you? I would have you know I don't do such things." He was laughing, enjoying her as he used to when he first met her in the highlands. "Free will," he told her. "You said, yes." He was thinking she'd said yes today and that one time as well.

"I need something to eat," she grumbled. "You are the one who said I *dinna* eat enough."

Laughing, he pulled her into his arms for another quick kiss. The contact was over before it started. He delighted in the way she gave herself to him leaving him weak with need.

~ * ~

Crissie folded her hands in her lap, watching her trembling fingers for several seconds. "I do like Rose."

His arm over Crissie's shoulder, he squeezed lightly. "Knew you would. She won't mince words with you. Don't expect to ever hide anything from her. I do believe she can read minds."

"I *ken* she is a woman who can see into one's heart as well as their soul."

Crissie wished for more time to talk with the lady, understanding she could tell her facts about Walker, things she would love to understand. She wanted to know everything there was to learn.

"The lady comprehends certain truths about me no other living person understands except perhaps my father." Walker laughed as he kept his gaze on what was passing by on the outside of the carriage.

"Don't suppose you would like to tell me any of those details."

She understood what she wanted to know was what was in his heart. When he truly trusted her, their relationship would change for the better. Knowing who he was as well as how he thought was important to her peace of mind.

His expression changed, his smile replaced by tawny brows drawn over golden eyes. His grip on her shoulder tightened. She looked away realizing she overstepped herself. He was not about to confide in her. Now he appeared the dangerous man she knew he was. Walker was always so sure of himself, at ease in any situation. He exuded confidence.

"You should not have called yourself my friend," he said softly. "Why?"

His gruff words surprised her. She regretted blurting out her thoughts. She was so very unsure of herself. When she said the words, she understood he would take issue. Still, that's how this situation made her feel. "I could hardly tell her I was your whore." When she heard the word, saw the look in his eyes, she regretted saying it.

"You are no one's whore, Crissie. Don't ever say anything so absurd again." Once more he stared out the window, his fingertips drumming softly on his thigh.

Stricken by the intensity of his statement, she was left with no words. If not his whore or his mistress, what was left to define her relationship with him. She reminded herself only last night she decided she was no longer going to dwell on that part of their lives together. She would enjoy his attentions for as long as he was amiable then deal with the consequences if there were any. After all, she loved him even though she also knew he would not take kindly to words of love.

"No, you're right. I'm not a whore and as I told Rose, I hope I am at least your friend. Can we agree on that?" Then she added, "The mother of your child as well."

"I didn't know lovers could also be friends. I crave more from you than mere friendship," he said sarcastically at best. The tenor of his voice was a grim reminder that he would dictate their lives together.

She best get used to it.

Shyly, she looked at her fingers winding into the fabric of her dress then to him. She touched his chin turning him so he looked at her. "We are hardly lovers. We've only been intimate once. Whether the coupling was ill-advised or not, it resulted in a child. I will never regret that. Except for a very brief moment when the shock of my pregnancy became clear, I've not regretted a moment of Ian's conception as well as his life."

Tenderly, his knuckles brushed across her cheeks. Their gazes held for several seconds. His eyes blazed with unspoken thoughts and feelings. She wished she had an insight into them. "I'm glad you're his mother. With all my heart I wish I could have been there for you."

As am I glad you are his father.

For the longest time she didn't know what to say to his gently spoken confession. She concentrated on breathing, inhaling one slow breath after another until she was suddenly light headed. He was right. She was not a whore or his mistress. They were not lovers, but to the latter she had to add the words not yet. Without a doubt they would be in time.

She wanted to experience the joining of their bodies as much as he did. Needed to feel her body melt into his when he kissed her while his energy wrapped around her, protecting and sheltering. Despite the knowledge of what would happen between them in the future, it was wrong. She knew they would truly be lovers soon. She would have to learn to accept the fact that was all she would get from him. Would have to learn it had to be enough. Knowing why he could never marry her would be nice though. What the devil did Rose mean by an archaic betrothal and marriage vows? Who?

They spent the rest of the morning wandering the streets, tasting food at various pubs and vendors along the way. A little after the noon hour he stopped at a pub. "Wait here."

His smile was endearing as well as mischievous. She could see him as a little boy about to undertake something he would get into troubled over. Could even see Rose reprimanding him.

She found a bench beneath a few trees before she settled on the seat, idly spreading her skirts around her. While she waited, she watched the people passing by. The air was unusually warm this early in the summer. Strange, that during all this morning she thought of Ian only a few times. Walker returned with two large tankards of ale along with a couple of meat pies.

"Thought you might be thirsty as well as hungry."

Her stomach rumbled. She was, yet she had not thought about her hunger until she smelled the pies. "Famished," she murmured as she drank long and deep before biting into the food. The pie was delicious.

"Are you tired or would you like to wander some more when we finish here?"

If she didn't have responsibilities, she would like to walk arm and arm with Walker for another hour or two. All morning he'd been such a gentleman. When she thought he would pull her beneath the shade of a tree and kiss her, he had not done so. She found she was disappointed that he had not.

Now he teased her. She certainly knew why. His softly spoken words reverberated in her brain.

I want you to beg for me.

Aye, that was what he wanted. She was sure by this evening that is exactly what he would get.

Remembering her embarrassment when she met him after his yearlong absence, she decided not to tempt fate. "While I would enjoy walking some more with you, I cannot."

He looked surprised and unable to think beyond the moment. One tawny eyebrow rose in speculation. "Why?"

"It's been too long since I've nursed Ian. I'm afraid," she plucked at her blouse before looking at him then catching his gaze of understanding.

His lustful grin was pure deviltry. She would well imagine how he got away with many things when he was a child. "I see."

"I'm sure you don't," she told him pertly then realizing he did. She felt her milk, the dampness of her shirt. Quickly, she pulled her cloak around her.

He chuckled softly, touching the bottom of her chin. "I remember that day all too well. We should go home. No more embarrassment for you. I would not want that."

No more embarrassment, ah, but she was sure he would always find a way to embarrass her even when he was not trying to do so. Just the way his lopsided grin made her crazy with longing caused her embarrassment.

Once they reached home, Crissie fled to the safety of the master chamber. Rose was playing with Ian. Rose stood up with Ian in her arms when she rushed inside.

"You stayed away a little too long I see." Rose waited for Crissie to put the damp clothing aside and don dry things before she handed the boy to his mother. "I will see you in the morning. Your trunks arrived an hour or so ago. They are in the adjoining room."

"Thank you, Rose. How was he?" She set Ian to her breast, which he took eagerly as if he'd been denied for several days instead of several hours.

"A perfect angel, my dear, absolutely perfect. Does not yet take after his father at all."

Before Rose left, she poured Crissie a cup of tea, setting the cup close so she could reach it. She closed her eyes now, resting, trying to absorb this new place and time along with her new role in Walker's life. She had thought Walker would have come to the room after Rose left. Perhaps he had business to see to.

After she put Ian down for a nap, she walked downstairs to find Walker. He stood on the porch in seeming argument with an older man. What little she knew about the father of her son, told her he was angry, despite his calm voice, furiously so. For a moment she thought to listen in on the conversation then changed her mind. Something like that would hardly garner his trust. Before she was anything else to Walker, she did want to be his friend, needed to be able to share confidences with him.

She turned, walking into the drawing room where she poured herself a generous glass of brandy. Crissie waited only a few minutes before Walker sat beside her with his own glass of brandy in his hand.

"Is Ian asleep?" he asked sipping.

While he asked the question, by the look on his face it didn't seem he would hear the answer. He was absorbed in thoughts that didn't concern her or his son.

"Yes," she told him. "Who was that man?"

"What? Oh, he's my or was my commanding officer. I've resigned, you know but they don't seem to want to let me go. He's the man I went to see last night."

Walker still seemed distant to her, his mind farther away than she'd ever seen him before.

"He had pressing business that couldn't wait?"

She couldn't keep the sarcasm from her voice. For some reason she didn't like that man, didn't like that Walker took orders from him. There was something nefarious about the man that made her skin crawl.

"He did."

"You were arguing with him."

She pushed too far too fast. She knew it. By the scowl on his face, he knew it.

"I told him the mission he's assigned me to would have to wait for at least a week. I wasn't going anywhere until I got you settled at Briarwood Manner."

"I could stay here."

"No."

Inwardly, she bristled at his autocratic command. He didn't even entertain a discussion. Once again, she was faced with the glaring fact she had no say in her life. "As you wish. How long will you be gone?"

Truly, she thought he could at least tell her that much after he gave her no choice in following him here. Now, he was leaving abandoning her in a place where she had no friends or family. She would truly be alone.

"I've no way of knowing," he murmured still deep in thought. "I don't want to go but I don't have a choice. If this mission is to go as it should, it has to be me. As I said, I won't trust anyone else to this assignment."

"Walker, why are you upset? Why don't you just tell the man you won't do whatever it is he wants you to do? Besides, I did recall you telling me you were a civilian. Just now, you said you resigned. Was I wrong about the meaning?"

He drank long and deep then set the glass on the table. "To answer all your questions is impossible. Just know I don't trust any other man

74

with this particular assignment. Even though you remember correctly and I'm no longer in the British army, in this there is no choice for me. I have to handle this matter.

They were silent for a while, Crissie plucking at her skirts, uncomfortable with the sudden distance between them. She knew it wasn't prudent at the moment to press him as to why only he could do this. In any case, he wouldn't answer her. "My trunks arrived today. If it makes it easier on you, we could leave for the country tomorrow."

"You in a hurry to see me gone?"

"No." She jerked, stunned by the venom in his words. "No, I don't want you to go anywhere. While I'm not enamored by my status where you are concerned, I want Ian to have a father. So, I'm reconciled as to my place in your life. Whatever that may be." Without giving more thought to her next words. "Perhaps you wouldn't be in this situation if you hadn't been so quick to leave the highlands behind. Mayhap you could have finished your assignment before you whisked me away."

"For more reasons than I can enumerate, I had to get you out of there. Too much danger for you." By the time he finished, his words gentled. He brushed his knuckles lightly across her cheeks. "There is much I don't know. Much you could tell me." He stood, pacing, running his hands through the tawny locks she loved, leaving them slightly disheveled. "If you could only be honest," he said softly. "I want to trust you, you know."

"Ask me. What do you want to know?"

She was taken aback by his words. Honest? She had always been honest with him. Didn't like the bent of his accusations.

He whirled on her, his fists at his sides. "I can't ask the questions I need to."

She rose, slowly walking to him, wrapping her arms around him. "Perhaps it is you who is not honest with me. I can hardly tell you truths when you don't ask, now can I? I could volunteer information yet I would probably not be telling you what you are so curious about."

Crissie rested her head on his chest as she ran her hands along his back. She heard the steady beat of his heart, felt each of his breaths as they feathered across the top of her head. It seemed the longer they stood together their hearts slowly began to beat as one.

"*Nay*, you cannot," he murmured, setting her gently aside, refusing her attempts to console and ease his anger.

"Come, it gets late. I've ordered a tray for the sitting room in the master suite. Let's go eat and talk about something that is not so confusing. Perhaps if I think on it long enough..."

"Think on what?"

"It might indeed be prudent of me to ask the question. You would have some insight on the tenuous danger of this assignment. If I heard your answer, it might ease all my fears for you. I don't want your family harmed in any way. Yet you are the most important factor in all this."

There had been nothing confusing he'd said simply because he failed to tell her anything until these last few words. She still knew exactly nothing of what he was going to do. Well, that was not true. She knew he wanted her to tell him something she couldn't tell him and he didn't dare ask. Which led her to the fact he wanted to know about her brothers along with their ability to shift.

Placing her hand in his, he walked with her to their room. His hand seemed to swallow hers. She felt the comfort and security in his strength coupled with the power she knew was his. She didn't want to think about his job on McKenna land had anything to do with her family. It was so much easier to believe he was still searching out the men who they called traitors to England.

They ate dinner in near silence. Ian woke. Walker played with him. If she didn't know better, she might be able to convince herself theirs was a happy normal family.

She knew better.

Walker put Ian into the cradle before turning to her. He opened up his arms, beckoning to her. Expecting her to come to him, "I'm sorry if I've been a little hard to get along with since this afternoon. I've a great deal on my mind."

Once again, she rested her head against his chest, understanding that whatever it was that bothered him earlier, he'd come to terms with it.

She pushed away so she could look at him closer. "I've been honest with you, Walker. If there is something I've overlooked and you want to know, please ask."

He set his fingertip against her lips. His touch was calloused yet tender. "Hush. If I dared ask, I'm sure you would tell me what I need to know. If I'm wrong, I don't want to create havoc where there is none. It is a conundrum I can't seem to figure a way out of."

"I would." She watched his eyes turn from warm brown to honey as he lowered his mouth to hers then parted her lips with his tongue. The tender sizzle of desire swamped her, heated every part of her. He knew just how to coax. She could drown in his heat, "I want you, Crissie. Tonight. I need you. Will you come to me?"

She swallowed the fear as well as the doubts simmering within, "I *dinna ken* if I can beg."

"Perhaps I just want you willing. You're not a woman who could ever humble herself to beg. Even the first time you did not beg. That was not well done of me." He brushed hair from her face before he pulled out the pins holding it in place.

"The problem is I'm too willing," she murmured as she wound her hands behind his neck tugging him closer until their lips again brushed against each other, caressed and stroked.

"You can never be too willing, lass." He swept her into his arms before carrying her to the bed. Gently he placed her on top. "Do you remember my rule for the bed?"

"*Nay.*"

She sat gazing at him as he began to shed his clothing. Yet, she did remember. She didn't think she could come to him naked. Didn't think she could disrobe in front of him.

"You may sleep in any bed you choose, but if you choose my bed nothing will come between us except possibly the sheets." His warm smile sent a cascade of warmth shuffling into the depths of her body.

Another fine shudder swept through her at his words, at the sight of his golden eyes deepening to amber when he gazed at her. Desire pulsed to all the erotic places she remembered where he touched and stroked with his hands along with his lips. Her heart pounded as he shed his last garment standing boldly in front of her. His manhood jutted proudly in front of him proclaiming his lust for her. She reminded herself his feelings for her were lust, not love

Yes, he did want her. That was blatantly obvious.

Yes, she wanted him even though he didn't love her. Still her fingers seemed frozen in place as he strode to the other side of the bed, snuffing all the candles save the ones on either side of them. He sat back, placing pillows behind his back, his hands behind his head. The grin on his face was broad as he waited for her to undress.

"I *dinna* know if I can do what you want," she whispered softly, feeling more nervous than she ever felt before. If she took this step, she would willingly give her body to him.

She did want him.

More than anything she'd wanted in her entire life.

By doing this she was for a second time giving up all her moral values that had been taught to her over a lifetime. The church told her it was a sin to lie with a man out of wedlock. She trembled anew.

~ * ~

General Abbot leaned back in the brocade wing chair by the roaring fire in the drawing room of his home. This evening a storm passed through. Wind wailed while rain pummeled the windows His whisky in hand, he watched the fire crackle, flames lighting the room while he listened to Andrew St. John present a very good case for him to stay in Ireland while Endicott left for the highlands.

Perhaps it was not such a great case. The man had ulterior motives that went beyond the pale although he did make some good points in addition to his obvious infatuation of Endicott's new mistress. Tonight, the young man seemed nervous while his leg bounced tightly, his heel leaving the floor repeatedly.

Drew's plan was selfish. But then most men of his age tended to be both selfish as well as greedy. While it had nothing to do with the military, it might help Walker's new mistress or lover. He couldn't be sure. One thing Miss McKenna wasn't was Endicott's wife, and she would never be unless the man made some major changes in his life. Andrew shifted in his chair before he finished off the two fingers of whiskey in his glass.

It was not well done of Walker to bring Crissie to his home, flaunting their relationship in the process. To everyone who counted in Belfast as well as the surrounding area he sent out a very fine and clear message. Endicott was an Earl. He couldn't do anything without the lords and ladies discussing his life the gossip ripe with innuendos as well as unpleasant speculation about the Scottish lass. She would be ostracized everywhere she went. He would have to keep her in seclusion from the rest of the world.

"So, you say you're in love with Crissie McKenna. May I assume she doesn't love you in return?"

He sipped looking at the young officer over the rim of his glass as he tapped his finger on the crystal, his snowy white brows drawn tightly together as he concentrated on the crackling fire. They did dance and play against each other in intriguing patterns. Perhaps this trio, one lady and two men, would eventually become just as captivating. "You say you fell in love while in the highlands."

"Yes, yes, I did. She's a very beautiful and fascinating young woman. A woman who could make a man proud to be her husband."

Drew sat up straighter, his spine seeming to stiffen. It would have to become rock hard if he were to go up against a man such as Walker Endicott. "It's my intention to pick up the pieces that Endicott leaves behind when he's through with the lady then make an honest woman of her."

The general chuckled softly, amusement at the young man's assumptions about the weaker sex. He always delighted in that phrase. Men seemed to have the need to make women honest when in truth they should be doing that to themselves. Too many took what they pleased, leaving damage to the lady's reputation in the wake. Few ever thought of the consequences of their dalliances, merely enjoyed. He knew the father,

Connal McKenna. Was surprised to hear The McKenna allowed Endicott to leave with his daughter without benefit of marriage. He let out a long breath of air, studying Drew. Ah, but a man should know his son. If rumors he heard were true, the young babe accompanying Crissie McKenna as guests in the townhouse belonging to Endicott was Walker's son.

"Do you believe she will be willing to wed you eventually?"

Andrew pushed a long breath of air though his lips as he studied his nails. "Not today. She's still half in love with the bastard. Well, she only thinks she loves him because he seduced her, took advantage of her innocence continues to do so. It's not right nor is it fair to her." Drew pushed at the dark chestnut hair falling across his forehead. "I'm going to see her tomorrow. Tell her how I feel."

"Then what? You realize of course, in this life few things are fair."

"Yes, that I do." He stood quickly, adjusting his pants then sat again. "I'm going to bide my time until Walker makes such a big mistake Crissie will leave him. He will too. There is no doubt in my mind she will eventually come to see reason along with the fact there is no other course of action than for her to leave the arrogant supercilious ass, who calls himself an earl, behind. When that happens, I will be ready and waiting with open arms."

"She will fall right into your open arms?" The general quirked a half smile. This man was just as pompous as Endicott. He didn't even hold a title in his name.

"Yes."

"You believe time will prevail for you."

The general thought the young man a bit impetuous even bordering on foolhardy to go up against a man such as Endicott. Still, where love was concerned, one never knew. He was curious though why Drew was confiding in him. Wondered too if he was seeking permission.

"Crissie McKenna is a proud woman. She will not want to live in the same home with the man's wife or in the same town as his mistress. While she might agree to something like that for a short time, I'm sure it will eventually grate on her nerves. Who knows what else could happen?

I trust in fate. Miss McKenna is not meant to be with that man. She belongs with a man who can give her a stable home along with a family."

The general was tapping his fingers on his brandy glass. "Yes, well where two women are involved one can never know what will happen. A mistress and a wife. Hmm... For that matter where one woman is concerned one never knows. I almost feel sorry for the man."

"I plan on calling on her tomorrow. I'll leave my card. Talk to her and tell her what I can offer her as soon as she is ready. Time is on my side, you know."

Ah, young love. He sensed heartache in this. Walker would not give up his woman willingly. There would be trouble for sure. Perhaps that was why Mr. St. John was informing him ahead of time. He needed to be forewarned. The altercation between these two might not be pleasant. Endicott still reported to him. The general cleared his throat as he contemplated his next words. "You believe you can offer her more than Endicott?"

He lifted an aging white brow in rising speculation thoroughly enjoying the game these two young stallions were playing. If it didn't involve a young woman's life, it would be much more enjoyable.

"I'll make her my wife not my whore." The man spat the words angrily, his fury as well as determination obvious. "He has no business disrespecting her that way. She deserves better. I'll give that to her. Even on his last day in the highlands he took advantage of her."

"Yes, he did bed her first. Also heard she ran after him. Gave herself eagerly and quite willingly to the young man. What was he to do? Turn her down?"

Nay, Endicott was a man in every way. Rumor spoke of countless lovers. Until now though there were no illegitimate children. With a lift of his shoulders, he proceeded, "Endicott would take what was readily given, without regrets, as I would have done the same at that age. Perhaps he loves her."

Drew's face turned a crimson shade at his words. What the general said was true. Crissie McKenna would not be easy for Drew St. John to win over. A lass coming from The McKenna himself would not give her heart as well as her body to a man she didn't love.

Drew sliced his hand through the air, his eyes narrowing as he seemed to be thinking about the general's statement. "No," he finally said, "I could not have turned her down either. However, if it had been me she ran after, I would have stayed and made her my wife. I would never have deserted her for more than a year."

"Playing the devil's advocate here, you willing to raise the bastard child of Walker Endicott?"

"Yes, but I'm sure Walker won't give over the child. So, the decision won't be necessary."

"If that's the case, the lady won't leave. Don't you suppose that is why she followed him to Ireland?"

Drew scrubbed his face with his hands. "I don't know what will happen, but I will have to try. A lady like Miss McKenna, cannot be expected to live as Walker is expecting her to live."

"As his mistress?"

"I mean to change that." Andrew's voice shook with pent up emotion coupled with a fierce determination to make Crissie McKenna his.

Chapter Four

Walker watched carefully while Crissie sat on the bed, her back facing him. Her shoulders trembled slightly, shuddered softly then drooped. Nerves he supposed. For a few seconds she fiddled with a piece of her hair that slipped loose from the bun wound at the top of her head. Perhaps anticipation or excitement, he laughed to himself. It seemed she was having a devilishly hard time abiding by his rules. The number one was that if she chose to sleep in his bed, she would do so naked. She inhaled a long deep breath then another, her torso expanding before she let the breath rush from her lungs.

Over one slim shoulder she turned her head to look at him, her brows knit together, her eyes wide. He could just see her hands as she clasped them together knuckles almost white. Lord but he wanted to get inside her head almost as much as he wanted to feel her sultry warmth surround him. She haunted his soul. Had done so for the past days as they traveled together, slept in the same bed without claiming her.

Seconds ticked by. She was still looking at him, her hands on either side of her now pressing against the bed, gripping cloth with her fingernails. Slowly, her tongue ran along her bottom lip, wetting the softness provocatively. Some of the meager candlelight shimmered on the moisture it left behind.

She had no idea.

Be patient.

With a breathy soft whisper that seemed to float in a fragile cloud around her, she spoke, her eyes closing for a sultry moment as if she anticipated his participation in her disrobing. "This would be so much easier if you undressed me. I," she moistened her lips again, drawing him even farther into the tangled web she seemed to weave around herself, "I can't seem to make my fingers move."

"I'm sure you'll find a way."

"I *dinna ken* how."

His grin widened as he reached out to touch the soft skin at the nape of her neck as he pushed her hair to one side, felt her body shudder beneath his tender caress. The movement was brief, barely discernible as well. Her words gave him pleasure. If this were not up to her, he would delight in undressing her, kissing each new portion of her he uncovered.

"If I did help you, it would be me seducing you, coaxing you to my will. To do that would break my bargain with myself. I won't do that. You have to want me as much as I want you." Again, her slight frame quivered at his words. Her head bent toward her lap until she looked up stiffening her spine.

"You know I do." She turned away sounding a bit petulant. "I wouldn't be sitting here, my nerves frayed to nothingness if I did not."

For a moment he thought she might leave. He cursed to himself. It might have been better to coax her, help her with her clothing until she lay quite naked beneath him. No, he would not. Would stick to his promise to himself even if it killed him.

"Not really. I've always seduced, touched you in ways I knew you would give yourself to me."

"Only once."

He remembered that one time as if it happened this morning. What he also remembered was last night, the way she fit so perfectly within his arms, beneath him. It took all his willpower to stop himself. He knew she would have given herself to him, there on the rug in the airless attic room.

She deserved better from him.

"Only once to fruition. I've kissed you though, touched you, known you would give yourself to me even while I knew your mind was screaming no. I could do that to you now, this moment. If I did that, I would never know the truth of your actions."

"It would be easier for me than undressing in front of you. I *ken* not how to keep from feeling the shame or the awkwardness," she said now facing away from him, her back a bit stiffer.

Perhaps she was gaining courage to do what he asked to perform the tiny task that would enable him to understand her true feelings for him. Leaning against the backboard, he placed his hands behind his head, the sheet covering him to his waist, failing to hide his arousal as it boldly tented the lightweight covering. He reached for his drink, sipping lightly as he patiently watched and waited. Now, her fingers fiddled with the crystal buttons running down the front of her gown. He heard a soft curse. The fabric loosened somewhat across her back as the crystals were slipped through their holes. His anticipation grew higher, his body understanding the fulfillment that would come its way soon.

She was trying. He would give her that much credit. She must want him. He knew, simply because he could see just how difficult this was for her yet she was slowly uncovering herself. Mayhap he should meet her half way or they would never be in bed tonight. He would be watching her back for hours if she continued at this snail's pace. No, he chuckled softly. It would not do to betray his vow to himself. She was not only wrestling with her crystal buttons but her shyness as well. This was new to her. In time Crissie would get used to her nakedness in front of him.

"Nothing you do is ever easy, Crissie. You understand that I want no coercion on my part where our relationship is concerned. It needs to grow as well as flourish at the pace you set." One slender white shoulder was now slightly bared. He willed his itching fingers to behave themselves. Setting his drink on the table, he once more placed his hands behind his head. If this evening continued as planned, there would be more than enough time to stroke as well as kiss the softness she was hesitantly revealing.

"I *dinna ken* if I can do this," she breathed, her voice husky now.

"You can. Already all those tiny beads holding the front of your gown together are unfastened. Are they not?"

His grin widened as he saw more of her back, her slim shoulders, the line of her backbone. The fabric clung to her arms, drooping down her back.

His breath hitched. His mind whirled. Enticingly the fabric pooled around her waist. Still there was a corset and chemise to be removed as well as a petticoat. It seemed to him women wore armor just to keep a man's questing fingers from finding all they sought. Perchance it was a good thing. Possibly, Crissie should have been wearing as much clothing that day so long ago as she was today. If she had, he would not have his son. The thought caught him off-guard, sent a sensation of pain to the pit of his stomach.

He found that his entire body shook with longing for her, for all the moments he missed with his son along with her, moments that couldn't be retrieved. When he reached for his drink, his hand was trembling. His breath caught in the back of his throat as she reached behind her straining to reach the ties holding her corset together. He longed to help. Knew he could not even if she asked.

For a moment or two her slim fingers fumbled with the tiny strings. Then, holding tightly and tugging, the ties fell free. With a small huff, she pushed the garment to the floor. Standing, she slid the gown away from her waist. With another quick breath of air, she took hold of the bottom of her chemise, tugging it over her head.

She wrapped her arms around her waist. Otherwise, she didn't change position. Just stood in that one tiny spot waiting for something.

For the longest time while he watched her, he couldn't breathe. No air spilled into his lungs or out. Her legs were long and slender, hips flaring provocatively from a narrow waist. He wanted her to turn around so he could look his fill, craved to observe the sweet bouncing of her breasts as she climbed into bed with him. It didn't seem she meant to grant him his request.

She was made from his dreams.

Bloody eyes but he was even more aroused now than he was a few minutes ago when he realized the first button was undone. When he appreciated the fact that soon he would once again hold her naked against his body. When he understood she was willing, along with the unmitigated statement there had been no coercion on his part.

"Will you undo your hair for me?" His voice shook when he spoke his request.

He craved to see it falling free, feel the silkiness as he wove the strands through his fingers, inhale to soft lemon scent pooling around the length.

She didn't turn as he hoped, merely nodded as her slender arms rose to unfasten the bun. In a matter of seconds, the long black strands fell around her shoulders, tumbled in curls to her waist. He gasped in a drought of air before letting loose of it slowly.

Now she would come to him, press herself against him. He would wrap his arms around her, touch her, taste her explore all of her until they were both sated.

Instead, she pulled the covers away from the bed, scooting underneath them without turning. Just as when she undressed, her backside was to him. She would make this more difficult. He would not be deterred though. She wanted him or she would not be here naked in his bed.

Now, what to do about her position?

"Shy?" he asked one eyebrow tilted upward even though he knew she couldn't see his amused expression. Her back intrigued him almost as much as her front. Almost.

Her head on the pillow now, she nodded.

"In that case, I will enjoy your back, unless of course you say *nay*. You wouldn't do that would you?"

He found the chuckle forthcoming in opposition to his best interest. Stifling the sound in the deepest recess he could find, he held a long strand of her hair. Her soft scent of lemons floated around him gently touching every nerve the essence of his soul. Pushing the softness away, he traced the length of her back with his fingertip reveling in the sensual tremor the caress ignited the expressive shifting of her muscles to bring her closer to him. Continuing his exploration, he softly touched her arm past her elbow to her wrist then along her side to her waist before sightseeing across her hip to travel down her leg to her exquisitely tiny feet. The return journey was more delectable than the first, her body reacting with delicious pleasure to his caresses.

The sweet rush of air from her lips enthralled him as he realized she might just be as pleased as he was. His lips followed the path of his fingers, tasting as he investigated, nipping with his teeth to generate more heat, more enchantment, bathing her with his lips and tongue. He burned to give her more pleasure as he ached to thrust himself deeply into her. Her taste was sweet and hot a savory delight to his taste buds. Her skin was flushed to a rosy hue as he realized her embarrassment continued. When he reached her waist, he nipped lightly with his teeth. She tensed, jumping a bit from surprise he hoped.

"Walker..." His name wobbled in the sultry stillness of the room. Perhaps he should have opened a window to let in the summer breeze. Needed the air to caress her just as his fingers were doing.

"What is it?" He did want her to question. Hoped to god she wasn't going to tell him no. Not when he was so aroused, he would be hard pressed to stop this journey.

"Should you do that?"

His lips were now on her rounded bottom, his kisses turning to tiny nips as he further enticed heat to flow rapidly within her shuddering body. Her hips were moving against him, her back arching as all that he did brought her closer and closer to the ecstasy he intended to pursue. Pushing the cover back, he found the underside of her leg, followed the same path with his lips as his hands did earlier all the way to her toes to return to her bottom, licking, kissing over and over again as her sounds of delight echoed in the stillness of the room.

When his mouth and tongue slid over the warm wet petals of her feminine folds, she jerked.

"Walker!"

"Hush, little pigeon. It's all good. I'm just loving every part of you."

He stroked her, reveled in the taste of her, the woman's scent that was unique to her. He continued to stroke with his lips and his tongue until she parted her legs even more giving him better access to her most intimate feminine parts. He thought he might truly die if he didn't find his way inside her soon. He'd waited so long for this moment.

"All good?" she whispered in question with a hint of awe in her voice. "You didn't—last time."

"No." He hovered over her. "If you recall, there was no time."

"Time," she murmured as she finally turned in his arms, the tightened tips of her breasts pushing against his chest.

A man's dream, at least this man's dream.

He settled between her parted legs, surveying her from a position slightly lower and above. Her breasts were white, perfectly rounded globes made perfectly to fit into his hands. The tips were a blushing shade of pale pink; that he wanted to take them into his mouth and suckle them was a given. They swayed slightly as she watched him, her fingers winding into his hair.

"Do I get to kiss you now?" he asked as he rose above her as his lips now hovered just above hers.

She closed her eyes. A small ripple from her lungs fluttered gently through the air to become a siren's purr.

"Is that a yes?"

He laughed softly as he threaded his fingers through her hair. He kissed her forehead, her cheek then the other side. He kissed the tip of her nose, drawing ever closer to her lips while he waited for an answer. She wet her lips, the slight caress of her own volition erotic to him. He craved to follow the path with his tongue. Would soon. When she gave him the answer he desired. Untrained and innocent, she sent him higher and higher, his body responding intensely to each simple gesture. She didn't know it but she was his rock, the sounding board for the rest of his life. He couldn't live without her. Her loyalty was unbound by tradition.

Crissie nodded, her eyes wide silver-blue pools beneath long dark lashes. He ran his thumbs across her cheekbones as he held her head, waiting for the words that would give him permission to continue on this carnal journey.

"Say the words, Crissie. Tell me you want to feel my lips against yours. You want to feel the caress of my tongue dancing with yours." His grin broadened as she nodded her head again. Wanting her, craving her, filled him. "That's not good enough."

"Kiss me, please," she whispered softly, her breath floating across his lips that were hovering slightly above hers, the heated warmth sending him more thoroughly into her magical spell.

Walker was reminded of their first time together. She asked him to make love to her. Perhaps he hoped for the same words this time too. Under the circumstances he didn't know if she would bring herself to such a bold point. Still, he could yearn for her to say the words and pray that in the future she would.

"Thought you would never ask."

Gently he touched her bottom lip with his tongue then his teeth. Slowly, his lips brushed against her, delicately, tenderly not wishing to hasten this sensuous contact an initial step in the first stages of their intimacy tonight.

Brazenly, as he taught her back in the highlands, she swept her tongue across her mouth touching his in the process, pushing his lips apart with her own. Unable to hold back his delight, he laughed, his heart now lighter than it had been in a long time.

"Impatient little thing yet endearing nonetheless. You must be patient, my darling. Rushing this ecstasy will never do. No, we won't' rush anything. Our love making will last the night through."

When his lips settled over hers, she arched against him, a mewling sound reverberating from her lungs creating a captivating song in his heart. "Please," the word was a whispered sigh in the passionately charged room.

Walker kissed her tenderly before deepening the kiss, taking her lips within his, exploring the dark interior, relishing the heat. She was warm and soft, calling to him in ways she had no idea. With a groan of impatience, he kissed her hard, touching her everywhere memorizing every part he caressed.

She was his.

Nothing would ever change that fact.

His hands moved to her neck, his thumbs caressing the underside of her jaw. He felt the puckered tips of her breasts push against the nakedness of his chest. The softness beneath him aroused with a supernatural passion he'd never known before. It was no longer Crissie who needed patience. His body pulsed, throbbing with his ever-growing need to sink within her mysteriously dark core.

Walker inhaled sharply, stunned and rigid, instantly tense and aroused beyond all measure. He swallowed quickly, felt the speed of his blood as it raced and bubbled through his veins, of the pulse that beat from his groin and echoed throughout his body. And oh, this! This most wondrous, most incredible love was his. For all that he'd done to her, the wrongs visited upon her, she could still come to him. Still give her body over to him.

He craved so much from her, asked so much, needed more from her than he could ever explain in a lifetime. She deserved better from him yet he could not, was powerless to do so. Would not let her go as she'd become an integral part of him, he would never deny. She was the fire, she was the light, she was everything that guided him now, that charted his course making him who he was. They would find a way through the maze of his life he had created through no fault of his own. This love was pain, it was fear, it was all encompassing. He couldn't for the very life of him put it aside nor could he refute the love shimmering inside of him for this beautiful Scottish lass who gave herself to him despite everything.

"Walker," she breathed at last, a cry, a desperate plea.

He reached for her hand. She gave it to him. He rose above her. He was so very aware gazing into the silver-blue depths of her eyes of the explosive power between them. He brought the hand to his lips, kissed her palm, traced the lines with his tongue. She was glorious in her passion.

He let his body come down upon her again, touching her hair, clutching her shoulders and pressing his lips ardently upon that bare flesh, where he held his lips warmed there for the long heartbeat of an eternal moment. His lips grazed her ear, the scope of her neck, wound around the hardened tip of her breast.

His whispered words came harsh and ragged. "Be sure this is what you wish for this moment, for if I continue longer here, I will not be able to stop. Tell me now that you want me. Show me how much. Open yourself completely to me."

She slipped her arms around him as she wound her fingers through his hair, pulling him closer to her lips, sweeping her tongue across his mouth. A harsh groan followed. He took control leading her further into the most resplendent pleasure. They touched again and again, parting her lips, nipping at them, coming to them again and finding a fiery meeting with his tongue.

His fingers wound into the glorious length of her hair. A glad and muffled cry tore from him. He was indeed lost in mercuric heat spiraling from her lithe body. She was pliant and hot beneath him. He started to speak. She stopped him with another kiss. "No more words this night," she whispered, her eyes alight with the passion he generated within her fragile beauty.

"No words..."

He agreed wholeheartedly as he knew there was still much to be said between them, secret truths he needed to reveal to her sooner than later. Ah, but tonight nothing would come between them.

Secrets still hidden, words unsaid and yet there was this.

He held her breasts, suckled them, gloried in the weight and taste of them as he kissed the peaks brushed his fingers and lips across them. They were swollen, ripe and waiting for his attention. She was sweet and innocent. She was his.

Lost in the enchantment of the night he no longer wished to delay the sexual ecstasy he knew he could bring to her. And to him. He knew it would feel as if he was lost in heaven's paradise.

To his surprise and delight she touched him again and again, losing all the shyness he'd observed earlier in the evening. She was bold and brash as her hands trailed down his chest then lower to his pulsing shaft. Her small slender fingers wrapped around him. He jerked and groaned beneath the tender caress of his arousal.

She loved him sweetly with her lips and kisses, loved him with a wild abandon he could never describe, never known before. Her wantonness coupled with the unbridled pleasure would have brought him to his knees had he been standing. She moved with him, then in opposition. Her hips bucked against his, her back arching as she begged for more and more. He entered her quickly, found the darkest part of her core tight, so very small, milking him, tugging him deeper and deeper. She was hot and so very wet, slick with her need. He moved slowly at first. Then, unable to stop himself, he drove into her over and over again until she was crying out his name in soft frantic pants.

He gave to her all of himself. He filled her, again and again, held her shivering, trembling, quaking, shuddering...faster and harder until she sighed against him and buried her head into the dampness of his chest, exhausted and spent. For the longest time, all he heard was the whispers of her soft breaths, felt them against his flesh

"Crissie..."

He didn't know what to say. This was the most beautiful and earth-shattering experience of his life. The power of their commitment to each other went far beyond their first joining. Didn't know how to describe what they just shared, so exquisite so filled with wild shared abandon. Yet he knew the words that needed to be shared with her.

I love you.

He could not, could not say the words until he was able to give to her the respectability of marriage. Still, they echoed painfully from his heart.

If ever.

Once more she touched her finger to his lips, shaking her head. "No words," she pleaded, almost sobbing. "No words tonight, I beg you. There is nothing you can say."

He cradled her tightly against his chest, rocking gently as if he could take the unspoken pain away from her heart. Despite the words not expressed, they were both aglow with satiation. His arms were strong around her. In time perhaps he would be able to say the words to her. In time perhaps he would be able to give her all she craved.

A loud wail brought him back to the reality of his life. His son. Had they woken him?

She pushed away from him, starting to rise. "He cannot be hungry. It is not even close to midnight. He sleeps tell early morn."

"No, he must want his mother as much as I do. Perhaps he is jealous," Walker said, laughing as he pushed the covers aside. "Stay here. I'll get him."

Walker rose, naked from the bed, striding to the far side of the room to the cradle and his son. He picked him up, snuggling him in his arms as he brought the boy to the bed where he and his mother had made incredible love to each other. He grinned at the erotic and pleasing image she made sitting on the bed, her hair tousled, wild around her shoulders, lips kiss swollen from his ardent attention. Her incredible blue eyes bright and shimmering. He could still taste her, smell the fragrance of orange blossoms floating around her. The sheets would carry that scent.

She held out her arms to him, even while she tried to keep the sheet tucked beneath her arms. "Rose said he was teething. Perhaps his little mouth hurts." She ran a fingertip around his gums. "I can feel just the barest hint of a tooth."

"So," he asked frustrated or confused, he wasn't sure. He found he knew very little about the ways of babies, "does he stay up all of the night?"

"No, at least I hope not. Rose gave me some oil of clove to put on his gums. It's on the dresser."

"That will help how?" he asked even as he rose, quickly striding to the dresser to return with the small vial.

"I don't know but I trust her advice. She says it will make him feel better, stop his crying."

Walker held his breath as Crissie put the oil where his teeth were trying to find a way to push through. Ian nuzzled close, dropped lower as if he searched for his food source.

"It will make him feel better if I let him suckle for a short while. He might fall right to sleep," Crissie said, cupping his head with her hand.

"I know just how he feels," Walker told her grinning as he settled down beside her to wait until mother and child were finished.

~ * ~

Beneath the covers, Crissie stretched lazily, her body slightly sore from the night before. The room was light although there was not much sunlight slanting through the window. She smiled to herself as she reached out a hand in search of Walker.

He was gone.

No surprise there.

While she had little to accomplish here in Belfast, Walker seemed to have no end of places to go as well as people to visit. Still, she wished he would stay with her. This first morning after seemed special to her, more than she would have thought. He woke her earlier to make love to her again. This time was so unlike the night before. Instead of fast as furious as if he couldn't get enough of her, this time was slow and leisurely. Then, it seemed he was gone with soft words telling her to stay in bed and sleep as long as she wished. She must be tired. Rest, he told her again after placing a tender kiss on her forehead.

Now, she was pleasantly awake. She sat up, holding the covers to her breasts as if he lurked in some dark corner of the room. Last night she'd acted wanton and brash. She surprised herself as she willingly acknowledged everything he wanted to give her. She accepted him in to her body more than once. He seemed pleased. Lord, but she actually disrobed for him, crawling into bed naked, asking him to make love to her.

He would expect the same this evening and the one after that as well as...

She took in a heavy breath of air then let it drift slowly from her lungs. This time was nothing like her first. There had been nothing painful between them. No, everything he did was pleasant, *nay*, more than pleasant. She lost count of how many times they made love, her body in desperate need of his, craving him.

Crissie rolled over onto her back, her arm flung over her eyes. Ian must be downstairs playing with Rose. It amazed her how everything, every part of her life revolved around her son. She didn't think she could live without him.

Just as she didn't think she could live without Walker. Both males made up an integral part of her life. She needed them as she needed to take in each breath.

He had secrets. She knew that. Someday he would tell her. He couldn't marry her. Why? Rose hinted at another secret. Spoke of a contract made.

"Would you be liking a bath now?"

A maid poked her head inside the room, a grin on her face. She was young. Her smile pleasant as her eyes sparkled with some unknown secret.

"Yes." Crissie beamed at the woman.

She wondered how the lady knew she was awake. It was nearly ten. She never slept in so late. Yet she'd never been so tired nor kept up through most of the night enjoying such delicious and delightful pleasures.

The ecstasy, the nearly painful indulgence...

Within minutes the water was poured and she was alone in the room. She started to slip from the bed. Glittering blue stones in the form of a necklace sat on the nightstand beside her. They were beautiful. She reached out a hand to touch them. The stones couldn't be real. She saw the note.

My dearest Crissie,

This token of gratitude is for the most memorable night of my life. I hope you will wear the necklace and remember how much you pleased me. It is with the utmost pleasure I give these to you. I'm looking forward to more nights such as the last one.

Thank you from the bottom of my heart,

Walker

Seconds turned into minutes while she stared blindly at the words on the paper. She didn't want gifts in payment of her favors. Tears welled in the back of her throat. This was exactly what she did not want to happen. She made love to him because she loved him, not because she wanted payments of any sort.

He degraded her.

Disrespected her.

She closed her eyes on a heart-wrenching sigh. Well, what had she expected? Giving herself to him was a mistake she couldn't take back. However, she could hold herself away from him tonight and every night after. Fool, of course, that won't work. All he has to do is look at you with his golden-amber eyes and you melt. If he touches you, you dissolve against his tall, lean frame. She waded the paper up. Threw it as far as she could. Watched the parchment as the little ball landed on the floor, rolling beneath a table.

"No!"

Her heart cried. In the past she'd scoffed at people who said their heart was broken. She had not understood the sentiment. Thought of it in literal terms. Hers was broken now. How dare he pay her for a night of lovemaking? The most wondrous night of her short life. She couldn't even look at his small symbol of gratitude.

She was nothing but his whore.

The gift of this small token gave her that title.

Why? Why couldn't he let it just be what it was? A union between two people who cared about each other, in her case she loved him. She thought she'd come to terms with her feeling and actions.

With her face in her hands, she let out a long breath of air coupled with a sob. She wasn't going to cry. What she was going to do was let him know how she felt about his token of gratitude. She would fling the gift in his face. He would know she could not be bought.

Where the devil would she wear something so extravagant? Even if she would accept gifts from him in payment of services rendered, she had no place to go in a necklace with more sapphires and diamonds adorning it than she could count in one glance.

Woodenly, she walked to the steaming bath stepping inside, feeling the heat soothe the aches and pains from last evening a sad reminder of what she allowed to go forth. Absentmindedly, she washed, scrubbing every part of her, unsure of her feelings or what she even wanted now. He would have to explain himself.

She would even have to listen to said explanation.

It was something she had no inclination to do at the moment.

Words would not stop the burning ache in her heart or the sensations curdling in her stomach. Her feelings ran the gamut of hate and love. More than anything she longed to hate him. Instead, she hated herself. Just as she had been on the trip here, she was confused and wary of what Walker wanted from her. He'd been so adamant that she wasn't going to be his mistress.

She wasn't a whore.

What was she? If he paid her in jewels or anything else she was certainly one of the two.

"*Nay!*"

Crissie fought the idea of keeping the necklace in order to use the money to return with Ian to her home. She pushed that momentary idiocy to the back of her head. The trip would be for naught, a waste of time as well as money. Walker would come after his son expecting her to return with him. Her mind and her heart warred with each other. Even now she recalled the way his hands lightly skimmed her body, the way his lips coaxed her to desperation in her need for him.

He was a wicked craftsman in this.

A fine pickle you're in, Crissie McKenna. Now, how the devil do you think you will ever find your way out of it? You're on an undeniable journey of sin.

There is no way out, not unless I was willing to leave Ian here and I'm not. Then you best make the most out of this situation.

She heaved a sigh of resignation as she slipped from the now cooling water to dry herself. Still nowhere near figuring out her course. As she sat near the fire dressed and combing her hair, a breakfast tray was brought into the room.

Hot tea sounded good. The food didn't. Thoughts of eating caused her stomach to sour further.

"Miss McKenna, you've a visitor downstairs. He says he'll wait." The pretty little maid bobbed her head in a mocking curtsey, the white cap dangerously close to falling off.

"A visitor?" She was surprised, *nay* stunned. She didn't know anyone here. "Who?"

"A man. Seems nice. Said he knew you in the highlands. Lieutenant Andrew St. John. What should I tell him?"

Crissie sucked in a deep breath of air. Andrew? Here? He told her several times he liked her. No, he told her he was in love with her. She told him she only wanted Walker. Indeed, she did only want Walker but she couldn't have him, at least not all of him, not the way she yearned for. He would hold his heart away from her. Andrew would have heard of her circumstances. She was sure here in Belfast rumors were ripe swirling around Walker Endicott and spreading fast. Would he feel pity for her? She didn't want anyone's pity. She did what she had to do. Walker did not give her a tenable choice.

"Tell him I'll be down in a few minutes. Have tea and refreshments brought to the drawing room, please. Tell him also I need to check on my son first."

Hurrying, she pinned her hair up. First, she would look in the nursery to see how Ian was doing. If he needed her. Quickly, she finished in the bedchamber then made her way to the upstairs playroom. Having fed Ian a few hours ago, she doubted if he would need her right now.

"Good morning," Rose stood then motioned to the soft blanket on the floor where Ian played. One toy horse was in his mouth as his toothless gum gnawed on the old wood. "Did the oil of cloves work last evening?"

"What? Oh."

She turned away from Ian, confused for a moment, wondering what the devil she was speaking of. Suddenly her mind coalesced around her. She finally remembered something besides the touch of Walker's lips. "You're right, he has a tooth coming in. After I smoothed the oil on his gums and nursed him, he went right to sleep."

"Good, good. Heard you have a visitor downstairs. Someone Walker knows?"

Crissie gasped slightly, her heart pounding. The question was intrusive. She'd thought better of Rose yet she supposed the inquiry might be innocent. "Yes, he was stationed near the McKenna castle at the same time as Walker. Mr. St. John was under his command."

"I trust you will enjoy seeing the man again." Rose watched her closely.

She felt obliged to say, "I've no idea why he is here. While he is nice enough, he means nothing to me."

"Don't you? I'm sure you can guess as to the reason for his visit," Rose asked as she sat down beside Ian. "You should think about it more carefully. You're a beautiful woman forced into an unorthodox situation. I find only one reason why the man has shown up here when Walker is gone."

"I *dinna ken*."

"Don't you?" Rose asked again. Her bosom heaved as she let out a long breath of air. "I suppose you might not. Part of your attraction to Walker is your innocence combined with innate sense of honesty."

"Still..."

"I'm sure the man is just as infatuated with you as Walker is. Don't give him a reason to pursue you. It is something you might come to regret." She waved her hands shooing Crissie from the room. "Go see the young man."

"I don't care for him," Crissie said in her defense. "I've never given him a reason to think otherwise."

"A woman as beautiful as you doesn't have to give a man a reason. Be careful, lass."

Crissie didn't truly understand what Rose was saying. She didn't play games with people's feeling. At least, she didn't believe she did. Well, Rose could be wrong too. This might just be a friendly call to welcome her to Belfast. Now, she wasn't at all sure about meeting with Drew. Rose made everything feel dirty.

Maybe she felt that way because of Walker's gift to her.

When she stepped inside the drawing room, Drew was standing at the window gazing outside. His hands were clasped behind his back. He was rocking on his heels as if he was nervous for some reason. She remembered Drew. He was a handsome man with startlingly blue eyes, the color of a summer sky. While he wasn't as tall or as broad as Walker, his build was sturdy, his legs long, his thighs well muscled as were his arms and shoulders. To Crissie it was his smile that always seemed to catch her attention. It wasn't as charming or as riveting as Walker's but it was nice.

"Lieutenant St. John?" She stood framed in the doorway, hesitant now that she was in the same room with the man.

He turned quickly, "Drew."

She cleared her throat taking a step closer to him. "Drew then. To what do I owe the pleasure of this meeting?"

"Always straight to the point, Miss McKenna."

"Crissie," she said, "Would you like tea? Something to eat?"

"Yes, please."

Feeling as if the air turned tense and so tight breathing was difficult, she poured the tea then took a seat, her hands clasped in her lap, studying the man. "How have you been.

"Well, thank you and you?" He crossed his legs, resting his hand with the cup and saucer on his knee.

She looked away, sensing there was something more going on here as she recalled Rose's words of warning. Honesty sometimes got a person into more trouble than a lie. She wasn't going to tell this man how she felt about anything especially not these living arrangements. She could pretend as well as anyone.

"I'm content," she said softly, focusing on a tiny bug crawling along the Aubusson carpet.

"Are you?" his voice was pointed, demanding without words that she look at him and speak the truth.

"What I'm feeling is truly not any of your business." She squared her shoulders, saying words that might border on rudeness. Mincing words was not her style.

"Of course it isn't. However, I would like to help out if you ever need..." He stopped as if he wasn't sure he wanted to finish. "Help."

"Thank you, that's very gentlemanly of you."

"It's nothing of the sort, Crissie. I know why you are here. Also know about the baby. He is not treating you right. Has you here under false pretenses. If you decide this isn't something you can live with, I would be pleased to help you."

"Drew," she rose, "you are taking this too far. Perhaps you should leave."

"Not until you hear me out."

"Very well, I'm listening." she sat again, feeling the agitation of this meeting to the tips of her toes.

For some reason she couldn't fathom she hoped he was gone before Walker returned. She didn't think he would appreciate Drew's presence at his home.

"I just want you to understand that unlike Walker, I would marry you in a heartbeat. Of course, I'm free to do so."

She blinked a few times, trying to understand why he would propose something so ludicrous. She tried to be calm, to hide the nervous energy sweeping within. "I don't want to marry you, Drew."

"You might someday."

"I don't think so."

"He will never marry you. He can't or hasn't he told you the truth?"

Crissie knew her eyes widened at his words. Another secret? She didn't know there was one about his ability to marry, just knew he couldn't. She spoke cautiously, "Walker has told me a few things."

Drew set his cup on the tray. A dark brow arched in disbelief. "That he's an adulterer? Ah, I see that he has not told you he's married."

Crissie thought her heart stopped. She swallowed painfully. Eternity passed by before she could finally form the word. "Married?"

"He keeps her in the country."

She was floating in a land that had no ground, a land where she could find no footing. Her voice seemed to come from far away. "He was going to take me to his country home." She couldn't allow it. Couldn't live in the same home as his wife.

Bassa!

"To live with his wife?" he sneered, his voice deepening with emotion. "He is no gentleman. I'm surprised he hasn't offered to put you up in the same townhouse where he keeps his mistress."

Mistress?

Truly she couldn't breathe. Her head spun. The floor seemed to be rising to meet her. The cup she was holding fell from her numb fingers. Drew was beside her, holding her, pulling her so her head rested against his chest. He smelled of spice and cigars.

It wasn't bad.

The scent wasn't Walker's.

She closed her eyes for seconds, kept them shut tight until she felt more herself. Pushing away from him she smiled weakly at him.

"I'm sure he will tell me in time. When he is ready," she said, not so certain she spoke the truth.

Walker did things in his time, no one else's. If he didn't choose to tell her, he never would. Dear God, he was really going to bring her to the home where is wife lived?

"When it suits him."

"We were leaving in a few days," she said wishing she could vanish into walls, dissolve away into nothingness.

All she wanted was to remain close to her son to watch him grow, nothing more.

"To live with his wife. Were the three of you going to share a bedroom?"

"I think you should go."

"No, not yet." He pulled out a card, handing it to her. He waited for her to take it before he spoke. "That is where you can reach me if you ever change your mind and want a real husband and family."

She took it, stuffing the card into the same pocket that held the necklace. "Yes."

"Don't lose it."

"No, no I won't. That wouldn't be a good idea."

"If you come to me, I want you to know that I will also raise your child as my own."

"Walker would never allow such a thing. He's made Ian his heir. So, you see, I will never come to you, Drew. It's not possible."

"Anything is possible."

"No, no it isn't."

"Why?"

She was taken aback at the harshness in his voice. "I can't live without my son."

Giving her no time to refuse, he pulled her into his arms, held her close. She heard the beat of his heart, the air as it slipped in and out of his lungs. When he bent to kiss her, she turned her head.

"No."

Rose was right, she thought as she watched Drew walk out the door. She needed to be careful. Her hand in her pocket rested on the necklace. She wanted to throw the offending token of affection in Walker's face. It was her intention when she first read the note, now the need burned like a fire in her veins.

~ * ~

Walker whistled while he strode down a busy street in Belfast to the home he had purchased for his current mistress, Monique. While he was looking forward to this final visit with her, he was also looking forward to returning home to the arms of his love, Crissie. Monique would not make this easy for him. He knew that beyond any doubts he might harbor. No, she would manage to wheedle more financial security for herself.

She deserved whatever she could get out of him. This was a necessary chore, one he had to do, better sooner than later. He was just happy to have a woman in his arms that he loved. Thinking of little else besides Crissie, he recalled vividly every time they made love last evening. She was so tender, giving of herself completely.

He hoped she liked the necklace, having bought it for her the first night they were in Belfast. He'd walked past a jewelry store that evening after speaking with the general. Unable to resist entering and purchasing something for her, he did just that. The necklace would bring out the silver-blue of her eyes. Smiling to himself he continued to whistle.

When he knocked at his Mistress' home, Monique's maid opened the door, a horrified expression on her face. "Something wrong?"

"Hello, sir. Monique was not expecting you." Fidgeting with the skirt of her gown she backed up a step.

"I didn't have time to send a message. I won't be here long." He stepped inside the door, placing his hat on the stand.

"I'll tell her you're here." The maid turned to rush up the steps.

Walker stopped her, his hand on her shoulder. She sounded frantic. He wondered about that for a moment only. "No need to have you tire yourself running up then down the steps. I'll show myself to her room."

"No! You can't do that." The maid's hands covered her mouth, her eyes wide in apparent alarm.

"Whatever is wrong?" Walker asked, stepping back to study the maid. Suddenly an understanding filled him, his relief tangible. "Ah, she is with someone."

The maid turned an alarming shade of red, her head bobbing. "Please, don't go up there. She'll never forgive me."

"If she doesn't forgive and forget, I'll hire you. No need to worry."

Grinning broadly, the answer to his problems solved, Walker took the steps two at a time on his way to Monique's room and the confrontation he was now looking forward to. This little faux pas would save him a great deal of money.

He couldn't be more pleased. Monique had already found herself a new protector. She could move out as soon as tomorrow. The money he would make on the sale of this townhouse would be put in a trust for Ian.

Perhaps he would stop on the way home so he could buy Crissie a pair of earrings to match the necklace. Never before had he found so much enjoyment in purchasing gifts.

Yes, she would like that.

He burst through the door without knocking, the maid behind him. "Monique! My you look lovely in your dishabille."

"Walker?" She was clutching the covers to her breasts. The man was blustering as he sat up, clearly naked beneath the covers.

"Get out!" he roared.

Walker had no intention of leaving, at least not yet. "Yes, it's me.

Who is that? Don't believe I've met your acquaintance. Are you new in Belfast?"

He pointed to the naked man beside her. When he first entered, they were in the midst of foreplay, the final intimacy soon to follow. Her tiny sounds of pleasure were all too familiar.

The man sat up. "Her newest protector I assume."

"How right you are. You've saved me negotiation time along with the *groats* I would have lost had you not been here so fortuitously. You can't know how much I appreciate your help."

"You could vacate the premises," the man said. "Barging in was not well done of you."

"No, while I understand I did barge in at a delicate time, it is you and Monique who need to leave, vacate the premises. You to find her a new home and Monique," he shrugged his shoulders, brushing imaginary lint from his frock coat, "well, Monique needs to be out by tomorrow morning. I will put the place up for sale."

"For your new mistress," she spoke out angrily clearly riled by the rumors she must have heard.

His lazy smile turned to a mocking one. "I've no new mistress, my lady. Even if I did, it would not be well done of me to place her in this home."

"That isn't what people are saying," she shot back clearly defiant. "You've also a bastard living in your home."

Anger rose quickly. Her defiance coupled with the gossip about his personal life was not to be permitted. He kept his anger simmering in the back of his mind. Giving more reason for gossip was not happening. "Just be out of this home tomorrow by ten. If there is anything of yours left, I will sell it with the house."

Walker turned on a heel, striding down the steps. He tipped his hat to the maid who was now standing by the door. "Remember, if Monique lets you go, come to me for help. I'll either hire you myself or find a suitable employer."

She bobbed a courtesy as he left. "Thank you, milord. I'll remember what you said."

The relief he felt traveled quickly all the way to his soul. This was one completed task. Now, he needed to get to his country home and his wife. The discussion with Charlotte was too long in coming. Again, the conversation he needed to have with Crissie was not something he was looking forward to but once again a necessity.

Before that, however, he would have to speak with Crissie about his mission in the highlands. He would have to ask her the hard question. She would be upset. There was no other alternative than for him to go. He would purposefully find nothing substantial. Would verify there were no shifters and give credence to the fact the notion was indeed archaic passed on by old women with nothing better to do than tell tales. He ran his hands through his tawny hair, knowing first hand that shifters did indeed exist.

As he decided earlier, he stopped at the jewelry store where he bought the necklace. The proprietor found the matching earrings. Walker wasn't at all sure why he didn't buy them the same day as the necklace. He also stopped at a nearby dress shop in order to cancel Monique's account then set up one for Crissie. Yes, they were leaving in a few days, but she might want to shop for some new things. He purchased a pale blue negligée with a matching robe. It was indeed a beautiful garment, one that would reveal as well as conceal all Crissie's womanly charms. His body throbbed in anticipation.

He didn't have to think very hard to imagine what she would look like. She would appear a goddess. Didn't have to fantasize how she would thank him. Perhaps they would make love first then eat. Ah, he picked up his steps, intending to reach home as soon as possible. Thoughts of sweet kisses in his mind, he stepped through the door.

She was waiting for him in the drawing room, sipping a glass of sherry. Her face was devoid of all expression. When she looked up, frown lines marred her forehead, her eyes flashed furiously. The silver color seemed to have turned to molten steel as they sparked losing their blue warmth. He paused midstride, hesitating for a moment before walking through the door.

Disregarding the expression, thinking only of the gifts he intended to give her, he grinned, spreading his arms in anticipation of her body pressed close to his. When the necklace hit him in the chest, he dropped his arms. His welcoming smile changed to perplexity.

"Is something wrong?" he growled.

"Bassa!"

Chapter Five

To say he was confused would not come close to Walker's feelings as he watched her race up the stairs, her skirt hiked almost to her knees. Slowly and feeling bewildered, he bent over, picking up the necklace. For the longest time his gaze roamed from the stairs to the piece of jewelry she hurled at him. This was definitely not the homecoming he expected.

What the devil?

He wasn't sure what to do or how to proceed. Perhaps he should let her simmer for a while before he went to talk to her. Clearly, she wasn't in a talkative mood. No, she probably simmered all day.

But why? He held the necklace up to the light. Before she tossed it at him, he imagined her wearing nothing but the jewels.

Striding to the sideboard, he poured himself a full snifter of brandy. Maybe he should go upstairs to see his son. At least the boy might smile at him. The lad's arm wasn't strong enough yet to throw anything at him. Right now, his mind was just to muddled to put a coherent thought or reason to her action. His previous joy this afternoon turned black.

He gazed at the steps again, then sat down.

"Thought you were home," Rose walked in with Ian in her arms smiling. "Thought you might want to see your son."

Setting the glass of brandy on the table one stride later his son was nestled in his arms. He ran a finger along the little boy's soft cheek. The boy cooed softly, blowing a tiny bubble.

"My God he's precious."

He sat down holding him and motioning for Rose to join him with a drink and hopefully an explanation as he waited for her to pour herself a glass of sherry.

After a small sip, Rose looked at him tenderly, "What is it? Known you for years. That dark expression on your visage doesn't bode well."

"Do you know what's bothering, Crissie?"

Truly he didn't want to bring others into a quarrel with Crissie, but he needed some idea as to what was going on with her.

Rose shook her head, "No, but she's been out of sorts all day. I've heard doors slamming as well as a bit of cursing. Didn't ask though. Wasn't my business. Have you tried asking her?"

"No, I'm a bit afraid of her at the moment. The way she looked at me when I walked in the door had me wishing I could run for my life. She might just bite my head off."

"If you want to know, you'll have to be askin' her yourself. Here, hand me back the boy. He will need to eat soon. Perhaps if she's nursing the *wee* one, she won't be able to bite your head off."

As Rose picked up the little one, she chuckled softly casting him a wry smile. Talk to her, she mouthed. "It might be good for you to pay attention to someone else's needs for a change."

Walker could do nothing but grimace as he listened to his old nanny trying to be neutral. He held up the necklace, staring at the way the light in the room caught and held in the costly gems. Slowly, he let out the breath of air he'd been holding in check. "I gave this to her this morning."

"Are you a bloody fool?" Rose asked him as she bounced Ian. "Thought better of you."

"What the hell does that mean? She threw it at me." He pulled out the box with the matching earrings. "I suppose I'm going to have to go back to the jewelers in order to pick out something different for her. She must not like sapphires and diamonds. I didn't think she was the kind of woman to be so picky."

"That might not be the wisest decision either. Your first instinct is right. It isn't the gems she has an issue with," Rose murmured making clucking sounds at him. "Can't you possibly think of even one reason she might fling the necklace at you beside the fact she might not like it?"

"Honestly? No." He found himself shaking his head, confusion growing as time passed and his feeble male mind couldn't sort anything out where Crissie was concerned.

Time and again, he searched for a reason and came up short. "I'll let her tell you. The words will have more meaning if they come from her lips. If I were you," Rose was shaking a finger at him, "I wouldn't expect to sleep with her tonight. And," following another short break in time, "I wouldn't give her the earrings right now. Perhaps save them for a moment when she isn't going to think the worst." Then she added, "If that ever happens."

"What woman doesn't like a gift?"

"Perhaps you need to be askin' yourself that exact question. Delve a wee bit deeper into your heart. Listen to the things she's been tellin' you since the day you drug her away from her family." One white but elegant eyebrow rose. "Put yourself in her place for a few seconds. Now that's all I'm going to be sayin'. Ian here is getting restless. He needs his mother."

"I never drug her anywhere. She always had a choice," he protested with a low growl.

"Untenable choices."

With Rose leaving his questions unanswered he was left with more questions than he started with. Downing his brandy in a gulp, he poured a second. This one he sipped slowly, going over everything in his head as he stared bewildered at the steps. Still, he held no viable answers or solutions. He ran the necklace through his fingers.

Not be sleeping in my bed tonight?

Not bloody likely.

She cemented their relationship last night. She came to him more than willing. He was not about to go backward. If he had to, he would remove the damn negligée himself. If he had to, he would carry her from her bed to his.

Given she doesn't throw the negligée in my face too.

He drank more brandy. Time slipped by as he stared into the amber liquid, pondering life and all the subtle intricacies of women that he didn't understand.

She should be pleased with the gift. All three of the gifts. There would be more too. She should count on that fact. He wasn't about to stop buying her things.

Instead, she tossed his gift to her in his face.

Would she do the same with the lingerie? Ah, but he wanted to have the pleasure of slowly removing the thin gown from her lovely curves to unveil the ripe fullness of her breasts. When he finally rose from the chair, he was half way to being drunk as well as starving. At the thought of food, his stomach curdled. At the thought of Crissie, he hardened, his erection pushing anxiously against the fabric of his pants. He found his anger festered deep inside throbbing just beneath the surface. Anger, fury, his gift shoved in his face unwanted. Well, he would make sure it stayed with her. He wasn't going to exchange it. She would wear the bloody necklace. He would put it on her himself.

He stomped up the stairs eager to confront her with rolling emotions. She was playing on the floor with Ian when he threw the door open. It banged hard against the opposite wall.

She looked up, her eyes wide with shock.

Ian wailed.

Crissie looked as if she was about to order him from his bloody bedroom. His bedroom. Instead, she picked up Ian, rocking him until his wails became tiny gulping whimpers. Guilt at upsetting his son swamped him. For a full second his fury vanished only to return harder.

He had not thought.

Frustrated for more than one reason, he propelled his hands through his hair. "I'm sorry."

"As well you should be," she reprimanded him her voice prim.

With Ian in her arms, she stomped from the room, headed he supposed to the playroom upstairs.

"Give Ian to Rose then come back. We've things to talk about."

He wasn't sure if she heard. Wasn't sure she would do as he bade even if she heard. Between this morning and the moment she rejected his gift something changed inside her.

Looking over her shoulder, she glared at him. Her eyes narrowed. He was sure she was about to tell him to go to hell.

"Is that a command or a request?"

Her voice was too sweet, too syrupy. She would retaliate.

He shrugged his shoulders thinking that yes, it was an order. "I suppose it is a command. If you don't come here, I will find you. Will bring you here where there is privacy. This isn't something the servants or even Rose should hear."

She whirled, her skirt flying around her ankles, pretty ankles, ones he'd like to see again close up.

Tonight.

He waited.

Ominously the clock ticked the seconds. More time passed as he paced the room. Where the devil was she? Was she defying him? Challenging him to make good on his promise.

She slipped inside, her back to the door looking as if he terrified her. *Bloody hell.*

Terror was not the reaction he needed from her tonight, not the reaction he expected when she walked through the door.

Bloody, bloody hell!

His mind reeled. "Crissie?"

"Walker."

She was stiff. Her voice strained. He didn't see tears. Yet he sensed they were very close to the surface. Through her anger she hid the real emotions pulsing through her veins. He just needed to figure out what exactly those sentiments were.

"If I did something wrong, I'd like you to tell me what it is. If I didn't, then you also need to explain what's going on. Why you don't like my gift."

Once again, he thrust his hands through his hair as he tried for an air of calm that didn't exist. Would not exist until he had answers.

Moving away from the door, she walked to the tray that had been brought up for them. She sat down. Poured wine. Drank deeply before speaking and ignoring his request. "Would you like to eat now? Nothing here will change if the conversation is left for a while."

"Hell no! I want to know why you flung the necklace in my face. It cost a small fortune, you know. You should be thanking me. Yes, you should show your appreciation. I can think of few ways for you to do just that." He wanted to shake her until she told him why. Wanted to fling her on the bed then bury himself deep inside her sultry core.

Craved her.

Craved her as surely as he needed to breathe.

"If you keep yelling, you'll wake up your son." Nonchalantly, as if nothing was wrong, she bit into a piece of cheese. Sipped more wine. Watched him with eyes narrowed, her lashes fluttering against her white skin.

This wasn't going as he planned. For some reason he was sure he said something else that she was taking exception too. No, he needed to take back control. He could be patient, wait her out until she was so eager to tell him why, she wouldn't be able to keep the words behind her teeth.

"We wouldn't want Ian to wake up and see his parents fighting. That is what we're doing. Isn't it Crissie? You don't play fair. You know what we're fighting about. I don't."

His voice was calmer now. He meant to carry on in that vein. Picking up a piece of apple he bit into it then chewed slowly savoring the juice.

"I'm not fighting with you." She sipped the wine again, peered at him over the crystal rim. Her eyes sparked when they met his gaze. "I just don't like the implications you made today."

Implications?

"Liar."

He smiled. Settled back, stretching his legs in front of him and waited. He ate a variety of the food on the tray, feeling once more in charge of this insane dance between them, one will pitted against the other. It would be so much easier if she would just tell him what was wrong. He could fix it. They could carry on as if nothing happened. He supposed she would always find ways to infuriate him. He also supposed he would always enjoy the end game. He looked to the bed then back to

Crissie. Saw the blush rise to her cheeks. He felt the first twinge of success.

"So, you did lie," he pointed out quietly.

"Are we fighting? I think not. I'm protesting what you did to me, the way you treated me."

"Made love to you? Are we talking about last night, all of last night, this morning as well? She needed to be plain spoken. "How exactly did I mistreat you?"

"No."

She was standing by the window now, her back to him. She ignored him.

He needed to see her face, read the expressions there. "No? No to what?"

Slowly she turned, her face having lost the color it once possessed. "I thought perhaps you would be more astute. I never took you for a cruel man. What you did was thoughtless as well as hurtful."

"Making love to you?"

"No."

"Crissie, the game has gone on far too long. What the bloody hell did I do to receive this treatment?"

His hands were on her shoulders, her breath wafted across his face when she looked up at him. She smelled of sweet wine. The taste would be on her lips in the darkest hottest part of her mouth.

There were tears in her eyes.

Something he did put them there. He cursed himself.

"I'm not your mistress."

"I never said you were. You mean far too much to me to ever be categorized as such."

"You gave me the necklace."

"Yes. Yes, I did. Was that wrong of me? If so, damn me to hell. I thought it was almost as beautiful as you."

She tried to turn away. He was still so confused he wanted to shake her. Perhaps she should shake him. The deed might clear his fuzzy mind because he was obviously missing some vital piece of this puzzle.

Her dark lashes swept momentarily across her cheek. "You paid me for the night, 'a small token of my appreciation' you wrote."

"I still don't understand. I treasured last night. Giving you something was my way of telling you that."

"Isn't that how you would pay your mistress?" she asked, stifling a sob with the back of her hand. "You would give her small tokens of your appreciation in thanks?"

Sucker punched would best describe what that one question did to him. "I didn't see it that way."

"Well, I don't want your tokens. Take the gift back. Throw the necklace out. I don't care but I don't want to ever see it again. I won't wear sapphires and diamonds for you to lord over me."

"No. When you're ready to accept me in every way, I'll give the necklace to you again."

He wasn't going to meet her half way in this, craved to see her wearing nothing but the necklace. "I like giving you pretty things. You're just going to have to get used to that fact. The gift has nothing to do with sex."

He pulled her into his arms. The side of her face was pressed against his chest. Tears soaked the front of his shirt. He wasn't going to let that dissuade him on his course. His fingers slid into her hair, disrupting the pins. They clattered on the floor. He wanted to kiss her, take away all the pain he inflicted. Craved for her to understand his motives were pure and simple.

Somehow, he understood they just touched on a tiny bit of what was bothering her. For a few minutes she accepted the comfort he offered. His hands roamed along her back, bringing her closer. The soft mounds of her breasts pushed against his chest. By the way she slowly began to relax, he knew she was coming around.

Until she stiffened, pushing away from him.

"Why don't you give it to your other mistress? She might be more accepting of your gesture."

His breath hung in his lungs until he finally let it sift out. "I don't have another mistress."

"That's not what I heard today." Her voice was accusing, leaving the air ripe with unsaid tension.

He didn't think she would believe anything he told her now especially since he never spoke of Monique to her. "Who? Who told you about my other mistress? I would know."

She waved her hand in the air, her eyes flashing indignation, "That's not important now that you admitted to the fact."

"I dismissed her this morning before I ran a few other errands. She will be out of the townhouse tomorrow by ten o'clock. She is gone. I don't want any woman except you." He pulled in a long draught of air hoping to maintain the air of calmness he sought.

"Your wife?" she queried in an even more reproachful tone.

"Crissie."

He couldn't breathe. Someone came here and told her things he should be telling her. Said things that were private. Things he fully meant to tell her as well as explain. He was looking for the right time. Evidently, he no longer had that choice. "Who was here?"

"So, it's true."

Walker understood a whole lot more now that all her fears were out in the open. He swept her into his arms. She wriggled trying to dislodge herself for a second then seemed to realize she wanted him to hold her. At least he hoped she wanted his arms wrapped around her. When he kissed her, he knew all her fury and impotent rage would vanish. She would melt in his arms as she always did.

She was his.

He settled on the wing chair by the fireplace with her on his lap. Her glittering lashes were spiked with tears. His lips brushed lightly against hers. Nipped at the corners of her mouth, ran his tongue slowly across her upper lip. She sighed softly as he absorbed her breath into his mouth.

She stopped him. Pushed against his chest. "No, Walker, don't kiss me."

He needed to kiss her until she became liquid in his arms, until she spun out of control with her need. "Alright, do you have any more questions? I'd like to explain about my wife."

"It's adultery. More of a sin than just sleeping with you. I can't be party to this. Don't know if I could forgive myself."

She touched a finger to the small dimple on the side of his mouth.

"I know." For an instant he looked away from her as he gathered his thoughts. "Charlotte has never been my wife in any way. She is more like a sister who I love as a sibling. I've always known her. As children we played together, at least until I was too old." He went on to explain everything. How their parents betrothed them when she was born. How she had never liked him. "She prefers women."

"She what?" Crissie blinked a few times then with unending question looked into his eyes. To Walker it seemed she had no idea what he was saying.

"This is probably more than you ever wanted to know. Charlotte doesn't want to sleep with me, have me touch her and kiss her because she would rather have another woman in her arms."

There, he'd done it. He shocked her to her very core. Now, he would have to make her understand Charlotte, that although she would never be his wife in any way, he was loath to hurt her. Crissie's eyes were wide, filled with confusion but also the realization of exactly what his words meant.

"Why didn't you get an annulment or a divorce? Surely the church would have granted you a dispensation to annul the marriage."

He ran a finger down her nose then across her slightly parted lips. They were warm and moist. He didn't want to talk. Desired to kiss her. "Until you, neither one of us cared enough to deal with the issue. Marriage was convenient for both of us. My life was fine as it was. Doting mamas stayed away from me. Young debutantes didn't pursue me. Life was exactly how I wanted it. Asking for a divorce or annulment would have changed everything between us."

"It was until now." Her words were a breathy whisper against his cheek. He could bring her so easily into his bed. Coax her with tender kisses. Sway her with the touch of his fingers. His lips could work their magic. Already, he felt the melting of her body against his. Heard the soft sighs as his fingers traced various paths across her body.

"I would have to speak with her."

"You could pursue those avenues now." The hesitation, the tenor of her voice all were poignant, "We could wed."

He was denying the fact to himself, afraid of further repercussions, afraid to make a lifelong commitment. He had been burned once. "There is much to be considered. I gave my solemn vow to my father, a promise I loathe to dismiss. He would be displeased to hear of the divorce or the annulment." Walker could never explain to his father the reasons. He thought on his father along with his opinions. Without voicing one complaint, he spent ten years wed to a vastly unsuitable woman. Perhaps it was time for a change. His father would understand especially now that he had his heir in Ian. His father would agree he needed an heir plus one. He could enjoy the creation of a second child with Crissie.

First, he had to convince Crissie he wasn't a cad of the worst sort.

Still, he had the reasons for traveling to the highlands to explain to her. It seemed there was someone visiting here who wished to tell her everything before he found a good time.

"Crissie?" He was trailing soft butterfly kisses down her throat, his hand now cupping a breast, his thumb rubbing the hardened nub he found there. Her sighs of pleasure spurred him too more daring caresses.

"Hmm..." She held his hand, stopping him from undoing her gown. "You shouldn't."

"Why?"

"I'm not ready."

His lips settled against hers again, one hand bringing her skirt higher, caressing the inside of her thigh, light teasing strokes. She parted her legs for him just as she was parting her lips.

"I would bet your honey is flowing. Would also bet you're more than ready for me. I can wait until you want me more than you've ever wanted me before." He bit, tugging on her bottom lip before soothing the tiny hurt with his tongue.

"No, really, stop. I want to know what you're going to do next."

To no avail, she pushed on his chest.

"I'm going to make love to you. Then perhaps we'll do it again and again for the entire night."

She purred softly turning in his arms still meaning to deny him. "About your wife. What are you planning if anything?"

"Don't want to think about her right now. Just you as well as how I'm going to love you until you scream with your woman's pleasure." His fingers stroked her intimately. She was hot and wet, slick with need. "I was right."

He swept her into his arms gently lowering her to the bed. They made love with a heated exhilaration. In his arms, she was wild and wanton, giving all of herself to him. He absorbed the very essence of her into him giving her the ecstasy they both craved before taking his own pleasure.

When they were finished, they were both still fully clothed. Garments had been unfastened. Some had been pushed aside and out of the way. Her head rested on his chest. She was unfastening his shirt, with her fingers playing with the hair on his chest. "You know that you don't play fair."

Walker sat up, bringing her with him. "Crissie, I'm not going to stop giving you things. You should understand that fact. I know you're not going to like this either, but I set up an account for you at the dressmakers with your name on it. Whenever we are in the city, you can buy what you want. Remember, I will always play by my rules. If that's not fair by your standards, I suppose you will just have to learn to live with it."

In his arms, he felt her bristle. He chuckled softly enjoying her independence as well as her determination to do things her way. She might fight him on this. She would need things, maybe not now but in the future. Without his money, she had no way to purchase what she needed.

"I've more clothes than I need, than I know what to do with."

"We shall see. For now, I did stop there this afternoon. Would you accept this gift from me? If I promise not to buy you anything tomorrow?"

"Walker, no..."

"Please."

She didn't answer. Now that everything had been explained, he felt confident she would accept. Reaching across her, he picked up the package he placed close to the bed. "Will you put this on?" He unwrapped the sheer gown, holding it up to the light. Her little gasp of surprise coupled with the sound of delight pleased him. "You will wear it for me?"

"I shouldn't." He heard the hesitation in her voice.

"I will enjoy taking it off."

When she appeared wearing the garments his breath caught in his throat.

~ * ~

Crissie knew she gave in too easily. She also knew she couldn't deny this man anything. He didn't truly understand why she abhorred his gifts. Nor did he understand why she felt so used when he gave her things after a night of lovemaking. He smiled like a little boy getting a Christmas treat when he handed her something new. With each new purchase she died a little inside, her heart breaking just a tiny bit more. In time it would be shattered.

Several days had passed since the episode of the necklace, since he confirmed what Andrew St. John told her about his wife as well as his mistress. She understood honor along with commitment. She also understood his deep-seated need to make everything right. He didn't say as much but she sensed he loved Charlotte, at least in the way a brother loves his sister as he told her. She felt love for her brothers. Her family traditions were steeped in honor, loyalty, commitment and so much more. She wasn't sure what she would do if he didn't honor her with marriage coupled with a commitment made in the church. Deep in her heart she understood she could never continue in this vein.

Hard for her to accept this role he placed her in, she merely gritted her teeth before continuing each day. Each night when she slept with him, she understood in some ways he did love her. Each morning when she woke up, she was so ashamed of her behavior, she wasn't sure if she could face the day. If not for Ian she never would have stayed.

Now they were on their way to a place he said she would love. He told her he wanted to make love to her there. She wanted to say no. Yet the moment his lips touched hers she wouldn't have a prayer of denying him. He was her heart. He was her soul.

The sun was shining, the day warm. A slight breeze ruffled the leaves on the trees. A mama deer and two fawns stood by the side of the road watching as they drove past in the buggy. Above on the wind drafts an eagle soared. She filled her lungs with the clean scent of summer air and wildflowers.

While he drove the buggy, one hand rested possessively on her leg. She knew he had ideas about finding places with his roving fingers where there was no fabric. Too many people traveled this road for him to do anything improper. At least she hoped so. He had this easy way of embarrassing her with his actions. He would chuckle and continue on as if nothing was untoward, as if no one knew what they were doing. He would tell her the blush on her cheeks was lovely. After that, he would ask if her breasts were the same color. Of course, by the time he finished the diatribe, she was shockingly crimson.

"Are you hungry, lass?" he asked while he gently squeezed her leg somehow finding a way to bunch the fabric of her skirt higher then higher still. "The cook packed a full basket of food. I made sure there were a couple of bottles of wine and crystal glasses to better enjoy our drinks."

"You want to ply me with wine so I won't deny your wicked advances."

She was able to laugh now a bit more easily. He skirted the issue of the annulment when she brought it up. Never talked about what he planned to do about his wife. Told her he couldn't tell her about plans he had yet to make. He supposed he could tell her what was in his heart, but he didn't want to disappoint her if his plans did not come to fruition.

He winked at her. "All I need is a kiss and you fall into my arms, my very willing arms I might add. The wine has no special powers as far as I can tell."

His hand slipped beneath her dress, found purchase at the top of her stockings, played with the ribbon holding it up.

"Walker, no, not here. Anyone can see." To no avail, she pushed at his hands even while they crept along her sensitive flesh.

"*Nay*, they cannot see anything, little pigeon."

His fingers roaming worked their way higher, higher still.

Her breath wobbled as she tried to keep her body from responding as he continued to explore. His fingers found more and more sensitive places. She thought about other things than the way he made her feel. Tried hard to think about Ian. He could turn over now. Push himself up on his arms.

"What was it you wanted to talk about today?"

"My assignment to the highlands but only after we eat then have a little romance."

"What if I want to talk first?"

She hitched in a breath. His fingers parted and stroked her. Just as she always did, she was turning to mush, no will of her own.

"You can try." His laughter rolled sweetly from his lips.

He was such a cad, a playboy. Too handsome for his own good. She understood he would always do what he wanted. Perhaps she liked that about him. Maybe she didn't. What she really wanted was for him to listen to her, for him to understand her position as well as how she felt. When they talked, he always pushed her words to the side as if his lovemaking would constantly count for more.

"I will." Her words held no value, not unless he stopped touching her. She tried to scoot away from him, but there was no room to move very far from his questing fingers. It didn't help either when she opened for him. She was a mess of tightly coiled emotions.

He laughed again, a full booming laugh, which spoke so clearly that he knew she wouldn't succeed, spoke of his male prowess. The buggy slowed to a stop. With his free hand, he turned her face to him.

"You're blushing," he said as his mouth descended on hers.

His tongue begged to enter her. She parted her lips. Touched her tongue to his while he continued the slow rhythmic seduction with his fingers.

"I should be. You should stop before."

"Someone sees us?"

"Yes. We're here."

"Oh, my."

Two fingers entered her.

He continued his not-so-subtle coaxing. She felt the magical enchantment he created so easily. One hand held her head. One continued stroking, caressing her intimately. His lips kissed her again and again. Heat spiraled. Fire raged while she was quivering in desperate need of release. The tremors inside grew. She shuddered in his arms while he continued taking her higher and higher to that rapture only he could generate. Her fingers gripped his shirt as her body climaxed arching against his trying to get closer and closer to him. She fell against him, weak from the love play.

"I love to watch your eyes, little pigeon, when I give you your woman's pleasure. They darken. The silver becomes bluer and hotter with each second.

Her breathing was raspy.

"I don't think I can move."

"You don't have to." He picked her up, jumping form the buggy with her in his arms. Beneath a tree he set her down. "Don't move one muscle. Don't do a thing."

She watched as he brought items from the buggy, a blanket to sit on along with the lunch basket. A few minutes later he had a bottle of wine opened and glasses in hand. He poured.

"A toast. To my lover and the woman I want to share my life with. And," he smiled, clinking their glasses together, "to the woman I will buy gifts for anytime it pleases me."

She frowned at him before drinking the wine. There was nothing she could do or say to dissuade him. This was not everything she wanted or needed in life. She knew it would come to an end, a bitter heart-breaking end. She simply could not do this his way for the rest of her life. If he didn't do something to change this horrible situation, she would have to leave him, take Ian from him.

"Now, tell me why you brought me all the way out here." The frown vanished. His little boy smile chased the foreboding feelings away at least for the moment.

"The scenery is beautiful don't you think?"

She nodded it was beautiful. Most of Ireland was green, breathtaking. It was very different from the highlands. "Yes, but I don't think we drove out here to discuss the scenery."

"Thought we could make love behind the waterfall over there." He lifted his glass high then drank. "Would you like that?"

"Is that all you think about?"

"*Aye*, when you're around."

If the water was warm, she thought the waterfall looked deliciously tempting. If the sun were hotter, it might be even more inviting. The day had yet to mature. Perhaps it would get warm enough.

"Why don't we talk first before we pursue other avenues of pleasure? When are we going to your country home? You know, I don't want to go. Not that my opinion has ever counted for anything with you."

"How you wound me." He placed his hand over his heart. "When I make decisions, I always think of you."

"'*Tis* the other way around and well you *ken* it, Walker Endicott. You're bringing me to the same home where your wife lives."

She didn't want to feel the anger boil up inside her. She couldn't help it though.

"Charlotte doesn't even live in the main house. She lives in a small cottage she prefers over the house. It's some distance away. One can only see it from the balcony."

"She can come and go as she pleases. When you're gone, she can walk into any room she chooses. I don't care if you think of her as a beloved sister. I don't want her coming inside the home where I'm to be living."

Crissie didn't like that idea. She didn't want to be stuck in the country somewhere all alone. She knew he was leaving after he deposited her away from civilization. Truly, she didn't understand why she cared so much. Where she lived in the highlands was fairly isolated. Still, there were people, family and friends.

She was never alone.

"The two of you will like each other," he ventured with the hint of a smile that touched a nerve in her.

She let out the puff of air she'd been trying to inhale. "I doubt that."

She didn't want to talk about Charlotte coupled with the strange notion they would somehow be friends. She would never be the woman's friend nor could she tolerate her.

He pushed a few strands of hair that came loose from her bun behind her ear. "Crissie, you know I have to leave a few days after we get there. You will have Rose and Ian to keep you company as well as a maid. You won't be alone. How you react to my wife is up to you."

"I want to go with you." She'd told him that more than once but he never gave her request any consideration. "I would see my family. Would love to reintroduce Ian to his grandparents as well as his uncles."

"No."

"No? Why? There is no earthly reason why you cannot take me with you. Just as there is no reason I should remain in Ireland while I try to be friends with your wife."

Her indignation coupled with frustration and fury rose quickly. She stood, wishing she had the nerve to toss her remaining wine in his face. If she did, he would retaliate in kind. The gesture would simply have no meaning.

"Danger, linked to the fact I'm going to London first. I've business with my father," he spoke softly, touching her cheek with the back of his hand a wistful sad look in his eyes.

"Your father would not like to meet your heir? I would..."

"He would, but not this trip. I've private issues to discuss with him. Things I don't want you asking questions about."

If he slapped her, she wouldn't have been more surprised. Of course, he didn't have to tell her anything.

Private issues.

"I see."

She was nothing to him. Would never have a place, a real place in his heart. She was simply the woman he wanted to bed at the moment. He must fear her brothers enough that he wouldn't set her up as his mistress. No, he wouldn't do that but he would treat her as his mistress.

His wishes, not hers.

Standing by the edge of the waterfall, she allowed the crashing of the water to soothe her strangled nerves. Since that first day he stole Ian, she knew what she meant to the man. He stood beside her now. His hand rested possessively on her shoulder.

"If it means anything to you, I'm sorry."

How could he sound so sincere? "It doesn't. Your apology means nothing to me." She sucked in a ragged breath.

"Come back and sit down, please. We've more to talk about. When we finish perhaps you will understand," he spoke softly, almost as if he could wipe away the hurt he inflicted.

To Crissie, it seemed she had lost her free will. He so easily molded her thoughts and actions to what he wanted. She nodded, fighting the rise of moisture to the back of her throat.

More to talk about?

Something else that would hurt her. It seemed each new revelation caused more pain and heartache. What more could he want to share?

She sat. He filled her glass then handed her a slice of cheese. "I doubt if food will make things better."

He lifted his broad male shoulder with an air of indifference. "Probably not. Food won't hurt though."

"What is you want to tell me now?" she asked stealing herself to keep her rolling emotions in check and her own hurtful words behind her teeth.

It would not do for her to grant him more power over her than he already wielded.

"Ask a question," he said quietly. "There is something important I need to ask you."

With no happiness in her voice coupled with the wounded feeling that went soul deep, "Go ahead."

She watched him carefully. It almost seemed he was reluctant to say anything; that he was fighting his own demons. Well, too bad, he could worry all night.

Placing her hand in his, gazing at her with a strange look in his amber eyes, "Are you a shifter?"

Startled, she gasped, pulling her hand back. "What?"

"Are you a shifter, Crissie? It's important you answer me truthfully." Once more her hand was in his.

She closed her eyes, willing a steadiness to her voice she knew didn't exist. He was so sincere, so all-knowing. What did he know? "I *dinna ken* what you're talking about."

"Don't lie to me about this," he spoke softly yet there was a hard edge in his voice. He was determined. She understood all too clearly he would keep on this until he was satisfied. "This is far too important for lies."

"I *dinna* lie," she persisted, knowing she couldn't reveal any knowledge to him.

That knowledge in the hands of the wrong person could be dangerous. Trusting him with the magnitude of this secret was impossible. The secret involved her entire family not just her.

"Yes, Crissie, you do."

"What is a shifter?"

His heavy sigh rattled already frayed nerves. It seemed he meant to humor her with a definition. "If you insist, a shifter is a man or woman who can change form."

She tried to widen her eyes in amazement. Tried for a look of astonishment. Knew she failed. When the frown lines deepened. "Something like that *dosenae* exist.*"

"We both know they do. So, tell me true. Are you a shifter?"

She looked away, fastening her gaze on the waterfall while thinking it would have been much more pleasant to make love behind the spray of water than continue the line of questioning she was on the receiving end of at the moment. She wasn't going to answer with another lie. Silence would have to be good enough for the man.

"Crissie?" He turned her so she was looking at him, lifted her chin until she had an unobstructed view of his heated amber gaze. "I know at least one of your brothers is a shifter. Brady, I saw him one day. He was careless. I saw him as a sleek black panther running without the benefit of cover. Watched him plunge into the loch then emerge as a man, a very naked man. He did that to hide the fact he shifted. He had no clothes nearby, nothing to wear. I gave him a shirt and trousers in my saddlebag before taking him to his clothing. After that I warned him to be more careful."

She was biting her lip, staring at him, tears filling her eyes. This was not supposed to happen. What would Walker do now? She answered him then, "No."

"No, what?" he queried, pushing her for more than she wanted to give. Always, he pushed her past what she felt were her limits.

"No, I'm not a shifter."

"Would you admit it if you were?" His question was hard, calculating even while his voice was soft. With the back of his hand, he caressed her cheek. "So soft, so very deceptive."

Tears running down her cheeks, she was shaking her head at him before trying to wipe away the moisture with the backs of her hands. "I'm not."

"So, you cannot make yourself into a cat? I'm heartily glad of that." He graced her with a tender smile. "I won't have to protect you from yourself."

It seemed he meant to believe her. She had no words, nothing to say. She wanted to understand what he meant to do with the information. He could have given her brother up when he was in the highlands. The clan all understood the English believed shifters lived there. Understood if one was caught, he or she would not be rescued. Most likely would be caged for the rest of their life.

"Is your other brother, Roby, a shifter?" He kept his voice soft, caring, wheedling as he always did with her. His hand circled her neck, his thumb rubbing gentle patterns there. He was coaxing her to his will, seducing her until her mind could not function. She didn't want this.

Anger flared against him, "You cannot possibly expect me to tell you something like that. Already, you know too much, so much that can put my family in jeopardy. You are going there, back to the highlands to hurt them, aren't you?" It seemed the realization hit her in the face. "Would you turn me in also? Is that your way of saving yourself of keeping me confined so I won't want to marry you?"

"Yes, I'm going to the highlands but not to catch and cage a shifter as you seem to think. I understood this conversation would not be easy. Comprehended too that you would jump to all the wrong conclusions before I could explain. Be patient and listen. Can you do that?"

She nodded just the briefest movement of her head, strands of her hair sliding across her shoulders. It must have been enough encouragement for Walker to continue. He picked up one of the pieces, rubbing the length between his fingers.

"I'm going there to dispel the myth, to keep your brothers and cousins safe while once again warning them to use more caution. Your father knows I'm coming. If they cannot keep their need to change form in order to run wild, they will be caught. If that happens there is nothing anyone or I could do about the situation to save them. I would also tell them there are places in America, untamed wild places they could go. They could run free as often as they wished without fear of being caught and caged."

"You are doing that to protect them?"

"*Aye.*"

"How can I believe you?"

"Trust," he told her.

She was shaking her head, more of her hair spilling form the bun on top of her head, strands sliding along her shoulders. Frustrated with her lack of power, she pushed them furiously from her eyes. "That's just it, Walker. I don't trust you. There is so much between us sometimes I feel chasms separate us, abysses so deep they cannot be crossed."

"You trust me with your body. You trust me with my son," he said softly leaning so close to her, his words whispered across her lips. He kissed her tenderly with so much gentleness she wanted to become part of him. He understood how easy she was. He took advantage every chance he got.

Unable to keep from shaking, she pushed away. "No, Walker, you can't solve all our problems with a kiss or even with a quick tumble."

She found that she was on her feet running from him, from the all too real threat he posed. All she wanted was to flee as far from him as she could go, run from the power and control he held over her. Just as she knew he would, he followed. He would catch her. They would kiss. She would let him do whatever he wanted with her body. After that she would tell him everything he asked.

She could not stop him. The only way she could end this was to leave. He would come after her. She would leave him again and again until he grew tired of following her. Until he didn't want her any longer. She knew that time would come, just as surely as he tired of his latest mistress replacing that woman with her.

Men were like that. They were until they found the one woman they could love forever. Obviously, for Walker, she wasn't that one woman. If she were, he would have ended his marriage by some means.

For now, she would give into his tender coaxing the delicious seduction of his lips. She would give him her body. When he left for London then the highlands, she would leave. She didn't know where she would go.

But she would leave.

~ * ~

Roby and Kit ran, exhilarating in the wild freedom, in the wind, the scent of the summer. They raced across the heather in the gloaming, the night sky darkening while stars were just beginning to twinkle in the sky. It was late almost midnight. A crescent moon cast more light on the two black panthers.

They knew and understood the dangers. His cousin Houston, Kit's older brother, had been caught in a steel trap while running as they were now, his foot mangled. That was several years ago. A young girl rescued him, released the trap. If not for her, Houston might be caged an exhibit for the Sassenach.

Even with that near escape in their heads, they both understood the risk. Felt alive because of the danger. Rumors abounded about the Sassenach searching for shifters. Unwilling to sacrifice freedom, they dismissed the tales as only rumors, in their minds relegating the gossip to just that. After all, the time was late and they were young. Immortal, Roby often thought. Sometime he believed he could live forever even though he knew better.

Roby looked at his cousin, meeting his gaze. Kit nodded then flashed a huge cat grin. He turned toward the rocky water tumbling down the crags, walked across the cascading liquid careful to stay on the rocks. When they reached the spot where the two young men had shed their clothing, they stopped. Roby understood this would be the last run in quite some time. Comprehended the caution that would be needed while Walker Endicott visited. Roby was on the verge of making a possible life changing decision. He hoped his cousin would go along with him. He wanted go to America.

Quickly, he felt the first tremors inside his body as his form changed. He shook his head, the sensations exciting. Giving this up would be harder than he could imagine. He wanted to find a land where he wasn't afraid to be himself. Where small-minded men who didn't understand different races didn't threaten him.

"Perhaps it's time to check out the land in America," Kit said as he slipped on his pants fastening them quickly. "I'm ready for a new adventure, tired of the ladies in our small village. If either of us is to find our mate, we'll have to venture farther than Edinburgh."

"*Aye*, I've had the same feelings. Seems you've read my mind. There is no one here for me. I *ken* it with each breath of air that enters my body. Yet I know if not here, somewhere my woman exists."

In less than a minute they were dressed. Silence coupled with deep thoughts seemed to swell around them, pounding in Roby's head. He was thinking of what he would have to do, of the words it would take to gain his father's compliance. In the end Connal could say no and still Roby would leave. He'd made up his mind.

"We can go anytime," Roby said, resigned to giving up his freedom here in the highlands if the Sassenach persisted in this conspiracy to rid the land of the shifters.

"What does Endicott want?" Kit asked giving him a sideways glance as they mounted.

"He says he just wants to talk. Don't know. It was a written message I wasn't able to read. Father kept it, tucked it into his pocket. Walker should be here anytime."

He did read it though. Walker's words of American were planted firmly in his head. They would sail out of Inverness hopefully before Walker arrived.

Roby was more worried about Crissie and how she was doing than being caught in his cat form. Walker Endicott was as ruthless as they came, hard-edged as well as tough. He took her, molded her to his will yet somehow it seemed he harbored a soft spot for Crissie. The look in the man's eyes when he walked out of the castle with his son a couple of months ago, a son he didn't know about; would have terrified him if he'd been in his sister's shoes.

What hell was she going through?

No one heard of a marriage between them. From time to time, he watched his father pace the battlements, looking out over the land they all loved. Roby knew his father's thoughts were focused on his daughter. At times, he found his mother crying softly in the solar. This was not a situation either one liked yet somehow Connal was unable to stop it or change the course.

Crissie would slowly die inside if she were forced to be Endicott's mistress.

"You're steeped in your thoughts," Kit said grinning. "Should we see if there's a willing lass or two at the tavern to lighten the night?"

Roby chuckled, understanding a good tumble was exactly what he needed to ease his dark mood. "It would keep my mind from brooding about my little sis and her problems. Talk of Endicott stirred those thoughts."

Chapter Six

London had changed little in the years Walker had been away. It was still dirty. The heat from the summer increased the smells wafting from the harbor taverns. The whores were out and about plying their trade. He didn't miss this. One purpose drove him here to see his father. That was to discuss the possibility of an annulment. His father would need to agree. Walker didn't think that feat would be too difficult in light of the truths he meant to tell him.

He had an heir. That would make Stephen happy. Perhaps he would even come to Ireland to meet his grandson. What he didn't understand is how no one knew what Charlotte was before their marriage, her preferences. He still wasn't sure anyone knew except for a handful of people. She must have been able to keep everything private. Either that or she didn't realize it herself until after the marriage and he tried to take her to bed.

His father would want him to stay for more than the three days he planned. Would want to visit White's, sit in on a card game or two, have a few drinks before he left. If he were to attain the annulment, he would have to attend to business before pleasure. He also wanted to see a friend of his, Hawk, before he left on government business. The two spent time in the army together, whored together, saved each other's life more than once. The man was still single as far as he knew.

All the way here, he thought of nothing but the look in Crissie's eyes when he asked her if she was a shifter. He couldn't rid himself of the deep-seated feeling that she might leave him. She didn't want to be considered his mistress even though that was not how he thought of her.

Bloody hell, but perhaps he should have taken her with him. She would be here, by his side. He wouldn't have to search for her when he returned home. He understood to some extent her feelings. She wanted to be his wife, legitimately his, just as her son was his now.

In his mind she was.

Not in hers.

Every gift he brought her she frowned, grudgingly accepting then setting it in a pile by the window seat. It was as if by not acknowledging the gifts, he hadn't really given them to her. He would marry her just as soon as he could arrange it. He didn't tell her though, just in case he couldn't get the papers. He didn't want to get her hopes up.

He talked to Charlotte in length about his plans. She didn't like what he proposed, craving to keep the status quo. She liked to be known as Walker Endicott's wife. Enjoyed the title that went with it. When he spoke with Charlotte, her mouth turned downward in a frown. If he followed through, her secret predilections would become much more obvious. People would take more than a sideways glance at the women who visited. As if she could stay his mind from his plan, Charlotte threatened him with his secret. She couldn't prove anything though. It would be her word against his.

This annulment was a necessity because he wanted Crissie to be happy, to feel cherished. He also wanted all his heirs to be legitimate. Ian was, only because of the paperwork.

When he reigned in at the Endicott townhouse on St. James Street, he swallowed a huge gulp of air, his nerves slightly on edge at the prospect of the coming discussion. He thought of the words he wanted to use to explain things to his father. There was simply no way to say the words without exposing Charlotte. She told him it wasn't well done of him to ruin her life.

Well, he could toss that statement back to her. It wasn't well done of her to ruin his life. He cared deeply for Crissie. Hadn't told her so. Couldn't until he could make her his wife. She accepted him on blind faith. He hoped that was about to end.

Before he could knock on the door, the aging butler opened it.

"Charles, you're looking spry."

"Lord Endicott, welcome home. Your father is waiting in the library to see you," Charles said, his smile wide. "He's eager to hear words of his grandson. We're not getting younger, you know. It is about time you settled down and did your duty as an Endicott."

"Well, I'm eager to tell him just how bright and handsome Ian is. Takes after his father you know," Walker said chuckling as he rid himself of his hat and coat.

"Yes, and that's a truth one cannot be kept hidden. He would have been more pleased if you brought the lad with you however," Charles said. "I would have liked it as well."

"You've always been an old softy." Walker headed for the library suddenly very eager to get this conversation out of the way. There was more than one important item to discuss this evening.

He didn't know yet if Ian was a shifter, but he was pretty sure the lad was. Already he saw the slight signs marking his body. He was surprised Crissie hadn't noticed the subtle tiger stripes on him as well. Still, most times, except the one time they made love at the waterfall, the room had been dark with only meager candlelight.

Even though he pried the truth from her about her abilities, he wasn't ready to tell her this one last secret of his. She wouldn't care but she would wonder about Ian. Since she wasn't a shifter, there was a chance Ian would not be. Ah, but once he told Crissie he was a shifter, he could mark her as his. Even if the annulment did not go through, she would be his through eternity.

My woman.

No one else would touch her.

He would legitimately claim her. When he did, she would understand the significance.

When he walked through the door, his father rose from his chair. Stephen held his arms wide in anticipation of a hug. They embraced. He stepped back looking at him from head to toe.

"Fatherhood agrees with you," Stephen said laughing before looking around the room. "You didn't bring the boy."

"Pretty rough journey for a four-month-old infant. I prefer to keep him safe and sound at home."

Walker poured himself a drink then sat on a brocade chair facing his father. For a few seconds he swirled the amber liquid in his glass, thinking of his life, all that he found when Crissie ran after him that day over a year ago. He might not have returned to the highlands. Hell, he would have. Deep inside he would have had to see her again, at least to discover if his feeling for her were real.

"You don't know all the motives for this visit. We've a great deal to discuss and I've important things to tell you as well."

"I can guess. You want to find a way to wed the Scottish lady who gave you your heir." Stephen was frowning while he drummed his fingers on the chair. His eyes were hard when he searched Walker for an answer.

"I do."

"I'm not going to agree to a divorce," Stephen said. "You made the commitment, vowed until death do you part."

"No, I didn't think you would. I'm not seeking a divorce just an annulment."

His breath caught in his throat now that he finally verbalized his intentions to someone other than Charlotte.

"You've been married ten years. The church won't look favorably on that. Could take years. What makes you think your request would be considered as anything but amusing?" Stephen asked. "We both thought she was your mate. The two of you were always close when you were children."

Walker recognized the fleeting look of pain on his father's chiseled features, his jaw set hard against what he was hearing.

"Not after I present the facts," Walker said finishing his drink. He didn't want to hurt Charlotte by making the reasons public. Didn't see another choice. "Christ, father," he began wishing he didn't have to give him the facts, didn't have to tell him that Charlotte only wanted to wed him to have a cover for her real sentiments. "We've never slept together. Not even on our wedding night. That evening she made it perfectly clear to me she didn't want to lie with me or any man for that matter."

He strode to the window. Looked down on the street. It was nearing evening. There never was very much traffic in this area of town. Not unless someone was having a gala affair. He enjoyed the quiet peace. Enjoyed his country home in Ireland even more. Crissie would be there now, coping with her identity and how she meant to carry on with her life. He slammed his fist against the windowsill. Damn, but he should have brought her. His gut turned over. It was almost as if he could see her packing up her belongings and leaving him.

She was gone. He knew it in the deepest darkest part of his soul.

"I thought you loved her," Stephen's voice was shaking, as it seemed he began to understand what Walker was trying to say. "I didn't realize..." his voice died away as he began to comprehend what he condemned his son to when he signed the betrothal contract so many years ago.

Turning, Walker rested a shoulder against the wall, watching, waiting. By the look in Stephen's eyes, it told him he understood the depth of the distance between Walker and Charlotte. Then the same tawny eyes as his own showed a hint of something else. Perhaps pity, Walker couldn't be sure. Pity was not an emotion he intended to deal with.

He poured himself another drink, one for his father as well while he thought on his feelings for Charlotte. "As a sister, I guess I do love her. I only agreed to marry Charlotte because of the betrothal contract. Didn't want to dishonor you. Also didn't believe in love. Not sure I do now. What I do believe in is the intense feelings I have for Crissie. If not for that piece of paper, a union between Charlotte and myself never would have happened.

"So, you plan to tell the church Charlotte sleeps with women. Her life will be ruined. She will be ostracized, cast from the church as well."

Pushing away from the wall, he moved restlessly through the room. "I'm aware of that." He spun on a heel, "Before I met Crissie I didn't care. I could have gone on for more years than I could count. Now, I don't want my life ruined. I found my mate. Crissie is my woman, the only one for me. Have to do something to make this insipid situation right before it blows itself apart."

Before she leaves me for good.

His father seemed to absorb every word, coming to his own conclusions. "I won't stand in your way if you're sure. There will be repercussions for everyone. It might well be more than a year before you can wed the McKenna lass."

"Never more sure about this." Relief coursed through him, joyous waves ebbed and flowed through his soul. One dark nearly insurmountable hurdle was just overcome now for the one he'd been putting off. Telling Crissie about his ability to shift would not be terribly difficult. He just needed the right time.

"I trust you've told your future wife you're a shifter." Stephen's tawny amber eyes seemed to pierce through him, probing for the truth, reading his mind.

"Not yet."

"She might take exception to the fact you're able to become a huge sleek tiger," Stephen laughed. "Tell her next time you see her."

Walker found a bit of amusement in his father's words. He flashed a huge smile, laughing. "The only exception she might take is that I'm not a black panther."

He saw the question in his father's eyes then another flash of understanding. "She's a shifter?" he asked as he arched a golden eyebrow skyward.

"No, at least she told me she isn't. I believe her. Many of her family are shifters."

"Black panthers? Well then she will have preconceived ideas but she won't believe you to be a freak of nature or mankind." Stephen questioned, a chuckle of his own. "Your son?"

"I believe so."

"And she won't be terribly shocked when she discovers the truth about her son."

"Probably not and while we stand here discussing that fact, I'm thinking of how I might show her who exactly I am. The possibilities are endless."

He grinned as his mind held a wealth of ideas. Yes, he would have to consider all the different scenarios. More than anything he wanted to surprise her with the truth, look into her eyes when she sees his tiger.

~ * ~

The days he spent in London were productive. He obtained the dispensation for the annulment. Hopefully, since all was taken care of away from Belfast, Charlotte would not feel the hurt and disdain cast upon her from those in the area. At least he hoped that would be the case.

Now he was headed to the highlands, his military purpose detailed in great depths. He was to find proof there were indeed shifters in the vicinity. He was encouraged to catch one, cage the animal, and bring it back to London. To avoid this all he needed to do was to convince the McKenna's to stop their midnight activities as well as some of their daily activities that would put the entire clan in danger.

Walker traveled quickly. He stopped only for short bouts of sleep, as he needed to get back to Ireland so he could undo whatever Crissie impulsively decided to put in motion. In a little less than a week he was on McKenna land.

He stopped in the same spot as he had two months ago before he rode down to the castle. He remembered that day as if it happened yesterday. So clearly, he recalled the depth of his emotions when he discovered he had a son, the joy, the fear, the excitement. On the other end of the spectrum, he'd never felt so helpless in his life when he first held Ian. He never suffered such rage when he realized she did not tell him of his son.

Now, all this time later, he knew his father withheld the letters. He should have confronted Stephen during this visit. It was just one too many things for him to deal with. He wanted to forget simply because it was in the past. Now, he craved living to the fullest, living with Crissie and their son. God willing, they would have another child.

Walker urged his horse forward. He entered the castle walls, handed the reins to a stable hand. When he walked into the main hall, he saw Connal and Wynnie sitting near the fire. She was sewing something.

He was sitting back, relaxed, watching her with hooded eyes. Walker knew that expression. Understood by the way his eyes seemed to darken and simmer that the man loved his wife

When Connal saw who was there, he rose. Motioned him to come over then found a maid to bring him a glass of ale along with a plate of food. Roby and Brady were nowhere to be found. Perhaps that was for the best. Questions about Crissie would be at the forefront of their minds. They would want to know if they wed.

So would Wynnie and Connal.

He'd told them before he left with Crissie he had a wife. Now he could tell them he obtained an annulment and meant to wed her as soon as she would agree. For some reason he wasn't sure of, he thought Connal might understand a little better than the brothers what they went through and would be happy for them. Connal might not be quite so ready to take him to task. After all, Connal allowed him to walk out of the castle with Ian and Crissie.

"Where is Crissie?" Wynnie asked, hurt shining clearly in her clear blue eyes. "Since you were coming you should have brought her with you."

"At home in Ireland. The trip was too long to take with the baby. We will come next summer. I promise."

His excuse was bland, held no substance. He should have brought them.

"So, why are you here? I'm sure it's not a social call," Wynnie asked obviously displeased with him then accusatory as well. "Have you wed my only daughter yet?"

He cleared his throat. His gaze passed between Connal and Wynnie. Standing in front of parents was new to him. It wasn't pleasant, he decided. Yet if he had a daughter, he would certainly want answers. "No, not yet. I couldn't at the time. As you know, there were complications." Before anyone could ask another question, he blurted, "You both recall I was already married."

"You were dallying with my daughter as a married man." Connal's voice rose in anger, his eyes darkening more so with the growing rage. It didn't seem forgiveness was possible.

"Hush," Wynnie said as she looked around the room. She placed a gentling hand on his leg. "We don't want anyone within shouting distance to hear you. This is private. Think of Crissie's feelings."

"Yes, but that will change." His hands ran roughly through his hair. "For reasons I don't truly want to go into here, I've asked for an annulment of my marriage. Received one. I'm no longer wed. So, I'm asking you for your daughter's hand in marriage."

"If I said no, you would still wed her." Connal's voice was hard still tipped with anger it didn't seem he could control.

It wasn't a question. Walker was sure Connal knew the answer before he asked. "Crissie is the mother of my son. She is mine." He almost told Connal she was his mate. It was too soon to divulge that information.

"That goes without saying."

Walker knew he wanted to ask if she'd been in his bed since they left here but he understood it wasn't his business, that the fact was between Crissie and himself. In any case he would never comment.

"I would only tell you *aye* if Crissie is willing."

"I believe she is," Walker said, hoping that by the time he returned she would still be where he left her.

He would wait for the perfect moment to ask. He wasn't about to rush in and propose. Creating a little romance between them might soothe any battered feelings.

Connal cleared his throat then stood. We should go to my private solar. Should have gone there before we began this discussion. I *ken* there is more for the two of us to speak of. You alluded to as much in the message you sent. They walked through the castle before heading up the stairs.

"What is the business you wrote about?" Wynnie asked as she lifted her skirts in order to keep pace with the longer strides of the two men.

"Brady and Roby should be here also."

If they weren't, Walker supposed he could live with that. Impressing Connal of the ever-present danger would be the most important person to convince.

"Roby is gone for a while. Brady doesn't live here. He chose not to come. It seems one of my sons along with his cousin took your advice," Connal said dryly.

Once more Walker sensed the older man's disapproval. "My advice?" he asked not remembering speaking with them or writing to them.

"Yes," Connal said blandly as if he didn't want to give away what he was really thinking. "The two got on a ship bound for Virginia despite my disapproval. Seems the randy pair wanted an adventure thinking they could do as they pleased there. Wasn't that your intention? Send them away so they wouldn't find trouble here?"

Walker smiled for the first time since entering the walls that held the bulk of the McKenna clan. That was one way to put it. He supposed he should own up to the suggestion, but it must have been Connal who gave them permission to read a private missive.

"Thought our correspondence was private."

"Thought it was too," Connal mumbled. "Sometimes my sons have different opinions on what is private and what is not. Brady read it then passed the advice on to Roby who was more than eager to disappear for a time."

"I suppose I should get down to the reasons I'm here. I insisted that I be the one to handle the investigation."

Walker studied the bland features of Connal McKenna. He didn't give anything away, no emotions. Now that the discussion changed away from his daughter, his features were honed from years of authority.

"Because you can be so objective?"

"More so than most of the English who simply want to rub the Scots into the dirt for whatever reason. I volunteered. Crissie and coupled with my son give me a vested interest in your family. I wouldn't want to see anything happen to any of you. It would devastate her."

Connal leaned back, crossing his arms in front of his chest. His eyes were hard as he breathed in all that Walker spoke of. The Laird would evaluate wisely. He would make his edict known to those who were affected by what Walker would set forth.

"I mean to make this as easy as possible for all those involved. I know that you and some of your family are shifters. Brady and Roby are shifters. With Brady I know first-hand. I saw him shift. Crissie has told me she is not. It is up to you to confirm Crissie's word."

Walker understood this would be another reason for Connal to doubt him along with his feelings for his daughter. He had to know for sure, had to be able to make the correct judgments where she was concerned. He didn't like surprises, not when the knowledge involved a life. Walker studied the ever-changing emotions on Connal's face.

"Crissie is not a shifter." He spoke quietly, a father's tenderness echoed in his voice.

"Would you tell me if she was? I posed the same question to your daughter. She told me no. Then tried to encourage me to believe her statement that she was not."

A hint of a smile formed on Connal's lips.

Wynnie's face turned white.

Connal cleared his throat. "No, I would not tell you. If my daughter wants your trust, then I suppose it is best she wins it. Much to my disappointment though, Crissie cannot change form."

"I will proceed in that vein. However, I'll not be pleased if this is proven false. Now, what the government wants is confirmation instead of rumors that shapeshifters abound in these hills. They have ordered me to bring them a black panther. If none exist well then, I cannot do as I've been ordered. If there is one out and about during my stay, I'll be obliged to capture the person. I trust that you will make sure your people are informed of my intentions."

While Walker spoke, Connal's expression was growing more and more grim. "I will do as you say. I cannot, however, oversee every person here. There are children as well as young men who have the common sense of an ant."

"It will be up to the parents to make sure they behave, a week only. There are no guarantees that someone else might return when I've failed. I do intend to fail and I hope you will help me in this."

Walker stood, not wishing to carry on further conversation with the McKenna.

"I will do my part."

"Then I'll see you at the end of the week. I've lodgings in the village."

"You could stay here."

Walker laughed softly. "No, that would not be wise."

When he reached his room above the small tavern, he flopped on the bed, his arm covering his eyes.

Crissie, where the hell are you?

~ * ~

Walker was gone less than a day when Charlotte made her presence known in the manor. Without preamble she moved herself into the master suite of rooms. Crissie found her trunk deposited in a third story room meant for servants.

Yes, Walker there is absolutely no reason why Charlotte and I cannot be friends. I will like her.

Hah!

Well, none of that was going to happen. She didn't even want to talk to the woman. Crissie pulled in a deep breath of air as she strode with purpose to see Rose. She carried Ian. She set him on a rug to play while she sat down.

Rose looked at her with an uplifted eyebrow. "You and the wife don't get along I take it."

"Would you like her? She's made it perfectly clear to me I'm not welcome here. It doesn't take a mind reader to understand she wants me as far away from this house as I can get. While she moved in here, she also told me not to dare take up residence in the cottage, Rose." She puffed a strand of hair from her face. "I'm leaving. No, you cannot talk me out of it. You can follow or not. The decision is up to you, but I would like it if you chose to come with me."

Rose chuckled softly. "I wouldn't dream of trying to change your mind. We both *ken* Walker will come after you. It is his way since you will have his son. He will haul you back here then set things to right. Charlotte will be living in the cottage again. You and Walker will occupy his rooms."

"She told me they wanted to renew their vows. Would do so when he returned, which is why she moved me out. She was wearing one of the gifts Walker gave me." She thought that incensed her more than most everything else even though she didn't want the gifts. Had told Walker too many times to count.

"You believe that bunch of nonsense?" Rose asked as she poured them both a cup of tea. She handed one to Crissie before she sat down.

Crissie wasn't sure how to respond. Didn't know what Rose knew about Charlotte. There wasn't a lot she could talk about unless Rose understood the woman would never be Walker's wife in every way.

"I know about her, dear. There isn't anyone in a close radius that does not. She doesn't keep her dalliances secret, at least her lovers are never short on words."

Depression and darkness filled Crissie. She needed to get away from this house. "I just don't know where to go."

"How fast do you want Walker to find you when you leave?" Rose asked as she added a touch of lemon and cream to her tea.

"I don't care. No, I do care. I want it to take him as long as possible." Agitated, she rose, swirling around the room, her breath ragged as she gulped in the air while her eyes brimmed with tears. "I don't want to leave at all," she spoke in a strangled whisper.

"Now, dear, we both understand eventually all will be fine. I've a boarding house in Portrush. We can stay there. He will most likely look there first for you and your son. At least you will have gotten your point across. You will have some time to breathe fresh air while you are able to truly figure out what it is you want. Perhaps you don't love Walker. Maybe you can be content to visit your son instead of live with him as you watch him grow up."

Crissie felt blinded by the sensations swirling around her assuming a death grip on her life. She was ripe with fears coupled with confusion. Sometimes she didn't believe she knew her mind. She certainly could make few guesses about what Walker would do, unless of course it concerned their son.

"I've no money," Crissie set her lips in a firm determined line.

"Come now. That makes no difference to me. I've three rooms on the first floor. You and Ian can each take one. I'll have the other. My borders occupy the second floor while the limited staff I employ either sleep on the third floor or live in their homes in town." She leaned forward, patting Crissie's hand. "This will work out. I promise you."

"Can we leave tomorrow? Don't believe I can last another day with Charlotte waltzing around the house looking down her pert nose at me. She knows I'm nothing more than her husband's mistress even though Ian is his heir."

Just thinking about Charlotte made her head spin. Dizzy, she sat. When she looked at Rose, she read the pity in the older lady's eyes. She didn't want pity as she understood exactly what it was she was doing. She was running away from a man who didn't love her, could never love her. If he did love her, under the circumstances of a failed marriage he would have remedied the situation.

"As soon as our trunks are packed, we can leave," Rose said softly. "I wish you would change your mind, but I also *ken* how you cannot."

"I never unpacked mine. Can we use Walker's carriage?" she asked realizing if they used the carriage, they would also be using his driver. "No, I suppose not. What does it cost to hire one to Portrush? I only have a few coins unless I sell that necklace he gave me." Then she remembered it wasn't hers to sell because she tossed it away.

"Don't worry about the money. I'll pay for everything. Besides, when Walker does come for you, he'll reimburse me. Everything will be fine, dear. You'll be happy again."

Crissie wished Rose would stop telling her that everything would be fine. It wasn't ever going to be fine. As for happy, it had been a very long time since she could remember truly feeling that emotion. Unfortunately, all the recent memories of happiness or even contentment revolved around Walker and Ian of course.

Nothing would ever be fine.

"Well, then I suppose I should go pack my trunk. We can be off for a new adventure first thing in the morning. Ian will love to see the ocean." She stopped a moment for a breath of air. "We will have to hire Walker's carriage to take us to the posting house. After that he can probably inquire about the destinations for each carriage. I'm sorry, dear, but we won't be terribly hard to find."

"If he even wants to find us. Perhaps he did tell Charlotte they would renew their vows when he returned. Maybe she promised him that she would sleep with him." Crissie tried to clear the tears away that were clogging her throat.

What Walker didn't realize was that Charlotte was an evil thinking person. She wasn't very nice.

"He won't. Charlotte is as a sister to him, nothing more. They grew up together although Charlotte has proved to be possessive where Walker is concerned." Once more Rose tried to reassure and ended up failing miserably.

Crissie didn't think she would ever feel confident in her relationship with Walker. "I just can't bear to wait for Walker here in this house. When he comes for me in Portrush and we return, Charlotte won't be in the manor. She'll be back in her cottage."

The night seemed to drag by. The seconds and minutes that she counted while she lay wide-eyed in bed left her remembering the way his hands stroked her, explored every inch. Easily she recalled the sweet taste of him, his masculine scent part spicy coupled with musk. He was both gentle and hard. He gave her so much pleasure. The thought of doing without that for the rest of her life was not something she wanted to think about.

She had never known anyone like Walker. She could only guess what life would be like if he chose not to come for her. Distressed as well as uncomfortable with her twisting thoughts she rolled over only to find the position was not any more soothing than the one she'd been in before. She missed his heat as well as his kisses coupled with the hard angles and planes of his body.

Finally, the dawn began to break. A few rays of sunlight slanted across the bed. She opened her eyes ready for the beginning of a new day. Sitting up she yawned then stretched. She would be glad to be away from this lonely place. Quickly dressing, she brought Ian to the first floor with her where the trunks were waiting. Rose already called for the carriage. It sat outside the front door ready to travel down the long lane toward the main road.

Crissie hoped this was too early for Charlotte to be up and about. She didn't want a confrontation with the woman. Didn't need to see the gloating look on the woman's face when she realized she had chased her from the home. What Charlotte didn't know was that she most likely was going to be gone for only a short time. Walker told her a month or so.

Luck wasn't with her.

"Where do you think you are going?" Charlotte asked, a snide smile on her face, her brown eyes flashing her victory. She was standing by the foot of the staircase, her hands on her hips.

"An extended vacation," Crissie said softly turning away from her before she could say anything damning. Just seeing Charlotte made her heart thump with dread.

Charlotte waved her hands in the air. "Well, no need to hurry back. Walker won't miss you one bit when he comes home. Walker will have me by his side. He will be pleasantly surprised he doesn't have to find a new home for you as well as a new protector."

Crissie bit her tongue trying desperately to keep her mouth shut. With her arms, she jiggled Ian who was beginning to get restless. He looked as if the last thing he wanted was to go on another journey somewhere.

She wasn't about to say anything more.

The trip to Portrush was as uneventful as it could be. They changed horses several times. Ate lunch in a rural inn half way to their destination. Crissie was pleased they were the only travelers. She was able to feed Ian without the embarrassment of trying to hide herself from another person while Ian suckled. She remembered when Walker uncovered her that first time. He didn't want his son smothering while he was eating. Remembered the way her milk let down, drenching her, giving her condition away to the man who irrevocably changed her life.

Well, if you recall the way you gave yourself to the man, he permanently changed your life long before that day, about nine months before.

Once in the city, they hailed a cab to take them to the boarding house where it sat overlooking the ocean. Today the waves were calm gently lapping at the beach. Seagulls swept over the ocean and across the land crying out plaintively. Farther out to sea fishing boats bobbed, rising up and down with the swells.

No, this was not a place that would take Walker long to find her. With Rose beside her, Walker could follow the path straight to her door. He said he'd be gone about a month. Well, less than that. A week was gone of that time. Ian would be five months old when Walker returned. The baby changed constantly. Every day he could do something new and different. His laugh was a small coo of delight when he saw something he liked. He was trying to say words. Ian would be the eleventh earl of Briarwood.

His honey gold eyes reminded her of Ian's father. His hair, the way his mouth turned up crookedly on one side when he smiled as well as the one dimple he possessed.

Ian was a perfect replica of his father.

Crissie hummed while she sorted through their clothes in the room Rose gave her. It was the largest of the three. Rose told her it was hers for when Walker came to bring her home. He might stay a few nights before they returned to the manor. Besides, Rose also said she was used to rooms that were a bit more comfy.

Ian's room was the smallest but it adjoined hers with a single door between them. This would be a nice place to wait as well as think about her life and what was to become of her as Walker's mistress. This month might well be the only serene month for her in a very long time.

She walked on the beach most days. Helped with the cleaning when the maids had a day off. She learned to cook a few dishes that Rose liked best. She found she enjoyed the kitchen. At other time she sewed new garments for Ian. He was growing so fast it seemed he outgrew his clothes within a week after they were made.

As the month quickly came to an end, she grew more and more restless. He would be here soon to claim his son. He wondered if he would even give her a choice to stay or go with him as he did in the highlands. He might want to be rid of her.

The month passed by, another week was slowly coming to an end. Restless energy consumed her as she took to pacing the small drawing room. Storm clouds gathered on the horizon. Best she get her walk this evening before the rain started.

"I'm going outside for a quick stroll," she called out to Rose.

"Take a rain jacket. Looks as if a storm is brewing,"

Yes, there was more than one storm brewing, one outside as well as one inside her. She slipped the cloak on before heading to the beach. The trail along the harbor stretched ahead of her. She rubbed her arms willing the sudden chill swirling inside her to go away. As the wind picked up, she felt Walker's presence. Her heart skipped a beat.

She turned quickly. No one was behind her. Yet, he was here, somewhere. She just couldn't see him yet. Unwilling to return, she picked up her pace, sidestepping stones and driftwood, trying to find the hardest packed sand. A few drops began to fall. The storm would be here and she would be caught in the midst of it. The tempest would be good for her. Perhaps she would soar with the wind. Maybe some of the helplessness she felt since Walker whisked her away from her home in the highlands would be expelled. When the storm ended, she might be cleansed of the fear of her future. Premonitions were not something she had often.

This terror she felt suddenly came from deep in her heart.

Unknowing when the culmination of their relationship would come, she had to move on. The fine watery spray of minutes ago turned to heavy fat drops. Waves rushed the beach, foaming mist rising off the tops of the breakers pounding beside her. She skipped away from a wave rushing toward her to bury her feet. The tide was coming in.

"You foolish woman. What are you doing outside in this weather?"

Pulling her hood up to cover her head, she turned slowly trying to regain the air that just rushed headlong from her lungs as well as steady herself. At the sound of his voice her knees threatened to give way.

He was here. Walker was standing in front of her appearing far more handsome and male than she remembered.

"Waiting for you to come for me and out son," she told him, her voice breathy the sound whisked away in the brewing tempest.

His eyes simmered with passion or anger. She never knew. His tawny hair had grown curling around his shoulders. The wind lifted and parted it while the rain flattened it against his head.

"You know why I'm here." He reached out to touch her tenderly with the backs of his fingers.

"To collect Ian."

"And you. If you want to come home with me."

"You're still giving me a choice?" she asked, watching the way he moved so easily as they walked.

The harsh wind seemed a spring breeze against him while she was bent over trying to push through the gusts.

"Always, little pigeon."

His strong arm wrapped around her as he pulled her into his body protecting her from the brunt of the storm. He stopped.

She found she was looking up into those simmering eyes. Anger wasn't the emotion she saw. Passion blazed from those incredible amber eyes lightly touched with honey. They were clear and firm as they bore into her, questioning silently.

He understood what was essential for her.

Because Ian would go with him, so would she.

The kiss was gentle yet strong, his hands easily holding her to the hard wall of his chest. All she wanted was to feel him, test the days' worth of stubble on his chin. He lowered his head until his mouth fit perfectly over hers. With slow gentle movements of his tongue, he melted her lips until they flowed apart beneath him.

The tiny serrations of her teeth fascinated him. He traced their edges over and over again before he allowed himself to taste the moist sweetness of her mouth. Just one taste, a single delicate touch of his tongue against hers.

The tremor that passed through Crissie was echoed deep in Walker's body, blood pooling hotly, hard flesh pressing against her belly demanding release. She understood all too well what he craved.

Once more Walker's tongue returned, slowly learning the honeyed texture of Crissie's mouth. Her hands on his back beneath his rain slicker tightened, urging Walker closer in silent invitation.

As the tempo of the storm increased so did the heat of his touch. His tongue returned, moistened with the drops of rain, water sluicing down their faces. When she followed his lead, she was rewarded with the velvet textures of Walker's mouth. Her tongue answered the teasing pressures of his, meeting retreat with boldness coupled with the wild abandon she always felt when he stroked her. He responded with a gliding, satin caress that drew tiny ripples from deep in her throat.

The kiss lasted until her heart was a madness shaking her. With no more coaxing, her mouth opened deeply to the pressure of Walker's against hers. Theirs was a dance, played in the tempest of the night coupled with the enchantment of what might come after. Even then the kiss continued, filling her softness and moist warmth with his taste, making her quiver with each ribbon of ecstasy swirling through her.

Despite the chill of the night the palms of Walker's hands were hot as they moved from her cheeks to her shoulders then along her arms to her fingertips. He threaded his hands through hers gently unwrapping her arms from around his waist.

Walker's fingers slid between Crissie's slowly, rhythmically, stroking the burning, sensitive skin, his thumbs massaging gentle circles on her wrists. His hands moved with ravishing seduction along the inner softness of her arms. The caress was as unbroken as the kiss, Walker filling her senses until she shuddered and drank his presence, wordlessly telling him of the pleasure surging inside her, ecstasy he had brought to her when she expected recriminations. Had expected commands. Had thought to be reminded of her promise to him to stay where he left her. After she left him, she had never been sure this time he would want her back.

The kiss deepened even more as Walker's palms slid over her skin. The sensitive flesh he freed from her gown the buttons causing just a touch of inconvenience. She ached to have his finger slide beneath the fabric and discover the softness of her flesh.

His hands continued a path of his choosing, sliding up to her ribs, now brushing the swell of her breasts across puckered nipples. His caress lingered there, learning the satin curves, coaxing her nipples into a tightness that ignited her as she heard her own ragged moan ripple in languorous waves of delight.

Only then did Walker release her mouth. His lips moved with slow heat across the taut skin of her neck.

Head tipped back, eyes closed, Crissie abandoned herself to the marvelous sensations Walker's caressing mouth and hand drew from her. His mouth slid with delicate care across the hollow of her throat, lingering long enough for his tongue and lips to sip the rainwater off her flesh. Primitive elements of the impressive tempest echoed what she felt inside. Thunder bombed above and around her while lightening slashed the sky lending silver light far out to sea.

When his mouth drifted over the curve of her breast then closed with melting gentleness over her nipple, Crissie shuddered and arched into the caress unselfconsciously, knowing only the delight Walker gave her binding her to him as thoroughly as he could. His teeth rasped lightly over the outline of her nipple beneath the smooth fabric of her gown. Rippling purrs of satisfaction vibrated deep in the back of her throat, telling him of her pleasure.

The sound seemed to tear at Walker's control. Her pain and pleasure combined to send a primal growl of male hunger into the night that delighted Crissie. Blindly Walker's fingers pulled at the remaining buttons holding the gown away from further exploration. Slowly, he let the fabric slide down her shoulder then from her arms. The rain slicker did little to keep the water from her or him. Yet it didn't seem either of them could stop what overcame them when they met.

Crissie sucked in a deep breath of air, holding it, craving nothing more than to feel the hot molten touch of Walker's tongue on her naked breasts. She realized what she was thinking and froze in surprise at the abandonment that Walker's touch called from her. In Walker's arm she never failed to act unrestrained as she gave everything of herself to the man.

She had meant to leave him, would when she could distance herself from this, from his lovemaking and from the fact she loved this man with all her heart. Rose told her she would have to come to terms with her feelings. Crissie didn't know if she could do that.

Not now.

Possibly not ever.

Walker seemed to sense the change in Crissie. She didn't want him to stop even though he held himself away from her.

"Walker?" Crissie asked, her voice soft, ragged. Waves of longing took Crissie by surprise. She leaned against him, shivering. "You make me weak."

"Wrap your legs around me."

"What?"

"Just do it," he told her.

When she did, he carried her across the sodden earth to what seemed to be the only tree. He set her back against it still kissing her. His lips pressed gently against hers.

Lightening streaked. Wind howled. Blue-white light coated the sky. She shivered. His lips moved over her face, caressing all the curves and hollows that he had already made his own. When his mouth brushed over hers, Crissie moaned then threaded her fingers into his thick tawny mane of hair that was now dripping wet. Her lips opened, craving him, needing him, hungry for the sensual excitement of his mouth coupled with the delicious feelings swamping her.

Walker's tongue slid between Crissie's teeth, thrusting slowly across her tongue retreating, thrusting again, inciting her with the primal rhythms of love. Her arms tightened around him, pressing her breasts closer. Her hard nipples swayed across his chest as she twisted and arched in his arms.

Sensual fire thundered through Crissie, causing her to whimper into the heat of his mouth. His arms tightened around her waist shifting her as he unfastened his trousers. She felt his arousal, hard as steel between her legs then at the juncture of her thighs.

When his hands returned from unfastening his pants, his fingertips caressed the smoothness of her inner legs. Gently, he stoked the liquid heat hidden in the most secret depths of her.

Eyes closed Crissie felt herself come undone all over again. Slow, liquid rhythms uncoiled deep in her core. She quivered, trembling as she melted over Walker, knowing only his touch and intense pleasure shimmering, gathering in her, longing to erupt in more ecstasy.

With exquisite care, Walker settled her on his hard arousal. Crissie kissed his chin as well as the powerful muscle of his neck. She felt the quiver of his response. She moved her mouth across the opening of his shirt, caressing him with her lips and teeth and tongue, glorying in the throttled growl that she felt as much as she heard.

Only then did Walker claim Crissie's mouth again. Filling her with a kiss so deep that she could merely cling to him, melting again, shaping herself to the hard male lines of his body as he pushed farther inside so deep, she ached with the raw, hungry pleasure.

By the time Walker ended the kiss, Crissie was making small sounds in her throat with each swift, shallow breath that she inhaled. When his lips left hers, she protested with a word that became a cry of intense, unexpected pleasure when his tongue circled the tip of her breast.

Tenderly he raked his teeth over Crissie as she arched against him, trembling while trying to bring his arousal deeper inside. He groaned, suckling her deeply while he held her hips as still as he could seeming to want to prolong this. She ached for him, for the mercuric culmination of what they began in the tempest that surrounded them. The storm had become as much a part of them as it was external. When his fingers found her liquid secrets then the hard satin knot, she cried out in rapture.

For long moments Walker caressed Crissie, drinking each soft cry, each hot shivering of her tender flesh.

Walker's fingers traced each petal softness, each curve and hollow of Crissie's passion until she was twisting in slow motion, her hips blindly seeking his begging him for more and more. Very gently he deepened the caress.

She shuddered and melted and clung to his touch, lost in the sweetness and intense excitement his caress called from her. He bent over her, drank her cries with ravenous lips as he slowly stroked her.

Crissie's soft mew of pleasure rippled from the back of her throat as muscles deep inside her body tensed, wildness gathering and melting through her in shimmering cataclysmic waves. Walker watched her with the hot molten desire she always saw in his eyes. She tried to say his name but could not form the word. Walker had stolen the ability to speak from her lips.

Chapter Seven

With a nearly soundless groan of pleasure, Walker opened his lips and drank deeply of the wild sweetness that waited for him in Crissie's' mouth. For a long time, he knew nothing but her taste and the supple heat of her body moving against his.

The hunger Walker kept savagely leashed threatened to explode, tearing him apart. His arms closed tightly around her, stilling the sensual motions of her body against his.

"You won't ever leave me again," Walker said, his voice harsh with the cost of subduing his elemental hunger.

He needed her promise even though he understood she might not keep it.

Crissie looked up at him. The smile on her lips was as old as Eve.

"If you don't give me reason to leave, I won't," Crissie said, her voice softly ragged against the heat of his mouth.

He saw the pain in her eyes with those words, understood what she was silently asking. His breath shuddered out of him in a long-ragged sigh. He wasn't going to give her a reason. He'd done everything he could to make her happy. Inside his valise was the dispensation granting him an annulment. He informed Charlotte when he arrived. Had to help her find a place to live if she didn't choose to go back to her father. He didn't want any more complications getting in the way of his life with Crissie.

"I promise you there will be no reason in our future. All will be well. Ah, Crissie... Crissie. How I crave you."

His voice was tight and low as he fought against the sensual promise of her body along with all the obstacles standing in their way.

Fewer now that he obtained the annulment. Still, this would not be easy. If possible, before they wed, he would hope to have gained her trust. *Nay*, he needed to learn to trust in her, in her word.

"Truly?" she asked.

"We need to get you back to the house, to warmth."

"Not yet, Walker please, I need you."

She rubbed her lips across the opening of his shirt, finding and stroking with her tongue whatever bared flesh she could find. Trembling, her hands found their way beneath his shirt, fondling the hardened muscles of his body running along his spine.

He looked to the sky, cursing softly. He didn't want to wait for his release. "Yes, I hunger for you now. I need you."

He allowed her to move against him, felt the contracting of her muscles. He growled low in his throat at the amazing sensations surging within. Walker thought of all the ways he caressed her, the intimate taste of her, the soft cries and liquid fire of her pleasure when she melted around him. She had come to him by her choice. Then she ran. Now she was back in his arms. If he could, he would never let her go.

Holding himself back, he thought of all the ways he had hurt Crissie. In the future he promised to make amends. She unraveled him as thoroughly as she spun her magic around him. His mind stopped when she touched him. He closed his eyes, knowing Crissie always gave everything of herself. She was sincere. Had told him the truth of her feelings without holding back. He grinned when he thought of the way she flung the expensive necklace in his face. Yet that very act of defiance angered him.

He needed to give her the same considerations when it came to giving of himself. He knew she loved him whether he deserved it or not whether he loved her or not. Never before had he known love from a woman. It was always what he could give to them. She didn't seem to be that way.

His vision clouded. He could think of nothing but the moment along with the woman who was so much a part of him, her sultry core inviting him ever more deeply. His hips moved tenderly against her then with her, telling her exactly how much he needed her.

She shuddered then cried out, twisting against him with wild, unrestrained abandon, instinctively running her hands along his back, cupping the hard muscles of his buttocks as she pulled him closer while he surged deeper within. Once again, his hand stroked down her body finding the liquid heat of her, a single touch that sent tiny passionate convulsion rippling through her body.

"Now, Walker," she pleaded her voice whisper thin carried away by the gusting winds.

"My sweet, little pigeon," he whispered against her lips, his tongue running along the seam, parting her more thoroughly.

Walker took Crissie's mouth and her body with the same smooth powerful motion, becoming a part of her, melting her around him. She burned him. He moved with aching care, afraid that he would hurt her in his hungry desperate need to have her.

There was no pain, no hesitation on her part. Walker fit her perfectly, hot and very close, caressing her even when he was utterly still within her. She smiled against his throat, murmuring words that had no meaning, simply sounds telling him of her exquisite pleasure.

Walker moved slowly despite the inexorable need hammering deep inside him, despite the tempest drenching them, despite the howling wind. He savored each tiny motion of their bodies so perfectly matched. Crissie's legs shifted. He felt the tightening of her muscles, the fatigue of holding herself in the position. His fingers flexed against the exquisite round shape of her buttocks holding her closer accepting her weight in his hands.

Her hungry seeking took Walker's breath away. Reflexively, he gave her what they both wanted, holding back nothing. With each speeding motion, each instant of wild abandonment, he knew he would never feel such amazing pleasure with any other woman.

Walker felt the intimate pulses of Crissie's release all around him. This coupling, this primal need for her was an act of binding her to him. His body arched into her, tearing a cry of ecstasy from her as well as from him. He shuddered then arched again and again, giving himself to her as deeply as she had given herself to him.

For several slow sweet seconds Walker and Crissie watched the rain sluice from the sky, his forehead just touching hers. In each other's arms they were spent yet drifting quickly back to an awareness that they were in the middle of a raging thunder storm and in a public place.

A tiny embarrassed laugh, a small shudder rippled through her as she seemed to realize what he was thinking. "We cannot stay here like this."

"I suppose someone else might be foolish enough to be out in this storm."

A small giggle escaped her lips. "Probably not."

Walker smoothed his lips against the tangled, silky fall of Crissie's wet hair. He kissed her temple, her cheek, the secret inner curve of her ear, the corners of her mouth, drinking up the raindrops off her face. Her fingers moved down his back to the powerful muscles of his buttocks. He jerked feeling another surge of need, of arousal hot and sweet.

"Ah, lady, what you do to me."

He craved her again and he was sure again after that. This would have to wait until they left the storm behind them to find the shelter of the boarding house. Warmth was something he needed but the subtle sense of her unexpected tightening of her body was nearly his undoing. If he didn't stop this now, they would never come in out of the storm.

Quickly, he adjusted her clothing then brought the hood of her cloak up around her rain-drenched hair, tying it securely around her chin. He settled her feet on the ground, holding on to her for a few seconds as she leaned into him. When his own clothing was completely refastened, he took her hand in his.

"Can you run?"

"I'll try."

"We need to race the storm."

Yet he thought it was the storm inside them they needed to race. The elemental sensations of their lovemaking exquisite, he stole a breath of cold damp air from the tempest.

Hand in hand and as quickly as Crissie could manage, Walker

guided her down the long path to the boarding house. She ran out of breath before they covered half the distance. He was afraid his foolish passion would cause her to sicken if he didn't get her out of the raging wind and rain. He swept her into his arms before dashing the remaining distance.

"Put me down, you brute! I'm too heavy." She was pounding on his chest but also laughing as he strode quickly up the steps into the back of the boarding house. He set her down when they reached the scullery. Their rain-soaked clothing dripped on the floor before pooling around their feet.

"Should I strip you here or wait until we are in our room?" he asked while thinking the sooner he rid her of the soaking garments the sooner he could make love to her again. They could always try to find a route through the house where no one would see them.

"You wouldn't dare," she told him primly. "I'm not undressing in the scullery. If I did, you would probably have me on the floor before I could take in a breath of the warm air. What would Rose say if she found us?"

He stared at her, thinking he would dare just about anything where she was concerned. Crissie was his responsibility. He'd be damned if he didn't protect what was his.

"Want to test me?"

"What are the two of you doing standing here shivering? When I watched Walker head outside to find you with the storm brewing, I knew there would be two frozen lovers dripping into my house."

"You know me too well, Rose." Walker laughed as he watched Crissie turn a delightful shade of crimson.

"The hot water will be upstairs in a few minutes. You two leave the rain gear down here then head upstairs. Put the wet clothes outside your door. Doesn't seem that the coats did the two of you any good. Land's sake what were you doing. What were you thinking? The two of you look like drowned rats." She hesitated then, looking from one to the other. "No, don't suppose I want to know what it was the two of you were doing. In a storm no less. Doesn't that beat all?"

Walker wanted to laugh. Crissie's gown was buttoned

haphazardly. Places where he failed to fasten the little devils gaped revealing tender white flesh. The curve of one, soft white breast showed more than the other. He grinned as his appreciative gaze traveled over her.

He took her hand, tugging her along behind him as he quickly led the way to their room, impatient now to rid her of the sodden gown. His luggage was there as well as a large tub. One, he thought, they would share. No reason to haul water for two baths when all they needed was to warm each other in the steamy hot water in front of them.

They barely had time to breathe when two lads with steaming water marched into the room, quickly filling the tub. He tested the water before he strode to Crissie, an eyebrow arched. She was dripping as well as shivering. Hunched over, her arms were crossed in front of her. She didn't look as if her fingers would move.

"You're freezing. What are you waiting for?"

"I." She tried to stop her shivering. "I don't know."

When the door closed, he tugged her arms away from her then set his fingers to the fastenings down the front of her dress. Half-heartedly she tried to push his hands away. She was shivering so hard she couldn't say a single word that made sense.

Her gown slid from her shoulders sliding soggily to the floor. He lifted the remains of her chemise over her head then let it too land on the floor. He didn't realize he nearly shredded the garment in his haste.

"Get in the water," he told her as he started to rid himself of his clothing.

It didn't seem she was going to do as he said. He wasn't sure if she didn't want to or her feet couldn't move. Easily, he lifted her from the floor. Within seconds, she sat in the steaming tub with lowered lashes, her arms once again crossed in front of her chest, hiding her breasts.

"There's no need to be shy," he spoke softly as he stepped into the tub, sitting behind her then pulling her back flush against his chest. He recalled the night she came to him undressed then slid into the bed keeping her back to him. He thought she was over the shyness. Apparently, he was wrong even after what they just did outside.

"W-wh-what are you doing?" Her teeth chattered alarmingly.

He rubbed her arms slowly moving up then down the outside then transferring his touch to the inside of her arms. Felt the shiver of desire begin anew. "You're ice cold. I'm warming you up."

She nodded, her hair freezing against his shoulders. He rung the excess from her hair before reaching out for one of the towels Rose left for them. A few seconds later, her hair was bundled neatly inside the towel. Cupping steaming water in his hands, he dribbled it over her shoulders followed with the lightest strokes of his fingers.

Crissie sighed softly, relaxing against him, now seeming to enjoy the warmth of his body. They spent the next few hours in each other's arms making exquisite love to each other.

She was his. Still there were shadows under her eyes. He understood she hated the position he placed her in by bringing her with him, insisting they live in the same home. She disliked Charlotte with so much intensity it surprised him. At those times he understood she held a part of him at a distance.

When they finally surfaced for food, Ian was crying. Rose holding the child knocked on the door.

"Seems someone else is hungry for you too," Walker said as he pulled on his breeches then fastened them as he strode across the floor to open the door. Before he did so, he looked back at Crissie. She was holding the quilt to her chest, covering herself. Rose would know what they'd been up to, but then he really didn't think anything got past the woman.

"Ian needs his mommy more than you," Rose said in a huff as she marched into the room. "Besides, it appears you should be sated for a little while."

Walker laughed as he took the boy from her arms. "After I give this wee one to his mum, I'll be in the kitchen to gather some food. What's for dinner?"

"Dinner's been served hours ago. I do have a bit of stew set aside for the two of you as well as some bread. If you be wantin' some wine, I've that too. Don't wait too long." With that said, she turned and left, leaving the door open.

Walker smiled to himself then closed the door softly. He leaned against the frame to watch, holding Ian casually in the crook of his arm. Crissie was plumping the pillows behind her back. He settled the boy into his mother's arms, watching as she bared a breast to feed the baby while unsuccessfully trying to keep the other one covered. The sight swelled his heart with pride. Watching his soon to be wife breast-feeding was beautiful and poignant. He didn't think he would ever grow tired of watching the two of them.

"I'll be right back with food. Don't go away."

"Now where would I be going?" she asked with a small laugh as she readjusted Ian.

Still, he was watching her. He loved watching Crissie feed his son. There was something so touching about the tender scene. Then with a long breath of air he turned and left closing the door quietly behind him. In the kitchen, Rose was setting out two bowls of fish stew. The dish was filled with clams and lobster along with cod. The smell caused his stomach to growl. The concoction smelled delicious. Walker couldn't remember the last time he ate. Had to be this morning before he started for Portrush. Perhaps he forgot altogether he was so eager to reach the town.

An open bottle of white wine sat on the counter. He placed it on the tray while Rose set two large hunks of bread on a plate after smearing them with butter. A pot of honey was set on the tray as well. On the counter, Walker found a large bowl of berries. He added the fruit to the tray thinking Ian might like a taste of something different.

"This should keep us for a while."

"Don't you be keepin' the lady up all night if you're planning on starting back first thing in the morning. She's still feedin' the baby and needs to keep up her strength. She needs more sleep than you."

"If it's alright with you, I'd rather stay another day. It will give Charlotte some time to adjust to the news I broke to her while she figures out where she's going to live."

He hoped when they returned, Charlotte would be gone from Briarwood. Now that he'd made the decision to end the marriage, he needed peace and quiet in his home. Gaining that state was impossible with both Charlotte and Crissie living so close to each other.

Not in the cottage I'm guessing?" Rose said then after a few moments of thought, "Not in the main house either?"

"Right."

"Then you were successful in your endeavors. Was it an annulment you received?"

"It was and I plan on telling Crissie after Charlotte has permanently left us. Until then I don't want you to say anything to her since I want the privilege of surprising her myself right before I ask her to marry me."

"Mums the word," Rose said her eyes twinkling. "I've waited a long time for this day, Walker Endicott, Earl of Briarwood. You go now and make this evening perfect for your lady. She deserves to be treated right after all that she has had to put up with from you. She must love you dearly."

"I plan on doing exactly that."

He leaned over to place a quick kiss to Rose's cheek as he mulled over Rose's words. *She must love you dearly.* He hefted the tray onto one hand thinking about the moment he would tell Crissie how things would be. He planned to take her to the waterfall on his property. Perhaps make love then ask her if she would do him the honor of wedding him. After she said yes, they would make love again. He had to buy a ring though. Nothing could be considered perfect unless he had a beautiful ring to give her, something that spoke of the deep tenor of his feelings. He would do that as soon as possible. Perhaps he should make a quick trip into Belfast first thing.

That would take another day.

He wanted the proposal to be faultless, to be special in every way. If that were to happen, he would have to make the sacrifice of waiting that extra day so he could purchase a ring.

When he opened the door with the tray of food, Ian was playing with his wooden horse. Lying on the floor, he was kicking his legs in the air while the head of the toy was in his mouth. Drool slid down his chubby cheeks. When Walker knelt down beside him, he stopped playing to stare at him.

He stood. "You got dressed?" He was disappointed to see she was covered from head to toe, all the buttons on the robe fastened. He was hoping she would be waiting naked for him. Well, that particular dream was in the future.

"Yes," she said as she arranged the folds of the robe around her. She sat on a chair near Ian. "I'll take Ian back to his room if you like."

"No, I haven't seen him in over a month. I want to play with my son." He set the tray on a nearby table. Walker picked up Ian, holding him while he walked to the chair next to Crissie's. Ian clenched his finger in his pudgy little hand as he brought it to his mouth.

Crissie laughed watching the two of them. "I can't believe how much the two of you look alike."

He snorted dismissing her words. "All Endicott males resembled their fathers. Does everything go in his mouth?" Walker asked while he felt the teeth coming through his gums. Two right in the front of his mouth. Then as if realizing something, he asked. "Does he ever bite you?"

She was shaking her head, grinning as her eyes sparkled mischievously. "No, not yet but I wouldn't put it past him to try sometime. Not sure what I'll do when he does."

"Scream?" he asked thinking of the times he bit her but his teeth were gentle against her nipples. At least he thought he'd been gentle. She seemed to like the way his teeth grazed over her but she was always aroused.

"Yes, I suppose so. I'll just keep hoping he doesn't get that particular notion into his head."

They ate in silence for a while. Walker wanted to tell her all his plans. Needed to tell her about the annulment but that wasn't part of his entire scheme. Watching her carefully, he understood she hated what he did to her. In essence he made her his mistress simply because he couldn't let her go. Couldn't curtail his craving for her. He wanted her day and night, every time he looked at her, caught her scent, saw the soft swell of her breasts beneath her clothing. As soon as they finished eating, he meant to take her to bed again.

She never complained. Seemed to like what he did with her body as much as he did. Not too long ago, he told her she would have to beg him. She didn't. No, she came to him more than willing if not a little shy.

They would have more children, as soon as he could slip a ring on her finger. He stopped in thought with a bite of stew half way to his mouth. Hell, she could be pregnant now. Neither one had taken any precautions.

His grin widened.

He hoped so.

His voice husky, "How about if we finish the wine in bed. I can pour little drops on your body and see how they taste coupled with the sweet taste of your flesh." He imagined drops of wine on her puckered nipples. They didn't need anything to make them taste sweet, but he liked the idea.

A rosy rush of color swept over her face at hearing his words. He thought her breasts must be the same color instead of the snowy white they usually were. In slow motion she ran her sweet tasting pink tongue across her top lip then the bottom. He heated from the inside out. He was glad he decided not to go home tomorrow morning because he meant to keep her in bed until midafternoon or longer. Maybe then they could go for a walk and find a secluded private part of the beach to make love. This night's tree wouldn't do in the sunshine on the public part of the beach.

~ * ~

Two days passed before they could get out of bed soon enough to take a carriage home and that was only because Rose brought Ian into the room as he was fussing for his mum.

Crissie was happy here by the beach. She didn't want to go back where she would have to see and maybe confront Charlotte. Seeing that woman even once a week was too many times. If she decided to come into the main house, Crissie thought she would scream. Hiding away wouldn't solve any problems between them either.

Walker told her things would be different when they returned. She wouldn't have to worry about his wife usurping privileges or power with the staff. That was all he said. He failed to elaborate about the details or tell her exactly why he was so sure what he was telling her would hold true. She didn't see how anything would be different once they were back. She would still be in his bed without benefit of a marriage. Charlotte would still live in the cottage while she pretended to be his wife even if in name only. For some reason here in Portrush, she felt more like his lover than a mistress. She didn't understand why though. Also didn't understand what the difference was except lover sounded better than mistress.

When they walked into Briarwood manor house, Charlotte was sitting in the drawing room sipping tea. Laura, her maid, hovered over her waiting, Crissie supposed for orders. Yet the woman had an unusual expression on her face. For some reason she looked a bit guilty as if she had been doing something she shouldn't.

Charlotte smiled prettily but the gesture didn't reach her eyes and it was wasted on Crissie. Then the woman focused her attention on Walker who was holding Ian in his arms. Crissie bit back the desperation she felt when Charlotte looked at Ian as if she wanted to hurt the little boy. Surely, she imagined the look wasn't meant that way. No one would want to hurt a small child. Still, it wasn't the first time she felt the malevolent stare from Charlotte.

"What are you doing here, Charlotte?" Walker asked as he sat in one of the nearby brocaded wing chairs, holding Ian possessively. He sported an air of arrogance coupled with determination. Crissie was sure he didn't like his wife's appearance in their drawing room any better than she did.

"Didn't your mistress tell you? I moved in when you left. We are married, so it is my house too. I've every right to be here. Someone had to see to the servants. Who better than your wife?"

Walker's jaw ticked furiously. A sense of relief washed through Crissie at the site of his anger. He would make Charlotte move back to the cottage. He would insist. The longest time passed and he didn't say anything. Crissie's heart seemed to be caught in her throat as she waited what seemed a lifetime. Walker needed to tell Charlotte she wasn't welcome. The silence unnerved her, setting her on edge as her nimble mind flew through different scenarios.

She tugged in a deep breath of air, filling her lungs with courage as her gaze roamed from one to the other.

"You can't stay here, Charlotte," he finally told her. "I thought we had an understanding. Take whatever things you moved here and move them right back to the cottage. Laura will help you. I'll get any other of the servants you might need. Do it now. I will speak with you tomorrow about other matters. No, perhaps I'll come over tonight. Although I believed you understood my position. We've things to talk about and I'm going to be busy all day tomorrow."

Crissie wasn't sure what to think only that she didn't want to ever see Charlotte again. If Charlotte fell off the face of the earth, she couldn't be more pleased. For the longest time Charlotte didn't answer Walker. Nor did she make a move to leave. Crissie held her breath, waiting.

Finally, after seconds with nothing being said between them, Charlotte spoke softly, "If that's what you want, Walker. I thought you would want me here."

"It is. Now," Walker turned his attention back to Ian, "I suppose it's time for a meal then a nap." He glanced at Crissie who held out her arms for the little boy more than eager to leave this distressing scene behind her.

"I'll be upstairs," she said softly, taking the lad. The palm of her hand moved gently over his tawny mane of hair.

When she settled down to feed him, she wondered what Walker wanted to talk to Charlotte about. He mentioned nothing to her when they were in Portrush nor did he say anything on the way here. Of course, Walker had been wonderfully distracted both places. She never realized he would make love to her in the carriage. She shivered at the thought of his warm lips languorously melting hers apart melting all of her apart.

Ian stopped suckling, looking up at her with honey brown eyes so like his father's. He was smiling at her almost as if he could sense how much she loved Walker.

She did.

More so each day.

Crissie walked with Ian nestled on her shoulder, waiting for him to burp. His eyes were growing sleepy. The trip must have been exhausting for him. Walker strode into the room, unfastening his shirt. He tossed his jacket across the top of the chair. In the next second Ian was tucked into his arm as Walker headed for the makeshift nursery. Now that they were back it would be nice to have a real nursery.

"Would you like to go for a walk?" he asked as he slid his shirt off, his gaze riveted on her as if he wanted to devour her again.

As if he shouldn't be satisfied by now. Crissie felt the same way. His eyes focused on her, roamed the length of her then back up, settling on her breasts. He was all male, his chest powerful, sprinkled with tawny hair but she already knew that. "What are you doing?"

"Undressing."

"Unless you go for walks naked..."

He laughed, startling her. "Changing my clothes to something a little less formal. So, would you like to go walking? It's almost time for the sun to set. We can sit on the porch like old folk, sip a glass or two of wine. Tell each other how our day went. There are rocking chairs there. Or we can sit on the patio and drink some wine. The cook makes these tiny little canapés that are delicious with a fine red bordeaux. What do you say?"

"You sound as if you are setting the mood for something." Truly she didn't understand what he was up to. He kicked out Charlotte but was going to speak with her tonight at the earliest or possibly tomorrow.

"The patio would be nice." She watched still fascinated as he slowly stepped out of the rest of his clothing, her eyes wide.

His grin was pure devil. He turned away, striding to the armoire. Then he was dressed. When he stepped up to her, he offered her his arm. She didn't accept it, just looked at him as if she didn't truly know him or what exactly she was supposed to do.

"Can't you wait until tonight, Crissie? Your eyes look as if you are thinking about devouring me in a single bite. They are huge, wide and simmering with the passion I always see when you kiss me," he said softly as he took her hand. He pulled her to her feet. She stumbled against him. "Ah, but you are going to have to control your baser needs until this evening. Later tonight I will let you have your wicked way with me. I plan on having a pleasant conversation with you this evening. Nothing more."

Wicked way with him?

He kissed her forehead before setting her aside. She felt the heat of the blush rising through her body. He was like that, delighting in embarrassing her. "Walker..."

"Shall we go?"

He led the way from the room, never turning back to see if she followed. She had no idea what he had in mind. Neither was she eager to find out.

"Walk first then patio or the porch?"

They were on the first floor. She felt as if she was running to keep up with him. "No walk for me unless you slow down. I can't keep up." She was breathing heavy and they only went down the stairs. "What are you up to?"

"Just a nice evening with you, little pigeon. You don't seem to be in very good shape. Perhaps the walk will take too much of your stamina. You will have to have lots of it when we retire for the evening. I mean to keep you up most of the night." His lazy dimple appeared giving more charm to his bad boy half smile

"I'm not going to have my wicked way with you."

She ran into his back when he stopped suddenly.

"Of course you are. If you don't, I'll have to work my wiles on you until you scream out my name."

"I won't do that."

He grinned. She knew he didn't believe her. She didn't believe herself. He took her hand in his as he kept walking across the patio then the lawn on to a wooded area behind the manor. She walked this way once when he was busy. Farther along there was a small stream. When she discovered it, she sat for about an hour watching the water rush by on its

172

way to the ocean. She mused about her life, about Walker and how he truly felt about her. This wasn't the life she once thought she would have. She longed for a husband, for respectability.

He found a log beside the stream, nearly where she sat the first time she was here. "What did you talk to Charlotte about?"

He stiffened, his face grim. Shaking his head, "I'd rather not talk about my…" he paused as if he was about to say something then changed his mind, "about my wife."

"No, I don't suppose you do. Not with your mistress at any rate sitting right next to you. You don't owe me an explanation or knowledge." She decided to switch the topic of conversation to something more palatable. "How was my family?" She'd been so busy with Walker she didn't even think to ask.

"Angry with me. Your mother especially as she believes I'm not treating you the way you deserve."

Well, she did agree with her mother on that score. "What do you believe?"

"You've wanted for nothing, Crissie."

For love. For respectability.

"Is that what you believe?"

She felt moisture gather in the back of her throat. Fought to stop the tears from rushing from her eyes. She was a fool. He would never give up Charlotte as his wife, at least not for her. He thought he was treating her with care. Trying to avoid looking at him, she sucked in a wobbly breath of air. At the same time, she started making more plans to leave. She would have to be careful. Going home would be the first place he looked. It wouldn't happen in the next few days but perhaps in another month or so. Rose wouldn't help her this time.

"It's true."

This wasn't a conversation she wanted to continue. "I suppose you believe so because you've gifted me with an untold number of gifts. I should be more thankful for your thoughtfulness. Shall we get back to the original question?"

She thought of the necklace. It was worth a small fortune. Finding a way to sell it for what it was worth would be difficult. For some reason she couldn't fathom she disliked that necklace intensely. Knew it would only bring pain as well as heartache.

"What was that question?" he asked as he tugged her into his arms. Her back rested against his chest. His arms were around her waist, her breasts resting atop his forearms. A tiny shiver of arousal swept through her.

"About my family. We got sidetracked when you brought up my mother's thoughts."

She wanted to learn everything about how her family was doing. About Brady and Lilly, about Roby and if he was still as reckless as always. "I'm sure father had a few things to say."

She wondered if Connal had been able to see into the future if he would have let Walker take her and the *bairn* without putting up a fight.

He cleared his throat as he idly ran his fingers along her arms, touching every sensual sweet nerve. "Not too much. He wanted to see Ian. Told him maybe next summer if all went as planned."

"What plan is that, Walker?" she asked turning in his arms, looking up into eyes that could make her melt with no effort whatsoever. They were tender when he returned her gaze.

He kissed the tip of her nose then moved on to her forehead. "I can't tell you right now. Have patience, sweetheart. I promise you will appreciate my efforts on your behalf."

"Since you won't speak of this scheme of yours can you tell me about my brothers?"

She realized she was homesick. The feelings went far beyond just the notion of hearth and home that she missed. She longed for the feeling of belonging as well as the sense of esteem she had in the highlands around those who loved her. Despite how Walker treated her with care and lavished gifts on her as well, it was not the same as being loved.

She didn't belong here with him.

"Let me think. Brady and Lilly I didn't see. They kept to themselves in a home they are building near the village. Nor did I see their new baby who is only a wee bit older than Ian. Do you think the new baby is a shapeshifter?" he challenged her.

She chose to ignore the jibe. She had no idea. If the *bairn* was a shifter, they would handle it well. "I wish," she sighed softly in his arms.

"What is it you wish for, little pigeon? If it is within my means, I will gift it to you," he asked as he ran his fingers through her hair dislodging the pins until the length tumbled down her back, curling around her waist. He ran his fingers through the length once more stirring feelings she could never control.

"I wish I could hold their child." She shivered as his hands settled on the bare skin near her neck, trailed across her collarbone leaving the moist sweet heat of the caress behind.

"I'm sorry. If I could change that, I would. My purpose there was not to visit with your kinfolk but to make sure there were no more rumors, no more wives' tales to stir up the English. I was supposed to put an end to the gossip."

"You were there to cage a shifter."

She found her anger beginning to boil forth. He had no tender concern for the people she loved. Everything was about Walker.

"*Nay*, lass. You jumped to the wrong conclusion."

He moved her hair to the side. His lips found purchase on her nape, increasing the fire smoldering within. "I was there to protect your family."

With shaking words, words of regret, "I *dinna* believe you, Walker."

His finger stopped their leisurely exploration as did his lips against the tender secret parts of her body. "I wouldn't lie about something so very important to you."

"Of course, you would. You want me to believe you have my best interests at heart while you seduce me, coax me to remain with you. You would say or promise anything to have your way."

He lied to her more than once. Led her to believe things she shouldn't.

She pushed away from him. He let her go just as he would when she bored him. Distancing herself from him was wise and prudent. She needed time to think.

"You can try trusting me, respecting my word as well as my promise," he told her almost wistfully.

"What was Roby doing?"

She was shaking her head, backing another step away from him, her arms crossed in front of her, closing herself away from him. She wanted to turn and run.

More than that, she needed to know about her family.

He was leaning against a tree, his hands stuck in his pocket. The only sign of his anger was the simmering of his eyes. "Roby is in America, at least that was his intention. He wanted an adventure. He traveled with Kit. Who knows exactly where they are right at this moment."

"Well, the two of them will most likely find a passel full of trouble. They always do."

She tried not to laugh. Roby was so precious to her. She was closer to him than their oldest brother, Brady. Roby was charming and witty. All the girls in the village were in love with him. He never failed to protect her when she needed him.

Except with Walker.

"It will be good for them to have a place to run wild without fear of finding themselves caught and caged. The two of them have a bit of growing up to do. Don't you think? Coddled by your father and mother will not help. They've always believed they could do anything they wanted."

She bristled once more at his critical words. By the look in his eyes, he wanted her to come to him. She didn't think she could recreate the soothing scene of him holding her in his arms a few minutes ago without seeking more from her. He was an enigma to her.

"We should go back. It's getting chilly."

She turned but he intercepted her, wrapping her in his coat.

"You didn't ask me about my father, Stephen," he reminded her.

"I don't *ken* what to ask."

"You don't care either." He spoke as if he was angry again.

"How can I care about a man I've never met? You've hardly spoken about him. All I know is that he was behind the betrothal contract

176

that gave you a wife of convenience, a wife you didn't love. He's the reason we cannot wed." She sucked in an unnatural draught of air. "Perhaps you don't want to wed. As you said the arrangement suited you along with your needs. It's pretty nice to have sex whenever you want with no responsibilities."

"Until now," he murmured holding her around the waist pulling her to him so she fit perfectly against his side. "I would like you to care about my father. Crissie, don't ever think you and Ian are not my responsibility."

"Your mother? You've never spoken of her."

She realized she never asked either. Perhaps she'd been too caught up in herself to think about getting to know Walker better. He was naturally aloof, held himself away from her. Perhaps she was as much at fault as he was.

She tried to push away from him. He wouldn't allow distance to separate them. "She died during childbirth. Father never remarried. He never talks about her either." His broad shoulders lifted slightly. "I never knew my mother."

"I'm sorry. I didn't know."

She had two parents, loving parents. She wasn't too sure his father truly loved him. What did she know?

Nothing, it seemed.

"There is nothing to know. Women who floated in and out of father's life brought me up. There was never another lady who took his fancy enough to wed her."

Just like he doesn't fancy me enough to fix this situation he's brought me into.

"I won't allow a hoard of women to bring up Ian. He's mine, Walker, and you best learn that."

His tawny brows narrowed, golden amber eyes simmering heatedly. He spoke softly yet she heard the darkly blunt message. "Ian stays with me no matter where you go. And Crissie, if you recall, you promised to stay here with me. Why do I get the sense you're thinking of running away again?"

Once more, she tried to distance herself from him. He held on to her, his fingers gripping her waist until the pressure hurt. She couldn't answer. She wasn't going to lie to him because tears clogged her throat. She was determined not to cry. It seemed he saw into her heart and mind better than anyone.

"I cannot abide Charlotte. Cannot live with her so close. You told me she would be gone when we arrived home. You lied. Your promise meant nothing. She was sitting in the drawing room sipping tea and making eyes at her maid. I wouldn't be surprised..."

"Hold it right there, Crissie. You go too far. Charlotte has a companion who she sees all the time. I'm sure she is not having sex with the servants. There are rules about that."

His voice was harsh but when she looked into his eyes, he saw the slight question.

"Perhaps what you speak of is true but Charlotte is far from gone. I don't think anything is going to move her from the cottage or your life no matter what you say or even threaten. Something should be done about it." Bitterness welled up inside. When she saw him at Portrush, there was something going on, something he wasn't telling her. He gave her reason to believe that perhaps her life might change for the better. Once she got back to Briarwood, she knew better.

The only changes are the ones I will make for myself.

"She will be gone. I promise." He ran his hands through his hair. "Just be patient. Give her a few days to adjust. This was a bombshell that I exploded on her. She has to get used to the idea of not living here any longer, of fending for herself."

Crissie wanted to say what about me? What about my feelings?

Instead, she kept her mouth closed even though she didn't think she had any more patience to give that woman.

When they reached the patio, dishes were set out along with crystal glasses coupled with both red and white bottles of wine. It looked as if he was planning on celebrating.

Or seducing.

They both knew seduction was far too easy.

"Going to Belfast tomorrow."

~ * ~

Charlotte lay in the arms of her current lover. Even the blissful sex didn't make her feel any better. She wanted to wring Crissie's pretty little neck until it snapped. How dare she barge into her life, disrupting everything she held dear, threatening her existence? Walker asked her to leave. *Nay*, he told her she had no choice.

Life here at Briarwood had been wonderful. Ten years of her life where she could come and go as she pleased. If she took lovers, Walker didn't care. The situation was good for him too. He had his mistresses. No debutantes flaunted their tiny waists and low-cut corsages to lure him into marriage.

With Crissie McKenna he was different.

Now, she didn't know what she would do. She certainly couldn't go back to her father's home. Didn't have enough money to set up a household for herself. Since there was no divorce, Walker wouldn't owe her financial help.

"Whatever has you so restless? I swear you are not yourself," Anne asked her as she leaned on an elbow in order to see her better.

Charlotte stood as she slipped a robe on over her naked body. Anne moved so the covers slipped to her waist, silently beckoning her back to bed. Charlotte would come to her if she thought for a second she could forget all her problems.

"Walker kicked me out." She went on to explain everything. Told Anne everything starting with Ian then to the fact that Walker must have fallen in love with his newest mistress. She hadn't thought that would ever happen.

"There is my place," Anne told her, smoothing the spot on the bed where Charlotte slept encouraging her.

"It's a dump."

"Well, it is better than nowhere," she said indignantly. "Perhaps I should leave."

"Perhaps you should. I need to be alone with my thoughts. Walker said he was coming over here tonight to discuss my leaving."

"Your father?"

"Not since Walker told him why he would never have grandchildren. No, he won't help. He thinks I could change my mind if I wanted. Perhaps I could but I don't want to change anything. I like my life exactly the way it is."

"You truly have no resources?" Anne questioned, slipping from the bed. She dressed.

"None that I know of."

"You will have to explain that to Walker. He couldn't possibly want you on the street. After all he's been pleasant to you for ten years."

"We were childhood friends. Did you know that? Possibly you're right. I might be able to strike a deal with him. All I need is a place to live along with a monthly allowance. Truly, I wouldn't ask for anything he couldn't easily afford."

"Don't think that would be too much to ask for," Anne said as she strode from the little cottage, Charlotte watching her swaying skirts as she walked away.

No, if they had divorced that would not be too much to ask for. Negotiation tonight might be in order. Walker had more money than he knew what to do with. He might be more inclined if she'd given him something to bargain with, even one night. She refused him on their wedding night. Told him how she detested men, which wasn't exactly the truth. She was afraid of the male species.

Bloody hell, but she did hate men, their arrogance, everything. They were hard, their muscles intimidating. When she was no more than fifteen a friend of one of her cousins raped her. She couldn't even remember his name having put everything from her mind. Particularly large men terrified her.

The night of her marriage, she tried to close her thoughts to the feel of Walker touching her. She went to this place where a velvet soft rose slowly opened its petals. Watching them open helped. She was so still, it gave Walker pause. When he realized he was forcing her, he stopped.

He swore. Asked her what was wrong. So, she told him. The wedding night wasn't pleasant. He left. When he came back in the morning, he smelled of ale and a harlot's perfume.

When sunlight filtered through the open window, they sat in the bedroom, each in a chair opposite from the other while she told him who she was and that she didn't want any part of him or a life together.

Once again, he yelled at her.

Why the bloody hell didn't you say something sooner?

She couldn't tell him anything except that she had to get away from her father. Had to find a life for herself so she could be the person she was comfortable with. The betrothal contract was the perfect out for her. There was no reason she could see that she wouldn't take advantage of the gift. After a time, they worked things out between them.

He never promised he wouldn't fall in love. Never promised that someday he might send her away from Briarwood disgraced with an annulment hanging over her head. The time was here.

Anne's buggy disappeared from view.

She hoped Anne would be back tomorrow.

Charlotte wandered inside the small cottage she called home for ten years, walking through the rooms memorizing them. Anne left angry. She might not ever see her again. Her breath caught in her throat. She didn't want to leave. When the front door opened, she wasn't surprised to see Walker standing in the opening.

"Hello, Walker."

"Charlotte."

She brought a bottle of wine and two crystal glasses into the drawing room. Without asking she poured them both a glass.

"You've come to make sure I leave in the morning."

"Yes."

"Where do you expect me to go? I've no money."

"Your father will take you in."

"He won't and we both know all too well why." She watched his brows draw together. "When I told you about my preferences, the words changed my life forever."

"What is it that you are asking, Charlotte?"

He sounded calm to her. Sounded as if he might be willing to negotiate something.

She sucked in a long deep breath hoping for the courage to ask the obvious question, "A house in Belfast or another country cottage and a monthly stipend. If you divorced me instead of seeking an annulment you would have lost a lot more financially."

"You might not have agreed to a divorce."

"True."

"I'll give you what you want as long as you never come here again. If you do, you will lose everything."

"That's fair."

Chapter Eight

When Walker returned from Belfast the next evening, all hell had broken out at Briarwood Manor. Rose met him at the front door a worried expression on her haggard face, tears streaming down her eyes. Two buggies were hitched on the hitching post at the cottage. Servants were running in and out the door, carrying trays and boxes. Maybe Charlotte was doing what he asked a day late. For Charlotte that wasn't too bad. She was always late.

"Where's Crissie?"

"In your bedroom with Ian."

"She and Ian are fine?" His voice trembled with concern coupled with a devastating fear settling into his gut.

"Yes."

Hearing Rose's words, the relief sweeping through Walker was more physical than mental. When he first arrived and saw the unusual activity his heart had been plastered to his throat, sticking there so long he couldn't swallow from the terror ripping through him. Now, with the knowledge that his soon to be wife and son were not hurt in any way he could breathe a bit more easily. The pulse in his ears receded to a dull roar.

"So, tell me what's going on." A sudden unexplained chill swept through him a foreboding.

"Crissie shot Charlotte," Rose said quickly, blurting out the news as if it left a foul taste in her mouth. "I *dinna* believe she would do such a thing. She *wouldnae* hurt a fly. No matter what she thought of that woman, she would not have done such a horrible thing."

His heart forgot to beat. The very air around him froze. "Why do you say she shot Charlotte?"

"There was a note in Charlotte's hand. The name Crissie was written on it. Otherwise, I would not believe the accusation. Even with this damning evidence a ring of truth is missing." Tears slid down Rose's cheeks. "I kept Crissie from running. She is so afraid."

He waved his hand in the air, fear riffling through all his senses, eating at him. At first hearing the news, he didn't believe it either. He would have to see the proof. Yet why would Charlotte implicate Crissie if it wasn't true? "How is Charlotte?"

"She lives but the doctor doesn't *ken* for how long. It was a head wound. Nasty business. You can make this right. If you told her your plans, none of this would have happened."

Rose was busy, picking up things, wiping the dust away before moving to another object. Walker knew it was Rose's way of keeping her mind off the disturbing news.

He understood he had to learn what truly happened here. Crissie hated Charlotte. She knew how to use a gun. From everything her brothers ever said she was an excellent marksman.

With a heavy sigh he rethought everything he knew about Crissie. Surely, she wouldn't be so stupid as to commit murder, would she? She was a crack shot. If she chose to shoot something or someone she wouldn't miss, wouldn't leave them wounded. She would shoot to kill. So why wasn't Charlotte dead? Questions throbbed in his head.

He raced up the steps, barreling into the bedroom with a loud crash. Crissie sat in the rocking chair, Ian in her arms. She was moving the chair lightly with her feet, singing to his son, a soft slow lullaby. Tears slid down her cheeks. He picked up Ian then took him to the nursery.

When he pulled up a chair to sit in front of her, ribbons of moisture streaked her face. Her eyes were swollen with the tears she'd been crying. He wanted to wrap her in his arms, hold her until she was no longer hurt. Craved to tell her all would be fine. He couldn't.

His callous actions had done this to her. Rose was right. He should have apprised her of his plans instead of hoping to surprise her. Unlike

Rose, he didn't think she was innocent. Didn't think Charlotte would write her killers name down if it weren't the truth despite how she felt about Crissie. His plans for their future felt like desert sand in his mouth.

She would hang for this.

Even if Charlotte lived...

Even if she lived, he would have to punish Crissie for the crime of attempted murder. While he never loved Charlotte as a wife, he loved her as if she were his sister. The ring box in his jacket pocket felt like a lead weight pulling him down while his heart was breaking in two.

Why did I wait so long? I could have told Crissie when we were still in Portrush.

"I didn't do it," she said, her voice a whisper thin echo in the silence surrounding them.

He saw the pounding of her pulse at the base of her neck. Saw the heaving of her breasts.

More than anything he wanted to believe her, trust in her words. She had every reason to kill Charlotte. The motive was there. Crissie was the only one who had good reason. Moisture clogged the back of his throat as he thought about all the two of them lost, what Ian lost. He would no longer have a mother.

He just didn't believe her.

Very slowly and with utmost regret, he said as his life crumbled down around him, "Stay in this room, Crissie. Don't go anywhere." He knew if given the opportunity she would run again. "Promise me."

"You don't believe me," she whispered, her eyes wide, frightened. Tears stained her cheeks.

Gradually his heart began to harden. He didn't want to say the words that would destroy her but he did. One thing that never existed between them was trust. "No, Crissie I don't believe you. Don't go anywhere."

He headed out the door, hearing the sobs wracking her small body. While he wanted to turn around, go to her, hold her, tell her he'd protect her that nothing bad would happen, he kept walking understanding nothing would be fine again.

Perhaps she was telling the truth.

The note was damning.

He was the bloody magistrate. He would have to take her to prison, would have to hand her over for trial. Would see her hang while he stood in the audience and watched. No other choices existed for either of them. Inhaling a shaky breath, he decided the note would be kept secret. She would pay but not with her life. He wasn't going to allow her to hang or go to prison. Left to rot in a prison cell she would die, her sprit along with the essence that was Crissie would vanish.

He couldn't bear that.

The time it took to reach the cottage seemed like an eternity. His thoughts mired in his head congealing. All his thoughts ricocheted around damning Crissie. When he finally stepped inside, the doctor was sitting by the bed. Charlotte was sleeping, her head bandaged.

She was alive.

For several heart wrenching minutes, he stood at the end of the bed. His gaze focused on the doctor then Charlotte. His voice gruff with worry, he asked, "How is she?"

"She can't hear or see anything. I doubt if she'll live through the next week or even the night. If for some reason a miracle occurs, she might remain alive."

"And?" he drug air into his lungs. "What aren't you telling me?"

"Charlotte won't ever be the same again. She won't function normally. Chances of her speaking are very slim. The wound was grievous. It should have killed her on the spot."

That was not what he wanted to hear. Now, he needed desperately to find the damning note with Crissie's name on it then destroy the evidence. As far as he knew Rose and Charlotte were the only other living people who knew about the note.

When he walked into the drawing room looking for the evidence, he saw the blood on the floor. Saw where the ball from the pistol planted itself in the wall. It had gone through her head, doing the damage. On further inspection the note was nowhere to be found. In Charlotte's bedroom he sat beside her picking up her hand.

Her face was pale, her breathing even. He pulled out the box holding the ring he bought for Crissie. Wanted to throw it as far as he could. Needed to never see the damn thing again. He was striving for the day of his proposal to be perfect.

It was perfectly horrible.

"I'll be back later this evening," the doctor said as he placed his hand on Walker's shoulder. "Get your rest. There is nothing that can be done for her. Time will tell the story. She will either begin to heal or she will die."

Walker could do nothing but nod his head at the doctor's grim words. He knew if he tried to speak, he would break down in tears. When they were children, she'd been his constant companion. He defended her from bullies at school, even into their teenage years. It seemed even then her peers understood there was something very different about her.

"Her maid is going to keep watch over her. She volunteered. You need to go home, get some sleep. Find out who did this to her. As magistrate here, it's your responsibility."

He nodded barely able to think. Of course, he knew it was his responsibility. He already knew who shot her. He needed to put Crissie in the jail in the village until he knew if Charlotte would live or die. He couldn't bear to put her in jail. Yet he promised himself Crissie would not be going anywhere. As of this moment, he didn't know how.

Walker couldn't get the horrible mantra from his head. If he placed her in the jail, in irons, everyone would *ken* she was the primary suspect. He didn't want that. Instead, he would find a way to make her stay in the house. Briarwood would be her jail. She would pay but she would pay his way.

He would keep her where she couldn't hurt anyone else. Where he could still see her and love her. Where she could stay close to her son.

How? How could he do that? He loved Crissie.

As he left the cottage and walked back to the manor house, tears poured from his eyes. The tears were for his lost life, he realized, not for Charlotte but for Crissie. What kind of man was he?

When he reached the house, he decided to confront Miss

McKenna realizing he also needed to distance her from his heart. He needed to find out why she tossed his generosity in his face. Why she tried to kill a defenseless woman. There was nothing defenseless about Crissie McKenna.

When he walked into his bedroom, Crissie wasn't there. On further inspection, he found her curled up in a ball on the bed in the adjoining room. She must have heard his footsteps or sensed his presence. She sat up pushing hair from her tear-streaked face.

"She's still alive. That's not good news to you, is it?"

He leaned against the cold fireplace. His feet were crossed as were his arms. His hardened gaze focused on her. He didn't want to care. She had to be dead to him if he were to survive the next days, weeks, years.

"I never wanted her to die, just out of the house as well as the grounds," she murmured. "I didn't do this."

"It seems we've already had this conversation. When you want to confess, let me know."

He pushed away from his resting spot taking one step closer, unknowing what he meant to do.

"Never!"

He heard the vehemence in the spoken word coupled with her seeming determination to draw this out forever. He slanted an eyebrow upward. "Confess or I'll have you settled in irons in the village jail filled with mice as well as spiders. Your new bed will smell of mold. I can assure you the wormy pallet there is not nearly as comfortable as that bed."

"You would coerce an innocent woman to confess something she had no part in. I *dinna ken* why you would believe I could do something like that." Her agitation clearly showing in the shaking of her shoulders, he refused to be drawn into her deceits.

"Again, a conversation we've already had. It bores me. Your lies bore me." He tossed her words into her face. "Stay here. I'll have a tray brought to you. Don't want my prisoner to starve."

Her eyes were wide pools of terror. He caused that. No, she caused it by shooting his wife, his annulled wife. This was the worst day of his life. Abruptly, he turned on his heels. With fierce strides he left the room to seek out Rose.

He found her in the kitchen, baking as he realized it was the way she relieved tension. A hot loaf of bread had just been set on the kitchen counter. A plate of cheese and meat was on the tray. Rose even included a bottle of wine. He wondered if the tray was for him or Crissie or perhaps both. What he did know was he wouldn't be able to share a meal with her. Not after this. His stomach churned.

"Where is the note?"

"I wish I could say I threw it out. Crissie didn't do this, you must realize by now. I'm as sure of that fact as I am of the next breath I take and that my heart will continue to beat."

"It's damning. There is no reason Charlotte would write that if it isn't true." His mind made up, he didn't intend to listen to any more nonsense nor did he intend to question his decisions.

"Other than the fact she hated Crissie for what she'd done to her life," Rose said, hands on her ample hips. "The two women never got along. From the moment you brought Crissie into this house then set her up in your bedroom, the sparks flew."

"So, they felt the same about each other."

Walker pondered that fact for a while. He walked outside for a few minutes inhaling as much air as he could. He stopped to focus on the cottage, which once again had a visitor. It must be Anne. He recalled the way Charlotte had been carrying on with her maid Laura the other day, remembered Crissie's instinctive reaction.

No, there was the damning note. He reminded himself once more questioning himself would get him nowhere. Crissie was guilty as sin.

He strode back inside. "Give me the note, Rose. Is there anyone else who knows about this?" He arched one tawny brow upward, his mood darker than ever before.

"What do you intend to do with this?"

"Give it to me, Rose."

"Well, I don't think so. Not if you're going to use it against the sweet McKenna lass when we both *ken* she didn't commit this crime. You think about it, remember her heart. Then you will have the answer and only then."

He didn't know any such thing. "Rose. Now I don't want to toss you on the ground and search your person for the note but if you don't hand it over this instant, you'll force my hand."

"Answer my question, young man." She was pointing a finger at him, jabbing at him as if she had authority over him. "You're not too old to put you over my knee and give you a good paddling. It's what you deserve."

He stuffed both hands through his hair, frustration coupled with anger eating at his soul. "She's guilty as hell. The note proves it. Now hand it over, Rose."

He stuck his hand toward her as if he truly believed his words changed Rose's mind. She brought her shoulders up as she stiffened against a glare that sent soldiers rushing to do his bidding.

"Don't think so. Not with you yelling at me."

She marched to the fireplace. After reaching into her bodice, she tossed the evidence into the fire, watching the flames lick the edges. "There, it's done. You're not taking her to the jail when you don't have proof of anything. Why the real criminal could have written her name on that note to implicate her. Use what little sense God gave you before it's too late and you've done something you'll live to regret, Walker Endicott."

With his hands behind his back, he watched the only evidence against Crissie turn to ashes. A smile touched his lips while relief filled his heart, "You didn't have to tell me about that note. You did, why?"

"I shouldn't have," Rose admitted grudgingly. "You got back sooner than I expected and I didn't have time to think the facts over. Now, you know well and good you're not going to hurt the lass. She is Ian's mother and deserves better from the father of her child."

"Perhaps I won't punish her as I've planned, not if she behaves herself and confesses to me, only me. However, she will remain a prisoner in this house. Rose, unlike you I don't have a doubt in my mind. She shot Charlotte. In case you haven't noticed Crissie has a temper. Charlotte could have done something to provoke Crissie. Even if that's so, she still has to pay."

"I know you. You're going to do something you'll regret, Walker Endicott. Think hard and long before that time. Think about all the repercussions of your actions."

"I will."

"Promise me."

"Promise. Now let me take that tray up to the room. This conversation with you has made me bloody hungry." For now, all he meant to do was keep Crissie confined to his suite of rooms. He would have a lock put on the doors first thing in the morning. There was no way he would allow her to remain free, in light of what she did.

If possible, he would coax her into telling her side of the story. He understood something must have happened between the two women. His heart went out to her as he tried to understand Crissie's point of view as well as Charlotte's.

When he strode inside setting the tray on a table, he found she was still curled up on the bed. She wasn't moving. A small moment of panic whipped through him. She wouldn't hurt herself, would she? No, Crissie was a fighter, a survivor. She would always find a means to land on her feet. Unlike Charlotte there was very little that was delicate or fragile about her. All he could see her doing right now was finding a way to get to McKenna land where she would have complete protection. He would not be able to reach her there. That was what the lock on the door would stop her from doing. At least he hoped it would.

"Crissie, stop pretending you're asleep. I know you're awake. I've food and I expect you to eat. If not for you for Ian, you have my son to think of." His words were harsh. He knew that. He watched the shudder sneak down her back. "Come on. Stop the sulk."

She didn't move one muscle intentionally. Still her shoulders shook with each tiny rasp of breath she inhaled. In her own way, she was defying him, making him angry. He wanted to shake her until she understood it wasn't prudent to gainsay him right now. No, she needed to appease him, tell him why she shot Charlotte as well as how. Still, she refused the smallest concession. On his part he'd done everything he could for her. He could feed her bread and water if he chose.

"Are you coming?"

"No."

"I'm not giving you a choice."

He stood over her, staring down at the woman he cared so much about. How did one lose what he longed for so quickly? He truly didn't know. Yet it was there in every breath he stole from the air, a deep-seated anger coupled with hatred toward what she did even while he craved to pull her into his arms then kiss the sweet fullness of her mouth, once more taste the essence of her that belonged to his heart. He wanted to feel her melt against him even while he wanted to feel the same pain he did for the part she played in the shambles of their lives. Her single action of vengeance ruined all his dreams. If she would confess, perhaps they could retrieve part of what they lost.

When he swept her into his arms, she came to life kicking out, hitting him with her fists. "Stop it! Just stop it, Walker!"

She swung hard with her fist. Hit him squarely in the jaw, hard enough to jerk his head backward. He didn't expect a fight. She twisted and squirmed in his arms until he thought he might possibly drop her. Abruptly, flipping her over he settled her stomach across his shoulder where he could better control her, his hand pressed firmly against her buttocks holding her in place. Her tiny fists pummeled his back while her legs swung heedless of what they might come in contact with. He grunted when the toe of her shoe hit his thigh.

"Put me down, you big oaf!"

He did. Walker dumped her into one of the brocaded wing chairs in his bedroom. Filling a plate with food, he handed it to her then poured a glass of wine. "Eat."

"I'm not hungry."

Even though she had no reason to defy him, she did and belligerently too. The firm set of her lips infuriated him to a point where he was sure to relinquish control to her. He couldn't let that happen.

"Yes, you are. I will find a way to make you eat if I have to stuff the food down your throat. You're feeding my son and I won't have you jeopardize your health out of pique."

She shot him a furious glare making no move to lift the fork he gave her. He thought for a moment she wanted to stab him with it, her eyes shooting such intense sparks his direction.

He stood over her, his hands on his hips, threatening in every way he knew.

When she ate a small bite, he understood he won this tiny round by mentioning Ian. Beneath lowered lashes she glared at him, her breasts heaving from the scuffle.

"I would never hurt Ian and you know that for a fact. The events of the day have made me nauseous. I might not be able to keep down the food. Do you want me throwing up on your nice blue Aubusson rug?"

"Drink the wine then."

He sat back, trying to enjoy the meal. She was right, this was not a meal he wanted to eat either. His stomach was sour from the distaste of today's events. Setting an example for her was more important right now so he forced the food down his throat while he watched Crissie nibble. All the while his irritation and fury grew.

She did drink the wine, too much it seemed. As he watched her refill her glass several times, he wondered if she didn't intend to drink herself into oblivion. He tried to cajole her into eating some more. "The food is very good."

"What are you going to do?"

With her fork, she moved the food around on her plate, toying with a piece of fresh salmon before attacking a few peas until they turned to mush on her plate.

"About what?" he asked smiling as it seemed her curiosity about her situation was overcoming her stubbornness not to talk to him.

He realized then he wanted her to worry. Needed to have her fear how he meant to go about punishing her.

"About me," she said, downing the rest of her glass.

While she waited for him to answer she poured herself another portion. Nothing more on her plate disappeared into her mouth.

"Ah, well that will be determined when you tell me why you did the deed as well as how."

He drank deeply of his wine watching her as she squirmed and twisted in the chair.

"I need to feed Ian." She started to stand, setting her plate away from her.

"Sit."

"Walker, he is crying."

"Rose will take care of him. You can do your part later. We both understand he only needs you for comfort. You can see the boy, after you've answered all my questions to my satisfaction." His voice was smooth, well-rehearsed. In his mind he practiced while he walked up the steps. He was determined she tell him everything.

"You just spoke of hurting Ian. He needs food too." Her fists were clenched at her sides, her lips set in a determined and furious line.

"He's more than five months old, nearly six and while he still nurses, he gets quite a lot of his nourishment from other means. I've already hired a wet nurse to be here if you refuse to relent in your unreasonableness to see what is best for you."

Even for this situation this was underhanded. He watched as her face paled and her breathing stopped. As if realizing she forgot to breathe, she gasped in a large gulp of air.

"*Bassa!*"

"Yes, well that pales in light of what you did."

"I *cannae* answer any of your questions. I *dinnae* shoot Charlotte. I *dinna ken* why she was shot or how or even when."

It didn't seem his threat was getting him what he wanted, a threat he could carry out, just not tonight. The breath he let out was long. This was going too far. He needed clarification. "Crissie just tell me. Did Charlotte provoke you in some way? Did she come over here looking for you, flaunting her relationship with me? If you tell me what happened, I can go easier on you."

"No. I haven't seen her since the day we returned from Portrush."

"Liar."

The more she persisted in the charade the angrier he grew. "This will not go well for you if you continue to lie to me."

She turned her head away, no words forthcoming. Her back was stiff, her shoulders squared.

"You leave me no choice. Tomorrow I'll have locks on the door. You won't be going anywhere." He waited for the longest time for a reaction. "Nothing to say, Crissie?"

~ * ~

Crissie stood on the porch of Andrew St. John's townhouse in Glasgow, Scotland. She drew in a deep ragged breath before using the heavy metal knocker. She checked the card Drew gave her that day so long ago at least ten times to make sure the address was right. Closing her eyes, she said a silent prayer that this would turn out in her favor.

The moment Walker told her she would be locked into his bedchamber; she knew she had to leave before the locks could be secured on the doors. No other choice for her was viable. She was innocent with no way to prove it. While he slept, she packed a small valise for her and Ian, stuffing the sapphire necklace and earrings into a pocket at the bottom. The moment she heard him leave the house, she rushed to Ian's room, grabbing him into her arms. She didn't even feed the poor boy. There just wasn't any time.

The sapphire and diamond necklace she sold in the village. She was sure she didn't get as much for the pieces as they were worth, but the money would get her to Scotland. Her destination wasn't to McKenna land because that's the first place he would search for her. She didn't know if her father would give her back to Walker when he came for her. Andrew told her not so long ago he wanted her, would wed her and protect her if she chose to forget Walker. Well, that was exactly what she needed now, a man's protection. Andrew wasn't as powerful as Walker but she thought he was just as wealthy.

Now it was up to him to decide what would happen to her. She inhaled a huge gulp of air sticking it to her heart for courage. It seemed she waited forever. Turning to leave she whirled back, deciding she needed to try one more time. This time she knocked harder. Her heart clenched when she heard a noise behind the door. She stopped breathing so she could hear more.

A tall slender man opened it. He sported a gray mustache that matched his thinning gray hair. The color of his eyes though was a startling sapphire blue. They would have matched the necklace perfectly.

His lips drawn together, he asked. "May I help you?"

Stepping back, self-conscious of her travel weary appearance, Crissie cleared her throat. "I'm Crissie McKenna. I'm here to see Andrew."

He looked over as if she was nothing, no one. "You mean Lord St. John? He's not home right now. Would you care to wait for him? The position has not been filled yet."

She had no choice but to bluster through this. If not here, there was nowhere for her to go except back to McKenna land. Perhaps that would have been for the best. She blustered through. "I will wait."

"Follow me." He turned, heading into the house.

She picked up the valise before adjusting Ian on her hip then wondered why the man didn't ask her why she was here. Maybe Andrew told him to expect her. Why would he do something so ludicrous? After all, she gave him no reason to think she would ever leave Walker.

Crissie followed him through the house to a kitchen that was empty. Confused, she wasn't certain what was going on.

"You may wait here."

"In the kitchen?" she asked growing more perplexed with each second that passed by.

"You are interviewing for the downstairs maid position aren't you." His voice was calm while she tried to think of something to say that wouldn't sound rude.

No, she was interviewing for the position of his wife, sounded crazier than she felt at the moment. One more time she cleared her throat. "I'm a friend. He asked me to come here a couple of months ago if I needed help. I do. Need help."

"You would rather wait in his office or the drawing room?"

It sounded like a question to her but she wasn't all too sure if the man already had the answer in mind. As if where she waited didn't matter to her, she lifted her shoulder slightly.

"I would just like somewhere private to sit and wait. I find I'm tired from my trip." She wanted to nurse Ian. Her breasts were painfully swollen. It had taken them most of the day to find a conveyance to take them from the docks to the townhouse. Ian had been very good, but he was exhausted and needed comforting as much as food. He needed a nap or even a good night's sleep.

Ian looked up at her before sticking his baby fingers into her mouth. She moved him to the other hip.

"Very well, the office is the most private of all the rooms. He might not be back until late tonight."

Crissie grimaced at the thought of waiting so long to find out her fate. She was hungry and needed someplace to sleep. The trip had been more tiresome than she remembered it to be. Instead of the usual ship that would carry paying passengers, she found passage on a fishing vessel. During her time in Portrush, she made friends with several fishermen. Shamus O'Riley had been more than willing to take her, especially when she told him she would pay. The fishing vessel had few places to sleep. What they did have was far from comfortable. A few sleepless nights was a meager price however to pay for her freedom.

She and Ian settled into the office, prepared to wait as long as necessary. It surprised her when the butler approached her with a tea tray that held a steaming pot of tea along with snacks that would tide her over for a few hours. At least she hoped Drew would not be longer than that.

A few hours later she and Ian were nestled together on a large chair facing the fire. The butler added wood for her, even covered her with a soft plaid. Her nightmares of the last week festered while she slept. She saw herself dangling from a noose. Saw Walker holding Ian, a satisfied smile on his lips.

She screamed when a hand touched her shoulder. Ian started wailing from the fright she caused him. Her gasp of air was followed by another then one more as she tried to place the room. For a moment she didn't know where she was.

"Hush, Crissie, it's just me, Andrew. There is nothing for you to fear."

She sat up just as Drew took Ian from her arms. "I'm going to have Charles put him in the nursery so we can have a brief discussion. I would have been here sooner if I'd known you were coming."

Hair dangled carelessly from the bun she wore. She pushed the errant strands aside trying to wake up, blinking the sleep from her eyes. Everything except the nightmare was hazy. She wanted to protest.

"Well, I assume we need to talk. Ian will be just fine."

Nodding, she watched the two of them leave the room. Ian seemed to like Charles. He was pulling the man's mustache and Charles was laughing. Her battered heart did a tiny flip-flop.

"Does your offer to wed me still hold," she asked fighting back the ever-threatening tears.

"Yes," he told her as he seemed to study her. His voice sounded solemn yet still filled with promise. "But you have to promise something first."

Crissie would promise anything if it meant her freedom. "Anything."

"Ah, don't be so fast to promise. This might not be easy for you." Gently he ran a finger along her chin. His eyes telling her he wanted more than a vow to be kept.

She held so very still trying not to flinch. "Since I owe you so very much, I promise. What is it you want?"

He smiled walking away from her. His back to her he clasped his hands behind his back, rocking for a moment on his heels. He didn't say anything. Seemed to be thinking.

After a few minutes he turned. "You must vow to forget Walker Endicott. I understand you thought you were in love with him. You might still be but some circumstance brought you to me. So, you're here now and if you're going to stay, I want all of you, heart and soul. You must have thoughts only about your husband. Can you do that? If you say no,

I'll understand then I'll make sure you reach your family."

The part of her heart still left to her after Walker's shattering denouncement of his trust in her withered. Closing her eyes, a tear sliding down her cheek, she swallowed hard.

"Walker is nothing to me nor will he ever be. He denounced me so, I will do the same to him."

The darkest part of her soul seemed to take over her body. With the words she shattered into a million tiny pieces.

"I *ken* it might not be easy for you. In turn I promise to be patient." Taking her hands, he pulled her to her feet. His fingers on either side of her head, he held her still while his lips tenderly molded to hers.

His touch was gentle, careful of her, non-invasive. She didn't melt even though the caress was pleasant. He didn't push her for more but set her aside as his sensuous lips formed on hers.

"Thank you," she said the words she truly meant from the bottom of her heart, pushing her feelings for Walker aside.

She promised herself she would do her utmost to make him the best wife possible.

"I'm going to assume you would like a bath before dinner. We eat at eight. I'll show you to your room. Ian is next door to yours and mine is down the hall. I'll have the servants take care of your bath. Ring if you need anything."

"What time is it now?" she asked.

"Nearly seven. Do you need a wet nurse for your boy?"

His light blue eyes studied her intensely. She wanted to cry out that she would never forget Walker. She had to pretend he was no longer in her thoughts. Had to convince Drew she didn't care about Walker Endicott, Earl of Briarwood.

"No, I still nurse him."

"If you change your mind, let me know."

She thought she heard a note of censure in his voice. He would care if she nursed another man's child. How could he not? Yet he was taking her in, giving her a home, providing for both her and Walker's son. Drew would be her husband soon. She would have to try her best to make him happy.

"I will," she said softly as he led her upstairs and to the rooms she would be occupying for the time being. It didn't seem he intended to rush her.

Her heart was breaking more each second. She had to do this. For her there were no other choices.

He turned her so she was facing him but did nothing else. "The bath will be here shortly. Remember, this will be your home as well as mine. You are not a guest."

She nodded, watching him leave. While she waited, she searched out Ian who slept peacefully in a crib just as Drew told her in an adjoining room. Pushing the moisture in her eyes away, she told herself this was for the best. Ian would have a fine and decent home. Drew would be his new father. At least she hoped so. He would want for nothing. She would be a good wife. The only problem was that she didn't think she would ever love Andrew St. John.

Not the way I love Walker Endicott.

This was not the time to bemoan her fate.

After she finished the bath and dressed in clean clothes, she checked on Ian who was still peacefully asleep. Trying to hold her head high, she walked down the long stairs. Charles seemed to be waiting for her. He nodded to the drawing room indicating she should go there. She understood Drew would be sitting inside expecting her to give him her heart. She didn't know how she would do that.

When she stepped inside, Drew rose with a handsome smile on his face. He extended his hand to her, which was warm, comforting in an elemental way. "Would you like sherry before dinner?" he asked politely.

"Yes, that would be nice."

Once more she wondered how she came to this. How she found herself about to wed a man she didn't love while she fled the man she did love. Thoughts of what she couldn't have swirled and mingled with the desperation sitting inside her.

This was all so polite as well as stilted. He motioned for her to sit as he poured the drink. She sat not knowing what to do so totally at a disadvantage. Her hand on the stem of the glass trembled. Her lashes lowered for a moment as she tried to hide her confusing emotions from Drew.

Andrew stood, leaning against the mantle of the fireplace, one booted heal resting on the hearth. He was acting so nice, so very gentlemanly as if he pretended there was nothing wrong with her being here, "Is the room comfortable? To your liking? When you are my wife, if you wish, you may redecorate. Make it your own."

She smiled. It seemed he was not going to ask her the hard questions just yet. "It's very nice. I don't think I would change anything."

A long silence followed. It seemed Drew was mulling over what he intended to say next. "You are sure you want to marry me now that you've been here for a little while?" he asked, his brows furrowed.

He was such a gentleman. There would be no passion, no desperate hunger. Yes, she was very sure. There was no other choice for her. Thinking of Charlotte as well as what the woman did to Walker, she answered with more information than she knew Drew expected. "I would like to be your wife in every way."

White shown out behind his suddenly broad smile. "That's good because I want that too. You must come to me willing. I won't force you. Make no mistake. I want you. Have wanted you since the first time I saw you. Do you understand?"

Forcing the words, she said, "I want you, too, Andrew St. John."

His grinned widened even more as he appeared pleased with her confession. Yet his next words belied that fact. Perhaps he was just amused at her quickly spoken words.

"Now why do I believe you are lying? I know. You were so in love with Walker when I first met you, you gave him your innocence without benefit of marriage. I don't expect those feelings will change overnight, Crissie. However, I pray that in time they will change. I don't believe you will ever love me as you did Walker. My only hope is that you will come to care for me."

She looked up. Her words perfectly controlled, honestly, "I want to love you with all my heart, Andrew. I promised to forget the man I now loathe with all my heart. Can we not mention his name again?"

"I do believe I would like that too." He took her empty glass from her, setting it on the table. "Shall we eat? We can speak of more pleasant things. Such as when our wedding will take place."

"More pleasant," she agreed as she allowed him to lead her into the dining room. All the while she wondered how she would ever stop thinking of Walker, seeing him in her dreams. She could only hope time would be on her side. The table was huge, menacing. "Drew, if it's alright with you, I would like to sit next to you instead of at the other end."

Her nerves were shredded into tiny strings. She didn't know if she could eat a thing.

"You need to relax, Crissie. You're shaking like a leaf in a tempest. I'm not going to devour you for dinner."

His tender smile she knew was meant for encouragement. He placed her hand in his.

Pulling her bottom lip beneath her teeth, she nodded. "I am nervous. This was not easy to do. I've been on tenterhooks for over a week now. It's hard for me to realize that I am safe now and with someone who truly cares about me."

"Come sit by me. I'd like you closer too." He pulled out a chair for her.

When he sat down next to her, he smiled again, his sky blue eyes shining with concern. The meal seemed to drag on while she tried to eat. She should be starving. For the last week she barely ate anything. Food didn't sit well in her stomach so she chose to forego eating. Now, with a full plate of food in front of her she could do little but push things around on her plate.

Drew didn't barrage her with a host of questions. Maybe he just wanted to wait until she volunteered information. She knew she should. If she were braver, she would tell him all that happened before she ran. He deserved to know why she changed her mind about Walker and came to him. He should know that he harbored a fugitive. For what he was doing he merited answers.

He placed his hand on hers. The warmth coupled with tenderness she felt from him surprised her. At that moment, she was truly sure Drew did care for her. She believed everything he told her as the truth.

He wants me.

"Would you like to retire for the night or would you like to talk some more."

Her hesitant guilt-ridden laughter seemed to cause his grin to widen. "We, we haven't talked at all."

"When you're comfortable we will. I won't force anything, even a conversation." His fingers hot around hers now squeezed tenderly.

She swallowed hard, gulped a frantic breath of air. He was so gentle and considerate. She was at a loss for words. In this same circumstance Walker would force her to talk. "He, he thought I shot someone."

Crissie knew her eyes were wide with the fear she felt. Drew could toss her out right now if he didn't believe her. He could send a message to Walker to come get her.

"Did you?"

Shaking her head, she forced the fear behind her teeth, slanted her chin upward. "No, I didn't. Walker didn't believe me."

"I thought we weren't going to mention his name again?" One dark eyebrow arched upward.

"Right. I'm sorry. Do you believe me?"

Despite the fact her voice was horribly shaky, she had to ask, couldn't let the question hang over her head. She would drown in worry if she didn't.

"If you tell me, you didn't shoot someone, of course, I believe you."

The weight of a thousand terrors slipped from her shoulders. A long soft sigh escaped from her lips before she could form the words. "He meant to lock me in the room until I confessed," she paused. "You do?"

"Yes."

"Thank you." Relief flooded her.

"Who does he think you shot?" He stood extending the hand that just covered hers with warmth.

With no hesitation, she answered, "His wife."

A bark of laughter followed her words. "Indeed."

"It's not funny, Drew." She shot back. For the first time with Drew, her temper flared. She had meant to keep the damn thing under control.

"No, it's not, not at all. For what Charlotte did to him, she deserved worse. Did she live?"

"As far as I know. When I left a week or so ago, she was alive. Which means I won't hang if he finds me."

~ * ~

At the mention of a shooting Drew knew Walker would find his way here. He also understood he would never allow her to keep Ian. If he meant to punish her or seek some twisted type of revenge, he would do his best to accomplish it. Walker was the type of man who would stand behind his beliefs until evidence changed them. Drew understood Walker needed to uncover more of what occurred that day before he could forgive Crissie for something she didn't do. Drew did believe Crissie didn't shoot anyone.

"What happened?" he asked hoping to discover more of the truths that seemed to elude Walker.

She was rubbing the palms of her hands with her thumbs, moisture clouding her silver-blue eyes so cold appearing they reminded him of ice. A chill seemed to sweep through her. "I don't know."

"Tell me what you do know." His gut reaction to this made him wonder how Walker could be so stubborn in his accusations.

She nodded brushing the moisture from her cheeks with the backs of her hands. "I was sitting in the bedroom, feeding Ian. Walker barged in asking me why I shot Charlotte. He told me that his wife wrote my name on a piece of paper. It was the incriminating evidence since I couldn't explain to him how my name got there if Charlotte wasn't telling everyone who committed the crime." She lifted her frail shoulders a bit as if she knew nothing more.

In truth, Andrew didn't think she did know anything else. He wanted to take the pain away as Crissie suddenly appeared so very pale, fragile too. Unlike herself. "So, someone is trying to frame you for the shooting. It's as obvious as the pretty little nose on your face. I'm surprised he didn't think of that."

"Why would someone want to frame me? I've never done anything to hurt anyone." Her heart cried tears.

"I've absolutely no idea. For now though, I want you to forget about that. Why did you decide to come to me? Not because you love me, I understand. Love will come for us. I'm a patient man as I look forward to the wooing just as much as the eventual bedding."

"He was going to lock me into a room, keep me there until I told him everything he asked. He wanted me to confess to something I didn't do. He was going to see me hang if she died. In the interim if I didn't satisfy his questions with appropriate answers, he threatened to have me tossed into the jail. I couldn't bear the thought."

"No, neither could I stay under those circumstances. You did the right thing by coming to me."

Crissie was tough from the top of her head down to her toes, but she would never survive long in a jail cell.

Feeling some of her pain, Drew took her hand. He led her to the patio outside her bedroom. His cook, Mrs. Alley, sent a bottle of wine along with two beautiful crystal gasses to her room per his request. Since she didn't eat much at dinner, he also requested a bowl of fresh berries along with cheese slices. Drew hoped she was slowly purging the man she once loved from her system. He'd seen them together numerous times. He didn't have any illusions about his relationship with Crissie yet he hoped in time she would come to love him as much as she once loved Walker. He had to be patient.

"Have a seat," he said softly. "The chairs are quite comfortable. They are even large enough for you to kick your shoes off then curl them up off the floor.

When she smiled at him, his heart beamed. She was everything he ever wanted, resilient as well as tough as nails. Her heart was soft. She was vulnerable and trusting. If she opened up to him, he would be the happiest man alive. He wasn't delusional, as he knew he had his work cut out for him. If luck held, he would have a lifetime with her. As far as he was concerned, the sooner they wed the better.

He leaned back sipping the wine watching every subtle nuance that passed across her features. He set the crystal on the table between their chairs. "We can wed in two weeks. Tomorrow, I'll have the papers prepared."

"Two weeks?"

"Is that too soon? Under your current circumstances, I assumed you would want my protection as soon as possible. Am I wrong about this?" He watched her, studied her eyes. The few lanterns on the darkening patio did little to help him see if she hid anything from him.

She twirled her glass in her fingers, seeming to study the dark red liquid as it moved. When she looked up, she said, "No, Drew, it's not too soon, the sooner the better. If possible, I would wed with you tomorrow."

"We could always go to Gretna Green. It's not far."

An aching wave of relief swept through him. While he waited the short few seconds for her answer, his heart pounded desperately. He understood until the ring was on her fingers and the papers signed, he could not take anything for granted. He also could not protect her from Walker's wrath.

Walker Endicott is a fool.

"I will take care of the arrangements tomorrow. There is a small church east of town. I would like to keep the ceremony small if that's alright with you."

He hoped she didn't have her heart set on some elaborate affair. If her circumstances were different, he'd give her whatever she wanted. That wasn't the case. If all went well over the next year, he intended to celebrate with a lavish anniversary party.

"Have I thanked you? You don't know how terrified I was when I first knocked on the door. Then you weren't home. I had to wait and wonder if you still meant what you told me back in Belfast."

"I think I saw your terror. You don't have to thank me. You're giving me my heart's desire by agreeing to marry me."

Indeed, she was doing just that. He intended to spend the next two weeks wooing her as she warranted. There were places he would show her, the theater, restaurants. They could take leisurely walks as well as parks to visit.

"There is a dressmaker not far from here. I'll go with you the next day. You will need a wedding dress among other things."

The small gasp he heard surprised him. "Truly, I don't need anything. I packed some things."

He waved his hand, smiling at her. "Not nearly enough. I assume you left most of your belongings in Ireland. Am I right? That one tiny bag you carried with you has Ian's clothes in it also. I'm sure you will need a new wardrobe. Ian will also need things."

"I *dinna* mean to impose."

"You will be my wife, Crissie. I've plenty of money to furnish my soon to be wife with clothing, nice fashionable clothes. Come."

He held out his hand, waiting for her to accept his hospitality. He waited terrified she might reject him.

Hesitantly, she placed her fingers on his palm. He curled his hand around her smaller one. Walking with her, he took her to the railing. The balcony from her bedroom looked out over a rose garden. A rock path led to a gazebo that could just barely be seen.

Drew wrapped his arm around her, felt the warmth from her body, noticed the fine trembling of her shoulders that he supposed traveled all the way to her feet. The evening wasn't a cold one. So, she must be nervous still. Slowly, he ran his fingers along her arm then back down. She shivered anew. He prayed the slight movement was because she felt something for him.

He wanted her so damn much. Not tonight though, he willed himself to an unsteady control. Their wedding night he decided would be the first time he would make love to her.

With his free hand, he pointed into the garden toward the gazebo. "Do you see the summer retreat?"

She nodded, "Can we go there?"

"Tomorrow we can have dinner alone there. Get to know each other better. I'm sure there are a lot of childhood tales as well as things you've done since you grew to maturity. What do you think? After we're married, I want to make love to you on the couch inside that gazebo surrounded by the scent of flowers."

Crissie leaned her head against his chest. He stroked the strands of her hair that had fallen lose around her face.

"I would like that. I would also love to hear about your past days. I bet you were a bit mischievous."

Some hesitancy clouded her words but this was a start. "I would like to kiss you? Is that okay with you?"

She turned toward him. A soft breeze ruffled her hair. The scent of orange blossoms filled his senses. "Yes," she sighed into his mouth as he brushed hers tenderly with his own.

Drew meant to take the kiss one step farther than he did earlier. He wanted to open her lips to him as much as he craved to have her open her heart. Slowly, he ran his tongue along her full bottom lip. Tasted the sweet wine she drank earlier. She brought her hands to his neck, her fingers running through his hair. With his teeth he gently tugged on the softness he just caressed with his tongue.

The tiny sound of pleasure delighted him. He ran his hands along her sides then down to feel the curve of her hips. She moved closer. He hardened further at the brief contact. He wondered if she felt him hard and so very aroused, craving her tonight. Scaring her away was not part of his plans.

Then she opened for him. He sensed more than felt the tenderness she was giving to him. His tongue swept inside the dark sultry heat that was all Crissie. She tasted sweet. Tasted of the wine. Savoring the sensation for a few more seconds as she let her tongue meet his, dance together for a few seconds. Then he set her aside. He rested his forehead against hers, touching her silken hair, caressing the spine along her back. He breathed in deeply.

"Thank you," he told her. "It's time you rested. I will see you tomorrow evening. We will stroll through the garden then eat. Perhaps you will not be so nervous as you were tonight."

Chapter Nine

A half-moon filled the September sky in Glasgow that evening. A soft breeze slipped through the coloring leaves while autumn flowers began to bloom. She'd been gone so long at one point he wasn't sure he would ever find her. One clue led to another.

Walker stood beneath the balcony where Crissie slept, watching, waiting. His heart raced at the prospect of seeing her one more time. Over the last two weeks his anger increased more rapidly each day he searched for her. By leaving him, she robbed him of his son as well as more days with her. Now she made her choice. He knew he could never have her but neither would anyone else. Now, more than anything, he would make sure she understood she wouldn't wed another man. When he found her, discovered she was to wed Andrew St. John, his plans came together with startling speed.

Charlotte lived if you could call remaining speechless and unable to leave her bed living. Anne, her partner, visited her occasionally, but she seemed to be losing interest in her. By the time he left, Anne seldom came to visit. Rose spent time tending to her as did her personal maid, Laura. Other than that, Charlotte was alone.

Restless energy flowing through him, He looked at his watch. It must have been the third time in the last five minutes. He slipped it back into his pocket. Once he discovered the fisherman she paid to take her to Glasgow, the rest was easy. She must have known he would come after her if she took Ian from him. She reneged on her promise not to leave. What could he expect from a woman who would shoot another person, one more helpless than she? Admitting to the truth, he would have come anyway, maybe not this soon. Perhaps he would have let her wed Andrew before he stepped in to make sure they would not consummate the marriage. No, he paused still thinking about Crissie. He couldn't do that to Andrew. The man didn't deserve a woman who would betray him, a woman who didn't love him. Despite everything he had no doubts Crissie still loved him.

He leaned against a tree, watching her room. The lamps had been on for what seemed like hours. He watched her walk back and forth with Ian in her arms, most likely in an attempt to put him to sleep. She'd put the lamp out about an hour ago. Still, he waited. He wanted to see Ian before he confronted Crissie. So, she needed to be sleeping when he arrived in her room.

He didn't care if he woke her, but he didn't want Drew or Ian to wake. This was his night with Crissie. He meant to enjoy every silken curve of her body, the sweet hot taste of her lips as well as the way she melted into him, giving him everything he asked for when he stroked her intimately. She might protest for a second or two. In the end, he knew she would give in to her desires and soften for him. Her honey would flow.

She was his, at least for this night as well as into eternity. Thoughts of claiming her flashed through his head. No, not until she would accept her fate. He would always find her, again and again if necessary.

It was time. Easily he swung himself on to the railing before he climbed onto the balcony. For a few seconds, he stared into the bedroom, his heart pounding from both the exertion of the climb as well as the anticipation of seeing her again. It appeared she was sleeping. He opened the doors she didn't bother to lock and stepped inside.

His heart thundering in his throat, he stood over her gazing down at her small form. Her dark hair was braided. Loose ends tussled from sleep lay haphazardly across her pillow. He remembered the way her hair felt between his fingers. He smiled when he thought of the molten silver shimmer of her eyes when she realized he was in bed with her.

Before he got into bed with Crissie, he strode the distance to Ian's room. Gently, he caressed his son's tawny head of hair so like his own. He meant to have his son back in his arms tomorrow morning, Crissie and her needs be damned. She never gave one moment's thoughts to her promise when she left. He never understood why. He supposed that would be the cruelest blow to her he could inflict. Stopping with claiming his son was not his intent though. In coming to Andrew St. John, she made a very bad mistake.

Undressing as he strode into the bedroom, he folded his clothing neatly on a chair, his boots beneath. Pulling back the covers, he settled next to her, bringing her fully against his chest. Instinctively as if there was nothing different, her small hands ran along his arms, entwining automatically into his hair. She sighed softly nestling closer to him as if this was something she was accustomed to.

Walker cupped her buttocks with his large hands, squeezing gently while he pulled her so close she should be able to ascertain his intentions when she woke. "Crissie," he whispered next to her ear. It's time to wake up and make love to the man who melts your heart."

He knew the second she woke. Her body tensed, her eyes widened, the moonlight casting across them. Her gasp of air rang in his ears. He placed his thumb at the pulse point on her neck, delighted with the frantic racing of her heart.

"Walker," she breathed her body rigid as she pushed on his chest. "What?" She heaved in a huge breath of air. "You can't be here."

"Oh, but I am, little pigeon" he felt his grin widen pleased with himself as well as her reaction to him. "I intend to stay the night."

"I'll scream."

He let her go. Rolling onto his back, he sat up, placing his hands behind his head as he relaxed indolently in her bed. Through slitted eyes he watched her, gaged her reaction.

"Be my guest," he spoke softly, daring her to do just what she told him she would do. "What do you think will happen when you wake the household? Hmm...they will all race in here, Andrew in the lead, and will see you in bed with me."

She clamped her mouth shut, staring at him her eyes blazing her anger. He wanted to tap into that anger, feel her passion as she twisted and arched against him with each stroke of his fingers. Ah, but he would soon. Just as the sun would rise tomorrow, Crissie would give in to her baser needs. It was just a matter of time and patience.

"Go away." She tried to leave the bed.

He reached out to stop her then drag her back where she was.

Her skin was as soft as he remembered. The expression on her face was harder, filled with distrust, maybe even loathing. "I'm not going anywhere until I get what I came for."

He smiled at her, his grin wide and wicked as he looked on the woman, he once thought would be his wife. He wanted her still. No woman runs from him, taking his child and gets away with the act. If she stayed, they might have found some way to work around the differences looming around them. She wasn't going to marry another man. If he couldn't have his mate, no one would.

But she ran

Crissie pulled the covers higher, not that it mattered. The prim white nightgown covered all her important parts, the parts he intended to stroke and kiss as soon as she understood the rules. He wanted to uncover every sweet part of her, kiss her everywhere until his lust was satisfied.

"What is it you want, Walker?" she gritted her teeth so hard the muscles in her cheek ticked.

He'd never seen that on a woman before all the while wondering if she'd be even more passionate than before. In her anger, she might...

He wasn't sure what to think, inhaling a long breath as he pondered her question. "What do I want? Hmm... 'tis a good question."

"Walker."

"All of you for one last night."

She was trying to back away from him while she was shaking her head, more of her long silken black hair coming lose from its confinement. He held her upper arms.

"No. I won't give in to your wishes."

"I think you will."

"No."

Her vehemence surprised him. He was ready for the upcoming contest of wills even though he knew who would win. She wouldn't be the woman he thought she was if she didn't fight him on some level.

"Yes."

He leaned forward, holding her head in one hand as he fit his mouth to a perfect alignment over hers. Against him, she shuddered. He felt the slow melting of her lips as they parted for his intimate investigation. He didn't want this to be too easy because prolonging this was in his best interest. Before he finished, she would find herself begging him for more. He pulled away.

She pushed away from him. He gave her some distance, smiling as he saw the gentle swelling of her lips. Watched as she unconsciously and provocatively ran her hot pink tongue across her bottom lip before her top teeth bit down on it. He would do that soon, nip her lips with his teeth.

"Walker, please don't do this to me. I'm getting married tomorrow." Her breathing was frantic small tiny sips of air.

"I know. That's why I'm here. I would never fuck a married woman." His voice was husky, so very deep and gravelly.

The dark thoughts centering in his soul would keep him going.

"After this, if I let you?"

She swallowed hard. He placed a finger on her throat as he watched with avid fascination.

"After tonight you won't bother me again?"

"Not if you're married."

He understood she knew she wasn't speaking to the same man she left three weeks ago. She changed him. He was harder and darker now.

"Thank God."

"You are agreeable with this?"

"No, you misunderstand. While I'm not wed yet, I'm engaged. It wouldn't be right." She sounded even more hysterical than before. "I don't want to think about you. Don't want to remember your name. Don't want anything to do with you."

Her fears wouldn't change his mind. "Not as bad as shooting someone."

With her hands pressing against his chest as if she could move him, she closed her eyes for a moment. When she looked at him again, "I won't do this with you. I'm not your whore. It wouldn't be fair to Drew."

His laughter was a short bark. He would possess her. "You will and when is anything fair?" he asked his voice husky with need, soft to cajole throaty with unleashed desire.

He kissed the corners of her lips, slipped his tongue inside her mouth, parting lips before he played inside her, touching all of her just as he would play elsewhere.

The shudders of her body against his didn't go unnoticed. Inside he smiled, pleased with this initial attempt to coax her passion to a frenzy. Little tremors rippling in languorous waves beneath him gave him good reason to understand her protests were verbal, nothing more. Crissie still yearned for him, despite the feeble objections.

His lips and teeth found the secret very sensitive part of her behind her earlobe, lathed and nipped while he enjoyed the twisting of her supple body beneath him, the brush of her small, feminine form against his. The way she strained against her desires to tell him no but failed. Her fingers laced through his hair, tugging him closer. She ran her fingers along his backbone down then up to find purchase in his hair once more. He kissed her mouth again, molded his lips against hers. Touched her deep inside when she opened for him just as a flower's petals would open for the sun. Pulling away, he gazed into eyes that seemed to beg him for more. He wasn't sure what she was pleading for, most likely for him to stop as well as for him to give her the pleasure she knew he could.

"Do you want me, little pigeon?"

It was a pure male question as the answer would feed his ego. They both understood he wanted her response, would wait until he heard what he wanted.

"No, I want Andrew," she murmured, turning her head away from his hard gaze as well as from his questing lips.

"Little liar," he murmured next to her ear as the moisture and heat from his words sent shivers throughout. "I'm going to have to do something to change your answers to something more pleasant for me.

"No, Walker, you can't do this to me." She did plead but her words were not the ones he wanted to hear.

"Just as you shouldn't have shot Charlotte." A rise of fury encompassed him. "You want concessions for yourself you're unwilling to give to others."

"I..." She licked her lips as she thought on what she meant to say, "I promised Drew I would stop thinking about you. I don't think about you. Don't want you."

He touched her cheek, his finger drawing with moisture on the tip. "What's this? A tear? And now you can't keep that promise. It seems you are never able to keep a promise such as the ones you made to me that you would not run." He sat back on his haunches, now straddling her. "I do think this nightgown is horrendous. It's time I removed it." His nimble finger had the gown unbuttoned then over her head before she could stop him. "Ah, just as beautiful as I remembered. You're every man's fantasy, Crissie. Did you know that? No, I don't think you do. You realize that's why Andrew wanted you, don't you?"

Bending forward, he bathed her collarbone with his lips and tongue, travelled lower so he swept wet kisses to the valley between her breasts then farther to her navel. She arched against him, silently pleading for more. Every unbridled move she made delighted him, did feed his ego.

Her hands rested against his chest, still with the pretense of pushing him away. Yet her nails scored his chest. "Admit you want me, Crissie. Say the words."

"Then you will leave?" she asked as her hand flattened against him, her palms across his nipples.

"I didn't say that." He lowered his head so he could touch one nipple yet didn't. Instead, he watched as the rose-colored bud puckered and tightened in anticipation of his lips, teeth, and tongue. She was so damn responsive, so passionate. He fought his own needs to contain himself to make this last until she cried out for him until she finally told him she wanted him.

"No, I guess you didn't."

"What do you want, Crissie. I know it's not for me to leave. I look at the response of your body, the clouding of your eyes and I know you are encompassed in intense desire that needs release. You don't want to spend the rest of the night quivering in desperate need of my kisses. Are you hot and wet, weeping for me in your most private places, places where only I have seen? Where no other man should discover, I wonder?" he asked as his hand explored the side of her body, traveling lower, caressing the curve of her hips then the outside of her thighs all the way to the tips of her toes only to repeat the process along the inside of her legs.

She moved slightly, her long supple legs opening marginally to give him better access.

He chuckled softly. "You are mine, Crissie, whether you know it or not, whether you will admit to the fact or not. Drew will never have you like this, weeping, crying out for your release, sweet honey filling his hands. With her legs parted he could see the cream of her wanting.

"Walker, please..."

"Tell me what is that you want."

"You *ken* what it is."

She twisted beneath him as he covered her, his weight solidly above her as he rested on his forearms, smiling down at her while he enjoyed this moment.

"*Nay*, tell me."

His tongue curled around the puckered tight bud pushing insolently upward as it begged for him to take it fully into his mouth to play with it. He did. Then sucked deeply, drawing her breast into his mouth, drinking harder as she arched against him, trembling quivering as he deepened the pressure. His fingers kneaded her other breast, twisting the tight bud between his finger and thumb. Beneath him she cried out her pleasure as she bucked against him without words, pleading for more.

Tears ran in rivulets down her cheeks. He knew she tried to deny her feelings, tried to put his touches along with the constant strokes of his finger to the back of her mind. He could almost see her thinking about Drew, trying to imagine if he could bring her to this ecstasy to this point of no return. She collapsed in his arm, her heart still harshly pounding, her breath erratic. He did nothing to soothe her as he wasn't done arousing her.

They still had what was left of the night to explore this mating, the raw vibrant energy coursing between them, something that was as old as time, elemental and primitive. He kissed her again, again and again as she slowly realized he wasn't finished with her. No, he'd barely started with her.

"You're mine. Best you don't ever forget that, Crissie McKenna. Andrew will never possess you the way I do. He can't give you this ecstasy," he whispered as he fitted his mouth over hers again.

He kissed her and kissed her, nipped and laved with teeth and tongue. He found the dark sultry parts of her, explored the sweet hot flesh that beckoned to him aroused him more than he wanted to admit. Before he finished with her this night, she would understand exactly who she belonged to.

"No," she moaned softly into his mouth. "Tomorrow I'll be Drew's, only his. After this evening I will never be yours. I will never ever think about you again. You'll be the darkest part of my life that I want to forget."

"Never. A ring and a few vows will not change how you will long for me in the middle of the night or think of me when you're in his arms, when he's touching you in all the sweet places that have up until now known only my possession." he told her softly as his mouth closed once more over hers driving her body to plead for more of the enchantment only he could give to her.

She twisted and arched beneath him. He wanted to drive her to another climax before he took his fill of her, before he encountered the velvet heat of her core. "You will always be mine, sweetheart, just as you have through all eternity as well as into the next."

Lower and lower his lips traveled until he reached the apex between her thighs. Of her own volition, she opened for him. He grinned. Loving her soft damp petals with his lips, kissing her, teasing her with his teeth and tongue until he moved higher again. He stopped just when he thought she might explode with the tremors of release that would bring her the rapture he knew she craved. His finger swept inside her, pushed as deep as he could before he held two fingers inside her his thumb finding the hard nubbin hidden between her secret folds. He worked her, teased her, loved the snaking and spinning of her body as she reached for the ecstasy she yearned for.

"Relax, sweetheart. Just let your desire reach its zenith as you did earlier."

His soft words seemed to send her higher, higher still. She was flying as her body thrummed against his hands. He pulled her to him, holding her tight against his chest, absorbing her pleasure into him. He settled his lips against her while he accepted her cry of ecstasy into his mouth.

Her slight frame shook against him. She trembled having given herself so sweetly so very completely to him. For a brief moment he felt a rise of guilt before he squashed the sensation. His beloved was a liar. She had no feelings for anyone other than herself. Perhaps not, she did love Ian.

Still...

I love you.

Cannot let another man have you.

I will move heaven and earth to keep him from knowing this sweet ecstasy from another man.

He ached; his pain so powerful now he wasn't sure if he could hold himself back so he could see her complete submission to him. Needed to know she would never forget him, never crave anyone else or want for their caress. Felt the most insistent craving to claim her as his. This woman was his soul mate. Yet he could not have her. Could not bring her home to rot in prison or to lock her in his bedchamber. He had to allow her to go to travel to her destiny bleak as it seemed right now.

Nay. A thousand times *nay.* He should have felt the release, the time to claim her before this dark moment in their lives. Perhaps he had and just not realized the extent of his desire for this woman.

Now it was too late for them.

She left him. Ran from him.

When she finally calmed. "Drew will be a lucky man if he can coax this same passion from your body," he murmured as his lips pressed once more against her mouth, swollen from his attention.

With a desperate need he began the assault on her senses once again. Kissing her deeply, drawing her into his web of intrigue and desire the magic insatiable. She enchanted him. He craved to leave his mark on her forever binding him to her. He continued the slow methodic seduction, holding her hands above her head so she couldn't drive him over the top before he was ready. If she touched him, he would surely explode.

Slowly, anticipation high, he spread her legs farther. Looking at her swollen petals of femininity damp, wet, crying because he loved her completely, he entered her sultry velvet depths. When inside he held himself in check, absorbing the gentle quivering of her need, her body pulsing around his, ever-drawing him deeper.

The movement was slow and richly vital. He watched her once more as she seemed to reach the crest of her deepest pleasure. Stopping momentarily, he let her fall to earth. He didn't want to pick up the pieces or cradle her when she fell. Yet he did, so he could begin the assault anew.

Crissie McKenna had already robbed him of all he held dear.

Still, he wanted her.

Needed her with a desperation he would never admit to.

"Do you want me, Crissie?"

She opened her eyes, moisture clinging to her spiked lashes. She shook her head saying no to his inquiry. He didn't believe her.

"So be it."

He drove deeper, harder and faster until he was beyond control. She spun against him curved, pulling him deeper inside than he'd ever been before. Frantic in his need, he no longer cared if he pleasured her. He knew she was beyond herself, beyond thinking. She would climax again.

His claws extended just as he reached the ultimate point in their ill-fated joining. He realized his folly, withdrew the claws that would mark her as his, that would tell her what he was. It was knowledge he could not trust her with despite the fact she might be a shifter herself as was her entire family. It was something else she lied to him about, he was sure of it.

He wanted to cry out her name, to yell out his release. Instead, his lips remained sealed against hers.

A woman he could never trust.

He emptied himself inside her. With a low groan of pleasure, he settled his weight on top of her, absorbing the warmth of her body for the last time.

The sun would rise soon. They spent all night having sex. He needed to leave before the house woke. She would deal with the consequences of what she was. She always did. This was no longer up to him. What happened to her after tonight, he would orchestrate. He yearned to keep her safe yet away from any other man. She was his.

Yet he couldn't help himself. "Confess, Crissie, and I can forgive you. You can come home with me. All will be fine."

Lord, but he already forgave her. This plea of his he understood was futile. She was a McKenna and she would stand by the word she gave him.

Tears flowed from her eyes as she was shaking her head adamant with her lie. "Believe what you will, Walker Endicott. You always do. I did nothing. I didn't shoot Charlotte. Will never confess to something that never happened."

His long sigh of discontent surprised him. While he knew she wouldn't acknowledge what he asked her for, he hoped. If she did, he wouldn't leave her here. He would forgive her the sin and pick up the pieces of their disheveled life. As magistrate of the county, he could find ways to protect her.

Without her confession, he couldn't begin to forgive. At that moment all his intentions changed. Anger once again simmered deep inside pushing to be heard.

"Have it your way."

He rose. With a heavy sigh he wasn't sure if it was regret at her obstinacy or the lack of courage on her part, but he knew now she would never be his soul mate. He was mistaken. He would never be able to claim a woman who didn't trust him.

"Have a nice life," he told her as he dressed. For a moment he stood in front of the doors leading to the balcony giving himself one final look at the woman he loved with all his heart.

Now, she could be nothing to him.

~ * ~

For the next few hours sobs wracked Crissie's body. She rolled over pulling a pillow close to her chest. The scent of Walker lingered there. How could she ever look Drew in the eye when she had betrayed him so? She should have told Walker no then stood by her word. Should have denied him everything he asked for. Denying Walker her body was never possible. She loved him so.

A small cry from the nursery startled Crissie from her melancholy thoughts. Quickly, she rose. She found her nightgown tossed haphazardly on the floor beside the bed. A small shudder, the memory fresh once more, ripped through her. Slipping the gown over her head she strode to Ian. He was hungry and she needed him, craved the comfort his tiny body gave, the unconditional love. She was surprised Ian was still here as she was sure Walker meant to take him from her.

Thoughts of Walker taking Ian away from her flitted through her head simply because she had not one doubt in her mind that he would. The only question was when.

A knock on the door startled her before she realized this was her wedding day. How could she get through the wedding night with another man?

"Bath water for you, Miss McKenna. May I come in?"

"Give me a second and I'll open the door." She didn't understand why she locked the inside door but neglected to do the same for the doors leading to the balcony. Juggling Ian between both hands she slipped on a robe.

When she opened the door a brigade of servants stood waiting with the tub along with steaming water. She sighed softly, knowing all too well how good that water would feel on her limbs after last night's unwelcome visitor.

"Now, you needn't hurry. There's lots of time before now and the wedding. Susan has your dress all pressed and ready for you to put on when we get to the church. She's going to do your hair as well. It will be a lovely day, a very fine day indeed."

"I have to feed Ian. Can you wait then take him with you to the nanny Andrew hired?" she asked as she sat down.

Crissie didn't want to think about Walker. She promised Drew so she valiantly tried to push thoughts of him out of her mind. When she looked at the bed, she remembered. When she closed her eyes, she felt his lips on her mouth, the stroke of his fingers on her flesh coupled with the warmth of his all-male body as his weight encompassed her. She swallowed the lump of tears threatening. It wouldn't do for her to have red swollen eyes when she stood at the alter saying her vows to Andrew.

He deserved better than that.

If she had not run after Walker that day when he left the highlands. If she had not gotten with child the first time she allowed herself to be intimate with a man. If her father had not let her go off with Walker without putting up a fight. If, she thought...none of this would have happened.

I would not be mourning the loss of a man who will never trust me or love me.

She would not be marrying a man she didn't love. She did respect Andrew St. John, admired him even for marrying her when he knew she didn't love him. Drew was a good man. He deserved better than her.

Ian finished so she handed her boy over to the nanny who was patiently waiting. "Will you feed him and dress him for the wedding?"

"My pleasure. This little man is such a dear one." She bobbed a little curtsy before leaving the room with Ian as well as his wedding finery.

With a heartfelt sigh, Crissie slipped into the soothing water. She relaxed, letting her eyes drift closed. So comfortable, she almost fell asleep. When her head lolled to one side, she jerked upward, her heart pounding. She was almost sure Walker was standing in the room again.

The maid must have been in and out of the bedchamber, since a day dress with all the frilly underthings that went with it lay on her bed waiting for her to get out of the bath and dress. Quickly, she finished.

Wrapping a towel around her body as well as her head, she strode around the room. She opened the door to the balcony, peering over the edge. He climbed up this? She would never have thought anyone would be so bold.

It took her almost an hour to dry her hair. When she finished, she dressed. She rang for the maid.

"I guess I'm ready to go to the church. Has Drew left?" she asked, wishing she could see him but understanding it was bad luck to see the groom before she walked down the aisle to meet him.

The wedding was arranged in such haste, she had no attendants. Her one and only marriage and none of her family would be there. Drew thought it best that under the circumstances the fewer people who knew the better. They would go see her mother and father in the highlands as soon as they could.

Drew's mother would be at the wedding but not his father. She didn't know if they approved or not. She supposed she should trust Drew's word that they liked her. If they knew what she was accused of, they wouldn't want her around their son. No, they would probably despise her.

On the way to the church, she sat across from Drew's mother. Crissie didn't know what to say so she spent most of her time staring out the window. She felt at such a loss for words. Nothing about the way she felt was right.

"Do you love my son?" Mrs. St. John asked.

Surprised by the sudden question she gulped air. She didn't even *ken* the woman's first name. "I..." She didn't want to lie but neither did she want to tell her no, she didn't love him. "Your son is a wonderful, decent man that anyone would love. He cares for me."

"You?" she persisted.

"Me?" She would have to lie. There was absolutely no way around it. "Yes, of course I love him. I wouldn't be marrying him if I did not."

His mother waved her hand in the air, her smile setting Crissie at ease. "It makes no difference to me if you treat him as he deserves. Most marriages are not created from love. I didn't love his father when we first wed," she confessed, a dreamy smile now on her lips.

"You didn't?" Crissie asked, surprised by the confession.

"No, I didn't even know him. Our fathers thought we would make a wonderful match. I was given no choice at all. The first time I saw him was at a special dinner the night before our wedding was to take place." She leaned forward, patting Crissie's hand. "Not too long after our wedding I did fall in love with him. Until he died, he was the light of my life. Things will all work out for the best. You'll see. Everything will be fine."

Crissie tried not to groan. She heard those exact same words so many times before she ran. To hear them now brought on thoughts of more bad luck. She didn't want more bad luck. Somehow, she knew her wishes would not come true.

Walker will do something irrevocable.

She realized now that she would never wed Drew. When they stopped in front of the small parish church, another carriage sat in front. She assumed it was the one that brought Drew. The St. John coat of arms was emblazoned on the door.

"Drew is here. Let's go first so he won't see you. Your dress should already be here. Would you like help with it? Since I have no daughters, I'd be honored if you would allow me."

"Please do," Crissie said wishing her own mother were here to help her. "I'd like that."

"Your mother would love to be here. What is her name?"

"Wynnie." Crissie felt the horrible prick of tears in her eyes. She didn't want to cry.

"Now, dear, be brave. I know you're frightened. Drew told me he met you when he was in the highlands and that he fell in love with you there. He told me that at least for him, it was love at first sight. I do believe that is the most romantic thing I've heard in a very longtime. Does he know your mother and father?"

Crissie nodded but couldn't get any words past the lump in her throat. Mrs. St. John was out of the carriage striding to the church. This was going to happen. It was truly going to happen. Her thoughts all collided in a tangle. She didn't want to hurt anyone.

If they knew...if they knew what I did last night...

Drew's mother was back quickly and opened the door. "Drew is with the minister in the back of the rectory. No one will see you when you go in the side door to the small room that was built for just this very reason." She slanted her another reassuring smile.

The coachman helped her out. They were inside the room. Her dress hung next to the mirror. The lady's maid Drew hired for her stood beside the dressing table waiting with a pleasant smile on her face.

Once she was dressed, her hair swept up onto her head, Mrs. St. John stepped forward. "I've a few things for you."

"For me?" Crissie was surprised once more, tears threatening again.

She couldn't take anything from this woman. Not when she had this gut feeling something very bad was going to happen. Not when she wanted with all her heart to marry Walker not Andrew.

"Yes, for my soon to be new daughter-in-law. I want to give you something very precious to me." Her eyes brimming with unshed moisture, she walked behind her, a sapphire and diamond necklace in her hands. "Drew's father gave this to me the day Drew was born. It's for you. I've no place to wear it. It will pass for something new as well as something blue. I don't have anything to lend you. I certainly hope that isn't an omen of bad luck."

Crissie was shaking her head needing to deny this present. "I can't except this."

It was so like the necklace she stole from Walker to use to get here. It wasn't the same one but it was so much the same her stomach turned sour. Not that her stomach wasn't already threatening to erupt.

"Yes, you must wear the necklace for your soon to be new husband. When Drew sees it, he will smile understanding I've accepted you completely into the family. I think he was afraid I would not. The circumstances were so sudden. He refused to explain everything to me."

"Alright."

She felt breathless and out of sorts. She knew this wasn't right. What could she do about it though?

"If it's alright with you, I'll walk you down the aisle. Give you to my son."

Crissie had no words. She could barely breathe. All she could do was nod her head then walk toward her destiny whatever that was going to be. She inhaled a long wavering breath filling her empty lungs.

"Are you ready?" his mother asked.

Once again, all Crissie could manage was a small nod.

"Everything will be fine. Don't you worry."

Then they stood in front of the preacher. Mrs. St. John handed her to Andrew. His fingers were warm, comforting in a strange way. He smiled at her. She wanted to cry again as she thought of the betrayal just last night into this morning. Only a few hours ago she was in another man's arms. She shuddered. Her knees felt so weak truly she didn't think she was going to be able to keep standing.

I broke my vow to you and I'm so very sorry.

She wanted to cry out that she couldn't do this to him. Yet she had to do just that in order to survive. To keep Ian. That was the only good thing about Walker showing up the night before her wedding. That Ian was still with her. When Mrs. St. John handed her to her son, his mother sat on the bench, holding a gurgling Ian in her arms. She smiled to her then nodded as if giving her much needed encouragement. At least Drew's mother didn't expect her to be in love with her son. Not yet anyway.

The hot sting of tears still threatened. When she looked into Drew's sky blue eyes, she tried to smile for him. She knew it didn't reach her eyes. Encouragingly, he squeezed her hands. The minister seemed to be droning on and on.

She wasn't listening.

She should be doing just that. What if the minister asked her a question?

227

Crissie tried with all her heart to listen. He was talking about God and how she was supposed to be a good wife. She would be. She promised. That was one sacred contract she would keep. From this moment on she would never give Walker Endicott, the tenth Earl of Briarwood a second thought or even a third. Forever and always, he was out of her life. She knew he would never come back.

Ian gave a high-pitched little scream of delight. He always cried out like that when he saw his dah. Crissie turned to look at her little boy. She smiled, loving her baby with all her heart and soul. Her heart caught in her throat as she gulped air in a rising panic. She closed her eyes telling herself she didn't see Walker negligently leaning against the door to the church, an indolent smile on his lips, lips that had been kissing her only a few hours ago.

Her throat closed around air that was too thick to breathe.

No, God no, no, no...

It can't be him. It's my imagination. Walker isn't here at her wedding.

She was dreaming. A nightmare it was.

What did he want?

She felt Drew's hands tighten around hers. Heard the minister drone on as if nothing was amiss. The minister was asking if anyone knew a reason why Drew and Crissie shouldn't wed. Any minute now her knees would give out. She would collapse to the floor.

"I object," Walker said, pushing away from the wall he previously seemed to be holding up as he strode to the front of the church.

His eyes blazed with passion and anger along with raw desire while he stared at her.

She sucked in a wobbly breath, didn't get any air as the floor whirled around her getting ever closer. Drew held her elbow, supporting her as Walker continued his long strides to the front of the church.

"Who is this man?" the minister demanded.

"He is no one," Drew said brushing Walker's sudden appearance here aside. "Ignore him and get on with the ceremony. If he has an objection, it doesn't amount to anything."

"Ma'am," Walker picked up Ian, cradling him against his arms. "This boy is mine."

So, he was taking her son now. Her throat closed tightly. Truly Crissie didn't understand why she thought Walker would not show up here today. What better place to seek his revenge, to make her pay for her supposed crimes along with her refusal to confess than at her wedding?

Walker held Ian now. She hoped he would leave and whatever nefarious purpose he might have planned he would forget about. It didn't appear as if he would abide by her wishes. Drew was holding her close, his hands on her waist now as if he understood she needed help just to stand.

"What do you want?" Drew asked, his voice not as confident as if it had been only a minute past.

"Thought you should learn some interesting facts about your fiancée, soon to be not so loving wife. Information you should know before you seal your fate this afternoon. It's for your good."

Walker's smile was boldly arrogant. Despite earlier sentiment, Walker's words seemed to pique Drew's curiosity.

"I know all about your relationship with Crissie. She has told me everything."

"Everything?" One lazy dark eyebrow arched upward, his gaze insolently raking over Crissie's body before lingering on her breasts. "Now, isn't that interesting. I doubt if she had the nerve to tell you what happened last night."

Drew turned her so he could see her eyes. She wanted to look away. "What happened last night? I would have you tell me, not this man."

She couldn't say the words that would incriminate her. When she opened her mouth to take a sip of air, Walker spoke over her.

"She would never tell you I spent last night in bed with her. If you go there, to her chamber, you'll discover the room ripe with the scent of sex. Did she mention it to you?" He grinned again. "She's a very passionate woman. I suppose you know that though."

Still, she was shaking her head as her knees slowly gave way.

"Walker, please, leave it be."

"You're lying," Drew said but the look on his face told Crissie he believed Walker. Believed she would sleep with Walker on the eve of their wedding.

She knew all the blood had drained from her face, maybe her entire body. This couldn't be happening to her. He wouldn't ruin her this way. When she looked at him, his eyes were cold, lifeless. He meant to extract everything from her. Drew would turn her away from him just as Walker turned her away.

"Ask her." He nodded in Crissie's direction. His amber eyes dared her to tell Andrew the truth.

She was crumpled on the floor, tears welling in her eyes, trickling down her cheeks. This was the nightmare of epic proportions, worse than anything that happened to her before.

Then Andrew's voice came to her, the condemnation, the knowledge that what Walker said was true. "Did he?"

She closed her eyes against the pain swamping her, welling up inside her. Both Andrew and Walker looked at her. Her body was vibrating with the intensity that had her nails biting into the palms of her hands so fiercely her knuckles turned white.

"Ah, she doesn't want to confess. And you want more than anything to believe her. I see the pattern here even if you do not."

"I think you should leave now. You've disrupted the wedding long enough," Drew said but he didn't sound as confident as he did before.

"No, not just yet. She climaxed twice before I even fucked her." His voice was harsh, held no hint of respect only disdain. It seemed he would not let this be. "She is so warm and passionate. Should I tell you all the ways I had her? No, I suppose that would even be too crass for me. I'm sure this evening she will show you all the ways I've taught her how to please you."

"Crissie?" Andrew's voice held a wealth of questions as well as disgust. "Is any of this true?"

Tears poured from her eyes, streaked her cheeks.

"You still don't believe me. Well, her room is quite lovely. The dark blue Aubusson rug coupled with the light blue drapes is very elegant. The bed, ah, the bed is firm but soft, the cherry wood nice. It's large enough for a man my size. Did you have it made especially for you? I want you to know you will enjoy it immensely if you haven't already. No, Crissie told me you were going to wait until the wedding night to take her."

Drew stepped away from her. The look in his eyes stole her heart, ripping it into shreds. "You broke your promise to me. The wedding is done, finished. Good bye, Crissie. You can have him if he wants you." Drew strode from the church, left through the back door. She saw his back. He didn't turn to look at her again. Walker's hateful words were even too much for Andrew to forgive.

Crissie knew the carriage would be gone when Walker was finished with her. Reaching behind her neck, she unhooked the necklace his mother gave her. She supposed the lack of something borrowed might had brought bad luck. Her laughter was shallow and clung to the back of her throat. When she felt steady enough to stand, she handed the beautiful piece to Mrs. St. John.

"I'm sorry. I don't think it would have ever worked out for us."

The woman looked ready to cry. Tears spiked her dark lashes. Her eyes were just like Drew's, the color of a summer sky with all the hope and love she wanted to give to her. That too vanished. She also left.

Alone in the church with Walker and her son, she had no words to defend herself nor to condemn Walker for what he did to her. All she dared was to wait to see what he would do next. Time ticked slowly. Walker walked to the back of the church. He returned with the valise she brought with her.

"What do you want from me?" She was finally able to ask.

"That's just it, Crissie. I don't want anything from you, not anymore. I got the annulment. I was going to ask you to marry me." For several seconds he stared at the cross in the front of the church. "I brought you the clothes you came to Glasgow with. They are all yours. The trunk, I will send to your parents. Once you are home, everything will be there."

"I've no way to get there," she said searching for some means to contact her father. "No money."

An annulment? He never told her.

"That's not my problem. Like the cat that you are, you always land on your feet. I suppose you will do so again. What did you do with the coin from the necklace you sold?"

"Do you expect me to walk?"

She had a few groats left. They were still sewn into the lining of her cloak. Perhaps there was enough left to pay for a trip to the highlands.

"I don't expect anything from you."

He was turning then, leaving her to her own devices. Yet she had so few. Didn't know if the few coins she possessed were enough to get her to McKenna land.

"I've no money."

"That's not true. Don't lie again. I left the coin you sewed into your cloak. The money you received from the sale of the sapphire necklace you didn't want. The one you stole from me."

"You gave that to me. The money is mine. I used most of it to get here."

"You flung it in my face telling me you didn't want it. You stole it, Crissie. It's another charge I could bring against you if I wanted. Still, I don't want you to suffer."

"*Bassa...*" she whispered.

"No, just a man who loved a woman who could not return that love. Use the coin to return home to your parents. I'll bring Ian next summer so his grandparents can meet him."

She wiped tears from her eyes with the backs of her hands. "Why?"

He cleared his throat as he looked away from her. "I promise you if I can't have you no one else will, Crissie."

Chapter Ten

In a daze, Crissie stumbled from the church, the small valise clutched in her hand, her cloak around her shoulders. The few coins in her cloak as well as her valise might be enough to get her home. When Walker showed up last night, she had a sick feeling about his sudden and unexpected appearance.

She never expected him to go this far. Never in her wildest thoughts expected him to set her on the road with no protection. What did he think? That the roads were safe for a woman alone and on foot?

In silent despair she slumped on the steps of the church and watched the carriage she traveled to the church in disappear down the lane toward Glasgow. Her heart caved in on her. She didn't know where she was. All she knew was that she needed to head northeast. If she couldn't find a posting house, how long would it take for her to walk home?

She didn't understand how Walker could despise her so much that he would leave her alone, defenseless. The only conclusion she could come to was that he wanted her to die. He told her he loved her. She loved him. Yet...

A fine mist began to fall. Gray haze covered the road as far as she could see. Even the weather was against her. Fumbling through the valise, she found her cloak and pulled the hood up. Just in case he lied to her, she checked the hem for the coins she sewed into the lining.

They were still there.

Walker's carriage rumbled around from the back of the church. How did he find out where she was to be married? He had connections. He was powerful and wealthy. The carriage rolled to a stop. He stepped out.

"If you would confess..."

He was giving her one last chance. She was so tempted to tell him the words he wanted to hear. He might take her in again, might at least make sure she made it home. She stiffened, her chin raising a notch. Determination loomed itself in her head. She would not lie, not to Walker, not ever, "I didn't say anything false, Walker. There is no confession to make."

"Very well, if that's the way you want to go on. The posting house is in the other direction."

She had no illusions he would somehow miraculously relent. At this moment she was more than willing to plead with him. "Can I see Ian now. Just to kiss good bye." At the word good bye, more tears pooled in her eyes.

She was shocked that he relented. "Yes, one last time." If she was not mistaken, there were tears in his eyes as well.

He handed Ian to her. She cuddled him in his arms, tears flooding down her cheeks. She kissed him. Kissed him again and again until Walker held out his arms. Frown lines marred his face. Tears slipped from his cheeks.

"Thank you," she stammered.

Her anger coupled with misery shook her to the core. She thanked him for giving her what was due to her.

"As I told you I will bring him to the highlands next summer so your parents can see him," he said turning he climbed inside. "Good luck, Crissie. If I hear of an impending wedding, I'll be there to stop it."

He would do it too. Although, she learned her lesson with Drew. She would never think to wed again.

She watched as her life faded away into nothingness. It would do her no good to wallow in despair. The sooner she started walking the sooner she would get to the posting house. He pointed her in the right direction. Never told her how far it was.

I should hate the man but I don't. I still love him. You best forget about him. Do what you promised Andrew. Don't think about him ever again. If only she could.

She was cold and tired. Needed a place to warm herself until she had the strength to continue. When she tried the doors to the church, they were locked against her. Strange that she didn't expect to find them open. She picked up the valise then started walking. She walked until no light from the cloud-covered sky lit the road.

With her cloak wrapped around her she found the shelter of a large oak tree. Sitting against the trunk she closed her eyes, only to hear her stomach rumbling in protest. Her feet hurt. Her body ached. Her head spun uncontrollably. She'd give anything for a nice cup of tea and chunk of warm bread with honey. Her stomach had been so out of sorts this morning. She didn't eat.

To make matters worse the rain began to fall at a steady clip. She pulled her cloak around her, huddled against the storm as well as the sinking sensation that she might die here and no one would miss her or even look for her.

She'd never felt so alone.

She'd never been so cold.

If the sky hadn't been so very dark, she would keep putting one step in front of the other just to go somewhere. Who knew, maybe something good would happen to her. No, good luck was not in her destiny.

When she woke, it was still raining. Mud clumped the road. Her feet stuck in the mud. She rubbed her face with her hands pushing the exhaustion away. Tilting her face to the sky, she hoped a few drops of rain would help her parched throat.

Two men barred her way. "Where do you think you're going, missy?"

"To..." she began but stopped as they both stepped closer.

The two men looked as hungry and as tired as she was sure she did.

"Your cloak looks warm," one said.

The other grabbed her valise. She fought but they were too strong. The man wrenched the valise from her hands as the other tore her cloak from her shoulders. "No!" she cried out only to see the men rushing away. She fought back the tears along with the curses. Now, she truly had nothing.

I'm not going to give up. If I have to walk all the way home, I will.

She trudged through the mire. By the time the rain changed to a mist and a tiny piece of sun hung between two dark clouds, she reached a village. She never saw a posting house. He would not have pointed her in the wrong direction or he had no idea how far by foot it was. Perhaps her mind had been so fuzzy from hunger she didn't see it. Dirt claimed what she wore as well as her legs. She hoped to find a tiny bit of work that might buy her a loaf of bread. There was no one about. Then she remembered it was Sunday.

When she arrived at a church, the doors were shut tight. They weren't locked though. She stepped inside. Sitting on one of the pews, she prayed silently, first for Ian—that he would lead a happy life and that somehow she would see him again. She prayed for Walker—that he would find it in his heart to learn to trust if not her then the next woman who might come into his life. She wanted him to trust her but that didn't truly matter any longer. She might never see him again. Crissie didn't think he trusted anyone except possibly Rose. Her heart bled.

She was so hungry her stomach no longer rumbled. Inside, there was only a dull ache of emptiness coupled with the rejection she felt so poignantly. Silence seemed to absorb her thoughts bringing them fully within her, smothering her. The loss she felt was unsalvageable.

"Are you alright, lass?"

She jumped, startled from her thoughts. Crissie thought she was alone. Her hand at her throat, she asked, "Who are you?"

"Just the cleaning woman. I've my lunch in a sack over there. Would you like to share? I always pack more than I can eat."

The woman was leaning on her mop smiling down at her as if she knew all Crissie's secrets. Her face was kind and Crissie didn't see how she could turn down food.

"Are you sure?"

More than anything she wanted to eat something, anything. If it hadn't been raining so hard, she might have foraged for roots and berries. Mushrooms she meant to stay away from since she didn't always remember which ones were the poison ones.

"You look as if you need it more than I do. When did you eat last?" She sat down blowing an escaped piece of hair from her face.

"I…"

She didn't want to sound too eager but she was literally starving to death.

"The truth now," the woman coaxed. "I won't be hearin' any lies."

With a heavy sigh Crissie looked at the plump-cheeked woman. Her eyes were a dark brown. Her nose was straight. When she smiled it seemed to reach across her face. She seemed sincere.

"Yesterday morning before my wedding but not much. I was too nervous." With a groan Crissie closed her eyes. Then quickly, "I wasn't married. The groom decided he no longer wanted me." She groaned again, her eyes focused on her hands clasped in front of her. "I'm sorry. That is more information than I'm sure you wanted to know. In any case it is more than I want to explain."

"Well, yes and no, it just sparked more questions. Probably can't do anything to help other than share my lunch, but I'm a good listener if you want to tell me what happened. I won't sit in judgment. In my mind your supposed groom is a fool. Despite the mud and the dark circles under your eyes, you're quite a lovely young woman."

Her laugh was brittle. Tightness gripped her lungs, compressing them, forcing air out when she wanted to suck it inside. "It's not my looks that were in question. It's my lack of character."

Without thinking, realizing this would help her heal, Crissie told the woman, Iris was her name, some of her story leaving out the worst of it. Leaving out the fact that the man she loved thought she shot his wife. Although everything to Crissie sounded sordid, as if someone wrote a very bad play.

No, Charlotte was no longer his wife.

"I'm a horrible person. I should have been able to tell him no then stand by my word."

"No, I believe you've been misunderstood. Men have this way of stealing our will and coaxing it to their way of thinking. I do hope you make it home to your parents."

"Can I stay the night here?" she blurted without thinking that this woman certainly would not have the right to give permission for her to stay within the church walls for the night.

The strained look on Iris's face told her all she needed to know. She understood her presence here for the evening would not be welcome. Trying to push the feelings of self-pity from her head, she let a whoosh of air escape her lungs. "It's alright. I can move on."

"Well just let me...no, you stay right where you are. The minister should not care. This is a house of God. We take in lost souls in order to help them. If anyone needs help, it is you."

"Just for the night. I'll be on my way in the morning. Can I help you clean?" Crissie asked hoping to give aide in some small way.

"After you eat half this food, I'll welcome the help."

The next morning was sunnier than the last. Iris left a loaf of bread for her. At least she thought it must have been the cleaning lady. She broke off a small portion to eat before putting the rest inside her pocket for safekeeping. She meant to eat it sparingly. Iris told her she was ten miles from the church where she was supposed to have wed Andrew St. John. The posting house was another mile down the road. She had not gone very far. At this rate it would take her forever to get home. She prayed she would continue to find people like Iris.

With a lighter heart she set out on her journey. Afraid of unknown travelers she stayed off the road, paralleling it. The weather remained mild that day as well as the next two. Crissie slept under the stars. When she couldn't sleep, she watched the stars above thinking they were the same ones Ian would see from his tiny crib while she tried not to remember Walker and how much she loved him. Star crossed lovers, that is what they were. She found a stream running alongside the road where she washed away some of the mud she accumulated on the rainy day. She drank deeply, the water filling her empty stomach.

She finished the loaf of bread. Each passing day, she traveled fewer miles until she didn't think she could take one more step. Near a village but unable to walk any longer, she crumpled to the ground. Her body slumped, powerless to do anything except rest. Her eyes closed, she listened to the beating of her heart, her slow uneven breaths. Heard the pounding of steps.

"Get up, lady. What you doing, lookin' for a handout? Bet you'd like one. You're not getting one from us." Three boys danced around her, tossing small stones at her. One kicked her in the ribs. She grunted incapable to do as they suggested. "Get up, lady, get up, lady." Their words sounded like a song.

"You're all dirty. Your hair is ratty. Don't you ever take a bath?"

She swallowed hard, forcing her legs beneath her as she tried to stand. A clump of dirt hit her in the face. She staggered then fell again. The boys continued to dance around her. Time stood still as she watched through blurred vision unable to defend herself against the mean viciousness of these boys. Her tormentors danced back and forth now circling her, throwing pieces of wood, dirt and larger rocks at her. She was on all fours unable to stand, unwilling to lie down and accept defeat. Unwilling to die.

She was going to die here, stoned to death by children. For the first time since she was a small girl watching her brothers shift, she wished she could do just that. If she could change into a sleek black panther, she would scare these hellions. It would do them good.

No reason to dwell on her inadequacies. No time to do anything at all. She crossed her arms over her head and prayed. Exhaustion claimed her as she slipped into blissful unconsciousness. Crissie sensed rather than heard another presence. The dull ache where their missiles landed faded yet still pounded a suffocating staccato. A cold wet nose rubbed up against her cheek, nudging her. A raspy tongue licked her face. She had a fleeting dream about the black panther she wanted to be.

A loud bark near her ear woke her.

"Ah, there you are little lass. You're finally awake. Dog here scared the brats off." It was a woman's voice, paper thin yet comforting. "If you can get your feet under you and help me out a little, I'll get you into my wagon. I'll take you home, feed you too. Everything will be fine. You'll see. Everything will be fine."

She wanted to scream that nothing would ever be fine again. Wanted to ask why people kept telling her that. Rose, Mrs. St. John, Andrew, now this lady. The only person who never told her that was Walker. Of course, he knew nothing would ever be fine for her again.

As surely as the sun set in the west, Walker planned her demise. No, he thought she had money. Thought she would be able to pay for safe passage home. Would be able to make it to the posting house. He didn't mean to leave her with nothing. Yet she had less than nothing.

Within a few minutes she was lying on the floor of the wagon, a blanket covering her shivering body and the dog lying beside her. The dog was warm, blessedly so, helped ward off the terrible chill snaking through and circling her body. This was the first time she'd been warm since she could remember.

Am I going to die?

Crissie didn't know if she said the words out loud or thought them. Since there was no ensuing response, she must have thought them. Perhaps her luck had just changed for the better.

Maybe everything would now be fine. *Nay*, she should not let her hope cloud the reality that was her situation.

The cart bumped along the road then turned off the main road onto something narrow and rutted out. She thought she would be thrown from the wagon from time to time as the cart lurched then righted itself before it lurched to the other side. The dog lying beside her didn't seem bothered. She closed her eyes tight while she tried to hang on to the boards beneath her.

What seemed like an hour passed by then another one before they ground slowly to a halt. She nearly groaned when she tried to move her arms and legs. Pushing herself up to see where she was, impossible. She fell back to the floor of the wagon.

"You just stay right where you are until I take care of Jazzy, my mule. The doggone animal needs to eat. Deserves to be fed too. Had to haul extra weight today. Thought we'd never get here. Don't move," she hooted.

Her laughter sounded more like a cackle to Crissie, but it was the first happy sound she's heard in longer than she cared to remember.

Crissie was fine with staying right where she was. Didn't know if she would ever be able to move again. Didn't know if she cared to even try. Didn't know how long the lady was gone. She lost the warmth from the dog when he left to follow the woman.

"Alright then, I'm back. You just scoot on over the edge of the wagon and I'll get you inside the cabin, warm you up and feed you. You're probably hungrier than the darn mule. You're all skin and bones."

When Crissie was finally standing inside the cabin, she realized it was not a cabin. It was more of a hut. There was only one room and a large fireplace. Bricks of peat were piled by the fireplace to be burned later. The old lady's lip twitched in what appeared to be silent amusement.

The woman helped her to one of two chairs that were sitting near the fireplace. She collapsed. She let her head fall back to rest against the chair as she closed her eyes trying desperately not to relive all that happened to her over the last days of her life. She concentrated on breathing while she listened to the slow, steady beat of her heart.

"You don't look so well," the lady spoke softly as she touched her hand to Crissie's forehead. "You don't have a fever though. That's good. Don't need you getting sick on me. No, don't need a sick lass to worry about."

At least she didn't tell me everything would be fine, Crissie thought to herself as she almost laughed but she didn't have the strength.

In any case, as soon as she regained her strength if she did, she would have to recount her story. Retell all the sordid details about her lost love, her desperation to love a man who couldn't love her back. She would have to speak of her determination to reach McKenna land realizing this old lady could do little to help her in her task.

"Two months along would be my guess," the lady murmured as she stirred the big pot hanging over the fireplace, tasted the broth added more herbs then continued to stir. "What is it, two or three?"

She held her breath, let the question stick in the back of her throat trying to understand what the woman was talking about. "Two or three what?"

"Well, bust my buttons. You didn't know you were with child. It's as plain as day." The lady heaped up a bowl of broth and vegetables then handed the bowl to her. "Can you feed yourself?"

"I'm going to have a baby?"

She almost laughed at the irony as the warmth of the bowl eased the chill she was feeling deep inside. Her fingers flattened against her mouth. Walker wouldn't know anything about this child. She would make sure he never took the baby from her because he left her to fend for herself. Would never ever tell him.

It would serve him right.

Aye, it would serve him right.

This baby would be hers.

"You think about it. We should have a better idea as soon as you start doing some counting of days. Think back. When was the last time you...?" she paused, the spoon still stirring and when she looked back to Crissie, "Guess you've been pretty busy with other concerns. What brought you to this point? Are you running from someone? The father of this baby of yours?"

"Later, I'll think later. Too tired to do it right now. Thank you for helping me and no, I'm not running from anyone even though the father of this baby is never going to learn about her conception."

She wanted to gulp down the soup. Instead, she sipped savoring every tiny spoonful, knowing if she ate too fast, she would most likely get sick. It was delicious.

"Were you raped?"

Crissie was shaking her head, a hollow thin laugh following, "No, nothing like that. I loved him and thought he cared a little about me. Turns out, he didn't. I was innocent, a fool on top of that."

When would she ever stop crying over Walker Endicott? Even now when because of his actions she nearly died she, still wanted his love. Craved to feel his arms around her, his kisses against every part of her body.

"Well, couldn't let those boys stone you to death, now could I? Dog here has a way of barring his teeth so that it scares the very devil out of some people. Looks like a wolf, doesn't he? People think he's part wolf too. He wouldn't harm anyone though. It's a good thing no one knows that for sure."

"I'll only stay until I get stronger," Crissie said feeling the results of the warm soup. "I won't be a burden and I'll work."

"Of course, you will. You're a good girl, dear. I can see it in your eyes. I'm not going to be askin' any questions or judging you for something that was out of your control. A man has got to take some responsibility for what he does. This man you think you love doesn't deserve you. Someday he'll figure it out and come looking for you."

"In this case, I hope he never discovers he has another child. He's not a good man. Once I thought he was. I learned though that he's ruthless and arrogant. He's so angry and distrustful, he would do anything to hurt me." She drew in a deep drought of air, feeling better for her efforts. "He can't know about this *bairn*."

"Odds are with you hidden away in this tiny one room shack, he'll never find you. He would have to be pretty determined. If you don't want him to find you here, he won't."

"He won't look for me. His feelings toward me have been made abundantly clear."

The lady must have heard her wistfulness in her voice. She looked at her, an all-knowing glint in her silver-green eyes, her lips moving as if she was thinking what to say.

Finally, "You still love the man." She held up her hands, her eyes giving her sudden compassion away. "Don't you bother to deny it. I can hear the truth in the sound of your voice and the look in your eyes. If he doesn't merit your love, try to forget he ever existed."

"I've tried. Forgetting Walker doesn't seem to work to well for me. It seems he's become a part of my soul."

Unfortunately, a part she could not stop thinking about no matter how hard she tried to do just that.

Crissie spent most of her days collecting peat for the fire. She made several stacks near the meager shelter where Jazzy was stabled. The weather turned chilly the end of October. The first snowfall arrived a few days after that. She thought about returning home. If Walker ever did look for her, he would look there first. Her parents would protect her. He had Ian. What more could he want from her. He already stole her heart and soul along with her son.

She didn't know what to do.

Torn between leaving and Walker discovering he sired another child tore at her. His discovery of her condition wasn't something she could bear to think about. He would steal this child from her too. Now she didn't have the choice of returning with him. She had no means available to her.

Gwen spent most of her days out and about the countryside, collecting herbs and wild vegetables. She certainly knew her way around the swampland. There were a few chickens in a shed out back that kept them supplied with eggs. In a boarded off spot in a corner of the tiny hut, she kept potatoes and onions along with carrots and a few turnips left over from the summer and fall harvest. Every once in a while, she'd come home with a rabbit she trapped.

After careful deliberation over the past months, Crissie figured that when Gwen found her, she was nearly three months pregnant. She was beginning to show. Her belly was rounded slightly. In another month she would have to try to let out the seams of her dresses. Gwen had a small supply of fabric so she was able to fashion a third dress for herself. She also needed to make crucial decisions about where she wanted to have this baby. Staying here in such an isolated spot might not be the wisest decision after all.

Gwen taught her about the herbs she collected. Some of them were medicinal, others were for flavoring the soups and stews they ate. Except when Gwen was foraging, Dog slept by the fire. This time of year, the days were very short and the nights very long. The wind howled down from the mountains, cold air seeping through the thin boards of the hut. When it rained there were a few strategically placed pots on the floor to catch the water.

Several times she thought to walk into the nearby village to send a message home. One of her brothers would come get her. She just wasn't ready though to be pregnant and without a husband for the second time where people along with her friends would judge her. This time she knew what she was doing, had made love with him more than once.

Her pregnancy the first time was impulsive.

This time...she simply could never say no to the man.

Crissie settled her hands on her stomach, pleased she would have her baby.

This baby is nobody's baby but mine!

If he ever tried to take this child from her, she would kill him with her bare hands. It wasn't going to happen. Yet she understood how feeble the vow was. Walker would do what pleased him. If taking this child from her gave him joy, he would do so.

~ * ~

Tears sliding down her cheeks, Crissie buried Gwen the end of February while she was swollen with child. She knew then she had to leave. If she didn't, she would have the baby here in the hut by herself. The time she spent debating what to do was long past and stupid of her. Fear coupled with desperation crippled her, swamped her to the bone. Tears she should shed were long past dry. She didn't know how she was going to survive. She no longer cared about herself, only the baby, only the little girl she carried in her womb. The baby whose kicks and restless moving begged for life.

Leaving this decision to the bitter end wasn't well done of her. By doing so, she risked far too much.

Before she died, Gwen told her dog would help her find her way out of the bogs. He would show her the dry land. All she needed was to ask the animal. She didn't have a lot of faith in that route, but she wasn't sure if she had a choice now. She had to get home. Gwen had enough coin in a basket in the hut to send a message. Perhaps even enough to buy a bit of food while she waited for her father to come for her.

Her baby was due the end of February to the middle of March. A small laugh erupted as she didn't truly have any idea when the babe would be born. She might have two weeks or two days if her calculations were wrong. Or she might have a month if her little girl decided to turn up late instead of early.

Gwen asked her to cover her grave with some huge rocks that held some kind of religious meaning to her. Despite her best efforts, Crissie couldn't move them. They were too heavy. The mule froze to death a week before Gwen passed on. She could have hooked the animal to the wagon then she would not have had to walk to the village.

Everything would be fine.

The weather had been frigid. So, she used most of the peat she collected to keep the house warm. She would have to get more. When she finally thought to check on Jazzy, he was standing beneath the shelter frozen solid. She didn't think there was anything she could have done about that except bring the old mule into the house. She wouldn't do that.

She knew for a fact nothing would ever be fine again.

That night after she buried Gwen, she cried more tears, just when she thought she had no tears left. Her sobs wracked her body so much that the baby growing in her womb must have felt it because she started kicking in what Crissie was sure was protest. She was sure the little one was telling her to stop feeling sorry for herself. So, she wiped the tears away with the backs of her hands then focused on leaving tomorrow morning.

Crissie didn't know why but she was sure her child was a girl. She also didn't know why but she started dreaming of Walker. She didn't want to dream about him. The nightmares only brought on more tears, the sobs wracking her body until she ached from the tips of her toes to her heart.

Anyway, now it was time to leave. She didn't know how Dog could lead her out of this quagmire when the poor old animal mourned for Gwen. Crissie would find him sleeping over the old woman's grave during the day then warming himself by the peat fire where she always sat in the evening.

Tomorrow morning, she would head out. Dog would just have to show her the way. Reality spiraled through her. Somehow, she knew she wasn't going anywhere. The baby would be born here on this land if she didn't do something to change that. She just didn't have any more thoughts about how to do that. It was too late to send a message to her father and expect him to arrive before the baby was born. She put it off so many times having never expected Gwen to die. Never thought she would be faced with birthing a baby with no possibility of help. Never thought she wouldn't be able to find her way out of the bogs.

The thought of having this baby by herself terrified her more than she could admit to herself. All these months she thought Gwen would be here for her. Thought she wouldn't be alone.

Here I am alone and unprepared.

At least she isn't my first baby. I've some idea what to do. On the tiny counter in a basket, she'd set clean towels along with a sharp knife. There was a clean blanket to put on the bed when it was time. She always kept water boiling over the fire as well as extra water from the well inside.

Crissie tossed one of the last pieces of peat onto the fire watching it crackle and burn, making a mental note to collect more tomorrow and stack them inside before she left just in case she couldn't find her way out. With a heavy sigh, she settled on the pallet pulling the cover over her shoulders. She would either find a way out of this tomorrow or she would probably breathe her last breath of air along with her baby here amidst the peat bogs.

When she woke the next morning, she spent time cleaning the house. She wasn't sure why but it felt important to her to keep it the way Gwen would have liked. She brought in from the stores outside all the peat she collected over the last few months before setting about the collection of a bit more. When she had the baby, she wouldn't be able to get more for a while. When she was finished, she scrambled four eggs then boiled the rest of them to take with her. She wasn't truly that hungry, but she was afraid she might not eat for several days. Two loaves of bread were wrapped in cloth then placed in a sac. There were a few coins in the bowl on the counter Gwen earned from helping ailing patients the doctors couldn't cure. She put the coins in her pocket.

She gave one last look to the small hut she called home the last six months. With a heavy sigh she called out for Dog to come. He barked then with seeming reluctance to leave followed her out the door.

"Well, you mangy mutt, you have to show me the way out of here. We both *ken* there is no road. So, what do you say? Gwen told me you could do it."

Dog sat on his haunches looking at her with soulful eyes.

"Go on, show me the way." She pushed her hands out as if the gesture would tell Dog what she wanted.

He didn't move.

"Fat lot of good you are."

Left with no other choice Crissie started walking. Dog followed her refusing to take the lead.

She tried to find her way around the bogs and the mires. Sometimes she found dry spots but more often she would sink up to her knees before she could turn around to find a dry piece of land. Dog stayed on dry ground. Just as Gwen told her he knew where not to step. This went on for several hours. Wet with swamp water, exhausted bone deep, she finally sat down on a dry spot of land, breaths in short pants, her heart thundering from the exertion of the day.

"I quit," she murmured softly wishing she knew how to find her way back to the hut. "I can't do this any longer."

Suddenly, Dog was beside her wagging his tail, licking at her face. He pranced away turned then looked at her as if saying what are you waiting for. Let's go home.

"Finally, you are going to show me where to put my feet. Very well, better late than never. At least the baby will have a roof over her head."

Roles reversed, Crissie followed Dog. She must have been traveling in circles because in less than fifteen minutes they arrived at the hut. All emotion seemed to drain from her the instant she saw where she was. The agony of having no control or power in her life led her to the ground. She didn't know how her life could get any worse.

Dog sat beside her, nuzzling her with his head, begging for pets.

"Yes, you're a good dog. You did bring me home." Even though this home was not the home she wanted to go to.

Shivering, she rose. Inside, the hut was still warm the fire still burning low. She put on a kettle of water to heat so she could wash.

Pressing her hands to the small of her back, she stretched. A small contraction seized her. She wasn't alarmed. When she carried Ian, she had lots of these early contractions. The midwife told her it helped prepare for the birth and that she shouldn't be alarmed. It was all perfectly natural. While she wasn't alarmed at this tiny contraction, she was well aware that she had to find a way to traverse the bogs surrounding the hut.

Tomorrow then, she would try again.

She had to, or she would have this child here.

Quickly, she took care of her needs then built up the fire. She wrapped herself in one of Gwen's hand stitched quilts. Still shivering and exhausted, she piled more peat on the fire before settling on the pallet to sleep. Another contraction hardened her abdomen. Startled by the intensity, she pressed her hand on her belly then settled on the bed. Vaguely aware of more contractions, she tried to sleep. She supposed she drifted in and out of a fitful sleep to wake when her stomach would harden again.

Oh, God, Dog was barking, pulling on her arm, tugging and tugging. His insistence surprised her. She pushed him from her. "Dog, lie down," she murmured, turning over to put her back to the animal. He pulled the quilt from her.

"Go away!" Then she cried out in pain a stronger contraction wrapping around her middle seeming to press upon her back.

Something was wrong. She sat up, searching the room, smelling the smoke. The house was on fire. Dog was trying to pull her from the flames. Slowly she staggered to her feet. Groping through the smoke, she found the birthing basket then the door, Dog behind her.

Frigid air hit her square in the face. Rain sluiced steadily from the sky. She sucked in clean air as another contraction sent her to her knees. Fear tore through her, ripping any pretense that she wasn't going to have her baby here and now. With as much determination she could muster, she opened the door to the hut so she could grab the old ratty cloak Gwen gave her that was hanging by the door.

Heart in her throat, she wrapped it around her, staggering toward Jazzy's shelter. Once inside, Dog sat beside her while they watched the flames sizzle and leap, smelled the acrid smoke in the air. With her head on her raised knees, she prayed in silence, tears streaming down her cheeks to freeze in the frigid weather.

She was going to die here. Her baby too.

As the last of flames seemed to diminish, Crissie looked beyond the fire, beyond what she thought was the horizon. It was dark yet the full moon cast shadows on anything moving. This time of year, light from the moon played along the moors. She watched as a horse and man gradually appeared out of the shadows, a dark rider. Her heart thundered beneath her ribs. Fear caught as her breath stuck inside her lungs. Every instinct she possessed cried out for her to run.

Yet she stood frozen in place.

Run before it's too late.

Run before he discovers your secret.

Another contraction seized her, as hand to her belly, she bent trying to will the contractions to stop. She cried out in pain, stumbling backward as she tried to distance herself from the apparition approaching her.

"No!"

Finally, her feet moved. She turned, lifting her skirts she ran as hard as she could. Stumbling to the ground once then twice, she pressed on. Tears streaming down her cheeks. Running from the past, fleeing a future she couldn't endure. One she thought she evaded.

"Crissie! Stop!"

Still she kept running, running for her very life for her soul for her soon to be born child. No, she couldn't let Walker catch her. Never. Never. He would rip her little girl from her arms then leave her behind to fend for herself. Once again, she would find herself homeless with no food and no way of reaching her family. He hurt her so badly. Hurt her pride. Ripped away her love.

"Crissie! I'm not going to hurt you."

She found herself whirled off the ground, caught by strong arms. Lifted into the air, her defenses crumbled. She was powerless against his brute strength. Hitting his chest with all her strength she tried to break away. He was off balance. She found herself toppling to the ground. Just as she was about to hit, Walker twisted, taking the brunt of the fall.

She was breathing hard, her heart pounding erratically, searching for a reason to stop. She cried out again, unable to stop the contractions that were now coming harder and faster. He was staring down at her, amazement in his amber eyes, a small smile curving his lips.

"You're pregnant," he said his voice filled with awe. "I'm sorry, Crissie. I acted like a beast. Don't cry please. I should have stayed and made sure you found the posting house. Dear God, what happened to you?" With his thumbs he wiped her hot tears from her cheeks.

"Just go away. I don't want you here."

She wanted to tell him he couldn't have this baby but why waste the words. He would do whatever pleased him.

"Not on your life."

She heard the emotions in his voice, the tender concern that was surely a lie.

"Get off me."

She pushed on his chest, fighting for a tiny bit of control over her emotions. Her breath caught. She didn't know whether to breathe in or out.

"Not yet, not until you tell me when."

"When what?" she asked, closing her eyes against the pain he so easily inflicted. She didn't want to scream. Didn't want him to know she was having this baby now. Didn't want him to know the contractions were coming too close together.

"When are you due?"

Possessively, his hand rested on her belly, rubbed lightly as if he wanted to feel the child they created.

It was too late for lies. In a few minutes he would figure it all out. "Doesn't matter when I'm due. I'm having MY baby now."

"Now?" There was a slight edge to his voice coupled with a moment of panic in his expression.

After a slight break in his thoughts, it appeared he grounded his emotions.

"Now!" she gritted out as another contraction hardened her belly and stole every last piece of air she inhaled. She screamed. Cursed him. Swore that she would never let him touch her again. Please just don't say anything more. She couldn't deal with his debilitating repugnance to her.

"You can't," he told her boldly seeming to forget when a baby decides it's time to come into the world no one, not even the imperious Earl of Briarwood had a say.

She almost laughed but she couldn't quite manage through the pain. Second babies didn't take as long as the first. Her little girl was eager to see the world even though Crissie never wanted her to meet her dah.

"Tell that to my baby. She's not waiting for your permission, Walker. She doesn't care a damn about you, what you think or command. Until now, she's never even heard your voice."

For a second, he appeared stunned by her words. Deftly, he rolled aside, bringing her to a sitting position. "You're sure? You..." He jabbed his hand through the tawny mane of hair, she loved. "Truly, you think she is coming now?"

"Not a doubt in my mind."

She nodded her head, clutching his arms as he brought her to her feet. He swept her into his strong arms, striding quickly to the old wagon sitting near the animal shelter.

"I would have never found you except for the fire," he murmured softly as he set her down on the bed of the wagon. "Thank God for the fire, but now we've no shelter."

"Just my rotten luck," she spoke softly even though she was relieved somewhat that she wouldn't have to figure out what to do by herself.

Even though it was Walker who was with her, she was relieved she wasn't going to have her baby alone. "You can take yourself off anytime. I don't need you."

"Liar. But I need you, little pigeon. I'm not about to leave you to fend for yourself." He kissed her nose, brushed rain from her face. "I'm not going anywhere."

With a few grunts and groans, he pulled the cart beneath the shelter before retrieving his horse. He placed the saddle behind her back. "Lean against this. What would you have done if I wasn't here?"

She screamed, clenching his hand, squeezing hard, her eyes tearing. When the pain passed, "What do you think? I would have had the baby."

"Of course, you would seeing there isn't much choice in this matter." He placed a blanket from his saddlebag over her then sat down beside her. "How did you end up here?" He sounded curious but she'd wager he already knew since he found her.

"As if you care," she told him bitterly, wondering why he asked. "What are you doing here?"

"What do you think? Looking for you," he shrugged his broad shoulders.

"I don't see why. I don't have anything you can take..." She suddenly realized what she feared the most was about to happen.

"It's not what you're thinking."

"I'm thinking you're a detestable mean hearted man. I'm thinking I wish this was only a nightmare and that I'll wake up to find you gone." Her words trailed off as her body contracted again.

She realized after she had the baby, she might truly wake up to learn both her child and Walker had vanished. He didn't need her. He would hire a wet nurse.

"That bad?" he asked. "Suppose I deserve that. A woman in town told me how Gwen rescued you from the delinquents. I'm sorry. Never wanted you to die. Was sure your family would come for you. That you would want for nothing."

"You didn't think past the end of your nose as you left me with no protection from those who would steal everything of value I owned. I was miles from McKenna land with no way to send a message. You didn't know you had another child so what do you want with me now?"

"No, I didn't, Crissie. Although now that I do..." he paused for several heartbeats as he seemed to wonder how best to answer. "Now that I do, I've one more reason to bring you home with me."

"I don't want to go anywhere with you. Nor do you truly want me. You only want the child. Because you believe I come with the child, you say you want me. What about the prison? The hangman's noose waiting for me? What about the confession?"

Yet she knew once more she would follow him wherever he led her simply because she would not give up her child. A small flicker of hope ignited inside her when she realized she might see Ian again.

"I'm sorry. I came to beg your forgiveness and to tell you I believe you didn't shoot Charlotte. I also want you to come home with me. We can work out our problems." To Crissie he sounded sincere but he lied to her before. He could lie to her now.

"Don't you think your apology is a little too late? I almost died."

"I will tell you time and again, I never intended for any harm to come to you. I just wanted you to understand that what you did to me as well as Charlotte was horrific and you had to pay somehow. I couldn't send you to jail so I found another way."

"What made you change your mind? Why do you believe me now?" She was more confused than ever before. Unless Charlotte remembered who actually pulled the trigger, there was no apparent reason for him to change his mind.

A low rush of air caught her attention. "You are not the kind of person who would resort to violence. I thought perhaps Charlotte provoked you but you denied that. Didn't know what to think except that I was positive you lied to me. Just be assured that I no longer believe that."

Crissie didn't feel reassured about anything. She didn't trust him any more than he trusted her. While she didn't want to admit that she was glad he was here, she was.

To Crissie, Walker still sounded cruel and calculating. Right now wasn't the time though to think about all the wrongs he committed. He squeezed her hand, touched her forehead, a sweet comforting gesture. The time between contractions decreased, the pain excruciating.

Silently, she cursed him until she could remain silent no longer. "I hate you, Walker Endicott!" she cried out, more curses following and directed at him. "You did this to me."

"I'm sorry," his voice was soft. "Just try to breathe. Everything will be fine."

"You're not sorry." Then she was crying out, angry with him for doing this to her and for telling her lies. "Why the hell does everyone keep saying that to me? Nothing is fine. You're here. Nothing in fine! Nothing will ever be fine again."

He'd pushed her skirts up to examine her. "Hush, sweetheart, breathe. Just take long slow breaths. Try to relax. The baby will be here any time now. I see the head."

"What do you know," she cried out then her words turned to a long scream. Now she was panting. Her legs were spread, her knees up and he was staring at her. "Walker... What-what's going on?"

"I've got the head. Push. Push hard."

Suddenly the pain vanished. Walker was holding the child in his hands. Her baby was crying now, her lungs just fine. "It's a girl." He set her in her arms.

"Of course, it is." Crissie covered the babe with her cloak. Quickly, she opened her gown so her child could nurse. For a few tense seconds the tiny baby girl rooted around looking for a nipple.

Walker seemed to know what to do as he cut the umbilical cord. After a few minutes of nursing, he said so softly she barely heard, "We should get her cleaned up, don't you think?"

Crissie didn't want to give the child to Walker, didn't want to let her out of her arms afraid something would happen. Yet she had to agree the babe needed to be cleaned. Walker rummaged through the basket and found the cloths she prepared. Dipped a few into the water at the well then returned.

She watched as he did everything her midwife did when she had Ian. When he finished, he wrapped another blanket around her before handing the little baby girl to her. "She's beautiful you know. She looks just like you. Have you thought of a name yet?"

"No, but I will by morning. I want to see what name will fit her."

"Now," he spoke softly. "It's time for both mother and child to sleep." He made a place on the wagon for the baby, close to the mother then he pulled out the rest of his bedroll. "I'm going to hold you, Crissie. You need my warmth."

"*Nay.*" Yet her voice wavered.

He ignored her wishes though. Just as he always did, "In the morning we'll leave here."

She couldn't figure out why but for some reason this time felt different.

~ * ~

Walker didn't sleep. Ever since he started on this journey, he had little sleep. The doctor told him only a few weeks ago when the note was mentioned that there was no way Charlotte could have written it. When the ball from the pistol hit her, she lost consciousness. Charlotte didn't open her eyes for another two weeks. Still, she couldn't write let alone move her arms.

All this time, he'd been a blundering fool. When he exposed Crissie at the mockery of a wedding to Andrew St. John, he had more than one reason. There was no way in hell he was going to allow Crissie to marry anyone but him. So, he turned up and made her life a living hell. He just meant to stop the wedding. Had not intended to drive her to this point where she had nothing. Christ, he loved her. Instead of leaving her at the church, he should have taken her to the posting house. Should have made sure she found her way to her family. Hindsight was never a blessing.

He didn't believe he could ever forgive himself.

Now he had to find a way to convince Crissie, he believed her, trusted her. If he had to grovel, he would. If she ever heard the only reason he came after her was because the doctor convinced him Charlotte didn't write letter, she might not ever forgive him.

While he had few doubts, she would stay with him, because he was once again determined to use their children as the means to bind her to him. It wasn't well done of him, but it was all he could think of. If he presented a possible engagement to her, he knew she would refuse.

As far as Crissie was concerned all they shared was amazing sex. She wanted more than that, as did he. Now, he understood the depth of his feelings for her even if the realization came too late.

He pulled her close to him. She snuggled in with a tiny sigh of pleasure, her small hand nestled against his chest. He could live a lifetime and never find a love such as this. He had no doubt Crissie was his mate for life. She was made for him and him alone. All he needed now was to convince her of the truth so he could put a ring on her finger.

Walker wanted to stay this way forever. Dawn would come though and he would have to take her and their newborn daughter from this god-awful place. Even if she complained, he would take her home to Ireland, to Briarwood Manor. It was her home, would always be. This time he would do everything right. There was nothing standing in their way except themselves.

The baby cried softly, whimpering beside Crissie. He didn't know much about newborns but he assumed the child wanted to nurse. Waking Crissie was not something he wanted to do just yet. The child could wait a little while longer. After the birth along with the trauma of the last months, Crissie needed her rest. Determined to give Crissie at least another hour of sleep, he picked up the wee babe.

She cuddled into his shoulder, her little head rooting around as if searching for the nipple he wasn't offering. He grinned a lopsided smile as he smoothed his hand over the tuft of soft black hair on her head. Just like her mother's hair he thought as he wondered if she would have the startling silver blue eyes of the McKenna's. Ian looked just like him. He had little doubt that this child would be a match for her mother.

For a few minutes, he stood by the smoldering remains of the small hut where Crissie lived feeling the regret of his past actions build even higher. The acrid scent of smoke hung in the air. Dog sat down beside him with a whimper as if he knew his life would change also.

Walker wasn't at all sure that change would be for the better.

With the baby he strolled around the exterior, watching where he walked. Dawn would be here soon. When the little one let out an ear-splitting wail that was followed by another and another, Walker bounced the child, humming little ditties that he knew were far from appropriate.

She wasn't going to stop her loud protest. Obviously, it was time to wake Crissie. Climbing up on the wagon, he rested his hand on her shoulder.

"Crissie..." He shook her slightly. "Crissie, sweetheart."

She sat up quickly, pushing hair from her face. "What?" The change in her expression told Walker it took her a few seconds to realize she'd given birth and she was sleeping in an old wagon.

"Think the little one needs you." He grinned at her, taking in the slight frown lines along with exhaustion clearly written in her eyes. "I would do it if I could." Just as he would take away all the pain he caused her.

If it was only possible...

Crissie reached out for the wailing child. In a few seconds the little one was sucking enthusiastically. Crissie was leaning back on the saddle, her eyes closed, breathing deeply.

Not entirely sure what to do, he brought her a cup of water before settling against the side of the wagon to watch her. He couldn't take his eyes away nor find a means to ease his wanting of her.

"Are you going to keep watching me?" she asked with a quiet resignation in her words.

"Not watching you. I'm gazing at my daughter."

He didn't look away. She was damn sure going to have to get used to him watching them. It was the most beautiful sight he could ever imagine.

She bowed her head. He would give most anything to learn what she was thinking. When she looked up, "What are you going to do now?"

He saw the pain along with the fear. She expected him to take the child from her. Expected the worst from him.

"When?"

"In the morning. I guess it's today. I believe I deserve to know."

She wasn't asking about him. She was asking about his intentions toward their daughter. He lifted his shoulders, still drinking in the sight in front of him. "As soon as it's light enough to make our way through these bogs, I'm going to take you and our new child to the village where we are going to stay until the two of you are strong enough to travel. I will send a message to Connal. If he and Wynnie want to see their granddaughter, they will have time to visit. Before all that though, I'm going to find a doctor to make sure the two of you are healthy and well."

"Thank you. After that?"

He was sure the rest of what he had to say would not receive a thank you from her thinning lips. With wary eyes, she watched him almost as if she was waiting for him to say something she would take issue with. Well, she wouldn't have to wait very long.

"I'm going to take you and our child home to Briarwood Manor. After that, you are going to marry me."

Her eyes flashed. Even in the dim morning light he saw the silver fire in her simmering eyes.

"No."

"Yes," he told her, grimacing when she looked away. "You will marry me. I'm not going to take no for an answer. Once you wanted to be my wife, well, now you will."

The bridges along the way that he burned loomed in front of him. He would get her compliance one way or another even if he had to seduce her to accomplish the deed. Once more she would melt in his arms. He was sure that had not changed.

"I *dinna* want to marry a man that is as mean hearted as you. I will never know what will happen if you disagree with me. Will you send me out on my own again, with not one *groat* to help me survive?" She spoke quickly, her voice low almost as if she thought the baby could understand what she was saying.

"Crissie, I promise you I will never hurt you again. I didn't send you out with nothing. You had coin to use. I made sure of it." His was a promise he intended to keep. He just didn't know if she would believe him. "I'll make you happy."

Tears slid down her cheeks again. It seemed he was forever making her cry. "Like you did before?"

The accusation gave him reason to wince. "I've apologized. What more do you want?" Most likely his blood.

Chapter Eleven

Walker was pleased when Crissie and Ilene Katherine, his little Kate, stepped into the foyer at Briarwood Manor. Rose immediately swept the child into her arms cooing over her and making little faces. While he knew everything between the two of them had not been settled, he was well aware of the fact he was making progress. Crissie would once again be his.

"The two of you are home. I'm so glad to see you," Rose gushed contentedly. "I'm so pleased Walker talked you into coming with him. Now we have another wee one. I'll ready the cradle for her."

Walker grimaced. Talking her into following him was not a problem simply because he gave her no choice. Yet he couldn't allow Crissie to take Kate away from him either. For them there was truly no compromise.

"I'd like to see Ian."

"His nap is almost over. I'm sure he'll be pleased to see his mama," Rose said happily, handing Ilene over to Crissie before hurrying up the stairs to fetch the little boy.

When Rose disappeared up the steps, Crissie turned to him. He knew what she was going to say. It was a conversation they had several times since he found her half-starved ready to give birth. What was one more time? Nothing in his mind changed.

"I'm not marrying you nor am I sleeping in the same bed with you. You are going to figure something else out."

Walker was intractable on both issues. "Maybe not tonight but you will. To both your statements." He waved a hand in the air dismissively.

"We're not talking about this again. In two days, we will wed. You will be in my arms and my bed. You want me, Crissie. Admit it."

He watched as her chin tilted defiantly in the air. She would admit nothing. He drew in a long deep breath of resignation. In two days, this argument would be done with. So frustrated with her position, he thought to pull her into his arms to show her just how much she wanted him.

"No."

Marching to the sideboard, he poured himself a snifter of brandy thinking he needed more than one drink to get him through tonight and the next few days. "Would you like something to drink? Sherry?"

"Brandy, a large glass. I'm going to need it," she said speaking stiffly.

He couldn't help the smug smile growing as he understood just how important her compliance was. When she took the glass, she drank in a large gulp, shuddered as the potent heat slid down her throat. The fire in the hearth crackled. Sounds of the house whirled around them. The first time he brought her to Briarwood it was under much the same circumstances. He wooed her gently. Now she despised him even more than the first time. What waited for them in the future? He prayed it would be love along with more children.

When Rose brought Ian into the room, he held out his hands for his, "Mama."

She closed her eyes, seeming to absorb the single word uttered by her son. Before he left to find her, he worked on that word but Ian wasn't able to say it. Rose must have continued the lessons.

With Ian in her arms, she cuddled him close to her heart, kissed the top of his head. "Thank you, Rose."

"I knew you would bring her back," Rose said softly seeming to soak up the warmth of the tender reunion in front of her.

In the village the encounter with the beaming grandparents was strained at best. Both Connal and Wynnie saw the reluctance on Crissie's part to return with him even though she tried not to show those feelings. This time, however, Walker was able to assure Connal he intended to marry his daughter. All he needed was her compliance, which he was working on.

Dog followed Connal and Wynnie home to the highlands.

Days passed without further confrontation as Walker watched Crissie settle in to the routine at Briarwood. They were married yet it was not all bliss. While she slept in the adjoining chamber, he never coaxed her into his big bed even though he knew he could. Just as the first time she was here in his home, he wanted her to come to him of her own volition. Holding the children over her head as hostage to his desires was not part of his plan this time.

Both he and Crissie spent an inordinate amount of time sitting with Charlotte. She was healing slowly but constantly. She finally mastered the use of her fingers and could write a few almost illegible words. However, she still didn't remember who shot her.

Much to his chagrin Crissie confronted him about the validity of the note a week after they arrived at the manor.

"Walker, how could Charlotte write my name on that note when she can barely write her name now? Was she lucid and able to see what was going on around her?"

That was a question he never expected from her at least not before he found the right time to tell her the truth. He always thought the information would be easiest for her to forgive if he told her. All blood drained from his visage while he tried to field a question he dreaded from the first moment he told her he trusted her and knew she wasn't the kind of woman who could commit violence.

He sucked in a cleansing deep breath of air, held until it rushed from his lungs. It was time for the courage he didn't feel but it was long past time to explain that he didn't come to the conclusion she didn't shoot Charlotte because of this new-found trust he had for her.

Softly, he said, "She couldn't."

"I don't understand." Crissie stepped closer to him as if his words were too softly spoken for her to hear.

If she wasn't holding Ilene in her arms, he thought she might be ready to do bodily damage. "Someone else wrote your name on that paper. Someone wanted to frame you for the murder. We might never know who."

It was her turn to lose all semblance of color. "Why?"

Walker saw the hurt in her eyes, was utterly thankful she hadn't as yet picked up on his perfidy. "That remains a question we cannot answer. While Charlotte is remembering bits and pieces of that night, she is the only one who can shed light on the real murderer. She doesn't remember."

"Is she in danger?"

Crissie walked into the adjoining nursery then set Ilene in the crib. When she returned to Walker, it appeared her mind was tumbling around all the information he revealed to her.

"If she remembers, I assume so."

He set guards around the cottage. Charlotte was guarded twenty-four hours a day. He wasn't about to take any chances on something like that happening again. "Whoever shot her has gone to great lengths to cover up the deed."

"You lied to me."

Walker's heart sank to the pit of his stomach. Deciding he knew what she was talking about and determining he might as well take the full brunt of her anger, he said, "Yes, to some degree."

"What degree might that be?"

She had her hands fisted on her hips, her eyes blazing as she challenged him.

He sucked in a breath before trying to give an acceptable answer. "I knew deep in my heart you would never hurt anyone no matter how angry I was. For the longest time I couldn't get over the fact that your name was on the note. I just couldn't see a reason for that. It didn't make a damn bit of sense." With a lengthy pause, "There you have it."

"Go on," she said her anger still fresh and vivid.

"Once the doctor told me writing would not have been possible, all my fears for you, all my doubts dissipated. Everything was clear to me. I was a blind fool."

"Probably still are," she muttered quietly.

"Do you forgive me?" he asked, holding out his arms while hoping she would run to him.

Cautiously, her hands at her sides she watched. "It would not do for me to give in so easily. What would you think?"

"I've waited quite a while," he said still holding out his arms. "You are my wife."

"Ah and you think that gives me reason to blindly forgive you?"

"What I think is that I've been patient with you. You are my wife after all."

"You have been patient," she admitted slowly walking to him. "I forgave you a long time ago, Walker. When you let my father and mother come to see Ilene, I would have given you just about anything you asked for."

"Would you?" he asked hopefully, his heart contracting painfully. With baited breath he asked the next question. "Why haven't you come to our bed? You know I want you there."

For a few seconds she looked away. Then with a little half-hearted sigh, "Because I didn't think you wanted me. Truly, Walker, you cannot expect me to read your mind."

"What in blazes gave you that idea?"

"You didn't act like you did before, all arrogant and all-knowing. I didn't think you wanted me as you never kissed me or even tried to coax me into your arms. It just wasn't like you. And," she paused, "the marriage was simply a convenience for you so Ilene would not be a bastard."

Shocked to the tips of his toes at her revelation, he said, "Come here, little pigeon." His arms open wide, he waited impatiently for her to come to him. "You have forgiven me. Now, it is time to consummate our marriage vows. Something I've wanted to do for what seems like an eternity."

"I haven't forgotten. I will never forget and Walker Endicott, if you ever hurt me again..."

"What?" he asked with a gentle smile on his lips, one he hoped she understood when she looked up at him, a fine sheen of moisture in her eyes.

"You won't survive what I intend to do to you," she said, looking away from him, her dark sooty lashes lowered, covering her eyes as well as her emotions.

He needed to see inside her soul. His thumb beneath her chin he slowly lifted. "I won't hurt you ever again, Crissie." One finger traced a path across her full bottom lip as he pulled her closer. "Don't ever think I don't want you. I need you, Crissie, more than I need to breathe."

Tenderly, his lips found hers and with a soft brush across her mouth that was so soft and warm, he promised her more, promised to see to her pleasure. "We can't right now. I wish I could take you upstairs. Wish we could stay there all afternoon then continue pleasing each other until the sun rises the next morning."

Reluctantly, he parted from her, his hands still around her waist. Releasing her, his knuckles gently stroked her cheek.

"I promised Charlotte I would talk to her," she spoke softly. "She's starting to remember things about that night."

"That's good," he murmured then with a soft chuckle. "Are the two of you friends now? I would have never believed it."

Her hands on his chest, "Walker, I don't think we, Charlotte and I, will ever be friends. She resents me for taking you away from her even though she couldn't be your wife. I guess I feel sorry for her. Anne has even left her. She doesn't come around to see her."

Walker knew that fact and often wondered why. At one time he thought the two women loved each other. Ah, but it seemed Charlotte had her maid, Laura-Beth. Crissie had been right about the woman when she saw the two together that day in the drawing room. Now it seemed the two spent a lot of time together even though Charlotte didn't need her as much.

"Laura-Beth stays with her at times," Walker said. "Did you know that? After the shooting she seemed almost guilty."

Those words stopped Walker cold. Charlotte's maid might have had a motive. He wanted to talk to Charlotte about that. Maybe it would spark a memory. Tomorrow, he would visit Charlotte.

"Odd, don't you think? Perhaps it was Anne or Laura-Beth who shot Charlotte."

"Well, we've no proof."

"You're right, suspicions don't mean anything," Crissie said. "I think I'll go talk with Charlotte."

"A confession from Laura-Beth if she did shoot Charlotte would be nice."

He wanted this over with, his mind spinning now that they were considering other people.

"I will see you for dinner in our room. I trust you will come to me willingly."

He dipped his head. Kissed her with a desperate need. For long seconds he held back nothing, coaxing her into complete submission. Just as always, her body melted against his as she leaned closer. She swept her tongue across his bottom lip. When he pulled a way for a moment, "Little tease."

"I don't want to wait," she murmured. "It's been so long."

Too long, he lost so much time with her. Had not been able to watch her swell with his child either pregnancy. He wanted to share that and so much more. He wanted to claim her, show her who he was, everything about him. He kept too damn many secrets. It was time for everything to come out.

The secrets had all been necessary. Ah, but soon the time would be right. After that he would show her what little Ian could do. Pleasure filled him. He found the perfect mate and he almost tossed her away.

Never again.

Unwilling to let her go, unwilling to wait to make love to his wife another second, he swept her into his arms. The rest of the world be damned. Everything but this could wait. He headed upstairs to their room. When he stood in front of the bed, he undressed. She watched him her eyes wide with desire. They were huge simmering pools of molten heat.

He settled on the big bed, patting the place beside him. "I'm just waiting for you, little pigeon."

His hands were behind his back, his legs stretched out in front of him while he waited.

"Walker..."

"What?"

"I don't know..."

Instantly, he was alert, wary. He didn't understand her reluctance. It wasn't as if he'd never seen her naked. "What don't you know?" He tried to hide the sudden unexpected anger bristling his tone.

"I'm not, well," it seemed she was struggling for the words.

He wasn't going to reply. She needed to tell him why a few seconds ago she was melting for him and now she was pulling away. His gaze raked over her. Her breasts were larger, filled with milk to feed Ilene. As he traveled lower, he saw the changes in her body and with sudden realization he understood her hesitancy.

"What you are is beautiful," he told her his voice soft caressing her with his words. "Almost two months ago you gave birth to a perfect little girl."

"Would you turn your back?" She was fiddling with the buttons on her gown. Her bosom heaving as her breathing increased.

"No, I want to see all of you. Not just touch you and kiss you. I want to understand everything about you as well as your luscious body."

If she insisted, he would turn his back but it was the last thing he wanted to do.

Her eyes wide, she stood beside the bed turning her back to him while looking over her shoulder to speak. "I just can't."

At least he would see her back. He loved her back, the gentle slope to her rounded buttocks. He loved the way her hips flared from the tiny waist. Supposed it was better than nothing.

She was magic to his soul.

"Are you also going to slide into bed backward as you did that first time?" He chuckled softly recalling that night so well. She did come to him a willing participant despite her reservations just as she was doing the same now despite her shyness.

"Yes." She was nodding her head, her black hair spilling around her shoulders as it fell to her waist.

"I'm waiting."

Watching her was pure torture. To Walker it seemed she took way longer to disrobe than she needed to. If she could have done this any slower, he would have been shocked to his very core.

She was naked, sitting on the bed. So she could slip beneath the covers, she had to turn to move them aside. He saw her breasts, large and rounded, coral-colored tips puckered ready for his attention.

When she was finally beneath the covers, he reached out for her, turned her so she was facing him. He rose above her, the covers falling around them. He saw all of her, meant to caress and kiss every part.

"You are so beautiful," he murmured as his lips closed over hers.

He kissed her softly at first, tenderly savoring every moment. He caressed the corners of her lips with his teeth and tongue. Followed every curve of her face with his mouth. The hard tips of her breasts lightly caressed his chest with each movement they took.

Only when her lips were kiss swollen and thoroughly ravished did he move on to slowly rouse more passion, to explore more of her. She enchanted him. Their lovemaking was pure magic.

He stroked the pounding pulse at the base of her neck, nibbled lightly as he was rewarded with her fingers winding into his hair to pull him closer as her vibrant body begged for more. She ran her hands slowly down his back, seeming to stop at each vertebra as they moved lower to eventually cup his buttocks.

She was twisting and turning beneath him, tiny little cries of pleasure rippling from her throat. He found that he'd been without her far too long. When she exploded in a climax, her body trembling desperately beneath his, he understood just how much she wanted him.

"Walker!" she cried out her pleasure.

His lips found one breast, nipping and licking as his tongue curled around a puckered nipple. He explored her intimately, massaging the silken knot hidden between her swollen petals. She was ready for him. Next time they would take this loving more slowly.

He pushed inside, driving faster and faster until once more he felt the quivering and trembling of her ecstasy.

"Crissie!"

He fell against her for a few seconds, his weight was almost totally upon her. He lifted on his forearms to look down at her sweat sheened body, saw the moisture in her eyes.

He suddenly panicked. "Did I hurt you?"

She flashed him a faint smile, "I've missed you, Walker. Not just this." She ran her hands down his chest.

"Sex?" he asked lifting an eyebrow high in speculation, loving the whisper of her voice so close to his mouth.

"Yes, but I've also missed you. Talking to you, seeing you happy, playing with Ian. I don't think you've been happy."

"Neither have you." He rolled to the side, holding her, listening as it seemed, their hearts beat as one.

"Because we've been at odds," she said as she rested her head on his chest. She was running her hands along his chest, stopping for moment when her palm touched a nipple. "I don't like arguing with you in any way even if it is in our thoughts."

"Unless you want to do this again, before you speak with Charlotte, I suggest you stop torturing me."

"Torturing?" she queried as she straddled him. He slipped inside.

~ * ~

Crissie left Walker as the sun began to set. The short journey to the little cottage where Charlotte lived occurred much later than she planned. It was hard to leave the bed, to leave Walker. When she finally left the bedroom, he was sitting on the divan, his shirt open to bare his chest, looking as if her leaving was the last thing he wanted. His breeches were on but unfastened while his feet were still bare. He was sipping brandy while he played with Ian. Ilenc slept on his shoulder. It seemed to be her favorite spot. The picture of his contentment was one she would never forget.

Crissie assumed Ilene liked his shoulder so much because she spent so much time there the first few weeks while they were still in Scotland while she was recovering. At that time, all Walker wanted to do was put food in her stomach. He felt guilty about her appearance simply because it was his fault she might have starved to death before she found Gwen or more appropriately Gwen found her.

Of course, her parents were more than pleased to meet their new granddaughter. They were also able to keep their harsh questions and criticisms of Walker behind their teeth when it came to their need to discover exactly what was going on with her and Walker. Both remained closed mouth about the facts surrounding their estrangement as well as the reconciliation. It wasn't their business. Connal had not wanted Crissie to leave with Walker. Despite her fears concerning him, she was willing to give him a second chance. She found now that he harbored a great deal of guilt. He was more solicitous to her needs than ever before, which made her feel guilty also. Their emotions seemed to be in a revolving pattern.

Rose, too, was different when she returned. She treated her with special adoring care. Part of it was because of Ilene and part of it because she never really stood up for her when Walker had her pegged as an attempted murderous.

They made love two more times before he finally let her go. She thought she was too exhausted to even move. Having promised Charlotte to see her this afternoon, she supposed being late would be better than not coming at all.

As she approached the cottage it was lit with what seemed like lights in every room. She could see Charlotte sitting in the drawing room. Charlotte had improved a lot even in the short time she and Walker had been at Briarwood. Laura-Beth usually sat with her this time of night. Since Crissie couldn't see her, she assumed the maid had left for the evening.

"Charlotte." She knocked on the door then opened it peeking her head inside. "Is it alright with you if I come inside?"

"Tea or sherry?" Charlotte asked following the question with a heavy sigh. "I do have need for company and a bit of small talk. It's driving me crazy not being able to remember things. I know this is the last place Walker wants to be. I can see it in his eyes every time he sits with me. He truly does regret what happened between the two of you."

Crissie leaned forward, patting her knee in hopes of encouraging her. "Not being able to remember must be awful. Perhaps it is just so traumatic your mind believes you are better off not knowing." With a slight lift to her shoulders, she went on to say, "Perhaps we all are. I'm not sure I want to know who tried to frame me for murder. Then again, maybe it's something I should know."

Charlotte handed her a glass of sherry, "You didn't say which you preferred. In any case, I stare out the window believing all of a sudden, my memory will return and in the process will *ken* who tried to kill me. Do you truly think someone is trying to kill me? Still? I've seen the guards even though Walker never told me about them. I'm sure he doesn't want me to be afraid."

Crissie didn't want to give false hope but then why would she know. "I certainly hope not. Walker is just being cautious. He would never forgive himself if something happened to you."

Crissie knew that to be the honest truth. He understood love for family, for a lost relationship. Crissie loved her siblings, but she also loved all her cousins. If anything happened to them, she would be devastated. Perhaps she should have understood Walker's feelings better.

If she hadn't run away from her problems...

At the time understanding had not been possible. She overheard him saying he was going to put her in jail and if Charlotte died, she would hang. To Crissie there had been no viable choice but to run.

"They make me nervous," Charlotte said, setting her glass of sherry on the table beside her.

She rubbed her temples, closing her eyes at the same time.

"Does your head hurt?"

Concern for Charlotte made a sudden and very unexpected appearance. While Crissie liked to think she cared, she had a hard time dissolving all her earlier animosity toward this lady who once had an iron grip on Walker's present as well as his future. They were both more than happy to continue the ruse.

Charlotte gave a tiny laugh. "Only when I try to remember. Then it aches like the very devil."

"I wish I could wave my hand in the air and have you remembering that night," Crissie said with a wistful little sigh.

They spoke for a while. Still there seemed to be no memory or any resurgence of clues. "All I can recount is that both Anne and Laura-Beth were with me. We were all arguing about something. I don't think it was very important. I do recall that I didn't understand their anger."

"You didn't remember that before," Crissie said as she set her glass of sherry on the table. "Maybe you can recall the argument."

"It's so close I can almost remember. That is when darkness closes in then there is nothing."

"They were both your lovers, weren't they?" Crissie pressed forward hoping that something would trigger another memory. "Were they jealous? Were you jealous?"

"No." Charlotte was shaking her head. "I don't think so. Oh, there just is nothing there. Anne stopped coming to see me, you know. I don't know why. Now Laura-Beth hovers around me as if I'm an invalid. She, too, is trying to get me to remember or maybe not. Sometimes I think she just wants to learn what exactly I've recalled."

"So," Crissie went on, "you don't think either one was jealous. Why do you think Anne stopped coming?"

Charlotte gave a brittle laugh before she drank down the rest of the sherry in her glass. "Isn't it obvious? I couldn't give her what she wanted."

"What did she want? Nothing is obvious where this incident is concerned." Crissie's curiosity was aroused.

"What Walker was giving me, us," Charlotte said. "Once the annulment came through, Anne understood I would be very nearly penniless. Under the circumstances I could never seek out my father for help."

The annulment... "When did you learn about it?"

Her heart seemed to lodge in her throat. If she had known, too, maybe none of this would have happened. If Walker told her instead of keeping it secret, perhaps he would have never thought she would try to kill Charlotte. He assumed she wanted to get rid of her by killing her.

"The first night he returned from his mission to the highlands he came to me," Charlotte spoke softly, her hands nervously winding in the folds of her skirt. "Told me I would have to leave the cottage. Explained to me that he would help me find a place to live and would give me a monthly stipend but only after I persuaded him to do so. Anne didn't think that was enough. After all Walker and I had been married for ten years. Anne thought he owed me a lot more than it appeared he was willing to give."

"So, Anne argued with you about the amount. Where does Laura-Beth fit into this?"

"Oh, I just don't know. It's so confusing."

Crissie rose, comprehending Charlotte had reached her limit for tonight. She should leave. Walker would be waiting for her. They were to have dinner in his, no their suite of rooms. Rose would have put the babies down to sleep.

"I will stop by tomorrow sometime. Perhaps you will remember a bit more," Crissie said suddenly eager to leave so she could see Walker so they could talk about the information Charlotte remembered.

"Thank you," Charlotte murmured as Crissie walked outside into the darkness.

She skirted the forest for a few minutes, drinking in the silence of the evening. While it was late April the nights still grew cold more often than not. It smelled of cold air and pine She rubbed her arms warding off the chill. She should have brought a cloak but she hadn't meant to stay this long.

"Put your hands behind your head." The voice reverberated from behind her, chilling her to the bone.

Crissie heard as well as recognized the voice, felt the pistol in the small of her back. With no hesitation, she followed the instructions. "Laura-Beth? What are you doing?"

"Keep walking. Head into the forest."

"No."

Crissie thought to turn, decided against it. Knew she needed to stall for time. Laura-Beth must have been the reason she was framed for

Charlotte's attack.

"You will or I'll blow your head off. Can't miss from this range now, can I?" she asked a smirk in her voice.

"Why should I go anywhere? You're going to shoot me anyway."

Crissie thought of Ian and Ilene. If this woman had her way, she would never see her children again, would never feel Walker deep inside her. After so long, they finally found each other again. She swallowed hard while she searched for a means to avoid what seemed to be inevitable.

The silence unnerved her, struck a dark chord in her heart. She looked to the manor. Nothing moved or stirred. Walker wasn't going to come to her defense. He wouldn't know what happened to her. He would miss her as the hour grew late. Would come look for her to no avail. He would find her body.

"Don't even think about screaming. I'll shoot you right then and there," Laura-Beth told her. "Keep walking."

Truly, Crissie couldn't think of a single reason why she should do anything the woman told her. She did start to walk, staying away from the shadows along with the trees. Trying desperately to stay where moonlight touched the earth. When she moved into the forest, it would be done.

I don't want to die.

No, she had too much to live for but she couldn't think of anything to do except walk. She drew in a breath of air then another. Each step she took brought her closer to death.

She heard the hoot of an owl then the chatter of a squirrel. The soft scent of roses filled the clean spring air then the scent of pine on the air caught her attention. All the scents and sounds smelled and sounded so much more vivid than she remembered. She recalled all too well the way the city, Belfast, smelled. While she liked the city, this was much better.

When she closed her eyes for a moment, she tried to remember her family, tried to think of the highlands, its rugged crags and roaring rivers walks in the gloaming. Remembered how her brothers teased her because she couldn't shift. She would give anything to be able to do so now. Wishful thinking wasn't going to get her out of this horrid situation.

This time when she looked to the manor, she did see Walker. He was standing on the balcony to their room appearing to look right at her. It didn't seem he saw her. She lifted her hand to wave at him, a final farewell she was thinking but felt the tip of the pistol ram against her back.

"Put your hand down and keep walking. Best you head into the forest like I told you."

Crissie stopped mid-stride then turned slightly looking over her shoulder. "What do you want, Laura-Beth? I can give you anything. You can leave here. Make a home somewhere else. I won't tell anyone what you did. You won't be punished, even though I paid for your deeds, almost died because of what you did. "I will never tell anyone you shot your lover."

"What I did? I tried to protect Charlotte from Anne. Anne was taking advantage of her. She wouldn't let her make decisions on her own. She wanted her to move in with her when she left the cottage. She told me she couldn't take me with her. She didn't have the money for a maid. Wouldn't be able to pay me. I know better. Walker would have given her the money."

"So, you were in love with Anne, not Charlotte," Crissie guessed.

"No, I was in love with Charlotte. I was just a horrible shot. I meant to hit Anne. They were in bed together asleep. Anne didn't know who did it because I drugged her."

Well, that gave her hope. If she ran, she might have a chance. Walker knew she could hit anything she aimed at. Understood she would not have missed. It was simply Charlotte's incredible will to survive that kept her alive. So, he thought she missed or not.

"You were jealous?" Jealousy had a way of making people do crazy ridiculous things.

"Yes, I hated Anne. She took everything that was good about Charlotte away from her. She took my life as well. As I said, when she had to move out, she could no longer afford me."

"I'm sure Walker would have let her keep her maid." Crissie was groping for things to keep her talking away to waste time so she could run. Perhaps the forest was her best chance. Laura-Beth would never be able to hit a moving target if what she said was true. She could lose herself then find a way back to the house after she lost Laura-Beth.

"I couldn't take that chance," Laura-Beth said, her voice soft filled with the tears she was trying desperately to hold back.

"Now, unless you let me go, you don't have a chance with Charlotte. I'm sure she still loves you." Crissie found herself groping for anything that might sway this mad lady to her way of thinking.

She turned, stopping only to look down the barrel of the gun. She gulped air then backed a few steps away from Laura-Beth, her hands held high and in front of her. Without a doubt she didn't know what else to do or say.

"Don't do this, Laura-Beth. Right now, Charlotte is alive. You won't be charged with murder. If you kill me, Walker will find you and see that you hang." Crissie held out her hand. "Give me the gun. Right now, all you've done is threaten me."

Laura-Beth held her arms straight, her hands trembling as she stared at Crissie, the weapon still pointed in her direction. "You are wrong. Walker will make sure I suffer. In his own way he cares about Charlotte."

"Yes, yes he does. He will be grateful that she lived. That you were a horrible shot." Crissie's voice was shaking, her hands sweating. She wiped them on her dress as she backed away from the pistol.

"I know. Everything you're saying is true, but..."

"But?" Crissie asked, understanding that her time was rapidly fading. She would have to make a mad dash soon if she thought to survive.

"Charlotte will never forgive me when she finds out I meant to kill Anne and hit her instead." She was shaking her head, her fingers quivering. "She will never forgive me. I know it. That's more important than what Walker will do." She seemed to be even more distraught than before. Her body trembling so hard, Crissie thought she might surely lose hold of the pistol.

She needed to act now or forget about survival. Whirling quickly with little thought to her welfare she dashed to the side, spun again then ran blindly toward the forest, intent on one thing—making it difficult for Laura-Beth to hit her. Her footsteps dodged to the right then to the left.

The loud roar behind her shook her to the core. Despite her intent she stopped. Spinning, she saw an incredibly large tiger leap upon Laura-Beth. The shot that was most likely meant for her ripped through the tiger' shoulder, grazing the fur.

Without reservation, she knew it was Walker. At the moment she didn't have the time for outrage at his blatant disregard for the truth. He kept so many secrets. Damn, damn him. She ran forward, picked up the gun and held it directed at Laura-Beth.

"I can take care of this." She nodded to Walker, hoping with all her heart he would understand what she was trying to tell him and leave. He could return in minutes. Having heard the pistol blast, the excuse would be evident. He would have come to check on her as well as Charlotte.

A smile on her face, she watched as he loped toward the manor. Her smile vanished. He was a shifter. He never told her. Gave no clue as to what he could do. She wondered if he ever meant to tell her. A horrible wave of dizziness passed through her. It was another truth he failed to share.

"Stand up, Laura-Beth. Unlike you I'm an excellent shot. I don't miss what I aim at."

"What was that?" Laura-Beth asked her, shaking.

"What was what?" Crissie darted a glance in the direction of Briarwood. He was gone already.

"T-tiger. It could have killed me."

"Your imagination is huge. There was no tiger, no animal. I overpowered you. That's all."

When they retired later for the evening, Crissie would have a few things to say to Walker. She meant to demand answers, not vague innuendos about his visit earlier to the highlands.

Next, when she looked toward the house, she saw Walker running toward them. His easy strides ate up the ground almost as quickly as when he was in his cat form. She wasn't going to make this too easy for the man.

"Heard a shot," he said as he stepped in beside her. "What happened?"

"Laura-Beth confessed to the attempted murder of Anne. She hit Charlotte instead. I'll tell you all about it later."

Epilogue

"We've exactly two hours before Rose brings Ian and Ilene here for lunch. What do you suppose we should do? I know what I want to do," Walker said as he leaned against the solid rock wall behind the waterfall.

"Lately, that's all you think about, Walker Endicott. No, I suppose that's all you've ever thought about." She pushed on his good shoulder. The other was bandaged where Laura-Beth's shot grazed him. He grabbed her wrist, bringing her to him.

"Not all, but I want to do something I should have done last night. I just didn't want to frighten you. I waited a long time for this. Kept secrets that should have been revealed. If you must know, I was a bit of a coward."

"I *dinna ken* what that could be. Seems we did just about everything two people can do last night."

"Well," he brushed a lose tendril of her hair behind her ear. "I want to make love to you."

"Yes, and that should frighten me? How?"

"I haven't claimed you as my mate yet. What do you know of such things? I doubt if it would be something your brothers would have spoken about. The claiming might hurt just as the first time we made love but different."

He was worried about her now, fear he would hurt her again even though it wasn't his intention. He put this off too long as it was.

"No, they never said a word about claiming. I suspected though, well I sensed..." she was mumbling.

"Our relationship will be different once I claim you. Since you are not a shifter it might be a bit painful. I'll try not to hurt you." He was terrified this would not go well.

"I should have known." She traced some of his markings with a fingertip. The lines on you are as obvious as the spots on my brother's bodies.

"They are subtle," he said. "Now..."

He watched her swallow, her silver-blue eyes wide with what could only be described as apprehension. "Is it necessary?"

"Yes."

"Why?"

"If we are going to travel through time after we pass into the other world to meet again, I have to claim you as mine in this time."

"Oh." She ran her tongue along her bottom lip. "Lilly must have survived the claiming. She never spoke of it. I wish I could talk with my sister-in-law or my mother."

His smile widened. He watched her, knowing how much he needed her at this second. The sooner he claimed her the better. All her apprehension would vanish when he did.

"I want to make love to you right here, behind the waterfall as we did that day last summer. Do you think we conceived Ilene then? No, perhaps not."

"Isn't it a bit chilly?"

"I will keep you warm."

"You will?"

His lips found hers, softly brushing against them. She tasted warm and sweet, her softness always amazing him. The way she fit him so perfectly never ceased to give him reason to wonder at the beauty that brought them together. They had been through so much. Crissie was made for him, only him. Just thinking of her aroused him. He kissed her again and again, nipping tenderly at her bottom lip deepening the pressure before backing off. He absorbed all of her into him. More than the first time he made love to her and took her virginity, she needed to be aroused to such a fever pitch she wouldn't notice the pain he had no choice but to inflict. He didn't like it but there truly was no other choice.

In no time he had her purring softly. She arched and twisted beneath him, begging for more and more. In his arms, she was liquid heat. When he thrust inside her, sure she would climax, his claws unsheathed.

"Walker!" she screamed when her body convulsed in heated pleasure, when his sharp claws pierced her flesh.

He held her. Rubbed her back trying to soothe the anguish he once again created. He hurt her. Hated himself. "Are you..." he closed his eyes. "I'm sorry."

Walker hovered above her, gazing at this woman he loved more than his life. He pushed damp hair from her face wishing he could have done this some other way.

"I saw you many times. We were always together," she breathed softly. "Once your hair was the palest gold and your eyes soft blue. You were different. I think you might have been a white tiger. Is that possible?"

He kissed her eyelids, the tip of her nose then her forehead. Softly, he brushed his lips across hers. "I suppose anything is possible. We need to get dressed. Rose will be here soon with our children."

"If she saw us this way she would know."

He laughed tenderly. "I'm sure she *kens* what we are about this afternoon." He rose then, dipped his shirt in the water. Cleaning the blood from her shoulders, he winced as he remembered the scream of pain. It was also coupled with one of delight. He wondered which one she would remember. He prayed the memory would be one of rapture.

"Walker," Crissie ran her hands down his arms then back to his shoulders. She trailed a fingertip along his collarbone before caressing his mouth.

"Yes?" He was sure his besotted grin would be amusing to her.

"There is nobody but you for me. Nobody but Walker."

"I love you, Crissie." He heard Ian talking to Rose before he saw them. "We've got to dress now. I've something else to show you." He pulled her to her feet then tossed her the chemise he'd taken off her earlier.

Quickly, he slipped on his pants. When they were both dressed, he led the way from behind the waterfall.

Ian ran to them arms outstretched, his little toddler legs whirring, giggling. Walker scooped him into his arms before twirling him around and around. Ian laughed, delighted with the daring play of his father.

Crissie grimaced, shooting him a look that told him he needed to stop. He didn't. Rose handed Ilene to Crissie before leaving. Over her shoulder she called out. "I'll see the four of you at dinner. Have fun."

Walker set Ian on the blanket they had spread out earlier. "Now, little man, why don't you show your mama what you can do?" Walker was unfastening his clothes. In a few seconds Ian was naked.

The little boy giggled delightedly. He shifted.

Walker heard Crissie's gasp of surprise and what seemed to be pleasure. "How long have you known?"

"A while. I understand you'll be angry I didn't tell you sooner. We've only been back several weeks. A lot has been going on. I wanted his unveiling, so to speak, to be special. Not tinged with other things, bad memories."

She stroked Ian's back. "You are a proud papa. I love you so much. Do you think Ilene will be a shifter?"

"If she is..." he shrugged then. "Time will tell. Crissie, for me there is nobody but you. Nobody but Crissie."

"How I love you, Walker," she sighed softly as she watched her son scamper around them in his cat form.

"As I love you as well as our children. We will have to take great care with him. He must understand the dangers inherent in this amazing ability."

"I'm sure you will teach him. Do you think the danger will ever go away?"

"No, most likely not. That is why we must stand firm in our love. No more lies between us."

"Just love, and trust me, Walker, as I do you."

"Always," he murmured softly as he gently kissed her.

Roby's Moonlit Night

Scotland 1749

The full moon hung low in the darkening sky. Silver light from the huge orb cast eerie shadows across the ground. Mist and dirty air clung to the path Roby McKenna and Kit Stuart rode. It smelled like autumn and tasted of smoke. Dried leaves coated the forest floor crunching beneath the horse's hooves. They were near Paisley, a small town near Glasgow. No breeze or sounds filled the forest as it was unusually quiet.

Roby felt as if something very significant in his life was about to happen. The sensation washed through him, leaving a trace of excitement. He and Kit had been away for two years. They were both eager to reach home. The McKenna castle was about a day and half's ride north of Inverness. While the travel was challenging, the land as well as the natives intriguing, neither man accomplished their goal. He was two and seven as was Kit with no mate in sight.

Well, what had he expected? Perhaps he just wanted an adventure he could tell tales about when he grew old and his muscles were weak. When he finally did find the perfect woman and have children, he could keep all entertained around the fire on a cold winter's night.

"What do you suppose that is?" Kit pointed to what appeared to be gallows rising from the ground. The dark black structure stood out as a silhouette in front of the brilliant light of the full moon, which encompassed the scene. Eerie sensations swept Roby to his core. Shivers swept up his spine. The noose dangled below the high beam. On the platform a small figure stood, a cowl thrown over the woman's head, arms bound in front of her. Another smaller form danced around the other. The animal chattered hysterically. When it saw him, it launched itself forward, swinging on tree branches, noisily claiming its displeasure.

"Appears to be a hanging," Roby said as curiosity caused him to spur his horse forward and faster. This seemed passing strange. The victim was either a woman or a child. The animal landed on his shoulder, covering his eyes with its hands. When it let go, it pointed seeming to think he should do something about the situation.

Absently he cradled the animal, a monkey, in his arms, making hushing noises as he tried to calm it.

"Too small to be a man. Why would someone be hanging a woman in the middle of the night?" Kit followed behind keeping pace with him. "In the middle of nowhere for that matter. What the devil? Did you just catch yourself a monkey?"

Roby nodded a soft chuckle escaping him. "Guess so."

At the sight coupled with the realization a woman was about to dangle from that noose, Roby's gut clenched his fingers tightened around the animal. Something wrong was happening here. He meant to find out what it was and if at all possible, correct it.

"Hello there." A man stepped down from the gallows, waving his hand. "Nice evening now, isn't it? Care to bear witness?"

"There's going to be a hanging here? How could this possibly be a nice evening when someone, a woman, is going to die," Roby asked, his voice filled with sarcasm as he brought his thoroughbred to a halt in front of the wizened man.

"Might not be a hanging. Not if one of you fine laddies wants to marry this lass." His wide grin showed yellowed teeth. The scent of garlic emanated from him. He looked back to the woman standing on the platform. "Either you lads up for the task?"

She was shaking, most likely terrified yet she held her head high, her narrow shoulders straight as if she defied the very act that was about to be perpetrated against her. Nothing she could have done could possibly warrant her execution.

"Marry?" Kit laughed as he leaned forward on the saddle horn to get a better look. "Not a chance. What about you, Roby? You want to wed this *wee lassie* to rescue her? Believe the animal would go along with her."

"What did she do?" Roby asked, his mind focused on the slight sway of the girl's body as she tried to hold herself still. She looked as if her knees would buckle at any moment. This had to be some kind of horrible travesty of justice. She certainly would not, could not have murdered someone unless it was in self-defense. The monkey leapt from his arms rushing to the woman. She bent down. The animal perched on her shoulder.

The man cackled. There was no other term to describe the noise. "Got caught eatin' a rabbit on Lord Bigley's land. He doesn't take to anyone poaching in his forest. Always says what's his is his and it's going to remain that way. Punishment he doles out is always harsher than it should be. She spent a month in the filthy pen he keeps outside his house near the barn before he finally decided that hanging was the best punishment, a life for a life."

"You don't say," Kit spoke, a bit of insolence in his voice. His horse nervously side-stepped.

Roby sickened at the thought a human life could be compared at the same value as a rabbit. The woman shifted from one foot to the other before she seemed to lock her knees to keep from falling, her body trembling hard.

"Why marriage?" Roby snorted still disgusted. "Doesn't change the manner of the crime in any way. Doesn't mean it won't happen again."

"Well, the old Lord Bigley believes that a woman should be molded by a man. It's his right to shape her into the woman she should be. If she's wed, well then she won't be gettin' herself into any more trouble. She won't have to ferret out her food. She'll be provided for now won't she? You wouldn't let your woman starve. She'll do what her man tells her to do. She'll have a protector a man to keep her to the straight and narrow so to speak."

"I see," Roby spoke softly his gaze still riveted on the woman as well as the monkey standing so very resolutely on the gallows waiting for his answer. He was her last hope.

"You do?" Kit asked, his head swirling to look at Roby and

sounding as if he wanted a better explanation. "What the devil do you see?"

"So," Roby's gaze ran over the woman's petite frame, taking note of her. It seemed upon hearing the conversation her chin rose higher. She was a proud lady. Hardly had the air about her of someone who would be reduced to fending for her food. "Allow me to get this straight. If one of us marries this lady, she will be set free. Her life will be spared?" The words on Roby's part were more musings than questions.

"That's what I said wasn't it?" the man asked irritably, rubbing first his head as if he tried to clear his brains before his hand found his crotch to do the same in his lower regions.

Roby chuckled before he wondered if he just lost all common sense. When he spoke, he was surprised by how clear and strong his voice was. This was something he'd never thought to do or that he would do what Kit did. Run the other way. He felt this strange calling toward her, a need to know her, to learn more about her. Very slowly and softly, he spoke, "I'll marry the lass. Does she have a name?"

"You will?" Kit sounded shocked as well as appalled. "You've lost your ever blessed mind, Roby McKenna. What will Connal and Wynnie say? They will be mortified, might even disown you. You are meant to wed your mate not some poor waif you found awaiting execution."

"For eating a rabbit." One eyebrow arched heavenward.

"Yes."

"My parents will bless the union if they believe it's what I want. I do want to marry this woman. Don't ask me why but I do. There is something about her that calls to me, to my soul, my heart as well." As every second passed he became more and more sure this was something he had to do. Wedding this lady he'd never seen before wasn't foolishness. It was written in the stars.

"Then, I'll just be gettin' out my bible. Come over this way. You can stand up here on the hangin' platform with the little lady. You stand right beside her now." The man pointed at Kit. "You come stand beside your friend. We'll be the two witnesses. Don't need more than that."

"Shouldn't you at least take the cowl off her head and untie her?" Roby asked his voice bland. He would do it himself if the man didn't agree. He didn't want the marriage to proceed any farther until this little matter was taken care of to his satisfaction.

"Well now, if you saw her before the ceremony you might have a change of heart. Wouldn't want that now would we? Don't want to see the *wee* little *lassie* hang for being hungry but I've got no choice or say in the matter. If I didn't do my duty by Bigley, I'd most likely find myself up there too."

"My mind won't change." With both hands, Roby gently removed the cowl. Stepping back, he stared into dark mesmerizing eyes that met his gaze with intensity. He wished he could see their color. She was gazing up at him, her small pert nose in the air, a defiant chin. Her hair hung to her waist tangled and matted, her face smudged with dirt. From what little of her he could see of her, her waist was trim, her breasts small and her hips curved femininely. The stench emanating from her was nearly unbearable. He grinned at her, knowing now he'd lost all sense of reality. With the full moon lighting the scene behind them, this had taken on an ethereal quality.

Still, she stood her ground. He reached to his boot, bringing up a knife. When moonlight glinted on the steel blade, she backed away. "I'm not going to hurt you, just get rid of this rope binding your hands. Don't think we should get married with you all trussed up." He paused, gently touching her cheek with his knuckles. "Do you wish to marry me, lass? If you don't...?"

She nodded after turning to look at the noose. He heard the swiftly drawn breath of air. Smiled. He decided she would do quite nicely even though he had no earthly idea what awaited him.

Thankfully the ceremony was nothing more than do you take this woman to be your wife? When he said yes, the old man closed up the bible and grabbed some papers from the pocket of his coat.

"Is that all?" Roby asked fairly unsure if the wedding was actually legal and binding. "You need to ask the lady or I won't consider myself wed. Don't want her to think she was forced in any way. I want to hear the words, I do, from her."

"Alright then, if you insist. Doesn't actually matter what she thinks though. Does it? Do you take this man?"

"Yes."

"Now, see, that was a waste of time. You got to sign these papers then everything will be in order. Don't go annulling this marriage or divorcing her unless you want to see her swinging up there. This all is binding. Lord Bigley has a far reach. He won't be likin' anything like that."

He found a semi-flat rock then smoothed the document out before handing him a pen, the bottle of ink already on the rock as if the man knew someone would come along to claim this woman as his own. Roby looked to Kit then back as he shrugged his shoulders. Kit was going to hand him an earful as soon as he got him alone, which wasn't going to happen anytime soon since he now possessed a wife.

With a flourish he signed his name then watched the lady do the same. For a moment he wondered if she would have preferred hanging to marriage. Well he did ask her.

"Very well then. The two of you are married. Let no man put asunder." He cackled again finishing the loud noise with a snort. The man stepped back. He collected his belongings then handed the document to the newlyweds. "Now, the two of you have a nice evening. Don't stop until you get to the other side of the river. That's where you'll be off Bigley's land." With another snort ending with a cackle, he mounted a nearby donkey. He vanished into the darkness and the mist.

Roby looked from the document he held in his hand then to the lady. He stuffed the parchment in his saddlebags. "Guess we're married. Let's get out of here. Can you ride?"

She nodded.

"Good, one less thing for me to worry about." With his hands around her waist, he lifted her easily onto his horse before mounting behind her. She weighed next to nothing. The monkey followed, resting in her arms. "You ever say anything?"

He felt her stiffen against him. "No, well maybe you'll warm up to me after awhile. I certainly hope so. I'd like the two of us to be friends." The devil but she was his. They would be lovers.

Kit wasn't speaking either. Roby could hear his thoughts clearly in his head as he wondered about the same things Kit was thinking. Ten minutes passed then another ten. They waded their horses across the stream to the opposite side, following the water until they reached a sheltered place to set up camp.

"We're going to stay here for the night. Why don't you go into Paisley? Find yourself a willing woman and get my new wife something else to wear. I'll meet you back here tomorrow morning. I want some privacy to acquaint myself with this lady."

"And you're going to...?" It seemed Kit didn't want to finish the question. "Sure, a new dress if I can find something."

"As long as it's clean, I don't care. When we get to Glasgow we can buy a few more things for her. She's going to need boots and a warm cloak to name some of the items."

"Probably needs a bit of everything," Kit said, a mocking smile lighting his face. He seemed to be enjoying this pickle he got himself into. The thing was, Roby wasn't the least bit worried.

He watched Kit ride away. Kit didn't put up an argument, just grinned as if he knew what was going to happen. It wasn't, at least not tonight. That was a good thing he supposed. Now, he needed to figure out just how to proceed with the woman who wouldn't speak, along with her monkey.

After dismounting he helped her to her feet. She smelled god-awful, a pig sty came to mind. Her first order of business was a bath. He hoped she wouldn't put up a fight. If she did, he would hog tie her and toss her in the small pond. Or he would bathe her himself.

"In case you're wondering, you wed Roby McKenna." *Of the clan Chattan and by the way I'm a shape shifter.* "And you are?"

For a second then another she looked at her feet. He figured she still wasn't going to talk. So be it, at least she didn't rattle on about nothing important. A silent female might be nice, practical in a way. He didn't need conversation.

"My name is Phillipa MacPherson. And this is Hypatia."

He was brought back from his inward thinking by the sound of her voice. "Ah, my fair lady does talk." He wasn't going to ask her anything else, at least not until he could breathe when she was nearby. Rummaging in his saddlebags, he brought out a towel and soap. "Here you go." He nodded to the pond. "You're going to take a bath."

"And where will you be?" Her voice quavered as she took the items, holding them close to her chest as if they would protect her from him. Her eyes were wide dark pools in a pale face.

"Right here. Need to make sure you don't decide to run off. I rescued you and I don't want that nullified." No, he certainly didn't. In fact he realized he truly did want to get to know this woman better. Needed to know what brought her to this point of nearly no return. "The monkey, Hypatia, can sit on the rock."

"Will you turn your back?"

"When you undress, of course. I promise I won't stare at you." Though, more than getting to know her better, he did want to see what she looked like naked. After all, she was his wife. Soon enough, he would see all of her. It would be his pleasure, hopefully hers as well to be seen in the buff.

While she walked to the pond appearing to be walking to her execution, Roby busied himself with starting a fire then setting up the tent they would sleep inside tonight. Hypatia now sat on a nearby rock, staring at him. When all of her body was beneath the water, he picked up her discarded clothing then he tossed them one at a time into the fire. Instantly, the air around him changed becoming sweeter smelling as the soiled rags she called clothing burned to nothing. When he looked her way, she was washing her hair. She ducked beneath the surface, foamy bubbles coated the top of the pond. He looked her way just as she was hesitantly backing from the water. When she turned slightly to see her way, he caught sight of her breasts. The air he inhaled jabbed in his throat. Her body was not as he'd thought. Good heavens, she must have bound her breasts. They were luscious curves that would spill deliciously from a man's hands, his large hands, crested with tight buds he wanted to taste.

He pulled one of his shirts from the saddlebag. When he reached her, she had the towel wrapped around her. He grinned pleased with her scent, the stench was now replaced with the smell of strong lye soap and woman. She was clean.

"Where are my clothes?"

"Burned them. You can put this on until Kit brings you something else to wear tomorrow."

"You burned them? That's all I had to wear." Her voice wavered yet she didn't sound angry.

"They weren't good for anything else. Don't tell me you intended to put them on."

"Was planning on washing them first." To his ears she sounded indignant.

"Foolhardy idea." He went about fixing a pot of coffee then pulled out a loaf of bread as well as an assortment of meat and cheeses. He held up a chunk of bread. "Hungry?"

"And why is that?" she was standing with her hands on her hips, her wet hair dripping onto her shoulders. She was shivering from the chill of the autumn air.

"Why are you hungry? Wouldn't know the answer to that question. Would you?" he asked grinning, understanding exactly what she'd been talking about.

"Why foolhardy?"

It didn't seem she was going to give up. He was enjoying her voice immensely. It was low, throaty a seductive burr in her accent coupled with rich low tones. He could well imagine how she might whisper to him, when he was giving her pleasure. Not a bad thing to think about one's wife, but he was hardly in the position to bed this woman he knew almost nothing about. He needed to like this lady he rescued from certain death before he took her to his bed.

"Foolhardy because first, there is no way you could rid the cloth of the stench by a mere washing. Second, because you would be wearing them wet and you would most likely freeze to death or take sick. The nights are chilly. Now put that shirt on then you can come sit by the fire. The heat will help dry your hair." He handed her his comb thinking he would like to comb her hair out for her. Perhaps in the future if they had one.

If there would be a future for them...

He certainly hoped there would be.

When next he saw her, she wore his shirt. "Thank you." She sat on a rock near the fire, his comb in hand. Her hesitancy didn't surprise him. To live she was putting an awful lot of trust into the hands of a stranger.

He watched her grimace as she constantly tugged at the tangles. Her arms must be tired from the work. He almost laughed before realizing this must be a harrowing experience for her. Only an hour or so ago, she'd been standing on the gallows expecting to die. If he had not come along when he did, she would be dead now.

"I am hungry as well as tired." Her arms dropped to her sides. "I'll work on this mess later."

He handed her a chunk of bread along with a couple of slices of cheese. "If you want I can comb your hair. Used to do it for my sister all the time. Do you trust me, lass?"

She looked as if that was the last thing she wanted. He watched her let out a long deep sigh. Sounding a bit reluctant, she said, "Yes, I would like that if you don't mind."

While she ate, he sat behind her. She was nestled between his thighs. As he worked she slowly began to relax. He felt her exhaustion, nearly bone deep. There were so many questions he needed to ask her. Wondered if she would answer.

He didn't ask.

"You can have as much to eat as you like," he told her as he bent close to her ear to tell her, wondering how she would react to this unasked for closeness. The shiver coursing through her thin frame was a good sign to him. The quivering wasn't from fear but her reaction to the warmth of his breath on her skin. While he wasn't going to rush her, he did want a true marriage.

She ate more then, "Thank you. You're very kind. Why did you agree to marry me?"

He paused in thought, setting the comb back in the saddlebag before he answered. "I don't know." He was shaking his head. "At the time I wondered if I had cobwebs for brains. In the end, I could not bear to see a woman hang for wanting to feed herself." He couldn't tell her how something about her called to him, enchanted him. If he said anything, she wouldn't believe him.

"A kind heart, do people take advantage of you often?" She was stroking her hand along Hypatia's back. The little money looked asleep if not that then content.

"Never," he murmured laughing, watching the way she moved. She was slim, too slim, but that was to be expected having spent the last month penned up. He liked the way she carried herself, the way her eyes shimmered in the light cast by the flames. Firelight danced across her face, casting it in shadows one moment, a warm glow the next.

"Confident as well." She sipped at her coffee, her eyes focused on his mouth. "You're a *verra bonnie mon*. I'm sure the ladies tell you that quite often. Do you often have coffee?"

For a moment he forgot to breathe. "Not in those words. Kit and I learned to enjoy the coffee when we were in America."

"I see."

"Do you?" he questioned wondering how much life experience this young lady had. Everything about her spoke of innocence yet she didn't voice innocent thoughts. He would feel very foolish if he assumed something that wasn't true. He decided to leave all judgments concerning the lady to the back of his mind then let time tell the story. She would show her true colors soon enough. He would deal with her as his wife.

"You can call me Pippa. My friends do."

He laughed softly then once more bending close to her neck, "You consider me a friend already? Suppose it's better than being your enemy. What happened to your friends when you were caught?" He pushed her drying hair to one side. The breath from his words brushed across her nape. He'd like to taste her there. Knew it was too soon.

"A friend in a husband would be nice. I've never thought about a husband except the one I *dinna* want." This time the shudder he felt against him was not a good sensation as he felt her fear shuffle into him become part of him. He didn't understand how he felt her emotions intuitively.

"The one you don't want?" he asked a bit puzzled but willing to wait until she wanted to tell him more. "That wouldn't be me, would it?"

"No, I'm not speaking of you."

"You want me for a husband?" For some reason he needed that answer to be yes now and for always.

"Yes, considering the alternative," she told him sounding sincere. She turned slanting him a bemused smile. "Truly, dying was not something I was looking forward to."

He was sure she evaded his question then wondered who the alternative husband was. Again, in time she would tell him. Demanding answers now would get him nowhere. "How," he asked, deciding to change the direction of their conversation, "did you end up fending for yourself?"

As she lifted her slim shoulders in a very feminine shrug, her nipples caught the fabric of his shirt. The rosy tips were dark beneath fine lawn fabric. When she stood to stretch her muscles, the silhouette of her legs and hips were clearly visible. She was made with lush curves, bounty that would fill her very new husband's hands. In time, in time he would reap the benefits of this hasty marriage. She might not be his mate, but they would do well together.

"Five years ago," she sat down again, smoothing the fabric along her legs, pulling it tight against her breasts, "I ran away. Couldn't stay where I was one moment longer." Absently she fed the little monkey pieces of cheese and bread.

"How old were you then?" Mesmerized and fascinated by her he craved more information.

Her hands clasped in front of her, she looked down, her lashes fluttering against her cheekbones. "Fourteen. I was fourteen the day I left. I gathered up a few necessities, took the coin I had in my room then never looked back. I've been on my own since. Of course, the money ran out very soon."

He let the breath he'd been holding out in a loud whoosh. "Fourteen you say?" The reason must have been drastic. She survived though. Roby found he was proud of her, the tenacity she showed.

"I suppose you'd be wantin' to know why." She looked up at him then, firelight glowing warm across her high cheekbones.

"Whenever you want to tell me. I am your husband. While I probably can't undo all the wrongs that may or may not have been heaped against, you I can always try. My family, the clan, is powerful. Perhaps we can help." He understood trust was fragile, giving of all her secrets to a man she barely knew would take time.

He was willing to wait however long it took.

"I would like that, Roby McKenna." She waited for a time, staring into the fire. "You spoke of a sister. Are there other siblings?" she asked as she poured herself another cup of coffee.

It seemed she wanted to change the subject again. He couldn't blame her. She already divulged quite a bit about her journey to this place in time. "Just another brother who is married. When I left, his wife was increasing. My sister has one child also. By now they might have more."

"And Kit? What about him and where is he tonight?"

"He's a Stuart. His father married my father's sister. As to his whereabouts," Roby cleared his throat unsure of how much to tell her. She should remember he went into town. Perhaps she didn't hear.

"Cousins, I gather. You think he's found himself a willing lass. While you are stuck with me, he's dallying in a warm bed."

Again and again she stunned him with her honesty coupled with her knowledge about the way of men. "Yes, Kit has a way with the ladies. Houston is one of his brothers, the oldest, then Kit and Riley is the baby of the bunch, but he would take grave offense if he were to hear any one call him the baby. He's nearly two and twenty."

"I'm an only child. Always wanted a brother or a sister. Guess it wasn't to be. However, I do have a cousin whom I despise, Harry Finchbottom."

A cousin she despised, he guessed there was more to this story also. "I see. Should I feel sorry for you or him?"

She laughed. The sound was low not a high-pitched giggle of most girls. He liked the way she laughed, the sound as well as the tenor. He wanted to hear more laughter.

"I'd like to say most assuredly for him. In two years I'm hoping that will be *verra* true. Until then it's sorry for me you should be feeling. Except now that I've found you, or more accurately that you found me, perhaps my luck has changed for the better."

"Now that you've survived the hangman's noose and you are clean as well, don't think I'll be feeling sorry for you right now. You've married me. True enough that fact might prove to bring you good fortune."

"I've had food too. You fed me as well as saved my life. I'm *verra* glad you came along, Roby McKenna, arrogant man that you are. Mayhap arrogance in a man is a good quality. I've yet to figure that one out."

"I like to call it confidence. Has a better ring to it." Roby was laughing, thoroughly enjoying his wife.

He was pleased he came along too. The first fat raindrop fell, hissing and sizzling on the flames. Before the coming deluge could soak them, he finished constructing the shelter he started earlier that they would use tonight, hoping she would not put up a fuss at the sleeping conditions. He was not going to get soaked while he had a tent to share with his new wife.

"Come." He held out his hand, studying her for any sign of reluctance. "You must be exhausted. Today must have been trying for you. We should go to bed now. Tomorrow will come soon enough and we've a long ways to travel before we reach McKenna territory."

She didn't acknowledge his invitation for a few seconds seeming to mull over his words as well as the tent. He watched her let out a slow puff of air, seeming resigned as she looked from the fire then back to him. "Are you going to stick your rod inside me now?"

~ * ~

By the look on Roby's face she guessed she shocked him to the core. Bluntly honest perhaps was not appropriate with a brand new husband. He stuffed his hands through his hair as he looked at the full moon still hovering in the sky. Drops of rain splattered and hissed on the hot rocks surrounding the fire pit. Seconds turned into minutes before he answered.

"No, Pippa, not tonight."

Her voice deepened as she tried for a calm she truly didn't feel. "I'd just as soon get it over with if you *dinna* mind. Isn't it what husbands do? What they want to do?" If he did do it tonight, they would be done. She would be his wife in every way then she would no longer fear the marriage bed with him.

"You think I would only want to do it once? Is that what you're saying?" he asked blandly. Once more he sounded shocked to his very core by her blatant but very necessary honesty. She meant to proceed this way in everything.

She nodded while she looked at her feet. "Isn't once enough?" she asked still moving one foot around in circles. She knew she changed from the confident woman of a few seconds ago to shy. Her voice shaking, she asked, "Are you telling me you would want to do it more than one time?"

His grin unnerved her to the tips of her toes, his even teeth flashing white in the moonlight catching more light from the dying fire. She was pleased they weren't yellowed and rotten. "Once with the right woman, one's wife, is never enough. Ah, Pippa, once we do make love you will want to do it with me all the time. You will ask me to take your warm body into my arms to fill you with my shaft as well as my seed."

She felt the color drain from her face. "I *dinna* think that will be true, Roby McKenna. Don't know what would make you think something so preposterous." Just the way he smiled, the way his gaze lingered on her eyes then swept slowly the length of her clear to her toes unnerved her heating her to an inferno. She smoothed the shirt she wore. Curled her toes.

"What crazy notions you have. Who made you think making love was something to do only once with one's husband?" he asked stepping so close to her she felt the heat radiating from his all male body. He smelled of the same lye soap she'd used and himself.

He was rubbing tiny circles with his thumb on the underside of her wrist. The strange contact sent spirals of heat coursing through her. A strange ache simmered between her legs. She didn't understand any of this. "*Ye* should not be doing that. It's not seemly." Her voice shook.

"It is very appropriate with one's wife." He brought her hand to his lips, kissed each knuckle before turning it over and pressing a tender kiss to her palm. "We shall go to sleep now. I promise you I won't stick my rod inside you tonight, hmm... You've nothing to worry about."

"Are you a *mon* who keeps his word?"

"*Aye*, come along now."

She nodded, unable to think of anything to say at that. She wasn't at all sure if she was relieved or disappointed in what he told her. Roby McKenna was nothing like Harry Finchbottom in face or form. Perhaps the act would not be as repulsive as she thought. She would have to give the idea some consideration.

He let her go inside first. As she bent over she was very aware of the shirt creeping up her bare legs. She tugged on the tails as she crawled inside, hoping to keep a tiny bit of modesty. It was all to no avail when she heard his words from behind her.

"You've very nice legs, long and slender. You're bottom is quite nice too," he told her, his voice so soft and throaty it sounded unnatural to her.

Heat flared on her face, on all of her body. She wanted to tell him his legs were nice, too, but she hadn't seen them without his trousers. Perhaps they weren't as nice as she imagined them to be. She realized she would like to do just that.

Look at his naked legs.

More heat. More funny sensations spiraled through her. I am a foolish ninny to be thinking things such as this.

Once she was settled, he crept inside followed by Hypatia who settled in a far corner as if she understood that would be her new place. She pulled the covers to her chin, felt him settle beneath them also. Next to her, so close she fought for each breath, he felt big and hot. She liked it. Pippa wasn't at all sure how she was going to manage to fall asleep. Heat from his large well muscled manly frame so close to hers was overwhelming all her senses. She didn't contemplate why.

His arm wrapped around her as he pulled her even closer. "Hush, don't protest. I won't hurt you. Relax and fall asleep. If I hold you, we'll both be warmer."

Her voice was a hushed tremble deep and low. "I don't see how a girl can sleep with you lying there all big and…" she gulped tiny bits of air. "You're not wearing your shirt."

He laughed softly as she felt his warm breath sweep across her cheek. "I'm making concessions for you along with your tender sensibilities. I don't sleep in my trousers either. But for you I'm wearing them."

She was on her side, spooned up tight against him, her thoughts a hazy muddle of confusion in her head. Afraid but liking the way she felt so close to him, she pushed back against him, feeling the length of his legs against hers. At the intimate contact, his big hand tightened on her waist, his fingers pressing into her. She closed her eyes. Listened to the patter of the rain on the canvas of the tent while she tried to tamp down the unnatural feelings that were zooming through her at a wild and reckless pace.

Heard more night sounds.

Listened to the wind.

This was the first time in so very long that she slept near to someone other than by herself. The fear was always so close and clear that it always cramped her stomach. She never knew what would happen to her during the night, nights at times that seemed to last an eternity.

Not much time passed before she felt Roby relax. The hand holding her body so close to his no longer stroked her. She wondered if she could go to sleep now that he seemed to be sleeping soundly. Wondered what the next days and months would bring. She should tell him that he should be afraid for his life now that he was her husband. If her cousin ever discovered she was alive and wed to someone else, he would act to change both those facts. While Harry would not kill her right away, he would certainly see to it after he forced a marriage between them after he inherited all that was hers. That fact meant that Roby could not continue to live.

She had a lot of telling to do.

A man like Roby McKenna deserved to know what he would be facing since he made that fatal leap of marriage to a woman awaiting death. Nothing for her changed. She still awaited death, this time at the hands of her cousin instead of the hangman.

She should not have divulged the private information about his rod. He would think she was a hussy or worse. What was worse than a hussy? She didn't know. Truth of the matter was that Harry told her he was going to do that to her until she was increasing. When it happened she would have to marry him. What Harry didn't know was that nothing he did to her would make her wed him.

He was a vile, loathsome man.

From the bottom of my heart, I despise you, Harry Finchbottom.

Pippa didn't want to think about Harry using Robby against her, to make her succumb to his plans. Not understanding exactly what was happening, she wriggled against the man behind her, pressing against him for the warmth he so sweetly offered. She discovered he was clasping her tightly, squeezing her waist. He was still breathing deeply, still sleeping. Could men do that in their sleep? The warmth of his fingers moved up her ribcage then downward to caress and squeeze her hip. Without thought, she pushed back against him, felt something hard against her bottom.

Closing her eyes she tried to put the strange and wondrous new feelings she was experiencing to the back of her head. Now he was trailing a fingertip along her arm then back down. A tiny unexpected sound rippled up from deep inside of her. To no avail, she tried to reposition herself so she wasn't as close to him. His breath tickled the back of her neck just before the palm of his hands brushed across the tip of one breast.

"Roby, what are you doing?" she asked the question even though she was sure he was still asleep.

"Sleeping," he whispered and once again the warmth of his breath whispered across the nape of her neck sending a myriad of shivers up then down her spine only to settle and throb deep in her most feminine parts.

"No, you're not."

"Go to sleep, Pippa, morning is going to come soon enough. Don't want you falling off your horse because you're too exhausted to do anything else."

"You go to sleep too," she whispered as he once again pulled her closer, his large leg covered hers. She found herself well and truly pinned against the man. *Baw* he told her, promised her he wasn't going to stick his rod inside her. What did he think to be doing at this time? Everything felt wondrous and unique to her. She didn't want him to stop.

"I'm sleeping now," he murmured against her ear just before his teeth tugged on the lobe nearly sending her jumping out of her skin.

"You're making me very hot."

"Hot is good. You can sleep better if you're warm." His hand cupped her breast, his thumb rubbing lightly across the hardened tip.

"I cannot sleep if you keep doing those things to my body. I *dinna ken* what you're about but you need to stop."

The long whoosh of air coupled with a groan that sounded as if he was in pain surprised her, but he stopped doing whatever it was he was doing. His hand settled on the rise of her hip but didn't move again.

She wished he hadn't stopped. Now she was hot and wet as well as unable to fall asleep the sensations in her body were so strong, pulsing and throbbing. She wished he would touch her more. Liked what he'd been doing. Pippa decided she would tell him as much tomorrow morning as soon as she found the chance to do so.

When she woke the sun was shining and she was alone under the tent. Even Hypatia abandoned her. Kit's and Roby's voices she heard outside. She couldn't quite hear what they were saying, just heard the warm rumble of men's voices she wasn't afraid of. Fearing Roby

McKenna was just not possible. Not when she liked him so much. As she also trusted him, she understood he would look after her.

He saved her.

She owed him.

Unsure of Kit, however, she decided to watch him closely, needed to take the measure of the man before she acknowledged him as she did Roby. The tread of boots on the ground neared her sleeping space. She looked up when the flap opened.

"Good, you're awake. Did you sleep well?" he asked his grin wide as if he remembered the way he touched her. She certainly did. She wanted more of the same.

"I did after you stopped tormenting me," she said looking up into his handsome face and hearing the soft chuckle humming from the back of his throat. Suddenly, she recalled she was lying. Before she slept, she wished for him to caress her more. She heard her little friend's chatter behind him.

"Torment?" he queried lifting one of his marvelous black brows into a perfect arch above gray eyes that shimmered molten steel. "You cannot fool me. I heard the soft little sighs of pleasure. The sound was a gift, I'll never forget. It was our wedding night after all. A husband couldn't ask for more."

"Was that pleasure you were gifting me with?" She caught her bottom lip between her teeth. She'd heard such things. She'd also heard of the pain of being forced. Pippa supposed she'd been lucky over the last five years.

Until she'd been caught with the rabbit.

His chuckle was warm, all-knowing. "You know it was." He handed her the clothing Kit brought for her. "You can dress in these. He wasn't able to purchase a dress but the pants and shirt will do for now. As soon as you're dressed come get something to eat and drink."

"Will there be more of that pleasure stuff tonight?" she asked then immediately thought she should not have done so when she saw the expression on his face. The shock turned to a wide grin, immediately relieving her of the notion that she was a foolish woman for saying something so forward.

"If you ask, you shall receive." With more laughter following him, he left, the flap falling into place as she picked up the clothing to examine the pieces. He brought a shirt and trousers for her and had apologized. What he didn't know was that shirts and trousers were her preferred form of clothing. She was pretty sure she hadn't worn a dress since the day before she left her home.

Inside the tent she scrambled to rid herself of his shirt then quickly donned the clothing he gave her. When she stepped outside the air was brisk. She ran her hands along her arms in a feeble attempt to warm herself. The coffee smelled good, the bacon sizzling on the campfire even better. She couldn't remember when she had two meals so close together.

A few minutes later she joined the two men. "I'm in heaven," she murmured as she sipped her first cup of coffee while she chewed on a piece of crispy bacon, in her mind cooked to perfection. "Such bounty, I forgot normal people eat more than every couple of days. Thank you, Roby McKenna."

"You don't have to keep thanking me." He looked from his plate of food to stare into her eyes. "I do believe I'm going to be the biggest benefactor in this relationship of ours. You enthrall me, please me very much."

"How so?" Kit asked still seeming displeased over what happened last evening in the moonlit night. "You need more than just sex for a marriage to work."

Pippa saw that Roby sent his cousin a blistering glance. "You know nothing of our relationship, Kit Stuart. I trust you to keep a civil tongue around my wife."

The air she inhaled punched her throat. For several seconds she looked away, trying not to retaliate with words that would serve only to hurt Roby. She would never want that even though his cousin didn't seem to care. The man was too quick to judge. She set her plate down suddenly not quite so hungry.

"Don't let Kit get to you, Pippa. He's only trying to look out for me. He has only good intentions. Don't you Kit? Now, before we leave here, I want you to eat everything on your plate. I didn't fill it so full as to give you too much. I *ken* you haven't eaten much for the last five years." He slanted a pointed look toward his cousin.

She did try to eat and managed most of the food even though it had lost the marvelous taste it should have had. Actually, the food tasted of sawdust. It was another half hour before they were riding again. Once more she sat in front of Roby. Kit rode ahead as if he meant to give them privacy. She wasn't all that sure what she needed privacy for, but it was nice to have her new husband all to herself. Hypatia swung from tree branch to tree branch until seemingly tired she settled on Roby's shoulder.

Finally able to relax she leaned against Roby's broad chest. "Ah, lass take this time for more rest. If you fall asleep, I'll make sure you don't fall off."

She turned slightly looking up at him. "You have silver eyes that are rimmed with light blue. They are striking." There were several blank seconds then, "Your lashes are far too long for a man. 'Tis not fair."

"And you possess the most beguiling green eyes with golden flecks I've ever seen. Last night when I," well he cleared his throat as if thinking better of what he meant to say, "When I first looked at your face, I wondered what color they were as I wondered at the color of your hair. Chestnut, I would say. Delightful. Very lovely."

"Flatterer," she murmured as she wondered why he was being so sweet to her.

They rode in silence for a while, Pippa trying to decide what part of her life she should tell Roby first. She could hardly blurt out everything all at once. Yet she had to find someplace to start. Not wanting to travel over ground she already walked on she remained silent.

It was a few minutes after she decided she would start by explaining why she ran away when his hand brushed across her nipple. Just as it had last night, the caress sent sensation raging straight to her core, in that secret part of her between her legs, at the juncture of her thighs. She gasped in a gulp of air as his fingers pinched lightly. As he switched his attention to her other breast, she pushed back against him, feeling that same hard part of him as she felt last night. She knew what it was as well as what it meant because Harry took great delight in embarrassing her and taunting her with his rod. While he never raped her, she understood if she stayed where he could get at her for much longer, he would force her.

So, she did the only thing she could do.

She left.

Pippa let her head fall against his chest. His lips made tiny forays down her neck, sipping and nibbling. She turned her head toward him. His lips swept so very lightly against hers she wasn't at all sure they made contact. Then she understood he was kissing her as his tongue touched her bottom lip, moved lightly across it.

"I find I cannot keep my hands to myself," he murmured beside her ear so only she could hear.

"You are a devil and a bad *mon*, Roby McKenna," she said softly as he continued the exploration that made her want more and told her she needed something else even while she didn't have the foggiest notion what that something else was.

"How can I be a bad man for giving my wife pleasure, for watching her eyes simmer with the passion she wants to bestow on me?"

"I *dinna ken* any of this." But she did understand that she liked all the delicious raw feelings he generated in her. "All I know is that I don't want you to stop."

He pulled his hand away when Kit turned to ride back to them. "Did you want to bypass Glasgow or go into the city to get her more clothes?"

"What do you think, Pippa? Would you be more comfortable wearing a dress?" he asked, as he seemed to be staring at her mouth. The kiss they shared was brief and so *verra* hot. She wanted more and wished Kit to leave them alone again.

She swept her tongue across her bottom lip as his hand tightened at her waist before creeping just a bit higher to rest beneath her breast. Pippa didn't understand why every contact with this man sent her senses reeling.

"I'm fine with what I'm wearing. You did say there is one change of clothing. That is more than I'm used to." It wasn't entirely true. During her stay with the gypsies, she'd wanted for nothing, even companionship. She'd thought herself in love. Now she knew what she felt for the boy, Aaron Rosamara, was temporary infatuation. With time the feeling would have faded. She would have to tell Roby about him as well as the few kisses they shared.

"When we reach home, you're going to get used to more, much, much more. I will bring the modiste from the village to fit you," he murmured close to her ear again, lightly grazing the tip with his teeth. "I want to give you anything your heart desires."

Kit let out a snort that to her ears was one of disgust. She stiffened realizing Kit knew exactly what his cousin was about. Roby chuckled sending waves of shivers down her arms. He was wicked, seemed to love to torment her in his devil's own way.

The next village is about two hours away. We can stop early or we can spend the night on the ground," Kit said, waiting impatiently for an answer.

It was abundantly clear he meant to ride ahead and out of the realm of any conversation they might have. That was fine with her. Kit had a way of disarming her, making her uncomfortable in her skin. While Pippa understood Kit's obvious contempt surrounding her, he shouldn't take his feeling out on his cousin.

"Let's stay at the inn. If I recall correctly, it's the Drum and Ox, a pleasant place, clean with good food. I for one would like to sleep on a bed with my new wife beside me," he taunted his cousin while his hand settled firmly on her waist. He was sending her a message. While she couldn't fathom why, she set the question aside for the time being.

She watched and she assumed Roby watched Kit as he spurred his horse faster. "Will he come back do you think?"

"As soon as he's worked off some of the anger he's feeling. As of yet, he hasn't come to terms with our marriage. In time he will." Roby allowed a long hiss of air to escape from his lungs. "I'm sorry for how he's acting and all. You deserve to be treated more kindly."

"I assume it's because you married a convicted criminal to save her from death that he is in such a bad simmer," she spoke softly understanding the words had to be said.

"No."

"Then why?"

"Because the two of us spent the better part of two years looking for our soul mates. We left the highlands to do so. Neither one of us was successful in that endeavor then out of the blue I decide to wed someone I've never spoken to. Speak o' the devil, the lass is a highlander. I had to come home to find my eternal woman. What he doesn't understand is that there is a strange and unique connection between the two of us. A bond I would like to come to understand better. I've a mind to believe you might indeed be that soul mate I've been searching the world for."

"Oh." It was her turn to be shocked.

Searching the world?

"Is that all you've got to say now that I've laid all my thoughts bare for you to demolish if you so choose?" He laughed then and pulled her close, teasing her with his male arrogance taking liberties that were best left to private intimate settings.

"I feel a connection of sorts with you too." She lowered her lashes, staring at his big hand that still held one of her breasts inside it. "I've never truly been close to a man before but everywhere you touch me, I want you to never stop." This was when she should mention Aaron Rosmara, tell him about the few kisses he stole.

"You have the most bountiful breasts. I want to stroke them, tease and taunt them until the tips harden into tight buds. More than anything I have this incessant urge that I cannot rid myself of to suck them deep into my mouth until you cry out your pleasure."

Truly he was the devil's own spawn. She swallowed the lump in her throat so she could speak. Still had trouble saying the words. "And what would you say if I was so brazen as to tell you that I want the same?" She paused to garner more courage to tell him honestly how she felt. "I would like to know how that would feel."

"I would tell you we can't get to that inn fast enough."

She sat up straighter, touched his forearm, marveling in its width, in the hard muscles her fingers surrounded. She tried to pull it away before she sighed softly and gave up. "We've things we should talk about before we carry this any farther. You might not want to stay married to me if you know the truth about me. Kit might well be correct in his assumption that I'm using you because I am. We both understand that fact. The difference is that you don't *ken* why."

~ * ~

"What does the letter say?" Wynnie asked impatiently as she paced the main room in the north tower where she and Connal had lived for the past thirty years. She was impatient to see her son again. He'd been away for two long years. They both missed him, were eager to tell him of all that transpired as well as hear all about his adventure in America.

"Says if all goes well, he'll be home in two weeks," Connal said as he set the letter on the table so he could pull his wife into his arms. He kissed her quickly as she pushed away from him knowing all too well the conversation would end if she allowed him to have his way with her. It always did. "*Ye* are too impatient, lady of my heart, my eternal love. Our son will be home soon enough, aggravating us as he always manages to do."

"Did he say if he found his mate?" she queried allowing Connal to hold her close to him again, trusting he would take this no farther while they still had things to talk about. She set her head on his chest, heard the steady beat of his heart against her cheek. The sound was wonderful to her. The years with Connal had been good ones. Now, she was eager to see her son fulfilled, to find his mate, to sire children.

"Says neither he nor Kit found someone they can call their eternal love. It seems my meeting with you so soon in my adult life proved me to be a lucky man. If you had not been running for your *verra* life, you would *nay* have run into my arms."

"You were a *verra* bad man then, Connal McKenna. First, you threatened to lock me away in a tower prison with mice as my companions. When that wasn't going to work for you, I found myself locked in your chambers with a different kind of rat to contend with."

"You wound me, Madam." Instead of placing his hand on his heart he cupped her breast in his hand with obvious intentions.

He was not satisfied. Lightly and oh so tenderly, Connal brushed his mouth across hers nibbling at the corners then sweeping his tongue across her bottom lip urging her to open for him. She met his with her own, touched the tip then explored the dark warm recess inside that which he offered.

His hand closed more tightly over her breast, stroking the sensitive underside through the fabric of her gown. Teasing and coaxing her to his will. It never took much wheedling for him to get his way. They both paused for breath.

"I'm sorry to hear the news. They had high expectations when they left." They all understood they journeyed from the highlands with more than one reason. It was no longer safe for any of the clan to shift and run wild among the heather. For young men freedom is a heady notion. One that can only be *coshed* with time.

"Wynnie, they wanted adventure along with their freedom probably more so than the idea of finding their mates. I suppose they needed to find out what kind of men they were. Those two could not do that here where everything they wanted was given to them."

She hit him on the shoulder. "Are you telling me I spoiled my son?"

"Along with your daughter and other son. I'm as much to blame as you. We both adored them, needed them to have everything they wished for. The journey was good for both men. I'm sure of that. They will come back wiser and braver than when they left."

"Are you now? So sure of yourself?" she asked looking to the bed and perhaps a small dalliance before they went downstairs for their evening meal. She would be amenable if he showed her that he wanted her other than the swift kiss they just shared.

"I am just as sure as the fact that I should carry you to our bed. No, on second thought now I take a few seconds to reconsider," he stopped talking for a few seconds. "I've the urge to make love to my wife on the soft fur rug in front of the fire."

"You would be making assumptions. What makes you think I would be amenable to such a situation, Laird McKenna?" She laughed as he further explored her, sucked in air when he found more tender sensitive places. "You're a bold one."

"You adore my boldness."

"Aye."

With the tip of his finger, he touched her nose then kissed the same spot. "By the wild passion I see simmering in the crystal clear depth of your eyes, I know for a fact you are wanting me. By the way your pulse is thundering right here where my thumb rests so I can tell what your body is saying to mine, I know your body is weeping for me. I *ken* you want me just as I *ken* I want you." He told her as he swept her into his arms, his mouth pressed gently against hers.

"Love me, Connal McKenna, as you always do."

"I will lass. We'll think of our son and pray for his safe return."

Other Books by Christine Young
Available at Rogue Phoenix Press

Connal's Eternal Love
Sweet McKenna Book One

A few days shy of All Hallows' Eve Connal McKenna, Laird of Clan Chattan stands on the parapets of his castle. Bonfires line the hillsides while his clan prepares for the upcoming festivities. Drawn by the whispering of the wind, Connal McKenna feels a strange restlessness in his soul. Setting out to discover the wickedness that is calling to him, he discovers his mate. With gentle words and sensuous kisses, the auburn-eyed highlander conquers his mate, the beautiful, defiant Wynnie Adair who he comes upon during an evening ride. She must ultimately put her trust in the only man who can save her from the ruthless plans of her father and succumb to his gentle coaxing.

In Brady's Arms
Sweet McKenna Book One

Forced to run from the only home she knows, beautiful, headstrong Lillian Townsends seeks shelter in the wild highlands where the McKenna clan live. Trying to avoid a betrothal contract signed by her stepfather to an aging lord, she is desperate to find a means to sidestep the inevitable, including a marriage to the oldest son of the laird. Lilly is enamored of the young lord who pursues her with unrelenting determination flashing his devilishly handsome charms. She is hard pressed to resist.

Besotted from the first moment Brady McKenna sees Lilly, he is determined to find a means to coax her into his arms and bed. With only the promise of carnal pleasure as his mistress, Brady relentlessly pursues the woman who has unwittingly forged a place in his heart. She is like no other woman, proud, defiant and enchanting. Despite his father's advice to stay away from her, he cannot. He boldly seeks her out and makes her his own.

My Sweet Broc
Bad Boys Book One

He's a bad bad boy...

Broc Wallace is a fun-loving rake who never thought any beautiful woman could melt his heart. He lives life in the present enjoying the camaraderie of his friends and the pleasures of his mistress. When Bliss races into his life, he is ill prepared to deal with her secrets or give up the tenor of his life. When the truth is revealed, he finds himself unable to forgive and forget the betrayal.

...but she's sweet for him

Bliss MacTavish knows she's playing with fire when she refuses to tell this bad boy her name. He tempts her with sweet whispers of seduction knowing her innocent nature will be unable to refuse all he yearns to give her. Deciding to follow her heart, she finds the repercussions more than she bargains for when she gives herself to this bad boy.

Crazy for Cam
Bad Boys Book Two

He's a bad bad boy...

Lord Cam MacEwen, Viscount of Rosehill, tries his best to be proper and court the lady of his dreams in the acceptable way. The feat proves impossible when the lady in question uses every means at her disposal to tempt him. He fights his jealousy for another man as well as the need to make her his own, finally giving in to her irresistible passion.

...but she's crazy for him.

Chelsea MacTavish wants the bad boy she fell in love with and kissed just before her eighteenth birthday. With feminine wiles and irresistible allure, the sensuous lady plans to best Cam at his game of hearts and make him forget his need to court her properly.

Falling for Flynt
Bad Boys Book Three

He's a bad, bad boy...

Fascinated by Hope's loss of memory yet haunted by her sultry beauty, Flynt is irresistibly drawn to the stoic miss—and into her troubles with the sultan who wants her for himself. When he discovers she is the sister of his best friend, his pride keeps him from pursuing her and making her his.

...but she's falling for him.

Raised in a harem but now penniless, alone and without her memory, Hope must discover a way to remember all that she has lost. She finds a way to continue with her life as a servant in Flynt's home. The first sight of Flynt steals Hope's breath as well as her heart. Can she overcome her fears and give herself to the man she fell in love with.

Dancing With Donal
Bad Boys Book Four

He's a bad bad boy...

Once a bad boy always a bad boy, Donal Chamberlin's carefree ways come crashing down around him when he meets the ravishingly beautiful Daryl MacTavish, the innocent little sister of one of his best friends. He is determined to win her heart as he sets his sights on marriage and an heir. His past gets in the way of his quest when a woman he once loved threatens Daryl's life.

...but she's dancing with him.

Daryl has seen the control her sister's husbands hold over them.

She yearns for a life where she makes decisions for herself. No man will have power over her. But no man kisses her the way Donal does. No man can make her forget all her goals leaving her helpless to give up her dreams. Yet Donal is determined to dance through all the barriers she thrust in front of him, pursuing her until she says yes.

Loving Leslie
Bad Boys Book Five

He's a bad bad boy...

Leslie Stewart, Duke of Southcliff is stoic, set in his ways, a spy who is used to having his life well ordered. He expects life to continue on in this perfectly conventional fashion. He assumes his bad boy status while keeping mamas and debutantes at arm's length. An heir is needed but Leslie has every intention of finding a woman who doesn't covet his wealth and tittle. He is irresistibly drawn to the headstrong young lady who becomes more beautiful as she develops into a woman.

...but she is loving him.

When Leslie kisses Lacie MacTavish, she knows even at the tender age of fifteen this is the man of her dreams. Forced to wait until she comes of age, Lacie withdraws into herself. Now she is eighteen and Leslie has returned from a mission for the British Government ready to claim her as his bride. She refuses him and he must find a way to seduce her and in the process create a burning passion within her, which she cannot deny.

Pleasing Arie
Bad Boys Book Six

He's a bad bad boy...

Arie Demir has never been denied anything in his life. He takes what he wants. What he undeniably yearns for is the beautiful redheaded spitfire he sees in a restaurant in Glasgow. At every turn, she confuses him by disputing his power over her. Alison refuses to accept the fact he owns her. While Arie tries desperately with patience and tenderness to drive her wild with new sensations, his scorching kisses ignite the fires of her very soul to make her understand he is all she will ever want.

...but is she pleasing him?

Alison Fletcher never expected to find herself kidnapped and sold to a whorehouse then bought by a Turkish sultan to become his slave. She vows to never surrender to the arrogant man who believes he owns her. She is stunned by the magnificently handsome man who awaits her compliance. Unexpectedly, she finds Arie the lesser of all the evils. The hidden depths of his mesmerizing dark brown eyes hold her into their power; his muscular embrace makes her weak with desire. She is his to do with as he wishes.

Graham's Wicked Kiss
Bad Boys Book Seven

He's a bad bad boy...

Graham Chamberlin is stunned to find three young boys dangling from the trees lining the drive to Runningmead Manner. On further inspection, he is astonished at their obsession to protect a young woman who has been brutalized by her pimp. The woman he discovers hiding in a third-floor attic room is gravely injured. He takes the silver haired stowaway under his wing. Clearly, Graham's new guest is a lady with many secrets. He is determined to unlock all the mysteries surrounding her.

...But she can't resist his wicked kiss.

The years since Ria left the convent where she was raised have been a nightmare. Her secrets are dangerous—as is the powerful man determined to find her. Handsome Graham Chamberlin is clearly a gentleman with secrets of his own, but staying with him could mean the difference between life and death for Ria. With each passing day, her handsome host turns Ria's convalescence into an increasingly sensual escape. Now her greatest challenge may be imagining anything less than a future in his arms.

Feeling Etienne's Love
Bad Boys Book Eight

He's a bad bad boy...

Etienne Dubois is the son of a wealthy vineyard owner who craves the excitement of putting his life on the line. Working with the French government and as a confidant of King Charles X give him reasons for living. An encounter with a beautiful young woman in a plush bordello in Paris has him rethinking his roguish ways. Etienne never expects to become a father especially from one encounter with an innocent prostitute who whispers his name and has him rethinking his well-ordered life.

...But she can't help feeling his love.

Elisa Moreau, the only daughter of Angelique Moreau, the owner of an exclusive bordello in Bordeaux, France, has loved Etienne Dubois since she was six. Unfortunately, until an unexpected encounter at a brothel in Paris puts the two of them in the same room, Etienne doesn't even know she exists. Confused but wanting Etienne and this chance meeting to never end, Elisa gives herself to the man who has held her heart in hands for what seems like her entire life.

Foolish for Piper

The pickpocket...

Piper has spent her life surviving the streets of St. Giles Parish in London, a den of iniquity and crime. Masquerading as a boy she escapes the whorehouses the young girls are sent to as they come of age. The day she encounters Brett MacLachlan begins the same as every other one. When she picks his pocket, she has no idea her life is going to change irreversibly.

...and the mark

Handsome aristocrat Brett MacLachlan has come to London for his amusement only to find his world turned upside down by a thief and her dog. From the moment he spots her, Brett knows there is something intrinsically wrong. In his arms, Piper discovers passion and joy. Yet secrets of her past haunt her, and a scar will tell the true tale as well as her identity.

Taylor's Destiny

She traveled to another time and place to change destiny...

Enjoying a day of sailing, Taylor Maxwell never expected after a suffering a concussion she would wake up in another century. A resilient independent woman in the twenty-first century, the blond beauty is ill prepared for life in the 1800s. Her first sight of the naval captain who rescues her makes her heart stop, giving her hope for her future.

His life is transformed by a woman who appears from nowhere...

Born to a life of ease, Reid Stewart defies the dictates of those born to aristocracy and chooses a life of adventure in the navy and as a spy for the crown. When he discovers a nearly naked woman on the bow of small sailing ship, his heart warms. His love for Taylor and his need to protect her from a man who pursues her might cost him his life as well as hers.

Caitlin's Duke

She played a fiddle in an Irish pub...

Caitlin O'Shea Is the most beautiful woman Roc Leighton has ever seen. With her blue violet eyes and long black hair she captivates him. In turn he mesmerizes Caitlin. Caught in the power of his gaze as he watches her, she is wise enough to know he desires her but will never give his heart to her. Caitlin has vowed to never be any man's mistress.

And fell in love with an English Lord...

Roc knows the first time he watches her play the fiddle and dance around the pub, she will be his next mistress. Despite her protest, he will find a way to convince her that her place is with him. While Caitlin's determination to keep her vows, fate takes a cruel turn and she is forced to seek refuge with Roc.

Catching Meara
Book One in the McKenna Clan Series

Meara Thorton was a feisty, world-class computer hacker—cornered by the FBI and shockingly given the chance to be their newly acquired technical analyst. Brilliant and intuitive, yet aching with the loss of everyone she has cared about, her restless heart led her to discover a love she fought and a world she didn't know could possibly exist.

Sweet Sexy Sadie
Book Two in the McKenna Clan Series

From the first time Sadie's eyes met those of Brody McKenna in the hot Sierra Madre Mountains, theirs was a potent attraction—not gentle, slow, and easy, but hot, hard, and all-consuming. The daughter of a dysfunctional family, Sadie had dreams no man could wrench from her with hot sex and an all-consuming passion. She'd challenge this alpha male with all the strength she possessed. But her red hair, fiery temperament, and indomitable spirit obsessed Brody...and he knew he had to find a way to show her he was more than he appeared and convince her to make a life with him.

Sweet Misbehavin'
Book Three in the McKenna Clan Series

Cast adrift after fleeing the home of Jokul, the ice demon, Atantsi, a firestarter, grew to womanhood as she moved through time to keep the demon from finding her. Though stubborn and courageous, she was ill prepared to use powers she had not been taught. Her first sight of the intoxicating Carr McKenna left her breathless, and her second encounter gave her hope for a future she never thought she had.

A playboy, a second son and a shifter, a man who thought his life would be carefree, Carr McKenna was shocked to discover the woman he'd paid as an escort is a firestarter who is running for her life. He is the leader of all the McKennas around the world and that he has multiple powers. His passion for Margo and the need to defend her might cost him his life as well as hers.

Sweet Talkin' Sugar
Book Four in the McKenna Clan Series

Lyonesse McKenna, was dreaming, or was she? From the instant Lyn saw Deacon McClain across a black jack table in a crowed Las Vegas casino the unmistakable attraction sent Lyn's senses flying into overdrive. Her family of shapeshifters believed in soul mates. She'd always been skeptical yet she couldn't help but question the way her heart sped when he looked at her.

When Deacon appeared in Las Vegas he knew his first job was to save Lyn from a Sea Demon, but the next order of business was to convince her he would someday mean more to her than she'd ever expected. But her stubborn nature and unbendable spirit consumed Deacon...and he had to chase away all the demons real and imagined in order to win her heart.

Sweet Surrender
Book Five in the McKenna Clan Series

Ripped from her family at the top of Infinity Cliff, Kimi McKenna finds herself thrust somewhere into the future. Dark elements threaten to destroy the earth unless Kimi can work together with the white witch to stop the destruction. Confused by her mate's role in the conspiracy, she refuses to acknowledge the connection. But amidst raging fire and attacks on the people she is coming to hold dear, she allows Maska O'keefe into her heart.

Maska O'keefe has loved the beautiful shapeshifter for years. Unable to save her life years ago, he vows to watch over her as he is given a second chance to convince her that even though he is a witch and not a shifter, they are indeed soul mates. Kimi's divided loyalties between her family and the cause she is now a part of will determine their relationship. Only the part she plays as the messiah can bring this to a conclusion in the final battle.

Dakota's Bride
The first book in the Lakota/Pinkerton Series

When Emma St. John received her brother's letter imploring her to escape her stepfather's vengeful scheme and to trust Dakota Barringer with her life, she was willing to chance it. But the handsome, brooding riverboat owner Emma found in Natchez a danger of another kind. For Emma soon found herself surrendering to an unrelenting desire.

Raised by the Sioux when his parents were killed, Dakota had been betrayed once before by a white woman. He wasn't about to trust another, especially one claiming that her stepfather, a powerful U.S. senator, had framed her as a murderess. But he couldn't let Emma's intoxicating effect on him. Now Dakota would risk his very life to protect the innocent beauty who had seduced him with her tender love.

My Angel
The second book in the Lakota/Pinkerton Series

A BEAUTY IN BUCKSKINS

When her father decided to send her to a finishing school back East, Angela Chamberlain refused to be confined to stuffy drawing rooms. Instead, the daring spitfire who could shoot like a man and ride like the wind longed for a life of adventure and romance—and she knew exactly who could give it to her. Devil Blackmoor was a hired gun with a dangerous reputation. But Angela was willing to go to the ends of the earth to capture the handsome devil's heart.

A DEVIL IN DISGUISE

He'd come to America looking for excitement, but Devil Blackmoor got more than he bargained for when he encountered a beautiful rebel who answered his kisses with a wild innocence that touched his very soul. Yet standing between them were more obstacles than either ever dreamed. For Devil had strapped on a gun for the wrong man. And that made Angela his enemy. Now he'll have to choose between his duty and the woman he loves more than life.

The Locket
The third book in the Lakota/Pinkerton Series

The year is 1894. Seeking revenge for crimes against his family, Misha Petrovich follows a path that leads straight to Ariel Cameron's boarding house in Mist Harbor, Oregon. A family heirloom in Ariel's possession leads Misha to believe she is guilty. The locket has been handed down to the oldest girl in the Petrovich family for generations. Ariel is innocent of wrong doing, but her father is not. Misha is torn by his feelings for Ariel and his need for restitution against her father. Knowing that the relationship between them is fragile, Misha does everything in his power to protect Ariel's father. His efforts are to no avail when her father is shot. Ariel comes to realize Misha's steadfast courage and determination to protect her and her father despite what has happened to his family. Ariel's love and devotion heals Misha's heart.

The Talisman
The fourth book in the Lakota/Pinkerton Series

Running from a marriage that lasted one night, Dr. Moriah McKeown discovers the land she has settled on is coveted by determined and lawless men. Yet the proud young woman who once vowed never to abandon her home has second thoughts when her adopted children are threatened. Her only recourse is to enlist the aid of a dark, dangerous gun for hire.

Haunted by the past and a betrayal he will never forgive, Ian Civanovich uses his fast gun and his reckless courage to forget the faithlessness of a woman in his past. He will trust no female—nor will he rest until the threat hovering over Moriah McKeown is put to rest.

Forever His
The fifth book in the Lakota/Pinkerton Series

Struggling to come to terms with the part she played in Jacob St. John's death, Etta Barringer resigns from Pinkerton Agency and seeks peace and solace in a Rocky Mountain Cabin.

Jacob has vowed to discover the reason Etta has betrayed him, sold him out to his enemy and left him for dead.

Isolated in their cabin, they discover their love for each other and learn to trust. But the trust is shattered when Jacob learns she is married to his sworn enemy; the man who left him in the desert to die.

Allura's Secret
Twelve Dancing Princesses Book One

Allura McClellan is horrified by her father's decision to take out an ad in the Times awarding her to the man strong enough and smart enough to win her hand and uncover her secrets. She's an intelligent young woman who takes great delight in the freedom allotted to her by her father. She's well aware that marriage would effectively curtail the adventures she's shared with her sisters and cousins.

Hunter Gray is nothing like the other men who've arrived to vie for Allura's hand in marriage and everything that goes along with it. However, he is the first to refuse to concede defeat and pursue her despite her attempts to disguise her true appearance. It's her temperament that is of more concern to him than her looks. Hunter has worked all his life with the hope of someday owning his own land. Now that it looks like there's a very real possibility that everything he's ever wanted is within reach nothing is going to deter him – including Miss Allura's disagreeable disposition.

Amorica's Wager
Twelve Dancing Princesses Book Two

Amorica Hepburn was sent to London to find a husband. Finding a man was the last item on her agenda. With her two cousins, Amorica wagers she can dissuade her suitor before the others. Despite her efforts she discovers a chemistry that cannot be denied. Suddenly she is the arrogant man's wife, pledged to a marriage neither desire. But swept off to his ancestral home above the Dover cliffs and into his strong embrace, Amorica is soon possessed by a raging passion for the husband she had vowed to despise...

Damian Andrews couldn't afford to trust the emerald-eyed spitfire who happened upon his secret. Amorica's hatred of all men of his kind only inflames the war that rages between them. Still, he can not control the intense desire his stubborn bride inspires, or make her surrender to his will until he has conquered the headstrong beauty on the battlefield of love...

Ravyn's Marriage of Inconvenience
Twelve Dancing Princesses Book Three

A REGAL BEAUTY

When the duchess decides to wed her to a wastrel and a fop, Ravyn Grahm takes matters into her own hands and declares her engagement to another man. Instead of fessing up and telling her great aunt what she has done, she goes through with the pretense. Ariec Lakeland is the bastard son of an earl and has a dangerous reputation. But Ravyn is willing to do most anything to keep the duchess from discovering the lie.

A DEVIL-MAY-CARE SMUGGLER

He'd bought land in America, looking to put down roots and end his life of adventure, but Ariec Lakeland got more than he bargained for when he encountered a beautiful heiress who made a promise she didn't want to keep. But the promise could not be undone and standing between them were more obstacles than either ever dreamed. Ariec had made plans to spend the rest of his life in America and that was at odds with Ravyn's plan of living in England and running her father's estate. Now, he'll have to choose between his dreams and the woman he loves more than life.

Christel's Sunrise
Twelve Dancing Princesses Book Four

He Made Her An Offer...

Life has thrown Christel McClellan some experiences that could have devastated a less determined woman. Beautiful, self-assured and fiercely independent, she is trying to forget the loss of her stillborn child. But is the child alive?

She Couldn't Deny...

Life is carefree for Ryder MacLaren who loves to see what is on the other side of the sunrise. Laird of Clan MacLaren, he is wealthy, handsome and happily unencumbered...until stunning Christel McClellan enters his life. When he hears her story, he believes the child she thought dead has been sold to a wealthy buyer.

Storm's Passion
Twelve Dancing Princesses Book Five

SHE MADE A PROPOSAL...

Life strikes Storm Graham a shattering blow when she learns her father has bartered her to a man she detests. Storm is beautiful, self–assured and fiercely independent, and refuses to be a pawn in her father's schemes, yet she can find no way out of this bargain made in hell. Going on the offensive she asks the wealthiest man on the eastern coast of England to marry her, never believing she might fall in love.

HE TRIED TO REFUSE...

For Hadden Johnston life has provided everything he ever wanted, including a sanctuary for homeless children. He is wealthy, handsome and happily unencumbered...until stunning Storm Graham marches into his life and proposes a marriage of convenience. Yet this type of marriage to a woman who inflames his senses is far from acceptable. If he's going to be tied down, he will move heaven and earth to have this woman warming his bed.

Gotta Have Fayth
Twelve Dancing Princesses Book Six

A regal beauty with raven hair and piercing blue eyes, Fayth Graham is unwilling to parade herself in front of the wealthy Lords of England during the season. Seeking a means to dissuade any man wishing to wed her, she seeks a way to ruin herself for marriage. When she unexpectedly meets a man with sparkling gray eyes and an infectious grin, she decides this is the man who will keep her from agreeing to obey.

He returned from six months at sea, looking for a few nights of pleasure with a willing lass, but Jarret Kinsley got more than he bargained for when he met a beautiful debutant who responded to his kisses with a wild innocence that touched his heart. Yet the obstacles looming between them might rip them apart. Both had vowed never to marry, so when consequences of their dalliances got in the way, Jarret would have to choose between the life he's always desired and the woman he loves more than life.

Ella's Pleasure
Twelve Dancing Princesses Book Seven

A WHISPER OF PLEASURE
Ella Hepburn was an auburn haired debutant from the harsh Scottish coastline—a wild innocent to be seduced and tamed. A spirited beauty, she captivated Drake Montgomerie's jaded heart—while succumbing to the smoldering desire she felt for her unyielding suitor.

A WHISPER OF DANGER
In Drake Montgomerie's glittering world of money and privilege, young Ella discovered passion and desire could overcome everything she'd been taught to resist—entangling Drake, the heir apparent, in a lethal coil of aristocratic family intrigue. But grave peril would only nurse the sparks of a love that knew no limits and a magnificent ecstasy that would not be denied.

Eveleen's Seduction
Twelve Dancing Princesses Book Eight

A WHISPER OF SEDUCTION
A brutal attack on Eveleen Hepburn's cherished island off the Scottish coastline leaves her shattered and bewildered. Learning a man she once trusted can kill as easily as he can breathe even though the deed saves her life, creates questions that need answers. An innocent beauty, she enchants Logan Maxwell's cynical heart—giving in to the raging passion she feels for her mysterious suitor.

A WHISPER OF INTRIGUE
In Logan's Maxwell's world of espionage and privilege, young

Eveleen discovers truths about herself she never expected, and a need for passion and love can overcome all her fears if she learns to accept certain truths. She finds herself entangled in a lethal battle for land that was once owned by French nobility, taken from them during the revolution and sold to Maxwell. But grave peril would unleash the flames of love that simmers, creating a magical union that cannot be refuted.

Tavia's Deception
Twelve Dancing Princesses Book Nine

WHISPERS OF DECEPTION
When her father decides to send her to London for her season, Tavia Hepburn resolves to see the world instead. The raven haired beauty decides to disguise herself as a lad and find employment on a ship bound for Barcelona as a cabin boy. But she never bargains on finding passion and love to a red haired sea captain who rescues her from certain death.

WHISPERS OF MURDER
For James Macmurra, the world is black and white until he meets a young debutante, who turns his world upside down. He's unable to deny Tavia's intoxicating effect on him. In a match tense with obstacles, unwillingness to divulge secrets, and unforeseen peril, irresistible desire and passion grows into undeniable love. James would risk his life to shelter and protect the innocent debutante who seduces him with her sweet love.

Larena's Fascination
Twelve Dancing Princesses Book Ten

WHISPERS OF FASCINATION
Fiery, free spirited Larena Graham never wanted to marry a duke. She is thrilled to be in love with the fourth son of an aristocrat, Gavin Broon. But when it seems Gavin ignores her, she set her sights on politics and bettering human life. Unsuspecting intrigue and a plot against her,

she continues her dangerous plans despite Gavin's wishes.

WHISPERS OF TRUST
Gavin has every intention of properly courting the beautiful Larena until he must leave the city in order to put his affairs in order. Returning to London, he finds the woman he means to make his own is embroiled in political protests that could lead to a prison ship. Larena must learn to trust the handsome Scotsman whose most pressing mission is to protect her and keep her from harm.

Tira's Education
Twelve Dancing Princesses Book Eleven

WHISPERS OF EDUCATION
Learning how to build ships is Tira Hepburn's only dream until she meets Jamie Lundin and her world is turned upside down. With her raven black hair and vivid green eyes, she tempts Jamie and pushes him to defy his vows. She never bargains on finding an irrevocable love and a passion to a man who cannot fulfill her dreams despite his burning desire for her.

WHISPERS OF A BARGAIN
Arrogant and self-assured Jamie is brought up short when Tira captures his heart. All his carefully made plans are put to the test when he decides to teach her the art of ship building if she will spend a week with him alone on his ship. He is unable to deny Tira's intoxicating effect on him. When Tira leaves him behind unwilling to live with him without the benefit of marriage, he races after her. Jamie will risk everything to shelter and protect the innocent debutante who seduces him with her sweet love.

Aidan's Love
Twelve Dancing Princesses Book Twelve

Whispers of Love

Aidan McLellan has loved since she first set eyes on him as a young girl. Spontaneous, wild and eager to grow up, Aidan haunts his waking thoughts day and night, insinuating herself into his life. With her fiery red hair and sparkling sapphire eyes, she seizes Blade's heart even while he tries to resist the innocent child until she becomes a woman.

Whispers of Courage

Blade has waited what seems a lifetime to claim the woman who captures his heart as a little girl. Claiming his inheritance before his younger brother takes what is rightfully his, Blade must convince Aidan of his sincerity after years of avoidance and wed her before his father dies so he can return home, securing his rightful place. Everything is put to the test when his life as well as Aidan's is threatened by the man who once called him brother.

Twelve Days to Love

When Archer Steele shows up at Calanthe Durand's failing plantation with an alligator over his shoulder, Cali thinks she's never seen a more handsome man. During the war she had to defend herself and her servants from both union and confederate soldiers. Independent and self-sufficient, she vows to never marry.

But Archer Steele has different ideas. The first time Archer sees Cali in town, he feels an instant attraction. He decides he will do everything and anything to convince the beautiful Miss Durand he is worthy of her love. During the weeks leading up to Christmas, he gives her twelve gifts in hopes she will fall in love with him. Yet they are faced with challenges they must overcome before Cali can commit to a marriage.

Door to Heaven

Jessica Lawrence is the stepdaughter of a woman born in the twentieth century transported back in time to the year 1868. An acclaimed suffragette, she raises Jessica to believe in the equality of women. Jess Law believes everything she was taught, and when the time is right she becomes a private investigator. Courageous and impetuous, Jess finds danger in her quest to save all women from white slavery. Her passionate mission results in a wedding to Roc Newman, a man she knows can steal her heart...

Roc can't trust the sapphire-eyed spitfire who invades his home in search of secret papers and knocks him flat with her karate moves. Jessica's refusal to obey his wishes serves to inflame the war between them. Still, he cannot control the intense desire his reluctant bride inspires, or make her surrender her independence, until he has conquered the headstrong beauty on the battlefield of love...

Rebel Heart

HER REBEL SPIRIT DEFIED HIS OUTSIDERS SOUL...She was velvet and silk, eyes the color of a summer storm and amber hair. Victoria DeMontville, because of a promise and a codicil to her father's will, was forced to marry one man to protect her from another. She hated Cameron Savage with a fierce passion. But to hold on to her genetic research and find a cure for the deadly Signe virus, she must pretend to love the enemy at her door, come with weapons of fire to melt her icy heart...

HIS OUTSIDERS TOUCH IGNITED RAGING PASSIONS... He wore a mask, disguised as the Phantom, a true legend come to life. Even as war and debate over new genetic research engulfed them all, he would find his greatest adversary in the beauty who'd branded him an outsider and barbarian, the woman he was born to possess, his soul mate.

Safari Moon

Solo St. John, a wildlife photographer, is preparing for a trip to Alaska. Suddenly, Solo finds women of all sorts invading his privacy, his home and his office, all cooing nonsense words and blatantly throwing themselves at him. Solo doesn't know why, and he has no idea how to rid himself of the persistent women. He finally decides to beg a favor of his best buddy Nyssa Harrington.

In love with Solo for the past ten years and knowing he doesn't return her feelings Nyssa doesn't want to talk to Solo. She knows if she accepts his phone call, she will not be able to resist the temptation to hope again.

Straight to Heaven

Running from demons, Alexandra McMurdie stumbles into Forbidden Ground where up is down and elements of nature are contested. Though a strong independent woman in the twenty-first century' she is unprepared for life in the 1800s. Her first site of the formidable James Lawrence makes her heart skip a beat, giving her cause to reconsider her desperate need to find a way home.

Born with a silver spoon, James' life was torn apart during the War Between the States. Moving west he vows to put the life he once knew in the past. When he discovers a half-frozen woman near Gold Hill, his heart begins to thaw. His love for Alexandra and his need to keep her from a man who has pursued her through time might cost him his life as well as hers.

A Valentine's Anthology

The Lending Library-a fantasy by Christie L. Kraemer
Faeries try to fit into the human world when the forest where they make their home is destroyed by a mysterious enemy.

Chasing Rainbows-a contemporary romance by Genene Valleau
An eccentric aunt, an inventive uncle, a mother who wears poodle skirts, and a brother who wears pearls provide a hilarious backdrop for the courtship of a young woman who yearns for a "normal" family.

The Gift-an historical romance by Christine Young

A man and a woman on opposite sides of the Civil War get a second chance at love after one final battle returns soldiers to their war-torn homes to rebuild their lives.

A St. Patrick's Day Tale
Christine Young, C. L. Kraemer, Genene Valleau

Tumble through time...

...to Ireland in 1817, when tensions are high between Protestants and Catholics and fae people guide the fate of villagers. A lovely Catholic lass stumbles upon the weakly ritual fisticuffing between Irish lads. She falls into the lap of a handsome young Protestant. Family ties, grudges, and two conniving faeries threaten their budding love. But the faeries outsmart themselves when they hijack a time machine that has mysteriously appeared in their forest and are whisked to...

...Eugene, Oregon in the 20th century, amid a property feud between the local faeries and night elves. The conniving faeries from Olde Ireland try to stir up more mischief. However, a warrior gnome convinces the magic folk to control their own destiny, and forces the intruding faeries to take refuge in the time machine again, spinning their way toward...

...A modern day castle in western Oregon. An eccentric inventor is determined to reclaim his wayward time machine and save his beloved wife from her latest misadventure. If only they can travel safely past the black hole...

a May Day Anthology
Christine Young, C. L. Kraemer, Rosemary Indra, Genene Valleau

Highland Miracle — Christine Young

HURTLED THROUGH TIME, Sean Michael Sterling, landed in the midst of a May Day celebration he didn't understand, assuming the role of Laird Sterling.

ILLIGITAMATE CHILD OF NOBILITY, Reagan Douglas searches for a way out of her half brother's house.

Defying the Odds — C.L. Kraemer
The night elves on the hill aren't happy without their magic. They concoct a plan to punish those who were involved in the act that rendered them almost human. Meanwhile, Uther, the rogue night elf, has returned to woo the Librarian to be his eternal mate.

Love in Bloom — Rosemary Indra
When childhood friends reunite it takes two fairies and a matchmaking daughter to help them admit their true love for each other.

No More Poodle Skirts — Genie Gabriel
After drifting for years in the innocent age of the 1950s, a woman struggles to join today's world by finding a career and a new love, with some help from her zany family.

Once Upon a Christmas Moon
Christine Young, C. L. Kraemer, Genene Valleau

TWELVE DAYS TO LOVE
When Archer Steele shows up at Calanthe Durand's failing plantation with an alligator over his shoulder, Cali thinks she's never seen a more handsome man. During the war she had to defend herself and her servants from both union and confederate soldiers. Independent and self-sufficient, she vows to never marry. But Archer Steele has different ideas. The first time Archer sees Cali in town, he feels an instant attraction. He decides he will do everything and anything to convince the beautiful Miss Durand he is worthy of her love. During the weeks leading up to Christmas, he gives her twelve gifts in hopes she will fall in love with him.

BOOTS AND BLADES

An ancient evil from the old country has arrived in the high desert of Oregon. Gnome children are vanishing then re-appearing, showing various stages of traumatization. Tiamoon, warrior gnome, will put her skills to use alongside Killian, a handsome warrior, also in need of a cause.

CHRISTMAS PAWSIBILITIES

With their world destroyed and their space ship malfunctioning, the dogizens of Planet Canid have little choice but to crash land on Earth. They face tortuous experiments at the hands of the Geeks in Green...or they can trust an eccentric inventor and his zany family to deliver the Canine Queen's puppies and help them celebrate new lives.